ELECTRA BITCHES

A novel by

MARJORIE DURYEA

SACADA LIBROS

For Chelsea

He who makes no mistakes never makes anything

—ENGLISH PROVERB

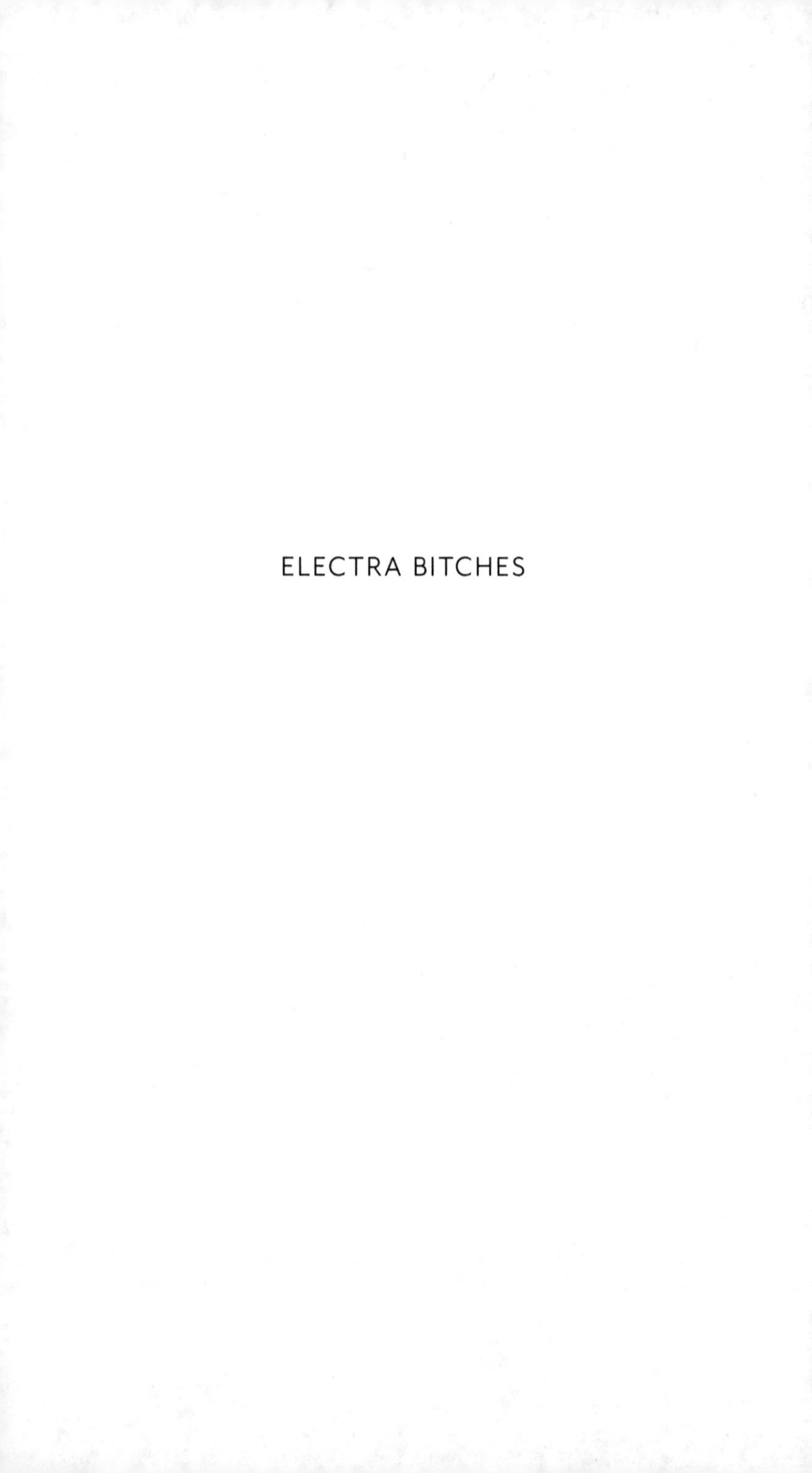

ELECTRA BITCHES

CHAPTER 1

ROSIE

I have no memory of my mother playing with me or taking me to the park when I was little. She says I'm wrong and insists she was the one who read me bedtime stories most of the time, not my father. The only thing I remember is when she read *Harold and the Purple Crayon* it seemed shorter than when my father read it. It was before I was able to read myself to know for sure if she was skipping pages and making up words. What was clear, in spite of my being illiterate, she acted like she wanted to finish as soon as possible. My father took his time, making faces and using different voices.

Dorrie says I only remember it that way because I'm a "daddy's girl." Dorrie has had this massive crush on my father since he spanked me and threw me over his shoulder in the park near our townhouse when we were both fifteen. He didn't hurt me and I probably deserved it, but it was humiliating. The only thing preventing further embarrassment and saving my father from getting a call from DYFS was Dorrie thought he was "a sexy caveman." Dorrie was a virgin at the time and I hoped this wasn't an indication of her liking kinky sex once she started doing it.

Luckily for my father no adults were present to see what he did, also ensuring he would not get a visit from social services. The only other people who had witnessed the act were PJ and Lewis; two boys who lived in the same complex as Dorrie and me. They also seemed impressed: "Rosie, your dad, rocks." It was only because they were intimidated. My father is a pretty big guy. They were afraid if they teased me about what happened or told someone about it, I might sic him on them. He could beat their puny little butts, but he would never have done that. His behavior was atypical that day. He had never raised his voice or laid a hand on me my entire life before the spanking, and he probably did it because of something my mother said to him. I blame her more for his actions that day than I do him.

I also find Dorrie's suggestion that the spanking was sexual in nature offensive. Daddy would never lay an inappropriate hand on me. I'm not a naive airhead though; I am aware of the fact that many people might find it inappropriate to spank a fifteen-year-old girl. But it was no way a sexual experience for my father or me. And I haven't developed a liking for my boyfriends to spank me when I have sex. I don't think my parents were into rough sex either. I do remember hearing noises at night sometimes when I suspected them of doing it (before I was old enough to even know for sure what *doing it* was). It was unlikely my father was spanking my mother though. He's too much of a lovable nerd; it was more likely the viper was spanking him. Dorrie ignores my father's true nature no matter what I say, and to this day the spanking in the park is an erotic fantasy for her.

"He was like Mighty Joe Young, Rosie."

"Who the hell is Mighty Joe Young?"

"This big, sexy ape. My mother has a set of classic films from the 1940's. I think there was a remake too."

"I never saw Mighty Joe Young in any movie, Dorrie. But my father is not a sexy ape. He's a sweet teddy bear."

"Yeah, like I said, you're a daddy's girl."

Daddy's girl, really? If you're a daddy's girl doesn't it mean he favors you over other women? He never takes my side when my mother's involved. He even defended her after she walked out on him. "I don't want to hear you bad mouthing your mother, Rosie. Am I making myself clear?"

It is clear, and baffling. And even Granny Nessie, my grandmother, made excuses for her when she left Daddy. Admittedly, it is understandable–she's her mother.

"She needed to find herself, I guess." Really? At fifty years old she hadn't found herself yet?

"And at least she didn't leave your father for another man." Nice to know some mothers defend their daughters. It hasn't been my personal experience. I did not say that or argue with my grandmother but I felt like saying–*just give her a little time*. She's only been gone a year; living in fucking Minneapolis. She's pretty far from us. Does Granny Nessie or anyone else know for sure what she does with her free time? How would we know now if she was with someone or not?

And I can't believe my mother hasn't found a man to replace Daddy. I've watched every boyfriend I ever had make an idiot of themselves when they first met her. They would stand there in a daze until they snapped out of it to ask (with their mouths open wide enough to catch flies): "Is that your mother?" I hated bringing my dates home and always hearing how she was "so hot" or "one sexy mama." Boys and men have been ogling my mother for as long as I can remember. How can anyone defend her?

My father baffles me, my grandmother irritates me, and my boyfriend Ben pisses me off. Shouldn't he of all people take my side?

"Why is it a side, Rose?" Leave your father alone. Your mother is his wife."

"Ex-wife."

"They're still married, aren't they? They're not divorced. And I thought you said your grandmother really believes your mother is going to go back to him."

"Oh, God forbid. I hope the bitch doesn't return."

"I can't believe how you talk about your own mother, Rose. Talk about bitches."

What? How dare he? Is he implying I'm a *bitch*? I'm no bitch, she's the bitch.

CHAPTER 2

SARAH

don't know why everyone was so judgmental when I left Joe. My mother thought I was mad, my best friend Paulee said I was "ungrateful" and Rosie called me a "narcissistic bitch." Rosie's statement was the least poignant, coming from a spoiled, self-centered teenager. She is also a *daddy's girl,* and naturally took a stand to protect her father. It's actually very sweet when I reflect on it. I love her father and was glad to see her fight for him, but my actions were never meant to be offensive moves against Joe. Rosie's comment had no basis in relation to my leaving, even if understandable. I wouldn't expect a teenager who was very immature for her age, as well as *spoiled* and *self-centered,* to speak otherwise. She could not be expected to understand the multi-faceted complexities of marriage and the dynamics between men and women. I do expect more from my mother and Paulee however. The true irony? The only person who has not been judgmental is Joe.

I left Joe and New Jersey for a full-time tenured position teaching mathematics at a private college in

Minnesota. I never asked Joe to come with me for several reasons. When I first broached the subject of my taking a job in another state, he said he didn't want to relocate. It was not the primary reason I didn't ask him if I am going to be honest though. I was on a quest, a search, a journey–whatever one wants to call it–and I wanted to pursue it on my own. I wasn't sure I wanted to remain married to Joe in spite of my love for him.

Joe and I have maintained a telephone relationship since I left. We speak on a regular basis every Sunday evening sharing our news. I never hear much from him for the most part. I do most of the talking; but in the early weeks after I left, he repeatedly asked if I was ready to come home or if I wanted him to move to Minnesota. I was evasive; not to be disingenuous or mean, I didn't know the answers to his questions. Eventually he stopped asking.

Paulee told me I was being "a cock tease," another judgmental observation. She told me Joe was really hurting and was "clinically depressed" –she was afraid he'd "hurt himself." I have seen Joe when he was depressed, he is not the suicidal type. I know him better than Paulee in spite of what she thinks. She may be my main source for information about most of his activities since he doesn't share it with me, but she is wrong when she tells me Joe is suicidal. The behavior she is describing is not a sign of clinical depression, only his nature. He also usually talks less on the phone than in-person which makes conversations more challenging and questionable if a person is not familiar with his phone-style. Paulee has known Joe for years but never had phone conversations with him until after I left. They're clouding her perceptions, but if I want to hear more about what's happening with Joe I have to talk to her about him. That means listening to some inaccurate takes occasionally and more frequently enduring her judgmental remarks. The current theme–*mistakes*. More specifically, mine. *I made one when I left Joe.*

◆———◆———◆

I began my research with two hypotheses. *Number one–I will discover that my life is more enriched without Joe. The conclusion–I am happier without him. Number two–I will discover that my life feels empty without Joe. The conclusion–I want to share it with him (in spite of any irritations I might continue to have with the stated person to whom I identified above).*

Now to the crux of the matter of Paulee's error. The fact that *number two* was confirmed doesn't mean–*I made a mistake.* It actually means I was *correct* because it was confirmed, which makes Paulee saying otherwise puzzling and unscientific. Her use of an emotional appeal to reinforce a flawed argument is also unethical–*Joe is dating a woman named Sharon.*

I hadn't anticipated Joe's proposition when I made mine. It was a shock learning it only days after my confirmation of hypothesis two. I had just told Paulee I finally realized I did not want to live without Joe and she says, "Well, I guess you made a mistake when you left him, Sarah. You know he is dating someone now." Her timing reinforced how unethical her methods were to prove her point. It was the first I had heard about it.

She and Joe never said a word to me. Paulee can be snarky but I am surprised about Joe. We are still married. We haven't even made a *formal* separation agreement. I implored these cogent facts to Paulee and she smugly replied, "I guess you leaving and recently telling him you had no intentions of coming back made it formal enough for him." She seemed to be relishing in my pain. I know Paulee loves me, she has been my closest friend for over twenty years. What is an odd dynamic though, she is also one of Joe's best friends. Telling me about this new unexpected development not only strengthened her argument, she gave me a slap on his behalf. My research was flawed but not in the way Paulee thinks. I did not do enough preliminary research before forming my thesis. It wasn't only Joe finding someone to date which I hadn't anticipated, I hadn't conceptualized a number of happenings.

I was trying to find a full-time teaching position at the college level for years after earning my PhD. It was my dream; like an actor dreaming of stardom or my friend Liz (who is a singer) longing for a career as a jazz vocalist. Getting the job was one of the greatest highs of my life. It was comparable to how Liz described her feelings when she landed a gig. I was offered an entire career though, not a few weeks of performances. It was a sustained natural high, but there were interruptions and that's the rub. The very nature of highs is that they don't last forever. Mine wore off after each teaching day. I found myself alone in my studio apartment smoking a joint trying to create an aberrant high to replace the natural one. Paulee would often snidely remark, "Maybe, you're just lonely or that professorship is not as rewarding as you thought it would be." She was wrong on both counts.

I'm not lonely. I have friends, and there have been men interested in me. I also continue to be happy about my job but I hadn't anticipated that some joy is lost not having anyone to share it with. Joe played a pivotal role in helping me earn my PhD; I want to share my joy with him. There's something different about having a history with someone. It took me a while to realize that. There's no denying the fact, Joe made me feel secure. I never thought he would leave me for someone else.

❦

Paulee met her; she told me she is a *mousy* little woman. I would find out later from Rosie she was someone I had met–she is the mother of her roommate at her university. She's very unattractive. If we are indeed talking about the same woman, Paulee made a poor word choice or an intentional oxymoron. Mice are cute. I cannot picture Joe with a little woman, cute or not. Won't he crush her? I'm having disturbing thoughts about them screwing; which I hope is not the case, but they are adults so who am I kidding. It isn't the real reason why it bothers me however.

Paulee asked, "Well, what's the real reason you're upset, and why is it unimaginable for Joe to be with a *mousy* little woman? He is not a superficial man, Sarah." I know that, but I can't imagine him with her because I can only imagine him with me.

Paulee plunged me into a deep depression of self-pity when she told me Joe was dating. She offered me a peace offering of sorts the next time we talked when she said, "Call him Sarah. He loves you, not this woman."

"I am not going to do that, Paulee."

"Oh, swallow your pride, Sarah, tell him you made a mistake, and you want him back."

I am not debating this issue with her again. I'm also amazed how little Paulee knows me after all these years. Refusing to call Joe has nothing to do with my pride or a self-centered choice. Is that why my daughter calls me a *narcissist*? Are Rosie and Paulee misinterpreting my actions?

"I won't call Joe because he obviously has found someone else with whom he wants to be with. I am not going to stand in his way, Paulee."

"You're making another mistake, Sarah."

CHAPTER 3

ROSIE

It was the end of my first year in college and my mother called me the day after my last final exam. I was spending my summer break at home, and I was expecting her and Daddy to pick me up in two days to drive me back to New Jersey. I figured her call was something to do with the trip, and I was right. She told me it would be just Daddy picking me up. She had moved to Minneapolis to accept a teaching position at a college in Minnesota. She left him. I told her she was a *narcissistic bitch.*

One thing about my mother is she never reacts when I call her names or throw F-bombs in her face. On one hand it is commendable she doesn't react; she can keep her cool. Dorrie told me if she ever talked to her mother like I did she would be killed on the spot. My mother not overreacting is a positive thing but on the other hand sometimes it feels like I don't matter to her. And after I called her a narcissistic bitch she non-reacted as expected.

"I knew you might be upset about this Rosie. That's why I waited to call you until after you took your exams." All said in a calm voice, I hadn't ruffled a single feather. She then proceeded to talk to me as though it was an ordinary call and not one where she had just delivered news about a life-changing event.

She told me she would not be able to visit for my birthday celebration because it was too close to her starting her new job. What did I think about visiting her? We could celebrate in Minneapolis, and I could check out her college to see if it "appealed to me." Perhaps I might consider transferring there? My classes would be free on account of her job. She and my father had discussed it–they would save a ton of money. There was no way I was transferring from a university in Miami to a little college in fucking Minnesota. She must be truly crazy; transferring was totally out of the question. But what really caught my attention were the words *they* and *discussed*.

"You're still talking to Daddy?"

"Well, why wouldn't I be?" She had to ask? It was ridiculous. She didn't act like a woman who just told me she left her husband. She was nuts or I was missing something. Discussion or not, I was not changing schools. I liked my classes and I had a lot of friends, but I was curious about Minneapolis. Didn't *Prince* live there?

"Is Daddy coming to Minneapolis to celebrate my birthday?"

"I doubt it." It was a *no* then too about visiting her. I would rather be with my friends Dorrie and Patty, but most of all I didn't want to leave Daddy. My poor father, she really is a narcissistic bitch.

I wondered how my father was doing; I was too nervous to call him directly so I called my grandmother. I didn't get much information about him from her because she wasn't doing well herself over the split. She said she thought my mother had gone mad and had lost all of her senses. She wouldn't stop crying and kept asking, "How could she leave such a loyal, sweet man?" I didn't disagree with her, but there was a little part of me that was glad my mother had left. Daddy needed a woman who cared more about him than herself. I also hoped she was wrong when she said she "knew in her heart" my mother would soon realize what she had done.

I couldn't express my true feelings to Granny Nessie because she's the mother of the bitch. I *knew in my heart* Daddy would be better off without her. I didn't want him to suffer any more than he had to, but he would eventually get over her and find a woman who would treat him the way he ought to be treated. In the meantime I'd do my best to be a loving daughter and try to distract him if he was sad. My father loves classic rock so I started to make a playlist we could listen to on our drive home. I was very nervous about seeing him; I hoped my rock of a dad wouldn't be crying like Granny Nessie.

❖ ❖ ❖

As soon as I saw my father I checked out his face before I said a word. He didn't look like he had spent sleepless nights or had been crying for days. I was still a little hesitant when I asked, "How are you, Daddy?" What if he broke down right then and there? I would not be able to handle it if he started to cry. He was the one who comforted me. He was my strong protector; if she had destroyed him I didn't know how I could be strong myself. He smiled at me and said, "Okay, baby girl."

I had two choices now: I could take him at his word and ignore the obvious or question him further. I decided to ignore the obvious because if he was really okay why should I discuss it; and if he was faking being okay, bringing it up would only make him feel worse. I soon forgot about it myself loading up the car with all my stuff. We had to clear out everything, including three months of dirty laundry. It was the end of the school year and I would be in different living quarters in the fall. Anything you left behind the school trashed.

Cleaning out my room was distracting, but now we were setting off for the long drive up to New Jersey. Would my father now reveal his true feelings if he was faking, "okay"? I was nervous for nothing though–the ride was uneventful. It was quieter than usual but it was only because it was my mother who normally did most of the talking, not my father. And he really seemed okay. Maybe he had already gotten over her.

Once we arrived home my father continued to act as though nothing was wrong. Based on his behavior I almost expected to find my mother standing in the kitchen. I soon realized he was thinking like Granny Nessie. He thought this was a temporary madness and my mother would eventually recover and return. If I said anything negative about her he shut me down fast. He didn't want to hear any bad mouthing about my mother. He made her sound like some beautiful fucking free-spirit, instead of a narcissistic bitch. "Your mother is a passionate woman and sometimes it makes her behave in overly dramatic or impulsive ways." I wanted to ask him if he had defended me like that when I was cutting classes senior year and the bitch grounded me, but he might think I was indirectly dishing her again. I didn't want to do anything to cause him more stress, even though he was not acting upset at all about what she did to him.

He also seemed to be enjoying himself because she was gone; drinking as many beers as he wanted and going to McDonald's as often as he liked without her being a pain in his ass. My mother hates fast food restaurants; she actually brags about not knowing how to order from the drive-thru menu–a badge of honor. Her way of showing everyone how infrequently she goes to these restaurants. Pretty lame to brag about not being able to use a drive-thru though, and she's someone who has a PhD? When I said that to her, she smugly replied it wasn't her specialty but if I didn't start doing better in school it might be the only thing I'd know how to do. What a bitch.

It also exposes her as a stupid snob; everyone likes fast food, Mom. At least she's being honest about not being a fan, I'll give her that. She hates grease. She only took me and my friends to McDonald's or Burger

King occasionally as a special treat, and she never let us eat in the car. Which means she didn't even have to order from the drive-thru.

Daddy loving fast food and Mom hating it is just one of many of their differences. They seem like an unlikely pair. I often heard people looking at my parents ask: why would a beautiful woman like my mother be with a man who looks like my father (with the exception of Dorrie who has a massive crush on my dad). I heard Anthony say it. He's Aunt Paulee's husband and he said it right in front of me which really ticked Aunt Paulee off. They started throwing F-bombs at one another and then what he said didn't matter anymore; even though his statement had been "an unfair and a myopic evaluation" of my parents. Something Aunt Paulee threw out between F-bombs and I agree with her. My mother is beautiful but my father is cute with a good physique.

Sometimes Daddy puts on a little weight–too much fast food, but he never looks fat. I once called him fat in anger but it was because I was annoyed at my mother for not telling me he was home. If I had known, I wouldn't have dressed in my micro-mini skirt and the blue top that showed off my tits which got his negative attention. I was more careful about what I wore if Daddy was around. My clothes drove her wild when I was in high school. This coming from a woman who wore: tight little suits; leggings that looked sprayed on; and blouses and tops that always showed cleavage. When I pointed that out to her she got pissed.

"There is no way I dress like you, Rosie, you look like a prostitute. But even if I chose to dress that way, it would be my prerogative." I had a quick response. "I don't think Daddy would mind; he doesn't mind you showing off your boobs all the time." It made her crazy. She really started screaming then. She does scream and gets angry frequently; only my swear words never bother her for some reason. "What don't you get here Rosie? I am your father's wife, you are his daughter. You are also a young girl, I am a woman."

She could be so stupid. I was only trying to annoy her. I always toned my dress and makeup down for Daddy. It wasn't because I thought he would react so violently like he had (when he caught me in the black micro-mini and blue top) but I never wanted to push him. It was more than that though; I didn't need to dress in outlandish clothes in front of my father because I didn't need his attention. He always gave it to me. I dressed the way I did back then to get my mother's attention. I always felt like I was invisible to her most of the time.

I also longed to look like my mother. People say I favor her but I never saw it when I was younger or now, and I have my father's curly hair and brown eyes. I can realistically assess my looks just like I can my parents', and I'm also able to get past it to see their connection. My mother is *movie star beauty* level and my father's *a cute guy who works at the gas station*, but the connection between them goes deeper than my dad's looks or blouses showing cleavage. That's what Anthony and other people who don't know them overlook. My mother needs my father; she is more emotionally dependent on him than he is on her. Not my original idea; something I heard Granny Nessie or Aunt Paulee say–and I agree. The first summer my mother was gone my father was working, going out to play golf with his buddy and flying his model airplanes; he was very happy. My mother in contrast was calling him on the landline practically every day, and she'd throw a fit if he wasn't there to take her call. She was an emotional wreck.

◆――――◆――――◆

Things changed in the fall, at least that's how it sounded. I was back in school and when I talked to my father on the phone he sounded very sad. My mother changed too, she was no longer making frequent calls; she only called on Sunday evenings. Was this an indication of her having found another man? Or was it simply because school started and she was busy at work? I didn't know, but hearing from her less may have been a reason for my father's change of mood. It wasn't my imagination, he sounded depressed in the fall; the way he had acted during COVID. When I told him I was planning to go to Chapel Hill, North Carolina with my roommate Leslie for the Thanksgiving fall break, I brought him down even more. He would be alone for the holiday. People think my father isn't social because he's not much of a talker but it isn't true. He likes to be around other people, especially if they're talkers; probably another reason he had gotten along well with my mother who never shuts up.

For the past several years my parents and I went to Granny Nessie's for Thanksgiving. My mother would make most of the food and we would take it to her house in Brick. I figured my father would be going there this year too in spite of my mother being gone. My father got along better with his mother-in-law than his own mother. I didn't know it when I made my plans with Leslie that Granny Nessie was flying to California to stay with my Aunt Penny and her partner for Thanksgiving, and wouldn't return until after New Year's. My grandmother was so upset about my parents' breakup that my aunt thought she needed a change of scenery and some cheering up. What about Daddy? His other options for the holiday made me depressed.

There was Aunt Lynne and my other grandparents, Mac and Jean. If Daddy didn't want to spend the holiday with his sister or his parents I couldn't blame him. Aunt Lynne was okay, but she and Uncle Scott were a little stern. Family meals at their house felt more like a gathering after a funeral than celebrating a holiday. Making it worse, Aunt Lynne never had enough food. One Thanksgiving she served the tiniest turkey I have ever seen for ten people. Daddy was still hungry after the meal and we found him in Aunt Lynne's kitchen dipping bread in the roasting pan drippings. My mother flipped out but he told her he couldn't help it–he was still hungry. He asked her if McDonald's was open on Thanksgiving, and we could stop on the way home. My mother was shocked that he thought she would even know their schedule, and she immediately vetoed the idea. She told him she'd make him something to eat when we got home, but we all needed to exit the kitchen before Aunt Lynne caught him "foraging through her roasting pan."

It was also totally understandable why my father wouldn't want to have Thanksgiving with his parents. First of all they never served turkey, only venison; the meat from a deer they had killed by gun or bow. It was one of my main reasons why I never wanted to go to their house when they were hosting Thanksgiving. I hated the taste of venison and I also didn't want to hear all the gory details of this animal's final moments which Mac always wanted to share with us. It probably wasn't the main reason why my father would decline an invitation though. The main reason was that Mac was very verbally abusive to my father–it was disgusting.

There was also Aunt Paulee. She wasn't a real aunt, and no relation to Daddy, but I've thought of her as a blood relative my entire life and she was Daddy's friend. The problem was she wasn't hosting Thanksgiving at her home but at her restaurant in Bergen County and there were negatives around that. One was Anthony. Daddy and Anthony don't like each other very much in spite of Daddy being best buddies with Aunt Paulee. The other was Aunt Paulee would be working as a hostess on Thanksgiving. How much time could she spend sitting with my father? Daddy would also hate to drive that far on a holiday. He also complains about driving on his off-time because he has to do it for work. In spite of that he drives me to and from school–he's a great dad. There was no way I was letting him spend Thanksgiving by himself, and my vacation was longer than the usual Thanksgiving break most schools have. Our fall break was as long as other schools' spring breaks. When they close for a week or more in March or April, we only have a long weekend. It was our school's strategy to protect us from outside influences. When hordes of students invade Florida in the spring, we are safely stuck taking classes most of the time. My father had planned that I would be home for over a week. He had taken off from work for all those days.

I told Leslie I couldn't leave my father. That's when Leslie and I came up with a great idea. She would ask her mother if my father could spend the holiday in Chapel Hill. Leslie and I would fly to North Carolina, Daddy would drive down to Chapel Hill, and after the break he would drive both of us back to Miami for school. It was not only the perfect solution for ensuring that my father was not alone for the holiday, it also set in motion our long-range plan of hooking her mother up with my father. Something we've been fantasizing about since my mother walked out on Daddy.

I met Leslie's mother during the spring semester when she was visiting Leslie's grandmother who lives in Miami. After she visited Leslie's Nanny, she came to our school to take Leslie out for dinner, and asked me if I would like to join them. I couldn't believe it; she paid for everything at a fancy seafood restaurant on Collins Avenue in Miami Beach. It was a real treat; I never went out to fancy restaurants growing up with my parents. My mother would have liked it but my father was not into that kind of thing.

Leslie is an only child like me and her mother is divorced. Leslie's father died from liver cancer when she was a junior in high school. Her parents had just divorced the year before his death. It made Sharon a kind of widow. Probably not in a legal sense since they weren't married at the time he died, but it sounded better, and what I told Daddy. It was only a tiny, little white lie to make her sound better. It won't matter; Sharon truly is a better woman for Daddy and when he finds out the whole story he'll be in love with her already.

From the very first day I met her I imagined what it would be like if she and Daddy were a couple. It was an idea even before my mother inspired me with her move. Sitting at that fancy restaurant across from Sharon–I wished she was my mother. She looked like a mother should look and I can remember every detail. She wore a black skirt just a little above her knee and a silk blouse modestly opened only three buttons down–no cleavage displayed. In truth I don't think she has much to display and Leslie is also flat chested. She's always whining, "I wish I had tits like you, Rosie." I don't know what the big deal is, I didn't even like it when I was thirteen and they popped out. Later, I didn't mind, but boobs are not that important to me. I hope they're not that important to my father–Sharon is attractive.

The only negative thing someone might say about her looks is that she wore funky glasses; glasses can be stylish, hers weren't. My father's glasses even look better but I think my mother picked them out, and he also wears contacts. He says he can see better with them when he's working on his model planes or playing golf. I asked Leslie why her mother doesn't get contacts. I even suggested we might give her a gift certificate. She said her mother had tried them but she didn't like them; she kept getting eye infections. She's still attractive enough without them. She's slim, petite and has nice legs. Is my father a leg man? Hard to judge because my mother has it all. But I reminded myself, it was more about personality than looks.

Leslie's mother goes to church every week and is very involved with her church, but I don't know if that would be a draw for my father. My parents aren't religious. My mother is a Lutheran but we only go to church with Granny Nessie for Christmas and Easter services. Daddy never comes with us even though he was raised Catholic. I asked him once why he didn't go to church; he told me he was a "retired Catholic."

Would he like to come out of retirement? He probably stopped going to church on account of my mother. Sharon is obviously a better person. She'd bring him back to the church. My friend Patty, who is Catholic, says: "Once you're a Catholic, you are always a Catholic. You can't truly leave." Leslie and her mother aren't Catholics, but any church is better than none.

Sharon being a religious person is a real plus for me but her best trait is how she listens to you. My mother never listens, she prefers to talk. What's worse is her choice of embarrassing topics no matter who's in the room. I often say, "Mom, I can hear you," but she won't stop. "You might be too young to do it but you aren't too young to hear about it. Sex is just a normal part of life, Rosie. We discussed things like this in my family when I was much younger than you."

◆━━━━━◆━━━━━◆

One evening Granny Nessie, my parents, and Aunt Paulee were at our house. We were sitting in the living room before having dinner to celebrate Granny's retirement. My mother was talking about some sex toy called the Pine Cone Vibrator. Granny would never initiate these discussions but would join in willingly. She and my mother were chatting away while the rest of us looked very uncomfortable–until my father said, "Can I speak to you in the kitchen privately, Sarah." He always said that, I don't know why he didn't just say, *shut up*. They went into the kitchen and when they came back my mother sat down on the couch and said, "Well, sorry, Joe wants me to change the subject." He then laughed and she punched his arm like they were now sharing some little private joke with each other–with an erotic overtone. It felt creepier than her talking about the Pine Cone Vibrator.

She can't control herself and growing up she didn't care if my friends were present. One time before my friend Kevin and I left the house she said, "Now no fooling around you two, only tongue kissing allowed." I was only thirteen and mortified. My father asked her to come into the kitchen with him that day too; we could hear them all the same.

"Why are you putting those thoughts in their heads, Sarah?"

"I'm not putting the thoughts into their heads, they're already there. I'm just letting them know, I know it." We were only walking to get ice cream at a nearby Dairy Queen and meeting some other friends. It wasn't even a real date, and I hadn't even done any serious kissing before she mentioned it.

She was worse when I was older. She could get real down and humiliating: wet dreams, masturbation and oral sex. My girlfriends didn't mind; Dorrie and Patty were always saying, "Your mom is so cool, I wish my mother was like her." It was my guy friends and dates who were uncomfortable. They were dazzled or dazed by my mother's beauty when they first met her. *Did they accidentally walk in on a movie set?* Then when she opened her mouth they probably thought it was a porno flick. That's how it was for Phil. Proms are supposed to be memorable and I'm sure Phil will never forget his senior prom thanks to my mom.

The night of the prom my father was out of town for work and my mother took over the traditional parent roles. She took pictures inside the house, at the door before we left and standing next to the car. We weren't fast enough getting into the car; she had to give Phil *the little talk*. Many fathers do that and Phil probably was not surprised that my mother was taking over the duty since Daddy was gone. He also thought it would be *normal* crap; he didn't know my mother.

"First of all, I want to remind you she is only fifteen years old. I've been reading about what kids are doing, and I don't approve, but I know I can't stop you." Phil just stood there staring, not saying a word; I was afraid he was going to split right then and there, but I didn't really care because I wanted to disappear. She wouldn't stop humiliating me. Her next move? She gave us a little gift bag; they were oral condoms: bubble gum, strawberry and root beer. She told us she didn't know how good they were because she and my father never used any kind of condoms. Before we left she reminded us once again, "Remember, I am not condoning or encouraging this behavior and those condoms are meant to be used only orally–absolutely no intercourse. Now go and have a great time at the prom."

We got into Phil's car and threw the bag in the back seat. I don't know what he was thinking, but I couldn't stop thinking about oral condoms. I never knew anything like that existed but I was only fifteen and a virgin.

Was I just naive? Phil and I did not talk about it. All he said to me was, "Your mother is very unusual." Yes, she is, and I didn't want an unusual mother. I want an average mother like Sharon.

My father did spend the week in Chapel Hill and then drove Leslie and me back to school after the break. Sharon was gushing how it was so generous of him; it saved her money not having to pay for airfare back to school for Leslie. I noticed a number of things during my father's stay besides Sharon frequently thanking my father for driving. She focused most of her time on him–almost exclusively; she wasn't as attentive to what Leslie and I were saying when Daddy was there. I gave her a break though, it was obvious she was interested– too many smiles, too many overtures to engage him in talk. It was a good thing, right? Exactly what Leslie and I had wanted. She would get a new daddy and I would get a new mother. I knew our parents would eventually marry; it was inevitable if they became a couple. Daddy was too honorable and Sharon was too religious for them not to make it legal. And after their marriage Leslie and I would become real sisters legally.

I went through a couple of periods in my life yearning for a sibling. One was when I was in early grade school and everyone had a brother or sister except me. I felt like I was being cheated out of something. It also bothered me because I was teased about being a spoiled only child. After I got older I didn't care. I didn't want to share the attention with anyone, and if that made me spoiled, I was okay with it.

Now at eighteen living away from home, and having been abandoned by my mother, I need more family connection; I yearn for a sibling again. More specifically, I would like Leslie to be my sister. We live together like sisters already being roommates at school; we both wish it could be for real. Strange how things have turned out and it's actually happening; pretty unbelievable to imagine that there is now a possibility of us becoming true sisters. It's not just a fantasy that Leslie and I share.

My father was not helping though. He was pleasant enough at Thanksgiving but it was obvious he was not romantically interested in Sharon. He kept interjecting comments all the time like: "my wife makes a similar dish as this" or "my wife would like that picture you have over your fireplace." What the hell was his problem? He also told me he would appreciate it if I didn't mention that he stayed in Chapel Hill to my mother. He didn't want her "to get the wrong idea." I wanted to scream: *she left you; your wife is gone; she walked out on you, Daddy. She's in fucking Minnesota.* He was not making this easy, and he was shattering my dreams.

◆———◆———◆

I have to thank my mother for helping to move things along and furthering her own demise. A year after she left she told Daddy she wasn't coming back. You can only push a person so far, even if my mother is doing the pushing. Daddy was not able to continue defending her actions, and he started to date Sharon. We will be spending Thanksgiving and the fall break in Chapel Hill again this year, with huge differences. The most significant is that my father and Sharon are a couple, but even more impressive is that my father doesn't care if I tell my mother where he is spending Thanksgiving this year. *Tough luck bitch.*

CHAPTER 4

SHARON

Thanksgiving should be reserved for close family and friends, but on Thanksgiving following Leslie's first semester at school we had unwanted guests–Rosie and her father, Joe. They didn't come uninvited and Leslie had wanted them there so it is unfair to say they were *unwanted*, but I had not been thrilled about them coming. I tried to discourage Leslie from inviting Rosie but I finally gave in. It was preferable to her asking to spend the holiday at their house. I would soon find out that was impossible because Rosie's mother had deserted her husband and family. They would not be hosting the holiday for anyone, and that's how a second invitation came about for Joe.

Leslie had grown very close to Rosie in a very short time. I was certainly not close to the girl, but she was not a complete stranger. I first met her and her parents at the start of the spring semester when my brother Pete and I were moving Leslie into her dorm. It was to be her first semester in campus housing because all the classes had been remote in the fall, and Rosie was moving in at the same time. Joe doesn't remember meeting me, and I don't think we talked beyond introductions. And in fairness, I can't remember any conversation with him. What I do remember was how he was carrying so many things up to the room. It made me think his daughter must be spoiled and it was my misfortune that she was Leslie's roommate. I also noticed it didn't seem to be very hard for him to carry all of her belongings nor did he complain. He was quite a big man and looked strong; like a lumberjack misplaced in Miami. He hadn't held my attention for long though; what had captured my eye was Rosie and her mother.

They were both wearing tops which showed too much chest. And the mother had a rose tattoo on her breast like some biker girl, not that I had ever met one. The mother made me uncomfortable and the fact that she was the mother of my daughter's roommate raised my concern for Leslie. I began to seriously consider making Leslie request a new roommate. I know she thinks she's all grown up now but she isn't. I did not want Leslie to be swayed by a roommate's unacceptable behavior. God forbid the daughter had tattoos like her mother.

I learned later that the daughter's name was Rosie; I wondered if her mother's tattoo was some sort of symbolic declaration of maternal love. I'm glad she loves her daughter but she should express it differently. It was a sin to deface your body, and she also showed disrespect for her daughter by the way she dressed. Bad enough young girls dress disgracefully these days, but having your own mother dressing like she was eighteen, especially at a school orientation, was shameful. They might be mother and daughter but I wouldn't be surprised to discover that they competed with one another.

Luckily Rosie's mother had not been aware of what I was thinking, and when she saw me looking at her she smiled. She told me her name was Sarah Janak and her daughter was Rosie.

I never met anyone like her before, and it had nothing to do with her tattoo. Rosie was pretty but her mother looked like an actress on TV or a model on a magazine cover; she was beautiful, no denying that. My parents would have called her *too fancy for their liking*, and I agree.

There had been no basis for my dislike, other than her looks and clothing; she was pleasant enough. It may have been due in part to my brother Pete. Sarah definitely was to his liking. He made a fool of himself, and I was very uncomfortable by the way he fawned and gaped at her. He had apparently overlooked the very large husband and I was anxious to finish the move. We had planned to drive over to Leslie's grand-mother's in Miami Beach after we finished to have a nice meal at my favorite restaurant on Collins Avenue. Pete had put the fear of God in me that we would spend the evening in the ER instead if he had a con-frontation with the lumberjack.

Thank the Lord that had not happened, but I did start praying more. I was not happy about Leslie rooming with Rosie. I prayed she would not feel outshined by this girl because young girls are so obsessed with their looks these days. It takes maturity to understand that beauty does not have lasting value. It didn't matter if Leslie wasn't pretty like her roommate. She was a good girl and a serious student, she made the dean's list her first semester. I wanted that to continue.

I prayed the Lord would protect her from being steered in the wrong direction by this Jezebel. There were boys to consider now since Leslie was living on campus, and her roommate looked like a tramp. I knew her type. She had an unhealthy interest in boys, and I wouldn't be surprised to find out she also drank and took drugs. I did not relax until I reminded myself, very seldom does a first-year student become friends with their assigned roommate in college. I at least learned that valuable lesson from my college experience. Leslie would probably not become close enough to this girl to feel outshined or misdirected. My first roommate in college was horrid. She was a slob, and it looked like there was an invisible line drawn in the center of the room we shared. My side: well-ordered and clean; her side: chaos–not a single surface which didn't have books, clothes or food wrappers. I couldn't wait until I could get a new roommate the second year.

CHAPTER 5

LESLIE

I feel like a twelve-year-old compared to Rosie. She's so sophisticated and worldly. I was sure when I met her she'd be a snob or a bully. She reminded me of Hayley, the head cheerleader at my high school, who along with her friends used to make fun of me. I thought that was going to end when I was in college, so my first glimpse of Rosie sent dread through my body. To my surprise Rosie was friendly and she didn't act like Hayley at all. She's also prettier than her, and instead of making fun of me she gives me tips and advice about clothes and makeup.

It didn't take long to feel a true connection with her. It amazes me to think I am really friends with someone like her since I never had many friends my entire life, and girls like Rosie were always bullies.

I'm happy now but I have a different sense of dread like it's all a dream and won't last.

CHAPTER 6

SHARON

To my dismay, by the end of February Leslie and Rosie were not only roommates but had become best friends. Now I had to monitor this situation. I was glad Edith, Leslie's paternal grandmother, gave me an excuse to visit Leslie. That had always been a consideration, even before Rosie came on the scene. Leslie, like most young people, wanted to go to college away from home. I had been the same but I chose a school closer to my parental home. Leslie wouldn't consider any of our state schools in North Carolina. The only reason I agreed to a school in Florida was it was near Edith's condo. I had a convenient excuse to drop in on Leslie when I visited her grandmother. I had never visited her very often before Leslie went to school in Miami, but we did have a good relationship. She even took my side when Mike left Leslie and me to move in with his tramp. She thought it was disgraceful how her son had left his family. She took Mike out of her will when he divorced me. She made Leslie her beneficiary for the inheritance that would have gone to him.

Edith's condo being close to Leslie's school meant she could also drive there if need be. Now it was a necessity. Leslie was in jeopardy of being tempted by forbidden fruits and Edith had to be my backup to keep Leslie focused on her studies. Leslie had hopes of becoming a lawyer. She did not take after me where studies were concerned, thank the Lord.

❖————❖————❖

I never cared for college and left after two years. Ironically, I had wanted to be a teacher but the problem was I did not enjoy the courses in the program. In spite of it, I am able to satisfy my aspirations by teaching Sunday school at my church (and the bible is superior to any book on pedagogy). I teach the seven through nine-year-olds every Sunday following the service. The Lord led me to my true path but it was a rocky road for a while.

I had no clue what I wanted to do after I dropped out of college. My mother told me I shouldn't worry about it because I'd "probably get married soon." I was not sure how that was going to happen. I was very shy and had never dated in high school nor had any success finding a long-term relationship in college. I thought Mother's memory was getting a bit fuzzy; she was confusing me with my younger sister Peg, who had no trouble attracting men. She must have forgotten, when I was a senior she asked my older brother Matt to escort me to my prom. I had been mortified and refused. Peg was the one who had dates for her junior and senior prom.

I had not been upset about not going; my good friend Connie, who was fat with a bad case of acne, had not been asked by anyone either. We planned to go to the movies on prom night, and that suited me fine, there hadn't been anyone I wanted to go with. No yearnings for an unrequited love or sexual urges, like most teens. I had not even shared much curiosity with girls my age about sex or virginity, even though they seemed to be popular topics amongst most of the girls I knew. Connie was afraid she would die a virgin. I told her it was a silly thing to be fearful about at eighteen.

Praise the Lord Leslie seems to feel the same way as me and she didn't even date when she was in high school. She was focused on her studies as it should be. I pray this will not change now because of Rosie.

CHAPTER 7

LESLIE

I don't know Rosie's mom so I don't understand their relationship. Rosie says she loves her mother but doesn't like her and that's why she doesn't want to talk to her. That's sad. I talk to Mom all the time about all kinds of things–except sex, boys or dating. She gets really uncomfortable with those subjects, and she makes me more uncomfortable. Rosie fills a necessary void.

Rosie doesn't just give me tips for makeup and clothes. She advises me on boys and sex, and she's helping me find dates. I never dated in high school so I'm at a total loss; I don't know what to say to a boy. I never had the opportunity to practice and it wasn't that I had no interest. I was really upset not going to my prom. When I tried to talk to my mom she just dismissed me. She said proms were for immature and silly people and I would realize that if I gave it more thought. I have given it a lot of thought but I still regret that nobody asked me. But like I said, it has always been impossible for me to talk about these kinds of things with her.

Now I'm in college and I like this guy in my American History class, but it's the same way it was when I was in high school. He doesn't notice me and I simply can't think of a single thing to say to him. Rosie is lucky because boys just gravitate to her without any effort on her part. She denies that and says she uses strategies to get attention and will teach me.

For starters, Rosie told me to tell my mother that the guy I want to date is named Noah to ease the way. "Noah is a big name in the bible. She might think his family is religious." I have no idea what his background is and I hadn't even considered my mother, but I would never say something to her if I wasn't sure. I doubted it would make an impression anyway. I don't think my mother wants me to go out with anyone until I finish school, no matter what their name is. The only thing she has ever said when it came to dating was it distracted from your studies, and quoted from the bible: "*For everything there is a season*, Leslie, and school is not the time for boys."

Rosie doesn't know my mom well, just like me with hers. I don't agree with her starter strategy, but I'm sure she'll come up with better ideas when it comes to attracting a guy. She has experience there while I have it with my mom. Rosie promises I will get Noah to notice me, and more–he will ask me out. And I believe her.

I find myself daydreaming now and lose track of what a professor is saying. Maybe my mom is right about *a season and a time.*

CHAPTER 8

SHARON

I hadn't cared if I remained a virgin forever and I maintained that attitude throughout college. I had no urge to touch or be touched. My relationships with most of the boys I dated didn't last long. The longest was a month with Charles from my computer class. I don't like to put people into categories but if I did, I would say Charles was a nerd. I only say it because most people considered me one. Charles was socially awkward and very smart. He wasn't interested in sex, or was too afraid to try anything. I'm not sure if that is characteristic of a college nerd, and not relevant to me. My lack of sexual enthusiasm did not end our relationship or the others with boys similar to him. They never stopped dating me because I wouldn't *put out* as some of the vulgar promiscuous girls would say; they dropped me when they discovered I wasn't a nerd. I was socially awkward like them but I was not an intellectual heavyweight. I was not above average in any area of study, nor was I interested in their knowledge.

Other boys I dated were not concerned about my brain power but they were interested in touching. I don't have much to touch on top but they would try to get their hands in there to check. Some also had the nerve to try putting a hand down my jeans. I ended those relationships myself.

Once I returned home from college my mother told me even though she was sure I would marry soon, I had to do something. "You can't just sit around on your duff all day, Sharon." I wasn't as confident as her of getting married soon or ever, and there wasn't anyone I met who made me want to marry. But I had no intention of doing nothing with my life; I decided to enroll in cosmetology school.

My mother couldn't understand it. I have very thin hair and I keep it in a ponytail most of the time. I've never styled it, but I didn't mind styling other people's hair. My mother was not keen on my decision to attend cosmetology school until I told her part of the curriculum was barbering skills. After I had my license I would be able to work as a barber and as a hair stylist for women. It made her feel better; there was a chance I might meet some men.

I did meet men, but most of them were happily married or very underage. It never mattered to me; I was very content and my mother still held hopes I would eventually meet someone. To speed that along she started setting up blind dates with the sons of her friends. That's how I met my husband, Mike. His mother was my mother's bridge partner. Edith had two sons–George and Michael. George was the oldest, settled and married with two children. Mike was her youngest but he was ten years older than me and still hadn't married. Edith was desperate for him to find a *nice girl*; she and my mother thought we were a perfect match.

Mike worked in a big insurance company in Raleigh as a claims adjuster. He made a very decent salary and was *good husband material* according to my mother. He was also a big lady's man. He wasn't handsome or even that attractive looking, but he was suave and a smooth talker. He reminded me of my father, who could present a very appealing front to strangers but was distant with his own family. Perhaps Mike reminded my mother of my father, and that's why she encouraged me to date him.

I finally reluctantly agreed, and he was very charming. Throughout our courtship he continued to be so. The problem was it did not stop with me. There had been several unfortunate incidents at the company before and while I dated Mike, when he had been too charming with young interns at work. He was encouraged by the higher ups to settle down or seek employment elsewhere. They preferred their male employees to be family men; it fit their image better.

I had not known any of this until Mike started cheating on me after we were married. That's when my mother told me about his checkered past. I asked her why she had set me up with him if she knew it. She told me Edith assured her he was ready to settle down. "Besides, men will be men," which was meant to justify her matchmaking and his cheating. In fairness to Mother she did not know he would cheat after we married, and she thought his background was an advantage since I had very little experience. "It's better if someone knows what they're doing, Sharon."

I don't know if Mike knew what he was doing or not but whatever he was doing did not increase my desire to touch or be touched. I was a good Christian wife however; I never refused him. This was about the time I became more involved with my church beyond going to weekly services, and when I started to teach Sunday school. I also started a weekly adult bible study group in my home. I knew my wifely duties as dictated by the bible; I only refused to do things which were not natural. That's why I still don't understand why Mike told me I was frigid. It only was his excuse to cheat, to which I chose to turn a blind eye. And I never stopped my obligations as a wife in spite of his philandering. I was blessed for it. I got what I wanted from the union–my daughter Leslie. I was able to direct all my passion and love towards her because I had none to give to her father.

When Leslie turned fourteen Mike left me for his secretary who was young enough to be another daughter. It felt like he had cheated on Leslie along with me, and she had adored him–*little girls and their daddies.* I had never experienced that connection myself growing up with my father, but such was not the case with Leslie. She loved Mike and was devastated when he left. It was the only reason I was upset when he was gone. It was for her, not me.

I had not cared that he had been unfaithful to me or that he had wanted a divorce. I was a Christian, not Catholic. Most people don't know that Adam had a first wife named Lilith. She left him and the union was dissolved. Eve was Adam's second wife. If a failed marriage was not shameful for Adam, it was not shameful for me. I shed no tears. What was shameful, Leslie being deprived of a full-time father–that had been on Mike. He needed to beg God for forgiveness or burn in eternal hell.

Two years after he left me, and one year after our divorce was final he died from liver cancer. I am not glad, nor would I ever say I was. All I say is God works in mysterious ways.

◆───◆───◆

Leslie still misses her daddy. I wonder sometimes if she is looking for someone to fill his shoes, and that's why she kept pestering me about inviting Rosie's father to our house for the Thanksgiving break. Then I found out about Rosie's mother leaving her husband. Leslie was distraught; she told me if I didn't invite her father, Rosie refused to come to our home for the holiday as planned. Rosie had not wanted her father to be alone. It was the first positive thing I was willing to admit about Rosie–she loved her father. But I did not like this new idea; it was bad enough I had agreed to having her spend the break with us–now Leslie wanted to invite her father?

He was a stranger, and based on his daughter I anticipated a crude, boorish man. He hadn't appeared that way when I saw him in the spring but he was busy carrying boxes. I had not been able to evaluate him in any meaningful way. Still, there was no way he could possibly be a decent man with a daughter like Rosie and a wife like Sarah.

Sarah leaving her husband reminded me of Lilith leaving Adam, although I was not suggesting Rosie's father was an *Adam*. I continued not wanting to invite him for the Thanksgiving break. I asked Leslie, "Doesn't Rosie's father have any other family he could spend the holiday with?" Apparently he did not, and Leslie became inconsolable when I said it was Rosie's duty to spend Thanksgiving with him in New Jersey. Leslie's a good girl and finally accepted my decision but she was so disappointed–I finally relented.

I was afraid of a *Romeo and Juliet Effect* developing. Nothing sexual in nature to be sure, I am not suggesting in any way that my daughter is unnatural, but I had a fear they would become closer if I discouraged their friendship. That's why I agreed to having Rosie stay with us over the break initially and would now reluctantly extend an invitation to her father for the Thanksgiving meal. But just for the meal. Leslie's school is off for an entire week; if he wanted to spend more time with his daughter he needed to stay at a motel. I had my limits.

I could think of nothing positive about seeing Rosie's father, but the one positive aspect about Rosie staying with us was I could continue my surveillance of their relationship. Having had the opportunity to know Rosie better these past few months, my fear of Leslie being negatively influenced had increased.

The first time I made a closer evaluation of Rosie was two months after spring orientation. I was visiting Edith and I called Leslie to tell her I was dropping over to see her. I'd take her to the fish restaurant we were so fond of. She asked if Rosie could come along, she didn't want to leave her. I told her I was sure Rosie could find something to amuse herself while she was gone. But apparently they had made previous plans to do something together that evening so I agreed. I was firm though, "You both have to dress properly; remember this is a nice restaurant, not a wild sports bar." I wasn't worried about Leslie naturally; it was the little tramp, and that evening was the first time I saw Rosie's smokey eye makeup. With those eyes and her wild curly blonde hair framing her face, she looked like a raccoon with a lion's mane. She was arresting and much prettier than I remembered her in spite of it, but that was probably because she was not standing next to her mother.

I should have mentioned makeup and hair to Leslie in addition to clothes but I had not anticipated everything. At least Rosie was wearing a proper top, but her skirt stopped in the middle of her thigh. I asked her if she had a skirt a little bit longer and she said no. I embarrassed Leslie, "Mom, it's a tutu skirt, everyone is wearing them." She wasn't and I hoped it wasn't something she would ever ask me to buy for her. I saved it for a later discussion, and I could not think of anything to say in response to Rosie saying she had nothing more appropriate to wear.

It could have been worse. I chose to ignore her skirt and her three-inch-high heels. They made her long tan legs stand out even more, and we had unwanted attention walking to our table at the restaurant that evening. I doubt if any of the men noticed her eyes or hair.

I don't like her. Not only how she dresses and her makeup, there's something hard and brash about her–a girl who has been around. That evening when Rosie went out to dinner with us Leslie was wearing a modest blue sundress with little white flowers and her cute sandals. She was fresh and innocent in contrast to Rosie. I just don't understand what draws these two together–they are total opposites, praise the Lord. Nevertheless, I have promised myself–if I ever see Leslie with eye makeup which makes her look like a raccoon, I am telling her she's transferring to a school in North Carolina. It would be futile to say: *find a new roommate*; they could still remain friends attending the same school.

CHAPTER 9

ROSIE

My roommate is a nerd but it doesn't bother me because I am the daughter of a nerd. Daddy indirectly influenced me to have a natural acceptance of them. And Leslie does not embrace her nerdiness making her more open to change. She listens to suggestions I make while other nerdy people I've known are stubborn and arrogant, with the exception of Daddy.

I look at Leslie as a naive little sister who I can teach the ways of the world. I'm making her my pet project along with classes and maintaining my social presence.

My mother said Leslie seemed like a nice girl, and reminded her of Dorrie. That's true. They both wear glasses and are nerds. It's too bad my mother likes Leslie. I don't want her to think I'm friends with her because she wants me to be. I was able to avoid that kind of thinking with Dorrie, but it was tough sometimes. My mother's admiration for her was often used against me.

"Why can't you try to be more like Dorrie, Rosie? I don't see her using garish eye makeup or dressing like you." Dorrie had no sense of style, like Leslie.

Leslie is going to be a challenge to mentor. I could not believe that sundress she was wearing when we went out to eat with her mother. It looked like something I refused to wear when I was four. No fucking joke.

CHAPTER 10

SHARON

The next time I saw Rosie was in May at the end of spring semester, around the time her mother left her father. She told me her mother left him to move to Minneapolis to teach at a college in Minnesota. I was shocked, her mother was a professor? Maybe colleges and universities are filled with subversive types teaching our children. I asked her, "What does she teach: film, theater, or art?" She told me she taught mathematics. I continue to be in shock over that and I hope Leslie does not have any professors like Rosie's mother. I can't erase the image out of my mind of her clothes; how does she dress? If similar to how she was dressed when I saw her at the orientation, I'm sure there are more boys than girls in her classes.

Rosie was very upset about her mother having left her father, and in spite of the woman being horrid, I could not believe how Rosie talked about her. I finally asked her not to use that kind of language in front of me. A shameless woman and an uncouth brazen daughter; it was completely understandable for me to have low expectations for the father.

But I would do anything to protect my daughter. If that meant keeping an eye on Leslie and Rosie's relationship rather than objecting to it and inviting *the* father for Thanksgiving, so be it. That's how I discovered this family was full of surprises. He wasn't a boorish, unpleasant man. He was–*Adam who was left by Lilith and shackled by her spawn.*

Two days after I told Leslie Rosie's father could come for Thanksgiving he called me. He said he hoped he wasn't putting me out, and he appreciated the invitation; he wanted to be able to see Rosie. She had been so set on spending the break with Leslie he hadn't wanted to insist she come home to New Jersey. Perhaps that's why she was so spoiled. It was the only thought I had about Rosie during the entire call. My mind went in many unexpected directions led by his voice, which was very deep and strong, but there was nothing threatening about it. He had a very measured and calm way of speaking which put me at ease. It was a voice I could trust. My father and Mike were very fast talkers. Their words often slipped right past me. I often thought it was their intent. I would ask Mike, "Why weren't you home for dinner?" and he'd reply that he had told me the night before he was going to be late–hadn't I heard him? He'd accuse me of not paying attention. The truth was his words were often too well-oiled to easily hold onto.

I did not have to grab at snatches with Joe; I could take my time because he took his time. That's when I knew I would have remembered his voice. I had never heard it; Sarah must have said, "This is my husband Joe," on the day we were introduced. He had never spoken to me that day.

❖

The girls flew up from Miami a few days before Thanksgiving and Joe drove down from New Jersey, arriving on Thanksgiving Day. He brought me a basket of fruit and nuts and a beautiful bouquet of multicolored mums. It was the first time any man had given me a bouquet of flowers. Even when Mike was trying to catch my fancy he never gave me flowers. If he had they would have simply been part of a master plan to try to bed or wed me. These flowers had no ulterior motive. They were only meant to express thanks.

My initial reaction to Joe when he stepped into my home was the polar opposite of how I felt about his daughter; I was drawn to him in a positive way. I found myself trying to block Rosie out for the rest of the day and evening, and in doing so I often blocked out my own daughter. If I focused primarily on Joe I could sometimes forget Rosie was even there.

At times I shamefully wished it were only this man I hardly knew and me. I was grateful that there were no other family members at my table to draw me away from him. After my siblings and I grew up, we went our separate ways; the holidays were a mish mash. We no longer kept a set tradition for visiting. This year my parents were going to Peg and Lenny's and Matt was spending the holidays with his in-laws. My brother Pete, who was divorced, planned to go to Peg's for dinner and afterwards to my house for dessert. I made better desserts than my sister who was always worrying about her weight.

The meal was very pleasant and I wished Pete was not coming over after he had Thanksgiving dinner with Peg. He was my brother; I couldn't uninvite him but I hoped Peg had made a good dessert this year and he would decide to stay there. She didn't and shortly after we had finished our meal I heard the front doorbell ring. When I introduced Pete to Joe there was no recognition in his face until he saw Rosie.

"Oh, hi, I remember you. You look like your mother. Where is she?" I couldn't believe he asked where Sarah was. The only consolation, Joe knew I had not been gossiping about his situation with my family. I do not gossip about people. Idle talk is the work of the devil. I have never even shared personal information about myself with anyone. I was not terribly close with other girls when I was younger, and I have continued to be private as an adult. I'm friendly but I only share general information with women friends: recipes, church news, gardening and quilting tips, and topics of the day. My friend Michelle is always telling me private information about herself and expects me to reciprocate. She often becomes annoyed when I won't do it.

It is surprising or often shocking what some women will tell me about their lives. I work as a hair stylist in a salon called The Hair Clipper four days a week. There are women clients who tell me very intimate details; I don't encourage them. I don't want to hear about their sex lives or their benign ovarian cysts. What is amusing though, while many of these women will gush out all this sewage openly in the shop, if they see me outside of work they snub me. Did they realize what was said afterwards and now are embarrassed? Many of them should be ashamed of themselves. Although these same women, as soon as they come back to the shop, will often spill it all out again.

I prefer my men clients–they seldom talk, like me. In addition to that I'm fast. These men are interested in getting a haircut and getting out of the shop as soon as possible. Other men who come to the shop looking for more than haircuts prefer the younger pretty girls. Which brings me back to what my brother said when he saw Rosie on Thanksgiving.

Did Rosie look like her mother? I suppose she did, but only because Sarah wasn't there. It was only a pale resemblance which would fade even more if they were together in the flesh. Rosie was about to pipe up immediately in response to Pete's question about where her mother was, but I saw Joe shoot a glance at her before she opened her mouth. She only told Pete her mother was in Minneapolis without any more detail and no disgraceful language. That's when I noticed her makeup, hair and clothing were acceptable. She obviously restrained herself when her father was present. There might be hope for her yet. Maybe her soul could be saved if she was pointed in the right direction.

Rosie did not say any more about her mother. It was Joe who picked up the thread telling my brother Sarah was teaching in Minneapolis and wasn't coming home for the holiday. He never mentioned he was separated from her, and I'm glad Pete changed the subject to a discussion about fall weather in Minnesota. I really wasn't paying full attention to the weather discussion–I was reflecting on how Joe used the word *home* when he told my brother about Sarah. He made it sound as though the separation was temporary.

Joe also mentioned Sarah in a positive or neutral way quite frequently which was strange, considering she left him. I never heard him speak a negative word about her. He did not have to talk badly about his wife–Rosie more than made up for it herself. It still was admirable on his part he never spoke unkindly about Sarah; I respected that. I had never talked ill about Mike either, and I wouldn't do that because Leslie loved him. Unlike Joe though, I try to refrain from talking about Mike as much as possible–when he was alive and since he's been dead.

One of the first things Joe said when he gave me the flowers was he hoped I liked them. He was going to give me a box of chocolates instead but his wife refused to eat sweets; maybe I was the same? He figured he was safe with flowers. Sarah and every woman he knew liked flowers. I liked both, and the flowers would be only the first of many gifts from him, including chocolates. I'm not Sarah.

CHAPTER 11

JOE

My sister Lynne told me she thought Sarah was a slut, and I'd be crazy if I married her–it wouldn't last. She was wrong about it not lasting. Things were rocky for the first couple of years but it will be nineteen years this coming December. I'll have to subtract some time from our years if she's still gone in December, or she doesn't agree to me moving out there with her by that time, but I'm hopeful I won't have to do that.

I never could understand why my sister thought Sarah was a slut. I was a pretty good authority on sluts since those were the kind of women I had relationships with for a good part of my life before meeting her. I hadn't been very comfortable or popular with girls in high school–no girlfriends or even dates. I lost my virginity when I was nineteen in a whorehouse in Anchorage, Alaska.

I was working on a commercial fishing boat for the summers and was the youngest member of a crew of eighteen men. They were a rough bunch, but after living with my father Mac they didn't bother me. I even became friends with a number of them. They told me they couldn't send me back home after the second season without seeing the sights of the city. They dragged me to this ranch-style house in a neighborhood called South Addition. I didn't know what was going on; how was this a sight I needed to visit before returning to New Jersey? It was clear what it was once we went in, but there wasn't a neon light in the window saying *Sadie's House*. Although the head lady, who looked to be in her early fifties, was named Sadie. The working girls were younger; they didn't look much older than me, but I was still scared to death the first time. For the next two years I continued to work on the boats in the summer and I was a regular customer at *Sadie's House*. After that most of my relationships were girls I met in bars. They often made me more nervous than the whores; I was worried about catching something from them. At least at Sadie's house they tried to maintain a good reputation.

The point is I knew what I was talking about and Sarah wasn't a slut. Why did Lynne say that? She told me "it was obvious by the way she dressed." It was true Sarah dressed in a very sexy way, but she was stylish, she didn't look like a whore. She didn't look the way Rosie did the day I saw her and totally lost my cool. I was ashamed about my behavior; I hate to lose control. There's no justification but I was afraid for her. I knew there were guys who would rape girls dressed like Rosie; their excuse was they had been asking for it. I heard some guys talk like that on the fishing boats. They were the lowlifes and I wasn't friends with them.

There was no justification for forcing someone to have sex if they didn't want it.

My sister had it so wrong, and clothes were only one thing; Sarah never behaved like a slut. She didn't even let me kiss her for six months. It was true she wasn't interested in dating me until then but many of the girls I met in the bars weren't interested in dating me ever. It didn't stop them from having sex with me on the same night we met.

I also never see Sarah coming on to men. It was another warning of my sister's: "Wake up, big brother, she looks like a tramp. Do you really want to be worrying about a wife cheating on you all the time?" I've never worried about that and I don't care if men look at her. Let them look all they want; she'd never let it go beyond that–I got the prize. I think Lynne is just jealous of Sarah. I never say that because I don't want to hurt her feelings, and I imagine many women are jealous–Sarah is too beautiful.

There was nothing in Sarah's behavior that justified my sister talking like she had; unless she hid a camera in our house to spy on private things between us. I was uncomfortable with some of Sarah's sexual preferences when we were first married, but it had nothing to do with her. I had hangups from things that happened to me when I was a kid. Sarah actually helped me get past them. She was sexually uninhibited; comfortable in her skin. She could walk around stark naked like an innocent child. Just being around her eventually made me more at ease in mine. Her skin is soft and white like a baby's too, but there's no mistaking she is a woman. I got lost smothering my face in her breasts. I might share some of the view with other men but never her feel or the whole picture. They see her rose tattoo on the top of her tit. Very sexy, but not as sexy as her pink nipples that look like rosebuds. I've been accused of sucking them too hard more than once.

Sarah excites me. I marvel at how she's so at ease with her body, and admit the only other women I've known who act like that were girls at Sadie's house. That's as far as the similarity goes, and Sarah definitely has more imagination than they had without a charge. I once came home to find her peeling carrots stark naked with only a little apron on; too small to completely cover her tits and ass. I asked her what she thought she was doing and she said "trying to spice up our sex life." She then slowly removed the apron like she was stripping and threw it on top of the counter over the carrots. She was taking her time, making me crazy. I thought it was going to take forever. I was more than ready when we finally made love on the kitchen floor. My sister would have flipped if she had heard that story. Sarah had enough brains to know she shouldn't share it with her, or highlights from some show about sexuality she saw as a kid.

My mother-in-law is also similar to Sarah. They openly talk about things like that show, but I never heard them do it in front of Lynne. If they had, Lynne would be calling Sarah's mother a slut too. And in spite of Lynne's dislike and warnings, she stopped bad mouthing Sarah once we were married. She started again when Sarah left me. She also began saying how I should have married Maureen.

◆——◆——◆

Maureen was the only long-term relationship I had prior to meeting Sarah. Her family owns a hobby shop where I buy my model plane kits and supplies. She was a manager there and that's how I met her. We started dating and she eventually moved into my townhouse with her cat Ollie. My sister really liked Maureen; she thought we were a perfect match: "She's very sweet, and reserved like you. She'd make a good wife. What are you waiting for Joe? Pretty soon you won't have the energy to play with your children." Lynne knew I wanted to settle down and have kids but I wasn't sure it was Maureen I wanted to do it with. I just let my sister talk; she wasn't going to sway me. I didn't think Maureen and I were a good fit.

It was true she didn't talk much in a group, like me, but she was a bit of a nag in private. I wouldn't have described her as sweet. We had a number of problems. She complained about my untidiness for one. I did not see a problem and it was my townhouse. Disagreements about socks and underwear on the floor were meaningless as I saw it since she didn't contribute to the mortgage or any tax or utility bills. She bought the food.

I didn't eat any red meat or pork in my home for the three years she lived with me. My lack of neatness and her food choices weren't the only problems. One of her biggest gripes was my refusal to attend church with her. She was a very devout Catholic. She asked me, "Joe, don't you believe in heaven and hell?" She was worried about my soul. My response did not reassure her I could be saved.

'Yes, but not after you die, Maureen. There's plenty of hell right here on earth though. There's heaven too, but not as much."

"Do you even believe in God?"

"No. I don't believe there is a god up in heaven, Maureen. Only people on earth who play around with people's lives like they think they're gods."

There is no point going to church when you don't believe in a god; it really bothered her. Especially when she went and I played a round of golf if the weather was good. She'd be so pissed she wouldn't talk to me for the rest of the day.

The thing that bothered her the most though, and what she nagged about every day was *marriage*. I wouldn't marry her. She was "living in sin" according to her, and that's what eventually ended it. I came home one day and all of her stuff was gone, except for Ollie; she left him. I liked Ollie but why didn't she take her cat with her? I went to the hobby shop and her brother said she left town for a while. I asked him, "What about her cat?" Jeff seemed really uncomfortable but he finally answered. "Look Joe, I like you, man. I really don't want to get between you and my sister. But she said if you came in here looking for her to tell you, you can keep Ollie. She said you're more committed to the cat than to her." Maybe she was right.

My father mocked me when he found out I was keeping the cat. He told me real men don't have cats for pets; Ollie made him reconsider that kind of thinking. Ollie was a Maine Coon cat and he weighed twenty-five pounds and with all his hair he looked enormous. When Mac saw him he was shocked; when he finally spoke he said, "Are you sure he's a cat? He looks like a fucking bear." A few months later I bought a second Maine Coon to keep Ollie company because I traveled so much. I named him Bear.

◆———————◆

I might not believe in God or we get our just rewards in heaven or hell after we die, but I do believe in luck. I was lucky a few months after Maureen left me when I saw Sarah on a two-lane road near my sister's house in Wall. She had a flat tire, and I stopped to see if she wanted any help. She looked like an angel; it felt like I had wandered into a little bit of heaven on earth that day. I was lucky too that she didn't follow her natural inclinations when she first met me. She wasn't romantically interested in me at all. She was open to being my friend though and eventually I closed the deal. The same with many prospective buyers; sometimes it's better not to be pushy. You have to have more patience with some people, just like fishing.

The last year working as a commercial fisherman I stayed a week after the job finished to do sports fishing. My buddies thought I was crazy, "Haven't you seen enough fish, man." I knew I'd never go back to

Alaska, and I was not anxious to return home. Halibut is one of the hardest fish to catch; it takes strength and patience. I landed one that summer and had a halibut tattooed on my right arm. My way of reminding myself that it takes strength and patience to get what you want. Some fish are harder to catch than others; Sarah was a hard catch.

I miss Sarah: her tits, her ass, her pussy and her brains. She hasn't changed from the first day I met her. She's still like a halibut and worth all it takes to recapture, but I also believe she'd return willingly if she started using those brains of hers. I might be wrong about that though. The problem may be an overuse of brain power.

Another reason my sister Lynne told me she didn't like Sarah was that she thought she was "too argumentative." I didn't understand that any more than her tramp and slut labels. Sarah is one of the most nonjudgmental people I know–another thing I love about her. I asked Lynne why she thought she was "argumentative."

"No matter what you say, she always has to come back with a different point of view." It was true, but she wasn't arguing. Sometimes I'd make a point and she would respond with five different perspectives. I'd finally say, "Well, what point do you agree with?" Nine times out of ten she agreed with the original point I had made. It was a waste of words, if you ask me. It mucks up your head, filling it with thoughts you don't need, and after a while you can't think at all. That's the reason I can't become angry at her for leaving me. I'm not being a "sap" like my sister says. I just know Sarah better than Lynne does. Sarah is too smart for her own good–sometimes it makes her think too much.

I also consider Sarah's age. She doesn't look old but she's around the age my mother was when she started to act crazy, hormones going wild which supposedly they call the change of life. I'm too uncomfortable talking to my mother about it but I decided to talk to my sister. "Do you remember when Mom was acting crazy when she was around Sarah's age? How long did it last?" That's when I was surprised to find out my sister hadn't gotten over her dislike for Sarah after all these years. "Please Joe, I hope you are not suggesting Sarah is comparable to our mother? I told you Sarah was a slut and a tramp and that you shouldn't marry her. But you did it in spite of my warning, and I knew it wouldn't *last*." If my sister was totally honest she'd have to admit, almost twenty years is pretty long. She was funny, and I might have even laughed it off but she had finally made me angry with her bad mouthing.

"Lynne, I don't want to hurt you, but if you ever say another bad thing about Sarah, I'm going to have to say something you won't like. You'll probably tell me to get out of your house and never come back again." She was upset at me for saying only that and asked me to leave. It was okay with me, but I wasn't going to get any help from her.

There's also Paulee. She is one of the few people I truly trust when it comes to my relationship with Sarah.

She likes and cares about both of us, but I don't want to talk about stuff like this with her. I might have to reconsider speaking to my mother. At least I know she likes Sarah. She was upset when I told her she had left. I didn't get any support from my father but that was to be expected. My father has always had a way of making me feel worse at times when I was already feeling bad. As soon as he heard the news he said, "That's not a bombshell, why did it take so long? I never could understand why a beautiful woman like her would be with a pansy like you. What's the matter, can't you get it up anymore?" My mother tried to defend me. She usually did but all the same I was surprised; I never heard her speak to my father like that before. "I wouldn't talk about people not being able to get it up if I were you, dear."

One might have expected my father to lash out at her, but he's a coward at heart. He knew if he ever said an abusive word directly to her or touched her in anger, she might come into the bedroom when he was sleeping and hit him over the head with a frying pan. Or season his food with some of the stuff they used to keep groundhogs out of their yard.

My mom has always tried to protect me and she likes Sarah. Two pluses, but talking about this topic with her is not something I can do. I'll research it by my own devices, but I'm no scholar like Sarah. I suggested she do a Google search for something when she was working on her PhD and she flipped out. "Joe, that is not real research. I'm not even allowed to use Google search." Google is good enough for me.

And I don't care what Sarah uses to find all the answers to my questions. I just want her to find them. The only thing she is sure about is she doesn't want me to move out there. Using my *strength and patience* I keep asking my same questions over and over again: why don't you want me to move out there; is this job going to be permanent; are you coming back or not? Her answer for them all is always, "I don't know." I was afraid to ask the ultimate question for a long time: *do you want a divorce, Sarah?* I don't know why I feared her answer. It was the same as usual.

◆————————◆————————◆

Sarah was more definite a year after she left. She is now certain she is not coming back but she still doesn't know whether or not she wants a divorce. I'm being played. I love her, but I don't feel like playing anymore. I am going to have to make a decision for both of us, like in my business.

Aside from those four years working as a commercial fisherman, I've worked in sales my entire life, selling wholesale air conditioner and heating units to businesses. They are big ticket items, requiring significant consideration at times on the buyer's part. They also provide big commissions for me. To make the most money, especially when you rely solely on commission for your income like I do, you have to know when you're just not going to close the deal. I need to know when to stop, when I am wasting my time. No matter how lucrative a contract might be, I'm losing other potential sales hanging out too long with a hopeless case. I've reached that point with Sarah.

Sarah has also toyed with me before. She didn't physically leave, but it felt very similar to how it feels now. Right after Rosie was born Sarah shut down. I thought at the time it was a normal effect after having a kid. I picked up the slack: cleaning, cooking, and caring for Rosie a good deal while still working at my job. I never complained, not even about her refusing to have sex for over a year. Some men feel they have the right with their wives. I never forced her. I would never do that, but she made me a celibate; she's doing it again.

Sex is not the only thing I miss. I miss having a woman in my life. It was not only thinking Sarah would come to her senses that made the first summer easier–Rosie was home. It didn't matter if she was out with friends, her presence remained in the house–I knew she was coming back. It was harder after she returned to school, and I need more than the mere presence of a female in my life. I need more than a daughter.

• —————— • —————— •

Sharon is the mother of Rosie's roommate at school. I met her at Thanksgiving last year. She seems like a nice lady. We started talking on the phone afterwards, as friends. After Sarah told me she was not coming back my conversations with Sharon changed. We didn't officially announce to our kids we were dating until August but we were more than friends before that. Sharon flew up here a couple of times and I drove down to Chapel Hill once. I've decided to sell the townhouse in Jackson because long distance relationships are hard, and I do like Chapel Hill. I never thought I wanted to move out of New Jersey. Sarah always said I never gave other places in the country a chance when I told her I didn't want to relocate. It took a long time but I'm finally in agreement with her.

Sex is different with Sharon. All women are different, but I haven't had sex with anyone besides Sarah for twenty years so it really seems strange. Sharon's body-type is nothing like Sarah's. The obvious is she doesn't have much of a chest to speak of, but I don't find her unattractive. There was a little Asian girl at *Sadie's House* who was built like her. I never went with her but I thought she was real cute. Sharon is petite and cute too, and it doesn't bother me that she has small tits. Only sometimes I get the sensation I'm making love to a very young girl. It makes me think of child molestation, and it's a real turn off.

I'm sure I'll stop thinking like that; Sharon is just so different from Sarah. It will take time for it not to feel strange. The bigger problem–feel is not the only thing nagging at me. Sarah's smell and taste are deep inside–a part of me. Sometimes I'm afraid thoughts of her will always keep getting in the way.

CHAPTER 12

SHARON

I like Joe. There aren't many men whom I meet I actually like. But the one advantage of not being very pretty is you're not bothered very much, which is a good thing. Most men from my experience only take notice when they want something. And if the something is sex, they don't pay much attention to me–which suits me fine. It was the same with my own husband, and eventually he preferred cheating to having marital relations. I didn't miss it then and I don't miss it now. My life is primarily focused on Leslie. Needless to say, she's less of a job now being in college and almost grown. I spend less time mothering, but I do have to monitor the Rosie problem.

And less mothering doesn't mean I'm idle. *Idle hands are the devil's workshop.* I keep busy with my job, the church, and caring for my home and garden. In addition to all that, I host the weekly bible study group, am a member of the Chapel Hill Ladies Flower Society and participate in a quilters club. The clubs work out well because they're seasonal. It leaves more time to devote to my bible study group which meets all year long. I don't need or want a man. That's why

I was surprised how often I kept thinking about Joe. He was different from other men. He was nice without an underlying reason and I was comfortable with him from the very start. He is the first man I have felt that way about in my entire life.

I never even had a good relationship with my father. The way he was friendly with strangers but distant with his children and Mother was unnatural. I could never see what she saw in him, but one never knows what goes on behind closed doors with couples. And they always seemed quite bonded; there must be something positive about Father. Maybe I was just unable to see it to feel comfortable with him. His aloofness is still off-putting.

Growing up with my brothers I always had a different kind of discomfort–unwanted attention. They were relentlessly annoying; putting worms under my pillow, sticking bugs in my hair and signs on my back. It was all a big joke to them and my parents never even tried to stop them from teasing. They were old school, believing I should learn to fight my own battles. I didn't do that very well, but survived, and we all are adults now. We aren't very close though.

I only see my older brother Matt a couple of times each year, and we seldom call one another. Card exchanges are sufficient to send birthday and holiday wishes. I see Pete more frequently because he lives quite near, but it doesn't mean I'm comfortable around him. His behavior is usually inappropriate. I never know when he'll say or do something to embarrass me–like the way he acted around Joe's wife on Leslie's move-in day.

Joe is not like my father, brothers, Mike or any other man I have ever met; he's sweet, considerate and very reserved. He even seems awkward at times, as though he doesn't know what to say. He reminds me of myself. I bet people called him a *nerd* like they did me in high school and college, but I don't think he's an intellectual. I am not saying he or I aren't intelligent, but he doesn't strike me as a scholarly type. He's a man with his feet on the ground, not his head in the clouds. Another reason why I was so surprised to find out about his wife being a professor.

Rosie told me her father did not push her to attend the university. He told her he'd be satisfied if she went to her community college. He thought four-year degrees had become "overrated." It had been her mother who pushed her about studying and school her entire life. She didn't like school and hated the way her mother was trying to turn her into a *scholar*. I did not think there was any real possibility of that happening, but clearly Rosie believed there was, "Just because she likes that shit doesn't mean I do." It was one of many occasions when I asked her to watch her language.

She also called her mother a *narcissist bitch* that evening. She was extremely angry because her father had paid for her mother's PhD and then she left him. That was not an excuse to use such language and I almost fainted when she cursed. I told her I really didn't want to hear any more about her family's private business. What she said stayed in my mind though.

Wasn't that what men did for years–ask their wives to put them through law or medical school, and then left them after they got their fancy degrees and careers for a cute secretary or nurse? In a perverse way I enjoyed hearing it played out in reversal, but I don't condone the behavior no matter who does it.

Rosie's mother is disgraceful. Her actions go against God's design for women. She will have to answer to him on judgment day for her blasphemous behavior, and I'm sorry it happened to Joe. I fear he has never been the stronger one in his marriage. He was unable to press his wishes when it came to Rosie as proof.

Joe had supported her choosing community college over the university but Sarah's wishes had prevailed. If Rosie had been allowed to do what she wanted she would be in New Jersey right now. When I replied, "it is a shame you were not allowed to do what you wanted," I meant it. She would not have met Leslie if she was attending her local community college–but I wouldn't have met Joe. As hard as it was, I had to reverse my original sentiment: I was grateful to Sarah for being the stronger one. I gave thanks to her for her strength in relation to Rosie's schooling.

I was too impulsive; upon further reflection I believed my meeting Joe was beyond Sarah's control or anyone else's. It had been preordained that I should meet him, and it was God who I owed my thanks. Rosie at the same university as Leslie, first roommates, then best of friends, Sarah leaving her husband and Joe finding himself at my Thanksgiving table. It was the divine plan. God has a divine plan for each of us.

◆————◆————◆

The more I talked to Joe I found myself wishing I had invited him to stay in my guest bedroom. It was free because Rosie was staying with Leslie in her bedroom. Joe had booked a room at the Rooster Inn; I was frightened for his safety. It was a local motel where prostitutes and addicts stayed. He was a big man, he looked like he could take care of himself, but I did suggest he find a better place to stay. He said it was only for a few nights and then he was driving Rosie back to school. When he offered to take Leslie too, I insisted he stay in my guest bedroom. It was the least I could do to show my thanks for him driving Leslie back to Miami.

There was no impropriety in my mind whatsoever when I offered him my guest room. Why would I extend the invitation in front of my brother if there had been? That's why my brother's behavior was inexcusable. Pete barged right in saying, "Oh, do I need to stay to be a chaperone for you two?" He embarrassed me, and I felt heat rushing to my face. I wouldn't have been surprised if it was a deep shade of scarlet. His remark did not seem to fluster Joe. He replied calmly, "No, I'm a gentleman," but that did not stop Pete. He became more offensive. "Yeah, I wouldn't be looking for pussy either if I had a wife who looked like yours." I was absolutely mortified and shocked by his words. I knew he could be inappropriate but never expected that to come out of his mouth. My anger became stronger than any embarrassment. I responded in a calm voice, similar to Joe's, "Pete, this is not some barroom, and there are young women present. If you are going to talk like that I'm going to ask you to leave my house."

"Sorry sis, I was just joking around. I had too much to drink tonight. My apologies to everyone. I forgot my sister was a church lady and ran a very proper home." He had not forgotten I was "a church lady," as he so rudely expressed my faith and devotion. This was exactly the kind of thing he did which is why it shames me for people to know he's my brother. Joe immediately stood up and said, "Let me help you clear the table, Sharon." He's a sweet man.

We were in the kitchen and I heard my brother and Rosie laughing. Joe heard it too and he abruptly turned his head towards the living room. It reminded me of a nature program on TV where a bear with cubs hears something, and is instantly protective of its young. I hoped my brother was behaving himself. Pete should be mindful of his safety; Joe struck me as a gentle man but one who would protect those he loved. Exactly as I would behave myself.

After dessert Pete left and Joe went to collect his things from the Rooster Inn, which was about a mile and a half from my house. I cleaned up the guest room while he was gone: changed the sheets; put away my quilting materials which were scattered around the room; and folded up my ironing board. I didn't have time to tidy it as I would have liked, but it was better than the Rooster Inn.

◆————◆————◆

The next day Joe took the girls to the mall for Black Friday sales. I preferred to stay home to putter around. It was with a sense of contentment; I didn't feel lonely or left out. While they were gone I gave the guest bedroom the thorough cleaning I had wanted to do the previous night, and spent the rest of my time quilting and reading the bible. My bible study group which usually meets on Thursdays was canceled on account of Thanksgiving, but I never skipped my studies; I chose Genesis 1: 27 to read. Lilith was on my mind: *"And God created man in his own image, in the image of God he created him; male and female he created them."* I planned to lead the discussion the following week on those verses.

I would email all the members my suggestion. Anyone could propose verses, and whoever emailed first was chosen to lead. Unless the same person was choosing repeatedly everyone agreed to this informal arrangement. I hadn't contributed in over two months so I was sure the group members would be amenable to my selection. Most of them were probably out shopping like the girls and Joe; bible studies were not what they were thinking about. I seriously doubted anyone would email before me.

That evening we had a left-over turkey dinner and on Saturday we went to a football game at Leslie's former high school. Joe insisted on taking us all out to dinner in the evening as a thank you for my hospitality. Joe ordered a big steak and fries at the restaurant. He also had a couple of beers and an ice cream sundae for dessert. He had a healthy appetite. I liked to see that in a man, but Rosie commented, "I bet you're glad Mom's not here. She'd be having a fit about what you're eating, Daddy." Joe laughed and said it was true, his wife always watched what he ate like a hawk. It made me wonder why it was so easy for Sarah to leave him and why Joe acted like she hadn't really left. Had she truly deserted him, or was this some twisted imagining of Rosie's to gain attention and sympathy by telling a fabricated family drama?

The next day Joe and the girls got up at 5 am in the morning to leave for Miami–it would take almost twelve hours to drive the girls back to school. Leslie called me as soon as they got settled back into their dorm room. I was relieved they had arrived safely. I only wished she had called me when Joe was still there. When I asked Leslie where he was she said he left as soon as he dropped them off. It was silly of me to be thinking about this man. It was only because he reminded me so much of Adam and the story of Lilith–if it was true that his wife had left him. God forgive me, I hoped it was true. Joe needed an *Eve*. He deserved a better woman than Sarah.

The following weekend after Joe drove the girls back to school he called me. He apologized for taking so long to thank me again for my hospitality. He had to catch up at work and wasn't much of a letter writer; and he didn't think much of emails as a way to say thanks. Another something I could identify with. He was very grateful to me for opening up my home, providing a family gathering for the holiday. Rosie was taking her mother leaving very hard according to Joe, "The holidays are tough for Rosie having her family all broken up."

So it was true, which made me want to ask: *what about you, isn't it equally hard for you?* Then I recalled that I had behaved the same way when Mike left–I thought about Leslie, not myself. I had made light of his being gone. There was a distinct difference between us though. Joe seemed to truly view Sarah in a more favorable light than I had Mike. He appeared to care for Sarah, and dismissed the harm she was doing to him.

He continued the conversation maintaining an up-beat tone and told me he was planning a trip to Disneyland for Christmas: "to get Rosie's mind off of her mother–start a new tradition for the holiday." Rosie never acted like she even loved her mother, and certainly did not respect her. Is that why Sarah could be replaced by Minnie Mouse so easily? As unfortunate as that might be it didn't matter as far as I was concerned. Disneyland sounded awful as a new family holiday tradition, and it's why I invited Joe and Rosie for Christmas.

He accepted, and it felt like the beginning of our new family unit. I am happy to note too that Rosie continues to restrain herself when her father is present–she's tolerable. All families have one or two black sheep; regardless–she is a cross I have to bear to shelter Joe. I am very protective of him, and I find it strange. The only person I ever felt protective towards was Leslie. Now I worry about Joe's safety. All the driving he does is dangerous; especially since he tells me he sleeps in truck stops. I know he is a large man but that seems to be tempting fate.

During the Christmas visit I asked Joe questions about work and his life because I was concerned about his health and safety. After he left, Leslie said I had sounded nosey. I hope Joe hadn't thought that. Wanting to protect him was the overwhelming motivation which drove me to ask questions, not curiosity. I was not trying to pry nor was I a busybody looking for material to spew out to others. And it wasn't that I thought Joe couldn't take care of himself, but he shouldn't need to is what bothers me. God gave men and women very different roles. Men are the providers; women are the nurturers.

God had to make a correction in his original design though–not that any mere mortal has the right to criticize the Lord, but it is true. When he first formed beings in his own image he made two equal ones–Adam and Lilith. Lilith was not a part of Adam and went off to pursue her own desires. The same way Sarah left Joe. God corrected the design by taking a rib from Adam's side to create Eve. Eve was designed to nurture Adam, not run off, thinking she was his equal.

Women's preordained role as nurturer is not a new idea or belief for me. I had nurtured Mike, but I never felt protective towards him as I do with Joe. Mike had too much of the devil in him; he was not sweet and considerate like Joe.

<hr>

After Christmas Joe and I talked frequently on the phone; two or three times a week. He missed his wife. But I grew to believe we were supposed to be together the longer Sarah–*Lilith*, stayed away. Joe would ultimately realize it since it was the divine plan. And when Sarah told Joe she was definitely not returning to him, a year after she left, he saw the light.

He started to call me daily, and one evening in particular he was very shaken. There were long pauses between his sentences; I hoped he wasn't crying. Each time his voice resurfaced I thanked God he seemed to be holding it together even though I knew he was in pain. I told him I could fly up to New Jersey or he could drive down to North Carolina if he felt he wanted to be with someone. Phone calls were okay but not as good as seeing someone in person. I only wanted to nurture him, be there for him. He said he'd like that; he would drive down–driving always helped him to clear his mind.

It was a Wednesday evening, he said he would leave early the next morning. He would arrive right around the time of my bible study group. I called my friend Michelle, who is another member, and asked if she could hold the study group at her home the next evening. It started a barrage of questions which I answered with as little information as possible, saying a person who was in need was visiting me. It wasn't enough information for Michelle, so I finally told her it was the father of Leslie's roommate–she was shocked. "The man who has stayed in your guest room? He's going to stay with you alone, without his daughter and Leslie?"

She knew that already because Leslie was back in school, and aware of the fact that she wouldn't be coming home until her semester finished. When she said, "he's married," before she was able to speak another word I told her I had to hang up. Michelle liked to hear herself talk; I reminded her of John 8:7 "He that is without sin among you, let him first cast a stone at her" –and I hadn't sinned. On the contrary, I was helping a friend.

I made a nice dinner for Joe: pork chops with gravy, home thick-cut fries, a salad and a chocolate cake from scratch. I knew, with the exception of the salad, they were things he liked to eat which Sarah seldom made for him. He needed to be nurtured.

After dinner Joe sat down on the couch. He said he had a headache and his neck hurt. He looked awful too. He had dark circles under his eyes, and his face had a strained expression which I imagined was from emotional as well as physical pain. I stood up behind him and told him to relax–I would massage his head and neck. I had learned how to do that in cosmetology school but never had the occasion to do it outside of the classroom. I had been glad because it seemed too touchy for me; working with hair was less intrusive on my sensibilities. I was surprised the thought of touching Joe wasn't off putting to me. I actually had the urge to touch him. He was the first man in my life I wanted to touch. When I finished, he took one of my hands and kissed it and said, "thank you." It wasn't erotic or in any way sexual in nature. His kiss was like the sweet kiss of a child, and I wrapped my arms around his shoulders and kissed the top of his head in response. He pulled me around in front of him and put me on his lap–I was the child now instead of him. I grew up fast when he carried me up to my bedroom. I now not only wanted to touch him, I wanted him to touch me.

Joe was very slow and gentle. I didn't know what happened. I was shaking and crying–a bomb exploded throughout my entire body. It mortified me and I was ashamed. I apologized to him and he took my face between his two hands and smiled. "What are you apologizing for? That's exactly what's supposed to happen." I believed him, because something so beautiful has to be in God's design; just as Joe and I becoming a couple was supposed to be.

◆————◆————◆

These past three months have flown by quickly with me traveling to New Jersey or Joe coming to

North Carolina. There is no doubt in my mind: I am his *Eve*. The Lord is casting the pieces falling into place: Joe has decided to sell his townhouse in New Jersey and move to North Carolina. We have not talked about marriage, but he told me he is asking *Lilith* for a divorce. I am content and patient. There is no need to pressure Joe; It would be presumptuous of me to try to rush the Lord executing his plan.

CHAPTER 13

SARAH

After Paulee told me about Sharon a gaggle of people joined her, notably my mother and Rosie gleefully biting at my heels. Why does my daughter seem to hate me so much? She goes beyond the acceptable level of annoyance with one's mother.

Joe in his fashion continues to not say a word. Will I be served divorce papers along with their wedding invitation? His obvious reluctance to say anything is one of the reasons I don't mention it. If we both say nothing, I can pretend it's not true and maybe Sharon will disappear from my family. I'm still amazed how I was so oblivious for over a year. I had no clue she even existed that first Thanksgiving when Joe stayed with her.

I asked Paulee if she had known and if she did why hadn't she informed me. "Joe asked me not to and they weren't dating then. I also thought I'd be wasting my time. You hadn't realized how stupid you were to leave him yet, in spite of all the pompous assholes you were meeting." I disagreed, they were not all "pompous assholes." And I hadn't been stupid–it was simply an early point in my quest the first Thanksgiving.

I had planned to spend it with Joe, Rosie and my mother, and booked tickets to fly back to New Jersey. I never told anyone I was coming because I wanted it to be a surprise. It backfired on me–they all made their own plans which didn't include me. My mother went to California to spend the holidays with my sister Penny, and Rosie was off with her roommate in Chapel Hill, North Carolina.

I presumed Joe was celebrating at his parents' house when I asked him what he was doing and he replied, "I'm covered, don't worry about me." Mac was an asshole, but Joe preferred insults with plenty of food to eat over starving with polite conversation at his sister Lynne's. I never discovered his true destination due to my presumption and his subterfuge.

I called him the Sunday before Thanksgiving but he didn't pick up the landline. I don't expect him to sit next to the phone waiting for my calls on Sunday evenings (that's what my daughter accuses me of doing). He has a life, I know that, but when he didn't pick up I called his cell. He answered and I asked him if his parents were serving venison this year. He said *yes*; I never directly asked him if he was attending–I made a *presumption*. He never expanded beyond confirming his parents' menu–I call that blatant *subterfuge*. And I was totally open with him about my invitation from Aunt Marion for Thanksgiving. I "was covered," and in addition to herself and Granny Laarsen, my aunt's daughter and husband and two teen children would be there–my father's family.

I had a place to go and should have been thankful. I reminded myself that they were my family too even though I had never met these cousins before. I told Paulee I would have preferred to spend it with Joe and Rosie–my *immediate family.*

"I guess you should have thought about that before you left him, Sarah." That had stung. Paulee continued to be upset over my leaving and her being torn apart by her allegiance to both Joe and me. Looking back on it now, Paulee was not as mean as I had thought at the time. She knew Joe was in Chapel Hill the first Thanksgiving; she did not say a word. She continues to insist that it was only because he told her not to, and it was futile for her to say anything at that juncture. I believe she was also wanting to spare me pain.

✦————✦————✦

There was no escaping pain the second Thanksgiving; not only did I know Joe was in Chapel Hill, thanks to Rosie, I knew every stinging detail. All puffed up she described them with great relish. "Sharon's house is small but there are three bedrooms. Daddy and Sharon are in one, and I share a bedroom with Leslie."

She sounded very free and easy when she said it, but her intention was clear. It was intended to bite regardless of her attempt to sound disingenuous. She was talking about her own father to her own mother, and we weren't divorced. I loved Joe and I wanted us to be together again. There was an obstacle getting in my way, besides my daughter's obvious dislike of me–

Joe was in a bedroom with Sharon in a small house in Chapel Hill, North Carolina. I took too long to realize I wanted him back. Rosie was making it clear with cruel words, disguised as casual banter, that her father had found someone else.

The second Thanksgiving I was with my mother in New Jersey–just the two of us. It wasn't a fun-filled celebration. I would have preferred to spend the holiday with Paulee and Anthony at their restaurant but I didn't want to leave my mother by herself. Mom believes Thanksgiving should be a home-made meal, but she did her best to make me regret my decision to spend it with her. Telling me, "You realized too late what you had, Sarah," did not make me feel better or create a festive mood, and it hadn't ended there.

"There are men who discard their wives like dirty tissues when they're old or sick. Some men wouldn't have stayed like Joe did when you got breast cancer. They leave their wives high and dry, kids and all. I wasn't even sick or old but it happened to me. I was left all alone to raise two little girls by myself."

I didn't know what she was talking about. My father was killed in a car accident. He didn't exactly leave her in the same context–he died. But it wasn't the entire story apparently. It took all these years to learn salient details that she had left out. He was in the process of leaving her; he had asked for a divorce. The fact that it had been interrupted by an untimely death didn't change his intention or mitigate my mother's feelings of having been abandoned. *Genetics*. Was it in my blood to leave Joe?

In spite of my mother making the Thanksgiving celebration a bummer, she encouraged objectivity which made me look beyond myself. Everyone has troubles and I brought this down on myself (even if I had been driven to it by my genes). Instead of feeling sorry for myself, I decided it was time to accept that Joe and I were done; it was time to move on.

And I was luckier than some. I was healthy, not terribly old, and my daughter was grown (it didn't seem like she wanted to have anything to do with me anyway). I was in a better position than my mother had found herself years ago when I was a little kid and my father *left* her. I also had to admit my culpability. I was the one who drove Joe into the arms of another woman. I refused to cry into my beer; but I certainly planned to smoke more pot. Joe is the one who likes beer.

CHAPTER 14

PAULEE

Sarah says she's not feeling "sorry for herself" but that's not how I see it. She professes to love Joe and wants to be with him again yet rolls over and lets Sharon take him without a fight. "Her culpability" crap is also starting to grate on my nerves. She acts like she wants to be a martyr. And don't get me wrong, some of my favorite saints were, but she's not going to be canonized giving Joe to Sharon.

"You're letting guilt distort your reasoning, Sarah. You can make it up to Joe later after you two are back together. Now you have to fight for your man." Hearing myself sounding like I'm spouting lyrics from a country western song makes me sick. I would also probably have better luck hawking my talents in Nashville than convincing Sarah she's wrong.

I'm not that surprised she is a challenge because she's not naturally a fighter or even adventuresome. Leaving Joe was probably the only adventure she ever dared in her life, and look what happened. Maybe she's suffering from PTSD in addition to guilt-induced inertia. She's also stubborn; that's why I'm often amused when she says Joe is "pig-headed." I never realized how stubborn she was until now and I've known her for a long time.

I met her when we were both teaching at a high school in Wall township, New Jersey. When I first saw her I asked my friend Irene, who also taught English, "Are you sure she is the new math teacher?" She didn't look like any math teacher I had ever seen, and she didn't look anything like Janice, the woman she was replacing. Janice with her little bun, thick glasses and ankles, and clothes which had not been in fashion for twenty-five years. An obvious difference, but it was also clear that the new math teacher would probably look good in a potato sack. We became friends in spite of her drop-dead gorgeousness, and Anthony, (my boyfriend then and husband now), continues to point it out–ad nauseum. Something I will have to endure as long as Anthony and Sarah remain in my life.

Anthony saw her for the first time when I invited her for dinner at my place. As soon as she walked in the door I called Anthony, who was in the kitchen making Dirty Martinis. He came out with the martini shaker in his hands, took one look at Sarah, and abruptly ran back into the kitchen. Anthony does not have a shy bone in his body so I had no idea what the hell was wrong with him. I told Sarah to take a seat and make herself comfortable and I went into the kitchen. In a hushed tone I asked him, "What the hell is the matter with you?" It turned out he did have a bone problem.

"Do you see how beautiful she is, Paulee? Jesus Christ, Mary, Mother of God."

"Oh, get a grip, Anthony."

"Sorry, I got hard just looking at her."

I'm not a man so she doesn't affect me that way, but I gave Anthony a pass because I could indirectly empathize with him. I sometimes feel like poking out my eyes when I look at myself in a mirror after spending time with her; not as much fun as a hard-on but definitely a visceral response.

It was understandable why Anthony wanted to keep seeing her, but why did I? She had to be a stuck-up bitch on account of her looks, right? It did not turn out that way. She was funny, honest, and down-to-earth–an *ordinary* person. I did not know her well enough then to add: stubborn, guilt-ridden and wimpy. It took time to determine that, but even though my overall first impression of Sarah had been spot on, I learned pretty quickly she was not so *ordinary* when it came to some of her sensibilities.

I am a curious woman but I have learned more than I care to know about human sexuality and a woman's sexual anatomy thanks to her. I'm not suggesting that I find her offensive though, and her material is usually educational, unlike Anthony's dirty jokes. In fact, I have frequently recommended her to people seeking information or advice, like the time I steered little Kathy to her.

Several years after Sarah started working at the school, we were both assigned as teaching mentors for two teachers right out of college. We all went out to get something to eat one evening and Sarah was chatting away about orgasms. She was dating Joe at the time and she was saying how she always had an orgasm; furthermore, she had one with every man she had ever been with her entire life. She left early because she had to meet Joe, and my newbie Kathy who seemed to be shocked into silence when Sarah was talking, now whispered to me, "Is that even possible for a woman to always have an orgasm? I'm not even sure if I ever had one."

All my orgasms are sandwiched in between premature ejaculations and the present–*I got her, I don't have to try, and I'm a selfish son of a bitch*. Sarah tries to comfort me when I complain about my sex life: "orgasms are not the only thing important in sex," (easy to say when you always have one). I do agree with her to some extent but qualify it by saying back to her, "sex is not the only important thing in life." I mean it too, that's why Anthony and I work, but I'm not clueless. I was about to say to the newbie–*if you had one, you'd know it*. Then I remembered Sarah talking about different kinds of female orgasms, with different intensities; maybe I was wrong. I told Kathy she should speak to Sarah. "Describe it to her; she'll be able to confirm if you had one or not." Sarah definitely has more experience than me in theory and practice.

Sarah's discussions while not downright offensive are graphic occasionally and she is cognizant of it; she tells me whenever I want her to stop to shout out. Discussing sexual topics was second nature to her and sometimes she wasn't even aware of other people's reactions due to how she was raised. I believed her after meeting her mother Agnes, who has a number of erotic books and romance novels scattered about her house. An old edition of *The Joy of Sex* is prominently displayed on her coffee table. Sarah says she remembers it being there her whole life. She would look at the pictures when she was little before she could read. I have a book on cats on my coffee table and my mother has one on botanical gardens.

Sarah and I would often throw parties on the deck of her mother's house which hangs over the Manasquan River. It is a great view, but not what caught Anthony's attention the first time he was at Agnes's house. We were on the deck when Anthony said to Sarah, "Hey, I really like your mother's reading material." She told him she was sure her mother would lend him a book. I told him to take her up on the offer, "Maybe you'll learn something, Anthony."

For all her open talk Sarah never acts like she's on the make for men. She doesn't have to go after them though; they come to her like bees to a flower, and Anthony follows suit. His constant drooling over her can get on my nerves, even though she is my best friend. How many times can one hear about how great her tits look in that black dress or the purple top? I finally retaliated. "Yeah, and did you ever notice what great biceps Joe has and the expanse of his chest? He looks like a muscle man; amazing what sweat and a few dumbbells can do."

"I see what you're doing, Paulee. You're getting back at me for talking about Sarah." It was true, but I do think Joe has a great body. The first day I met him he was wearing a tight t-shirt where I could clearly see his biceps. He reminded me of *Mr. Clean*; I had fantasies about that character as a preadolescent girl. I met Joe on a double date with Sarah, who at that point was not even interested in him; she didn't even notice his build. "Sorry, Paulee, I guess *Mr. Clean* never did it for me, and the only thing that comes to mind when I think about him is his bald head."

After that initial meeting, Joe, Sarah and I started to hang out together as friends, and before they started dating I continued to have a small crush on him. It was clear he was enamored with Sarah though, not me, but I could still appreciate his great physique. I saw him washing his SUV one day without a shirt and I stood there like an idiot with my mouth open. I never seriously considered pursuing him though; I had Anthony after all–who is always talking about Sarah. I once joked with her about Anthony and I doing a threesome with her. She was appalled at the idea–it was only a joke for God's sake. Does she seriously think I'd take my clothes off and be compared to her?

In spite of Anthony's drooling, and Joe having ignored my initial feelings for him, I always cherished my friendship with Sarah. There are more positive things in our relationship than negative–but no relationship is perfect. Sarah has an outstanding flaw. *A classic tragic flaw*–and what makes it a tragedy? She's oblivious.

The tragic flaw paradigm goes this way: the hero or heroine has a talent or strength (in Sarah's case it is her beauty). It starts out as a positive characteristic but mutates–culminating into hubris. Hubris surfaces when the heroine becomes too proud about her positive characteristic. I have already pointed out that Sarah is not vain about her beauty. She's not stuck-up or bitchy to people on account of her looks. That's why she has many women friends along with male admirers, but I am not saying she doesn't have hubris. Hers is an innate quality; it bypasses her radar and drives her to act in ways that a person who looks like me would never consider. The reason she's not aware of it is due to her making presumptions based on her previous experiences. Simply put, she has gotten away with things most women in the world would not have been able to get away with.

◆————◆————◆

She wasn't very happy when she first married Joe. *Married to Joe* didn't measure up *to dating Joe* apparently (big surprise–the same for most of us) but Sarah was depressed. She complained nonstop and smoked too much pot. She also refused to have relations with him for a long time–over a year. I kept asking her– "aren't you afraid he's going to cheat on you or leave?" What made things even worse from my perspective was Joe took care of the house, did the cooking and still maintained his job to support her and Rosie while she was behaving this way. When I asked her my questions, she said she wasn't worried. She believed Joe would never leave her regardless of what she said or did. Last year when she left him, she told me Joe would wait for her–*that's hubris.*

Sarah and Joe aren't divorced and I don't believe she would commit adultery, but she had a few dates with men in Minnesota. She called these dates *meetings.* I wanted to ask her if she had told Joe about her meetings but I never did. I feared she would say–*yes.* She stopped when the last man made a serious pass at her. It was also about the time she finally realized she wanted to be with Joe. She was a little late, she hadn't counted on Sharon.

Even if one is not familiar with the tragic flaw paradigm, they might see this was not moving in a favorable direction for Sarah. Which brings me to the last part of the paradigm–*the nemesis.* An agency or force that ultimately brings about the downfall of the heroine. Sarah's nemesis is fucking her husband.

I met Sharon in August after Sarah told Joe she was not returning to New Jersey. I was in my old neighborhood in Jackson to visit my cats. When Anthony and I moved to Bergen County I asked Sarah and Joe if they could care for them (the apartment we were moving to did not allow pets). It was supposed to be a temporary arrangement but it took a while to find a place we liked where I could have them. I periodically came down to Jackson to visit my babies and it was my primary reason that day. I also wanted to feel Joe out about me taking them back. His foster parenting had been longer than anticipated; if he was too attached I would let him keep them permanently.

I took an instant dislike to Sharon and it wasn't because I loved Sarah and Sharon was on her turf. This woman had only been dating Joe a short time but she was possessive and too familiar for that stage of a relationship. If one didn't know better they would assume they were a long married couple. She was even talking for him. I asked Joe if he minded me taking the cats and before he could say anything Sharon butted in. "Oh, take them. I can't stand all the fur. You can take the dog too while you're at it. The doggy smell is awful even though we keep giving her baths."

Joe loved his little dog but he didn't say one word, and Sharon would not let up. She told me how Joe never noticed the smell because he's used to it. "He said it was my imagination until the realtor showing the house agreed with me. She told him to put air fresheners around so prospective buyers won't smell it." I never owned a dog, but I never noticed a *doggy smell* in Sarah's house (even when they owned the big lab). Joe and Sarah have a little Maltese named Holly now. The only scent I smelled in the house was heavy and cloying from cheap air fresheners. It was overwhelming; I was a little nauseous, not refreshed. I wondered if Sharon had picked them out. It wasn't the smell that made me feel sick to my stomach though; it was hearing Joe was putting the townhouse up for sale.

I didn't see Sharon again until I went to Jackson to pick up my cats a week after Thanksgiving. This was the second Thanksgiving to be clear; a new year, not like the one prior when Joe asked me to keep his holiday plans a secret from Sarah. "You know how she imagines stuff, Paulee–better not to tell her anything. I don't want to upset her." I replied, "Why not?" She had needed a serious *wake-up call*, but he refused to change his mind. I should have insisted or told her myself.

This year he didn't care what I told Sarah. And he wasn't reluctant to share with me that he had a buyer and was planning to move to Chapel Hill. In the interim, Sharon had seemingly installed herself in the townhouse. I would later find out she was only visiting after she and Joe drove her daughter and Rosie back to school after Thanksgiving break; they came up from Miami to New Jersey. Sharon was helping Joe pack. She walked around the townhouse like she owned it, touching Sarah's things like they belonged to her–including Joe. She kept reprimanding him about the dog: "please don't let it jump on the couch, Joe. I just cleaned." This sounded serious, not like casual dating. I tried to make Sarah appreciate the situation but she refused to call Joe to tell him how she felt.

It was a case of pride or stubbornness or perhaps what she said–she didn't want to stand in his way if he wanted someone else. Which is also another way of playing the martyr. Whatever her reasons, she was not even trying to fight her nemesis. I had to do something.

I asked Joe to give me a call later as I was leaving– "I need to speak with you about something." Before Joe could respond Sharon piped right in, "Well, you can talk to him right now, why don't you stay for dinner. Joe and I would love you to stay to share a meal with us before you leave. I made a casserole." I wondered if she used the dish I gave Sarah that I found at a garage sale. I always teased Sarah for making casseroles like some 60's TV mom. She said it was only because she was so busy teaching; she could make them ahead of time and then pop them in the oven when she came home.

I envisioned the white casserole dish with the blue flowers and I had a strong urge to say– *this is not your house or your dog, bitch, and Joe isn't your husband yet. The casserole dish does not belong to you either and I want it back*. Instead I said, "Kind of private, between me and Joe." I knew she'd stew on that one for a while because she looked visibly upset when I said it.

Sharon was not the only person upset. Anthony was angry because I told Joe to call me; he said to stay out of his life, it was not any of my business. We then exchanged a few words like always.

"Don't tell me to mind my own business, Anthony. Sarah and Joe are my best friends and they love each other and should be together." Anthony was never a big fan of Joe's, and could never understand Sarah's attraction to him.

"She's better off without him, Paulee."

"Okay, let's imagine that. It doesn't mean she'd go with you if she were free if that's what you're thinking, Anthony." I knew that would rile him and it did, but I was annoyed by his accusing me of interfering.

As the evening wore on I wasn't upset with Anthony anymore. I was a nervous wreck over Joe. I hadn't heard from him and began to regret getting involved; maybe Anthony had been right. Then shortly after midnight Joe called. Using every acting skill I learned from years of directing the school plays I expressed Sarah's desires as I felt she would have if she wasn't a stubborn wimp. I also made it really clear that she wanted him back before she even knew about Sharon. He took a long time before he responded, that's the way Joe is sometimes, and I had to ask twice: "Are you going to call her?" He finally said: "No."

Well, there it was. I tried. I at least tried to fight the nemesis, but it wasn't enough consolation. I felt weepy and was in the middle of saying good-bye when Joe said: "Hold on, don't rush me, Paulee. I need to think. I have to take Sharon to Newark to catch her plane tomorrow at eleven; and then I'm going to head out to Minneapolis right from there. Let's keep it between us though, okay? Don't tell Sarah, Paulee."

Is it possible the paradigm for Sarah's tragic flaw story can be changed? If so, I helped to bring it about. I'd thank God every day I hadn't listened to Anthony and minded my own business, even though I don't usually listen to Anthony most of the time.

CHAPTER 15

JOE

When Paulee told me she had something private to tell me I knew it was about Sarah. It could be anything: Sarah met someone and she told her she wanted a divorce; or Sarah had finally come to her senses–she wanted to be with me. It could even concern Sarah's health; had the cancer returned? I didn't know whether or not this "private" information Paulee wanted to share was good news or bad. It was one of the reasons I took my time calling her back. The other was I didn't want to do it in front of Sharon so I waited until she went to sleep.

Sharon is a pretty light sleeper; as soon as I got up I heard her say, "What's the matter, where are you going?" As though she had not been sleeping at all. Sharon is a nice lady, but she is a real nervous type and it makes her nosey and pushy at times. When you have an edge, making you feel overly anxious all the time, it messes up your head. People like Sharon are always fearing the worst.

I told her I needed to call Paulee; I was going downstairs so as not to disturb her. She said I didn't have to leave, it wouldn't bother her. I told her I'd prefer to be alone when I made the call. She asked sweetly but it was obvious she didn't like me saying that very much. "Are we keeping secrets from one another now, Joe?" I told her some things did not concern her; there would always be "secrets" as she called them. I can be understanding up to a point with her nosiness but if our relationship is going to work she has to give me privacy. I was with Sarah for over twenty years and I never told her all my thoughts. She could be insistent sometimes when she was looking for answers but overall she respected my privacy.

Sometimes it seems like Sharon's using me to fill a void in her life with all of her questions, and she hasn't developed a life apart from her family. She mostly talks about her daughter and I feel a little bored around her, which is wrong to say. I shouldn't fault her for not talking about a variety of things when I'm the same way. I don't bring much to the table myself, I never did. I depended on Sarah for that when we were together.

Sarah often took my lack of comment as not listening. Fault me for not contributing much but she was wrong about me not listening to her. I enjoyed what she had to say about all kinds of things because she's so smart. I'm sorry to say I am guilty of not listening to Sharon very much–she's not Sarah. Which reminded me that I needed to call Paulee; it was already late.

I told Sharon I wouldn't be long and she turned away from me in the bed. No more discussion; I went downstairs to make the call. She was annoyed but I knew in spite of it she wouldn't hold a grudge for long. As soon as

I came back to bed and put my arms around her–she'd turn back to me. Unlike Sarah, who could hold a grudge for years. But to be fair, I haven't known Sharon for years to honestly compare them on that point.

The call didn't take long but I needed some time to gather my thoughts before I could return to Sharon. The news had been good. I had wanted to hear it for more months than I cared to remember, but the timing is off now. It complicated my life just when I was starting to feel comfortable moving in a new direction. There wasn't any doubt in my mind though. I liked Sharon; I loved Sarah more than any complication.

That didn't mean I was going to go upstairs to tell Sharon. I trusted Paulee as a source, but my wife can be all over the place sometimes with her thinking. For all I and Paulee know she may have changed her mind already. That's why I am not saying a word to Sharon or calling Sarah right this minute. Whatever Sarah is thinking I want her to say it to my face in present time–I need to see her.

I went back up to the bedroom. I wanted to make love to Sharon but I knew I wouldn't be able to get Sarah out of my mind. Recalling her image only reminds me how Sharon feels like a young girl; I just wouldn't be able to keep it up. I got into bed and put my arms around her and she turned to me, "Is everything okay, Joe?" She is really a sweet little thing. I felt guilty when I said, "I hope so."

The next morning I retrieved my heavy winter coat and gloves from the back of the hall closet. Sharon asked me why I was dressing so warmly. "What's the matter with the coat you usually wear, and why gloves?" I told her you never know if the weather might change and you're faced with an unexpected snowstorm. She said she didn't think they were predicting any storms in New Jersey. She kept on it like a dog gnawing a bone. "Have you heard something about a storm on a weather forecast?" I told her I hadn't checked. It was the truth; I hadn't checked for New Jersey or along my route to Minneapolis. I was familiar with the route to Minneapolis though, and the weather can change fast out there.

I was glad I kept an emergency overnight bag in my car so I didn't have to pack or explain why I had a suitcase to Sharon. I'm often too lazy to pack a bag; Sarah had always offered to pack for me but it was easier to keep one ready-to-go. It bothered her. "Well if you insist on keeping a bag in the car at least change your toothpaste." She was afraid it would go bad because of the temperature changes. It's probably frozen now, but I don't know what she means by *bad*. I don't eat it, and I'm not going to worry about the ill effects of toothpaste. I did have to call my mother-in-law about keeping the dog a little longer though.

Since I started dating Sharon my mother-in-law has cared for Holly a number of times. Sharon is like my mother, she doesn't like pets in the house. My sister and I were never allowed to have them. We did have a rabbit; one of the few good memories I have of my father is when we built the hutch in the backyard together. If Sharon and I do eventually live together, I'll ask Sarah if she wants Holly or maybe my mother-in-law would like to keep her permanently. She's practically her dog already, and Holly doesn't trigger her allergies. They were meant to be together.

I will miss having a cat or dog, but if there's a choice between a pet or a woman in my life–I'm going for the woman. I would have the woman and the pets with Sarah, but we aren't there yet–if ever again.

I made a point to take the papers from the hall table which I needed Sarah to sign for the closing. I waited until Sharon was out of the room so she wouldn't see me picking them up and ask about them. I would have had to tell her I was going to Minneapolis. I didn't want to tell her, but that doesn't mean I'm a lying low-life; I didn't say anything because why upset her for no reason? I don't know what's going on, and I'm not that anxious to find out. I'm glad I'm driving instead of flying. It will take me about eighteen hours–plenty of time to think, and delay what might be a negative experience. I'm not going to deliberately delay the commute; storms are a real concern. I plan to make as few stops as possible but I have to pull off the interstate to crash in a motel at some point, because it's too cold to even take short naps at truck stops. I'll freeze like my toothpaste otherwise. But it doesn't matter how long the trip takes; Sarah doesn't know I'm coming.

The last time we spoke she told me she's working and won't get a break until January. She usually works right up to Christmas with her classes so I expect to find her home. I may not be sure about her mindset until I arrive, but I'm sure once I reach Minneapolis our relationship will be resolved. I want us together but if she doesn't want that and wants a divorce–okay with me. I don't want to be with someone who doesn't want to be with me. What I won't accept is hearing another, "I don't know." If she says it, I'm finally asking her for a divorce; just like I told Sharon I would months ago.

The trip was uneventful and I didn't run into any storms along the way. I hoped I wouldn't be walking into one. I found her apartment building easy enough but it was hard to find parking. They were not keeping up with snow removal around here. I had to park in an in-door parking complex nearby. It wasn't a far walk, but I was glad I had my heavier coat and gloves. Sarah's building had no outside locked door. I didn't bother to call her; I just went right up to her apartment and rang her doorbell. It took her a while to answer. I heard her say, "Joe?" before I saw her. She must have looked through her peephole, but she sounded like she wasn't sure if it was me or not. It's only been a year and a half; did she already forget what I looked like?

Then she opened the door. There was light from the windows in her apartment that cast a bright curtain behind her. It was like the first time I saw her–she looked like an angel. An angel wearing a baggy white sweater with long sleeves that came to the middle of her thighs. Other than that she was bare legged, barefoot and bra-less–I could see her nipples through the sweater. We just stood there looking at one another until she said, "Joe, if those are divorce papers, just hand them to me. I'll sign them, but I don't want to talk about it." At first I didn't know what she was talking about until I realized I was holding the closing papers in my hand.

"Is that what you want Sarah? Do you want a divorce?" She answered in this tiny little voice, "no" and I could hardly hear her.

"Well, what do you want, Sarah?"

"I want you, I want us to be together again." She then started crying and I didn't think she was going to stop any time soon. I picked her up and carried her into the apartment since she was acting like she couldn't move.

It was the only time I felt like I had complete control of her for the next few days. She soon recovered and was back to her usual self–running the whole show.

CHAPTER 16

SARAH

had been working since early morning, correcting papers and doing grades. The end of the semester is crunch time. It was 2:00 pm and I was calling a break time for myself. I'm amused sometimes when I hear people say a professor or teacher's schedule is easy; how not true. I don't teach every day, but on the days I don't–I'm doing paperwork.

I jumped into the shower and turned the hot water on my aching neck and shoulders. I had already showered for cleanliness first thing in the morning. This shower was solely for the benefit of having the water relieve the tension in my sore muscles. I no longer had Joe to give me a massage.

After the shower I planned to stretch out my break: smoke a joint; drink a little brandy; and masturbate on my fake animal rug in front of my fake wood burning fireplace. I needed to smoke slowly, savor every hit; it was my last joint. I never knew for sure when I would have another one. I told my student Daniel to stop putting rolled joints in my mailbox in the faculty office. He was discreet–he put them in a manila envelope–but I continued to be nervous about it. I had been promised tenure but had not received it yet. I certainly wouldn't get it if they thought I was buying pot from one of my students. I was not doing that–the joints were gifts.

One day I was talking to Daniel after class; his eyes were blood-shot and it took a longer time than usual for him to answer my questions. He looked a *mess*. Correction–he looked stoned and I casually mentioned it. His response was, "I wish," and I said without thinking, "me too." That's how it started.

I told him after the second time I found three rolled joints in a manila envelope in my mailbox that he had to stop giving me pot; (perhaps I should have told him after he had done it the first time). But I made it very clear to him initially that he couldn't bribe me for better grades.

There was also my concern over its cost. I should be giving him money, and I was absolutely not doing that and I told him so. Daniel replied, "I don't want any money from you, and I'm not trying to bribe you, professor. Just keep wearing that black suit of yours and we're square." I have continued to wear my black suit (it has nothing to do with pot), and I also continue to find three rolled joints in my mailbox twice a week.

I was appreciating every inhale of my joint and enjoying my very expensive brandy from Spain. I've recently started to drink brandy instead of wine. It takes less booze and time to get a buzz. I then chose one of my sex toys to masturbate. I'm trying hard to stop saying "masturbate" though. My new female friends act like masturbation is dirty–in spite of them being highly educated women. It makes me wonder, wasn't Minneapolis one of Dr. Ruth's markets? If it had aired here there was no long-lasting positive effect. People are definitely more conservative than in New Jersey. I am training myself to think and say–*practicing self-love*. When I now say, "I need a little self-love" my female friends think I am talking about giving myself a pedicure.

◆————◆————◆

I felt very mellow; I was lying there in front of my fireplace, having finished the joint, the brandy and the self-loving when the buzzer from my apartment door jarred me to attention. I did not want to get up. Besides, I was only wearing a baggy sweater that reached down to the middle of my thighs and no clothes underneath. Whoever was there would go away I thought, but they kept buzzing at my door.

I decided to at least look through my peephole to see who was at the door. What I saw froze me to the spot. It was Joe and he was standing there with papers in his hand. If it hadn't been for those papers I wouldn't have gotten upset. On the contrary I would have been pleased by how powerful my thoughts were. I had been fantasizing about him when I was self-loving. Had I been able to conjure him up in the flesh merely by imagining that I was screwing him? How great would that be? If it wasn't for him holding those papers.

I knew they were divorce papers; it would be just like Joe to feel he had to see me in person to tell me he wanted a divorce. He would never choose to call me, mail me, or have some person other than himself serve me with papers. He would feel it was the decent thing to do–to hand me the papers face-to-face. Screw that, he could slip the papers under the door (not enough space with my door though); okay, he can hand them to me and immediately leave. I didn't want to talk about it. That's what I said when I finally opened the door but he wouldn't stop talking about it, and I started crying uncontrollably. He then put the papers in his pocket, walked over to me, took my face in his hands and kissed me. He said, "don't cry baby, these are papers I need you to sign for the closing on our townhouse."

Why the hell didn't he say that in the first place instead of torturing me? I was so relieved; I didn't want Joe to divorce me and he wasn't carrying divorce papers–but I couldn't stop crying. He then picked me up and carried me into my apartment like he used to carry me up the stairs to our bedroom. I had my head on his chest and my arms around his neck. He asked me where I wanted "to light." I didn't have a bedroom; my couch was my sleeper bed so I pointed to it and that's where he set me down.

In every one of my mother's erotic romance novels when a man carries a woman into a room he then rips off all her clothes and makes passionate love to her. Joe put me on the couch and asked me where my bathroom was–he always has to spoil the mood. I had to get this story back on track. There was no time to open up my sleeper couch. I took off my sweater and went over to my antique Victorian settee, which looks like a sleigh. It has only one side and I placed my left leg over it when I laid down. If there had been more time I would have put a blue velvet ribbon around my neck to match the royal blue upholstery of the settee to set the stage. I still hoped, being stark naked with my legs splayed open, I'd look like a provocative courtesan posing for a painting; or a naughty postcard from the 19th century. The settee was in direct view from the bathroom.

Joe would definitely see me when he came out of the bathroom, but it was taking him forever to do it. My heightened anticipation was making me impatient, and my leg that was thrown over the side arm was starting to cramp. When he finally came out, he stood there staring at me until he asked, "Are you trying to tell me something, Sarah?"

"No, Joe, I'm trying to get you to do something."

I told him to take his clothes off slowly. He laughed at me which was not exactly a response which enhanced the mood I was trying to create. He then asked me why I didn't have any blinds or curtains in this place. Really Joe? Your wife–who you have not seen or fucked for a year and a half is offering herself to you–and you are concerned about the window dressings? I didn't say that, but I told him to forget about the curtains, nobody can see us. He said he didn't care, but he thought I might.

Was he getting me mixed up with Sharon? I wouldn't care if someone saw me having sex from across the street. The only thing which would concern me is I wouldn't want them to figure out what apartment I lived in when they were spying on me–I didn't want any uninvited visits. They could look though–free show and I'm not an exhibitionist. *Free shows* are dependent on context and variables.

The three buildings across from my apartment are all new construction and have not been rented yet-*context*. I also bared all when I sunbathed without my top in college. This was an example of *context* and *variables*–everyone was doing it. As a more mature person I agreed to have my breasts painted along with Paulee when we were in Key West on vacation. I never told Joe but he would probably not have been upset if he had considered the *variables*. The first was the guy who painted them was very, very gay. Another, his work was so good it looked like we were wearing bathing suits. I still didn't walk around all evening like Paulee without covering up. I was not as daring as her and what if it rained? The third variable.

It was the painter himself who made me consider the rain. He was aware of what a shower would do to his boob art. He asked us if we would like to preserve it more permanently with a photograph (which we could purchase for a modest additional charge). This was before all cell phones had good camera apps. The painter took a picture of us and Paulee bought it. After we returned home she showed it to Joe. I was very upset with her, "Why did you show him the picture, Paulee?"

Paulee is one of my best friends, and we have a long-standing friendship which has spanned decades. But she has a habit, resulting from our years of intimacy, of butting into my affairs with Joe without asking–head down and charging. A small part is simply due to her personality. The greater part is because she cares about both of us, and she has never evolved past our original trilateral configuration.

In the beginning, we were all just buddies hanging out together. After Joe and I became a romantic couple things changed. Our trilateral ceased being a democratic one. Sometimes I wonder if Paulee realizes she no longer has the right to an equal say in every context. The three of us still share a relationship together, but the configuration is now more one of a shifting bilateral between members. I have no idea why Paulee felt she needed to share the boob art with Joe. I thought she stepped out of bounds; she thought I had overreacted. "Relax, Joe thought they were bathing suits, Sarah."

I don't know if that was true, but Joe never said anything to me. It didn't even matter; I don't know why I got upset with her. I was familiar with Joe's policy–*look all you want but I'm the only one who can touch*. He has held to that since the day we began to date, and it was exactly one of the things I was growing impatient for him to do–*touch me*.

I regretted having told him to take his clothes off slowly, but it did give me time to check him out. Paulee is always saying Joe has a great body. Was it true I had never appreciated what was right in front of my eyes? He definitely looked better than I remembered. I was wet, hot and ready and Joe just stood there at attention, until he said, "You don't expect me to do anything on that little couch, do you? I'm afraid I'll break it." He had a point; I never considered his size when I chose to lay on the settee.

We had to choose a position that Joe didn't like very much; he refused to do it for nearly a decade of our marriage. It wasn't one of my favorites either; I like to see the people I'm having sex with, but I hadn't had very much time to stage my seduction. The settee had seemed like a good idea, and it was workable after I maneuvered into a different configuration. I held onto the side of the settee with both arms extended and was grateful it was a reproduction and not an antique. It was a moderately priced knock-off but able to withstand the force of the thrusting. And since it wasn't an expensive antique, I wasn't upset about the semen stain on the upholstery. I could probably remove it with hydrogen peroxide. If not, I'd cover the stain with a scarf; or leave it as a visual declaration of our love.

We only used the settee one time during Joe's visit, favoring other locations: the couch closed; the couch opened up into a sleeper; on the rug in front of the fireplace; and standing up against the closet door. Joe thought the settee was problematic, so are doorknobs.

◆——◆——◆

My emotions were in high gear–I was so happy Joe and I were together again. I'm sure he was happy too, but as soon as we made love that first time on the settee he playfully spanked my butt and said "hurry up and get dressed, baby." He then proceeded to dress in a flash; a complete contrast to when he removed his clothes. He was anxious to find a notary so we could sign the closing papers. There was no time for cuddling; at least he called me *baby*.

Later Paulee scolded, "I can't believe you're already complaining about Joe." I wasn't complaining, I was disoriented. Joe did not act like a man who hadn't seen or fucked his wife for over a year, or a day ago was moving to North Carolina to be with another woman. And the glow after our lovemaking dimmed quickly for him. His mind was on the mundane.

One of which was the closing that would be in a couple of weeks, and he had to clear out our townhouse. He was going to make more than one trip moving our things, and there would be more than one stop before there was a final destination for our belongings. He was planning to store stuff at my mother's and make several trips to Minnesota. He told me he had time to think about things driving from New Jersey to Minneapolis, and to consider different outcomes. He said, *"I got the one I had hoped for* but that means you have to start looking for a house immediately." It definitely was not a strong romantic offering but I'd take it, even if I was displeased over some of his ideas.

Joe is so tight with money; he refused to hire a mover. He was renting the biggest U-Haul he could, but it would still take more than one trip to move

everything. He insisted it wasn't about money directly–
he thought most moving guys were "crooks." Crooks
or not, it was unlikely I was going to find a house in the
time frame we were talking about. We had to come up
with other ideas. That's when it was decided we would
visit Aunt Marion the next day with two objectives:
to introduce Joe, and to ask her if we could use her
barn in the event I did not find a house *immediately*.
Aunt Marion's barn was big, clean and empty, "only
filled with memories these days," she liked to say. I
was sure there wouldn't be a problem about us storing
our things in it.

I strongly disagreed about not hiring a moving
company, but Joe was stubborn; there was no point
arguing about it. I had a greater concern. What about
Joe's job, what was he doing about that? He said he had
asked for a transfer a year ago when I first left. His
company had an office in Minneapolis. He told me he
had even worked there for a while years ago before we
were married. It was one of those times he was working with a client outside of his market. He would have
to reactivate the request to transfer, but he didn't think
it would be a problem. Joe certainly was organized. It
filled me with a sense of calm like I was safely nestled
in a warm blanket. Joe made me feel safe; I realized
that had been missing from my life since I had left him.
I linked arms with him and willingly allowed myself
to be swept along as he orchestrated the day.

After we went to the notary we went to a little
fusion restaurant walking distance from my apart-

ment. Joe was not a fan of restaurants as a general rule, and he definitely didn't like food he considered "exotic," but he would eat Chinese food. I knew he would be able to find items to order at the fusion restaurant. I often got take-out delivered from them, but if the weather was nice I preferred to eat inside. I had become friendly with the owner, Jimmy, and when he saw me he came over to our table. "Hello, professor lady." He always called me that and when I introduced him to Joe he said, "I'm glad to meet you, professor lady's husband." I asked Joe if he minded being addressed like that. He said no; but he would have preferred *professor lady's banker* since he was the one who had paid for my PhD, enabling me to be a "professor lady." Ordinarily his words would have greatly irked my feminist sensibilities. It was true he had paid most of the bill for the cost of my doctorate, but not all. I had also used my entire savings from years of working. His words only registered a mild pinch, because I continued to be too wrapped in a safety blanket savoring the feel of his protection. There's a flip side to protection. We protect those who are not strong enough to care for themselves.

We were settled at our table but my feet continued to be cold from walking outside. I kicked off my boots and wiggled my toes to encourage circulation. After I was sufficiently warmed up, I took my foot and ran it slowly up the inside of Joe's leg until I reached his crotch and began to tap my toes. There was no one near to see and we were in a booth but he stopped talking and grabbed my foot. He wasn't quick enough. I had felt him. I doubt Joe considered it beneficial but I was not the only one who had increased circulation flow to an extremity in Jimmy's restaurant.

Joe told me to keep my feet to myself. I replied, "I was simply engaging in a little tactile flirting." I did not win him over completely– "save it for home, Sarah." I stopped, and demurely placed my foot back on my side of the booth. It really was more than simple flirting; had Joe sensed that? I don't even think I believed it was innocent. It was a need to express my strength in our relationship–I used my toes to do it.

After the restaurant we made a stop at the small grocery store two blocks from my apartment. Shopping for groceries was a necessity; my refrigerator was almost empty. I cooked most of the time for our entire relationship but living alone I had been fine with canned tuna, baked beans, toast and some fruit, or ordering from the fusion restaurant. After the refrigerator was filled, there was very little reason to leave my apartment.

Aside from visiting Aunt Marion the next day, Joe and I didn't venture outside over the four days he was with me. We were content to stay in. I cooked and occasionally he would, but our primary activity was sex. I was surprised he and I were holding up so well. I continued to have an overabundance of energy driving me. I don't know what drove him, with his lackadaisical attitude. He's also three years older than me but it felt like we were young and on our honeymoon. The kind we should have had twenty years ago.

Joe had hang-ups about sex which surfaced after we were married. It made our real honeymoon miserable. We were starting afresh when Joe carried me over the threshold for the second time. We were not just reuniting after a year and a half separation; we were having a second honeymoon–Joe failed to see that.

There's a plus side to Joe's placid demeanor. It contributes to that safe and secure feeling he instills in me, but the negative is sometimes I want to shake him. I shouldn't complain. It was an almost perfect second honeymoon–but not flawless, and I am not referring to Joe's placid attitude in any way contributing to the less than perfect score.

On the very first evening after making love on my sleeper, I cuddled up to Joe. I was all dewy with the afterglow of lovemaking, expecting him to stroke my face or fondle my tits, as he usually did, but he seemed removed from the moment. I looked intently at him, yet he wouldn't turn his face towards me until he said, "I have to tell you something, Sarah."

He sounded ominous, but Joe always sounds ominous because he uses the same voice whether he tells you something good or bad. I'm not suggesting he's robotic, only that the words he often chooses to communicate with affect the relationship and understanding of his meaning more than his inflection. I can't explain it, I only knew I didn't like his tone or his words so I am not sure why I said, "Well, what do you want to tell me?"

"I love you, Sarah, and I know for some reason you needed to leave to find something you were looking for; I don't understand it but I get it. But if you ever leave me again, I'm not coming after you. And I want to make this very clear, even if you want to come back to me, I will not take you back." That's when he abruptly ripped the warm safety blanket off my body.

I was stunned. I always thought Joe would want me, and now it was a matter of pride. Did this mean he would rather be with Sharon? I wasn't jealous. She was a mousy, flat-chested little woman with glasses. Why would I be threatened by her? The thought of Joe being inside of her made me crazy, and the idea he'd prefer to kiss and fondle her instead of me was upsetting, but I wasn't jealous.

I didn't say anything after he spoke, and when he finished he put his arms around me and began to kiss me. He acted as though he had said nothing unsettling, and if he was aware of how I felt he gave no indication of it. It appeared he had no idea his words would linger in my mind for the next three days. *Linger* is too gentle of a word; it was more like–*stuck in my brain*. Like a barnacle to a rock–impossible to remove. Every time we had sex, I couldn't stop thinking about him having sex with Sharon. Nobody had told me they had had sex. Rosie only said they slept in the same bedroom. I had to sneak into the bathroom and call Paulee to discuss it with her.

I began our conversation in a hushed tone. I didn't want Joe to overhear me from the other room. I asked her how familiar she had been with Joe and Sharon's relationship. "Were they having sex Paulee?" I stunned her, "Are you joking, Sarah, or have you gone completely bonkers? Of course they were, but you are back with Joe now. He's sleeping with you, not Sharon. So stop hiding in your bathroom and acting like an idiot."

What Paulee said didn't make me feel better. Joe's words haunted me. Did he mean if I left him he would divorce me and marry Sharon? I ignored his point about me leaving; it became irrelevant and overlooked. I dwelled instead on what was hard to accept–the idea Joe would prefer a woman like Sharon instead of me; it was incomprehensible which made me curious.

My curiosity messed up our second honeymoon. It was the last night before Joe would return to New Jersey the following morning. We again made love on my sleeper couch and we were cuddling. It seemed like the perfect time to ask: "So tell me Joe, how is Sharon in bed?"

"I will not talk to you about that, Sarah. So just get it out of your mind."

"Why not?"

"Because it's not any of your business." What did he mean by that? I told him I hadn't slept with any man since I met him. But if I had, I would give him all the details if he wanted to know. He told me he was glad to hear I had never been with another man, but he wouldn't want to hear any details–it was *my* business. I totally disagreed with him on what was or was not "my business."

"It's *our* business Joe, I'm your wife."

"Yes, you are my wife, Sarah. And you left me, remember?" It was true, but I hadn't slept with anyone.

I needed his assurance that he wanted me, preferred me, to Sharon. There was no reason for him to become defensive. I was not attacking him; I said it very sweetly, "You know Joe, you did commit adultery."

"Are you kidding me? I think the legal word for what you did is abandonment. And you not only told me on the phone you weren't coming back, I saved the email where you put it down in writing." I became enraged. I had no idea what email he was referring to, but had he saved it in case he needed it for divorce proceedings? I screamed at him:

"Just tell me one thing Joe, did you use a condom when you fucked her? And don't you dare say that's none of my business because you've been fucking me for four days without one."

Joe sat up in bed; he started to rub his face and eyes with his two hands like he was trying to rouse himself from a nightmare. It was an uncomfortable amount of time before he finally turned to me and said, "Yes." I was not really afraid I had caught something from Sharon via Joe. It was more about saving face. I at least now knew I was closer to him than Sharon had been. There were no barriers between us.

Joe got up and put on his jeans and went into the bathroom. He was there for nearly twenty minutes. It was the only room you could use to get away from someone you didn't want to be with in my studio apartment. It gave me time to think. I knew Joe hated gossiping; is that why he wouldn't tell me anything about Sharon? He had overheard Paulee and me talking about someone one evening and said it was a good thing he didn't believe in hell. He would worry about us if he did– "you two are earning points to get there." It was a theory for his reluctance to talk about Sharon, but in my heart I knew it wasn't about gossip, or him being an honorable, good man. I had to face my fears. He cared about her. It didn't matter if she was flat-chested or mousy. I had almost lost him.

When Joe returned to bed he sat on the edge of the mattress with his back to me. On my knees I walked on the bed over to him like a penitent sinner and put my forehead between his shoulder blades. "I'm sorry Joe for asking you about Sharon. I know I can be a real bitch sometimes." He didn't turn towards me, he only said "no problem." Did he mean it was no problem that I asked questions or that it was no problem I was a bitch? Or both? I would have appreciated more clarity. Or better yet? I would have preferred it if he had said–*ask all the questions you want, and you're not a bitch, Sarah*. It was too much to contemplate and then he added more to ponder, "sometimes I just wish there was a little less drama, more *quiet*." I understood his subtext, Rosie had told me Sharon was "a quiet, well-mannered lady" –not a big mouth like me.

The problem was I wasn't sure I could be quiet and Sharon was like a piece of sand stuck in my shoe. She would continue to resurface, irritating me, every time I was irritated with Joe. It wouldn't even have to be about her. If I was annoyed because he forgot to recycle his beer bottles or refused to go to the movies with me–I might bring up *Sharon*. It was just me. I can't forget things, and I really want to put her behind us.

I stared at Joe's back for a long time before he finally turned around to face me. We went to bed, side-by-side holding hands. We watched a movie and snuggled until it was time to sleep. He put his arms around me and I fell asleep deeply, surprised it was morning when the alarm went off. It was pretty early; the sky wasn't bright yet. Joe wanted to have an early start driving back to New Jersey.

Joe talked less than usual that morning. It made me feel insecure. I hope he will continue to want me in spite of not being *a quiet, well-mannered lady*. At least three times when we made love over the past four days he put his hand over my mouth, "Sarah, your neighbors are going to think you're being murdered in here." I bet Sharon doesn't behave that way; but I don't know. Joe won't say.

CHAPTER 17

JOE

've loved Sarah from the first day I saw her broken down on the road with a flat tire, and I'll probably love her until I take my last breath. It doesn't mean that sometimes I don't want to throttle her, or take her over my knee and spank her. I would never do that, and knowing Sarah, a spanking wouldn't humiliate her. More than likely it would turn her on. It humiliated Rosie, and I hoped I wasn't doing it again when I broke up with her roommate's mother.

Driving to Chapel Hill I realized this will be the first time in my life I broke up with a woman. Far easier to be dropped if you ask me and I'm not looking forward to it. I had to tell Sharon face-to-face too. She's a nice lady, and was a good friend these past months. I'm going to miss her friendship, and her cooking. I always teased Sarah that she was trying to starve us with rabbit food. I was only joking but there was a big difference in their cooking styles, and other things.

Sharon's content with making a home and caring for her family. Not that Sarah did not take care of Rosie and me or our home but it never seemed like it was enough for her. She was discontented much of the time. That mind of hers–too smart sometimes. I'm not saying that Sharon is dumb, but she doesn't overthink things like my wife. I know if my sister had met her she would have said she was a better match for me than Sarah. She would have been wrong again. Loving someone has nothing to do with tallying a scorecard–you can't pick who you love.

I doubt that ending my relationship with Sharon will be an emotional scene–she's not an emotional type. Still, I know guys who would have preferred to end it with a call just in case, but I can't do that. My friend Rocky told me, years ago before his marriage and cell phones, he would end a relationship with a call when he knew they weren't home. He'd leave a message on their answering machine. That's cold, but some guys simply disappear–that's worse. I couldn't even do that with prostitutes.

I had to let them know at *Sadie's House* I wouldn't be coming back to Alaska to work on the fishing boats again after that fourth summer. I didn't want to simply disappear. It bothered me that they might think I was going somewhere else when they didn't see me any-more. There were three girls I went with on a regular basis depending on who was available. I had to tell each one personally it was my last summer. When I told Lorraine I was leaving she said I was one of the sweetest guys she ever met, and some girl was going to be so lucky to get me. She offered me another on the house. I was younger then; I was able to take her up on the offer easily.

Sarah nearly killed me these past few days, and she isn't so young herself anymore. She'll settle down; it was only because of the emotional nature of the situation. That also made her act differently when we made love; for the first time there was a neediness or urgency in her I had never seen before. I've always felt like I loved her more than she loved me, but we never talked about it. Sarah would complain about "scales not being balanced" when it came to parenting Rosie. I never agreed with that, but I had always felt a love imbalance between us.

Now it finally seems more level; even leaning more in my favor. It took years and there's no guarantee it will stick. Always hard to figure out my wife's next move, and I'm no expert on women. I would be very reluctant to give any man advice about them, with one possible exception. I know from personal experience that prostitutes are much easier to have in your life than wives or girlfriends.

CHAPTER 18

SHARON

had been baking cookies for Christmas for weeks. Homemade oatmeal and chocolate chip were staples that I always had in the cookie jar, but now I was making the holiday favorites. I knew what Leslie liked and made a note to ask Joe what his favorites were. He and Rosie would be spending the Christmas holiday with us again–like a family. I wouldn't bother to ask Rosie–the black sheep, her cookie preferences. I was making a big enough variety that she would certainly be able to find a cookie to her liking. I tried to avoid talking to her if at all possible, and did not feel guilty about it. It was enough that I tolerated her.

Holiday cookies were important but so was the meal. I planned a nice one, but nothing fancy: ham, creamed pearled onions and mashed potatoes. For dessert there would be pecan pie and Red Velvet cake. Joe liked my Red Velvet cake when I made it for Thanksgiving.

Joe called me two weeks before Christmas making me tweak my holiday menu. He said he needed to see me. It was about something he couldn't say on the phone. I was sure it was about the divorce and a marriage proposal. The holiday menu had to be more special, more festive. I would add whipped horseradish cream and a parmesan crust for the mashed potatoes.

After he called I had to also plan an immediate dinner for his arrival. After looking at a number of cookbooks I chose his favorites: pork chops smothered with gravy and macaroni and cheese. I wished there had also been time to make a cake but there were plenty of cookies, and I had to prepare myself.

I am not a vain person but I asked Georgia, another stylist at the shop, to pin up my hair. She was very patient and I was grateful; my hair is so fine it took her over a hundred pins to hold up my French twist. After I returned home I set the dining room table and lit candles. I was beside myself waiting for Joe to arrive so I calmed myself by preparing my response to his proposal. I did not want it to sound rehearsed like I had expected him to propose, but I wanted the evening to be memorable. It was.

What Joe said was the last thing I had ever expected and will always stay in my memory–because the bible was clear. *Lilith never returned to Adam.* How did this happen?

Joe was a weak man. It hadn't come as a complete surprise. I had suspected it when I saw the tattoo on his arm the first evening he made love to me. I believed it had been Sarah's doing so I forgave him, even though tattoos are a sin. She had persuaded him to mark his flesh against the word of God. Leviticus

19:28: "Ye shall not make any cuttings in your flesh nor print any marks upon you." Lilith made him mark his arm but I will not let her mark any other part of his body. I will not let her ensnare his soul. I pray I'm not too late.

I have often questioned how it came about that he was ever with her. I finally concluded it was to be expected, physical attraction was the obvious reason. Joe is no different than any other man. Men are really the weaker sex when they're pitted against the wiles of women. I saw that in my life when Mike yielded to his homewrecking tramp. I only need to look in the bible for more examples–Samson and Delilah; David and Bethsheba. Their stories attest to the superior strength of women. Joe is too weak to battle Lilith on his own. I have to help him, and that's why I know our story is not over. I must be strong for him and have faith in the Lord. Isaiah 40: 31: "those who believe in the Lord will find new strength."

God answered my prayers that night; he gave me the comfort and strength I needed. As upset as I was, I did not cry. I told Joe I wanted to remain friends and asked him to stay for dinner. I also offered my guest room for the night; I didn't want him to go to the Rooster Inn. Joe accepted my hospitality. He enjoyed the dinner I had prepared for him and stayed in the guest room while I turned to my bible. I had to find the answer. Why had Sarah returned?

I was rewarded with a new insight and understanding of the scripture. It is true that Lilith never returned to Eden in the form of a woman, but some believe she returned as the serpent. The serpent that tempted Eve and Adam from paradise. This revelation made Sarah's return clearer, and Joe's plight more dire. He had been too weak to fight temptation. The fight was not over though. I was willing to die or kill to protect Leslie and I felt the same about Joe. I had to save him from Lilith. I would not let her win. I don't know how I am going to do it but I know I will have help. I am not alone. God works in mysterious ways.

CHAPTER 19

JOE

It wasn't so bad. I hadn't anticipated a big emotional response and Sharon did not seem that upset. I'm glad I went to see her in person. Women are still hard to figure out. I tell Sarah I don't want a divorce and she starts crying like a baby; I tell Sharon I'm ending our relationship and she doesn't shed a tear. She still made me feel like a louse because she had made this great dinner. If this had been in reverse with Sarah, I might have refused to eat it. I'm not implying she'd poison me but she would spice it up somehow to make it inedible. She was angry at me one time and added red chili pepper to some stew she gave me; it nearly blew my head off. She insisted it was a mistake; she thought it was paprika–I didn't believe her.

Thinking about that stew, I hope Sarah never finds out I stayed the night at Sharon's. I called her as soon as I left Sharon's house–and not a minute too early. She was concerned because I hadn't called her since leaving Minneapolis. I didn't lie when I told her my cell phone had been in the SUV and I was too tired to retrieve it once I settled in for the night. It was a good thing I left it on the passenger seat. It would have rung in Sharon's house, and I would have been reluctant to answer; it would have been awkward. Sharon at least knew I was back with Sarah, but how would I explain to my wife why I was in Chapel Hill? She'd probably scream–*stay there*. She wouldn't mean it and we would recover but who needs all the drama. I had enough for the week already as it was.

I had been surprised Sharon asked me to stay over; begged me really. But it was all above board; I stayed in her guest room. I had been so beat from driving I couldn't refuse. She explained she had to do it: "You can't sleep in your car at a truck stop in these temperatures, Joe." North Carolina was way more warmer than Minnesota but I still offered to go to a motel. She insisted it was not necessary, "we're both adults," and she understood how I was "compelled to go back with Sarah."

I don't know why Sharon phrased it that way–no one was forcing me to reunite with my wife; I was doing it willingly. But I was not talking about my marriage or Sarah with her anymore, even if she wanted to remain friends. We used to talk about stuff like that after Sarah told me she was not coming back. Things are different now.

I'm okay with maintaining a friendship with her though. She had been a lifesaver when I felt like I was going down, and she was the mother of my daughter's roommate. But there would be limitations; I'm definitely not going to continue discussing personal things–Sarah would throw a fit. She seems really threatened by Sharon, and I have never seen her act that way in all the years we've been together.

Sarah is reminding me of Maureen, which is a shocker, but with some major differences. Maureen had been threatened by all women–even those not really in my life. She was jealous of porn actresses. It was another reason I hadn't been sorry she moved out of my townhouse. Sarah likes porn; she was my porn buddy. We watched it together and then made love. Sometimes she didn't even want to wait until the film was over. Who knows, maybe she was in competition with those women on the screen, but I liked it.

Maureen used to have a fit when she found nudie magazines in my car. She said *"masturbating* was a filthy habit and I was going to hell." The hell part was not surprising but her saying "masturbating" was. The only comment Sarah ever made was in the form of a question: "Why do you need those magazines if you have me?" I told her when I was on the road I didn't have her. That's what gave her the idea to pose nude for photos in our living room. "The living room has the best light, Joe." I wasn't going to argue with that or had any wish to stop her from traipsing around naked posing for me.

I spent an hour taking pictures of her with my Kodak Ektar, taking my time setting up each shot like a photographer doing a magazine layout. Sarah was a natural but I found it hard to keep my mind on taking photos. When I finished we made love on the oriental rug where I had taken my last three shots. I still had some film left but no more self-control.

I used those pictures for years until I accidently left them at a motel in Maryland. I was afraid Sarah would be angry when I told her. There she was nude for anyone to find–they were *porn worthy*. She laughed, and the only thing she said was: "Well, I guess you saved some guy from having to buy a magazine to jerk off, right?"

After I lost the pictures I wanted to take more with my phone but she wasn't keen on the idea–she was afraid somehow they would find their way on the internet. "What if they got out there somehow, Joe? It might jeopardize my job. You might lose your phone this time." She's smart, but she didn't think about how someone could take pictures of those lost photos using their phone and she might still end up on the internet one day. I could have also pointed out how the photos had been taken more than ten years prior when I lost them; I chose not to question her logic. If I had said that–it would have opened up another line of unwanted talk: *what, you don't think my tits are as perky now as in those photos?* Telling her they were perky enough for me wouldn't satisfy her. And she did look really good, but her body and face did not look like they had when I took the photos. That will remain a closed subject forever.

She gave me a subscription to *Playboy* after she refused to let me take more pictures. She didn't have a problem being compared to the *playgirl-of-the month* because she looked like one of them. She still does, with a little air-brushing. She's a great looking woman even for her age. But taking nude pictures of her is something I'm not keen about anymore. After losing her this past year and a half I'm not wanting to chance sharing her with anyone if I did lose her pictures. And today I can find plenty of porn on my phone or the computer. Porn continues not to bother Sarah–but Sharon does.

Once I got home from North Carolina I went to Agnes's house to pick up Holly. Agnes had been one of my staunchest supporters after Sarah left me. When I told her the good news she started crying. It took some time for her to recover; now I know where Sarah inherited this crying trait from. If memory serves, I think Agnes was crying most of the time at our wedding.

It was a relief to walk into my townhouse, even if for the most part it was filled with moving boxes. I hadn't moved a single thing out yet. The closing was one week before Christmas and I had to start moving stuff into Agnes' garage and a storage pod she let me put in her driveway. The garage and pod were fixed but now my destination was no longer North Carolina. I planned to start hauling our things to Minnesota after the holiday, but I didn't have to worry about that today. I was happy to be able to crash out on my bed–alone, with no women. I was glad I was back with Sarah but the only female I wanted was Holly.

She was allowed back on the bed since Sharon was no longer there to object. I had tried to follow her rules even when she wasn't in the townhouse for Holly's sake because I did not want to confuse her. I hadn't given the dog much thought in the past few days, but now I suddenly realized–*I no longer have to find a new home for her.* I stretched out and called her, patting the bed encouragingly. She hesitated before she jumped up to join me. She could not understand why now she was being asked to go on the bed after months of– "no, down." I felt like saying–*Yeah dog, what is going on?* Hopefully there won't be any more changes for both of us for a while.

Our answering machine on the nightstand was still hooked up and I listened to my messages. There was one from Sarah– *"Where are you, Joe? I know you can't be home yet but please call me as soon as you get this message since you don't answer your cell phone and I've called at least eight times and your voicemail is filled."* The return call to Sarah had already been taken care of and next was a message from Paulee. She congratulated me, "I knew you two would get back together. I am so happy for you both, Joe." I guess Sarah had already given her the news. I not only appreciated her good wishes, I was glad she didn't cry.

The last message was from my buddy Rocky. He called me to find out how it went with Sarah and asked me to give him a call back. I took a shower and a short nap before I returned his call. I told him we were back together and now I was moving my things to the northwest instead of the south, and I hoped he was still willing to help me with the move. We didn't talk long but I did tell him how Sarah had been pretty upset about Sharon, and I couldn't understand why. "We're back together, Sharon is no threat." Rocky said it made no difference, "you were boning this woman."

"I was with women before I met Sarah and it never bothered her before. I also went with Sharon after she told me she wasn't coming back. I don't get it."

"Maybe because she's a dog. Sarah met her, right? Pretty insulting that you would prefer that to her. You know man I really thought you were out of your mind doing that downgrade." I liked Rocky but I did not like the way he sometimes talked about women. When I objected he would always respond, "just kidding, man." He did not say that when I told him I would appreciate it if he did not bad mouth Sharon; "she's a good person, Rocky." He didn't say another word about her.

I really don't fully understand why Sarah seems so upset, but I'm not a fool. That's why I didn't tell her I was going to North Carolina and would never tell her I spent the night at Sharon's house. I wouldn't have done it if I hadn't been so tired, and the big meal had made me sleepy. Not an excuse and too late now to retract my decision to stay, but I'm not volunteering the information to Sarah.

I also know I could never convince Sarah that Sharon and I can be just friends. We were always more friends than serious in my mind, even with the sex. I was moving to North Carolina because I wanted to sell the townhouse; it reminded me too much of Sarah. And North Carolina is a more affordable state to live in than New Jersey. It was also near Sharon, and I hadn't ruled out the possibility of us eventually living with one another–to save more money. Marriage had never been a serious option though. We were a long way from that, if ever, and from the way Sharon acted when I ended it–a pretty safe bet she had felt the same.

And if she says she wants to remain only friends–she's sincere, she offered her guest room instead of her bedroom as proof of it. Being friends is okay with me too; I like her, she's a nice lady. She also strikes me as being a clearer thinker than Sarah, who thinks more with her heart than her head. Sarah's thoughts shoot off into all sorts of directions, and I just hope she stays on track with me this time. I'm like Holly, I'm getting a little old for changes; too confusing.

CHAPTER 20

SARAH

'm an emotional mess. It was only a little more than a week that I had finally accepted the fact–*Joe and I were not going to get back together.* I wasn't happy about it, but I accepted it. Then ninety-six hours ago I was tossed and turned from being usurped by a homely woman, almost divorced, and reunited all in a matter of minutes. I am thrilled over the outcome and still blistering from the woman. Joe and Sharon are the primary reasons for my distress, but all the changes, even the positive ones, are playing havoc with my equilibrium. I could not sleep at all last night and I need to work today.

I'll be okay in spite of my restless night after I lie down with two wet tea bags on my eyes for fifteen minutes and splash cold water on my face. I'll then apply my makeup, and put on my black suit with the red silk blouse. I love the blouse but it has a V-neck. It means I'll have to check for love bites.

Joe gave me one once and I was totally unaware of it until a colleague pointed it out. I was embarrassed and asked her if she had any under-eye concealer. She did and I immediately ran to the ladies' room to cover it. I hoped none of my students had noticed it before she did. When I got home I chastised Joe. His calm retort was, "I don't see what the problem is. Your students are in college; they're adults, right? They know you're human." My being human had nothing to do with it. I told him—"from now on, put your bites only in places the public won't see." I still continued to check carefully because I didn't trust him then, and still don't. Joe is a biter.

I also planned to wear my new red heels, in spite of having to carry them in a tote until I put them on in my office at school. Minnesota weather made it necessary to wear winter boots in transit from home to work. It was worth the effort. I liked these heels and they only pinched my toes a tiny little bit. That won't bother me; nor thoughts about Joe or Sharon when I stand in front of my classes.

I will be confident, knowledgeable and in command of myself and my students. I am Professor Janak or Professor J or Dr. Janak—whichever my students wish to call me. In the many years of teaching, I have only had two students address me by my first name and I told them to stop. They were males; regardless of my age and status my gender made them regard me as their equal. I squashed it; I was strong and self-assured. It wasn't a facade. Something magical happens when I stand in front of my classes. I only wish I could be more like Professor Janak or Professor J or Dr. Janak in my personal life, especially with Joe.

I have a vague memory from years ago of Joe saying, "Please don't talk to me like I'm one of your students, Sarah." I'm ninety-nine percent sure he said it but it is a faint memory so I can't be absolutely sure–maybe I should ease up on the pot. Joe also doesn't like me smoking it, and when he was here he remarked, "it smells like you're still smoking dope, Sarah." He's right, and I had just finished a joint before he rang my doorbell. His choice of words was annoying though, and he's been delivering the same line for two decades. Hearing him one would think I'm some out-of-control dope addict instead of a recreational user who is in perfect control of herself. And on reflection, I'm sure any memory issues I might have have nothing to do with me smoking grass. My mind becomes muddled when I'm stressed. It was also a long time ago when Joe said I was talking to him like he was one of my students–and maybe he never said that. I might be confusing him with Rosie.

I have no doubt about her responding in a similarly negative vein. The last time I told her to apply herself more in school she said, "I'm not one of your students, Mom. You can't talk to me like that; and I'm in college, remember?" I assured her that I don't speak the same way to her as I do with my students. I added, "save your breath and use your energy to do your work instead of arguing with me." Rosie makes me laugh sometimes. Young adult children who attend college thanks to their parents embrace a false-independence. They have to be reminded that being in college was not a valid argument–until they start paying for school themselves.

I do hold a semblance of rank over my daughter, even if she is uncontrollable at times. She knows she is not my equal. With Joe there's a difference; always has been. I have struggled with feelings of not being his equal for our entire relationship. It might speak more about my self-concept than actions on his part but the dynamic between us for whatever reason remains the same–it can reduce me to a blubbering idiot. I can feel like an out-of-control child sometimes–as laughable as my daughter.

Leaving Joe was due to a perfect storm generated by the low and high pressures of my insecurities and fears. When I left him a year and a half ago it was more about me than him; I never meant to hurt him.

For most of my working life I have been struggling with self-esteem issues. Which is understandable when you are an adjunct professor. In the eyes of my students I seemed powerful, but an adjunct professor is one of the lowest ranks in the teaching hierarchy. I never taught at schools where there were graduate assistants teaching classes. If I had, perhaps I would have been raised higher in the caste system, but it's not part of my work history.

My rank was low in the academic community at large. I spent years working, as well as all my savings and Joe's money, to earn my PhD to make less money than the maintenance workers at the schools where I was employed. I'm not suggesting I am intrinsically better than the non-teaching staff. They were working full time which is why they deserved their higher salaries with full benefits. I understood it on an intellectual level, but the knowledge did nothing to improve my self-worth. After years of schooling and spending loads of our money, I earned less than someone who was cutting the grass on campus.

My self-esteem has also taken a beating from Rosie since she turned twelve. She had never been an easy child because Joe spoiled her. But I do have great memories when she was small: baking cookies together; painting her toenails; reading her stories, and all of her beautiful sentiments– "You're the prettiest Mommy"; "I love you Mommy"; "I want to be just like you when I grow up, Mommy." She turns twelve and before her eyes I suddenly morph into a *cunt* or a *whore* (and now a *narcissistic bitch)*; expletives pour out of her mouth as freely as her sweet sentiments once did.

She learned her colorful language from her grandfather Mac–who is a pig. Even though I knew where she had learned the words, the first time she used them was a shock. I am not overly sensitive when it comes to language, but I started to question myself as a mother. What had I done or not done that would make my daughter act like she hated me? Had I neglected her?

I was busy when I was working on my PhD, and I could not afford to stop teaching while I was in graduate school. One semester I taught at several schools simultaneously in my attempt to achieve a semblance of a full-time salary, and took classes at night. I had to stop doing that but I never stopped using the TV as a babysitter. I might have also said, "Not now Rosie, Mommy's busy," too often, but I always continued to make time for her. I believed in the merits of quality over quantity, but maybe she needed more.

In some ways I mirrored my mother who had worked full time my entire childhood. My sister Penny and I were latchkey kids: we came home to an empty house, made our own snacks and did our homework until our mother came home. I never remember my mother playing with me or reading a single story. We didn't even have a father, and Penny and I turned out okay. More importantly we never disrespected our mother.

Rosie's experience was different from mine; Joe or I were always there when she returned home from school to greet her and make a snack. And I always asked about her day and homework, told her to change into her play clothes, and asked her to straighten her room before going out to play. My mother had never done any of that. Yet Rosie made me feel like I was an awful mother, making me question myself.

Joe helped to create an imbalanced family paradigm. He was a big problem–no surprise Rosie resents me. I have always tried to teach her and discipline her–to be her mother, not her friend. Joe on the other hand was *Father Fun* when she was a kid; he indulged her. We often had heated discussions when she was younger but one at age four stands out. He denied *his poor parenting skills* as usual:

"I don't indulge her, Sarah. I'm not even sure what that means."

"Really, Joe? Let me explain. You let her color the tattoo on your arm with magic markers."

"She's four. And they're water soluble; they wash right off."

"I don't care. I would never let her near my tattoo with magic markers."

"Well, yours already has color, Sarah." That really had been off point, and he still indulges her today.

◆――――◆――――◆

Rosie's hostility towards me ramped up during the time I was contemplating leaving Joe. Coupled with the insecurity about my career–I needed an ego boost. When I was offered the full-time tenure-track position to teach at a small private college in Minnesota, it was the long-sought affirmation I had been longing for my entire career. My self-esteem grew. I might be a lousy mother, but at least I was not a failure as an educator.

Accepting the teaching position doesn't explain why I left Joe. He might have relocated if I had given him a chance. It was fear, along with insecurities, which blew into a storm shaking my marriage. I was afraid he'd refuse to relocate to Minnesota, and I'd never have this opportunity presented to me again. I was not young, just starting a career. A fear of mortality also blindsided me.

Not the prospect of death itself; I had wrestled with that specter when I had breast cancer. It was the apprehensiveness of regret on my deathbed–*I did not achieve my goals.* Joe in the paradigm of my life was also a factor. Would I regret having stayed with him? We were never a perfect match.

Joe was never anyone I had imagined I would marry. We started as friends which they say is a good thing and then love grew out of our friendship. Sex changed the dynamic and my mind got all mucked up. Joe says that's my real problem, I overthink things too much, "and sex is never the same after you're married." He's probably right but overlooks another complication in our relationship–he has a mucked-up mouth. It prevents him from speaking effectively. We are not compatible when it comes to communicating. My difficult situation was never all about sex. Sometimes it feels like I'm on a game show trying to solve a puzzle when I'm talking with Joe. He is very stingy with words and I have to figure out the subtext to understand his meaning. I've been with him so long I'm good at the game. I can decipher his message and feel proud; I can also find him amusing occasionally. Other times I'd like to hit him over the head to see if more words will fall out of his mouth.

Ironically I hadn't handled my departure well due to my own poor communication skills. It has no bearing on my recommendation for couples with lingering doubts about their relationships though. If I re-evaluate leaving Joe in its entirety it was a positive action. I urge couples experiencing stress like I had to take a vacation from one another. It's like airing out a room filled with stale air, and I realized after being away from Joe that I missed him more than he annoyed me.

There is a caveat to leaving that must be pointed out though–it's risky. I miscalculated and thought Joe loved me unconditionally. As long as I did not ask for a divorce–I was safe; analogous to airing the room out but not burning the house down. I believed he would wait for me as long as it took to confirm or deny my doubts about our relationship. Paulee believes in this *unconditional love* bullshit, which reinforced my miscalculation. She now says I was "just lucky," but maintains her position for the former.

I know I was wrong, even though Paulee won't concede her stand on unconditional love. We must have different definitions for *unconditionally.* I'll agree with her on this point: Joe said he'd love me always, but here's the rub: he added that he wouldn't take me back if I left him again. *Unconditional love* shouldn't have disclaimers. He should take me back no matter how many times I leave him. What an error on my part thinking I was safe staying away so long. Little had I known my time had been running out like a parking meter.

I was ready to reunite earlier than some would say, but I wanted to keep my job in Minnesota–which brings me to my culpability. And I'm not even sure it was my poor communication or simply being too stoned. My student Daniel gives me some very strong grass. My memory is a bit blurry on all the details.

I am very aware of Joe and I talking that rainy Sunday evening. I was lying naked on my rug in front of the fireplace, sipping brandy and feeling no pain. I told him I definitely was staying in Minnesota. Then he asked me if I wanted him to relocate or did I want a divorce. This is where it becomes confusing because I don't remember responding. I was mesmerized by the flame in my fireplace; it was my primary focus. Joe insists I answered "I don't know" but I can't swear to it. And since my memory is vague, it's hard to dispute. It grows more complex however because in our subsequent phone calls I never received a clue from him that I had uttered any life-changing statement. He didn't seem upset by any previously said words I might have uttered in my grass induced haze–not a single hint about the subject from him at all. It's also fair to add I was out of practice deciphering Joe's puzzling communication style.

After this *meaningful* phone call when I was stoned out of my mind, I became distracted by work. I had been asked to teach summer classes, and I was trying to come up with syllabi. Students often take them thinking they are easy–*only five weeks*, then complain about all the work. They don't realize that a full semester of class assignments is being crammed into a five-week session–they are not abridged courses. These sessions are also challenging for teachers who agree to take them on, but I couldn't refuse; I wanted tenure.

My mind was not on Joe or my marriage one iota. No need; *unconditional love*, remember?

It wasn't until I was finally prepared to teach my classes that I was able to focus on other things–like my marriage. I wanted to reunite with Joe. I told Paulee first, only because Joe never answered his phone, and that's when she told me he was dating Sharon. She delivered it with a tone that felt as though she stuck her tongue out at me when she finished. The way she treats me at times I wouldn't be surprised to discover she had been a bully growing up, taunting other little girls.

I was upset and Paulee was not supportive. I called my mother and she asked, "What, did you expect him to wait for you forever, Sarah?" –no support from them. Paulee has allegiance to Joe preventing her from committing to me fully, and my mother can't stop being a mother. I often felt as though I had time traveled back to my teenage years when I talked to her about my marriage–she was always critical of my behavior. And she continues to criticize me like I'm sixteen if I broach my relationship with Joe. She's a far cry from a traditional mother-in-law forever taking his side and pointing out my culpability. She told me to "grow up," when I told her he was dating Sharon–reinforcing my sense of ambiguity about time.

◆　◆　◆

Now she tells me to stop brooding over what happened, but to thank God I came to my senses– "you should have never left him in the first place though."

She can't stop criticizing, but I am trying to heed her advice–I have stopped obsessing about why I left. I can't rest easy about the security of my marriage though no matter how hard I try.

I felt fine teaching my classes after Joe left Minneapolis for New Jersey. It wasn't until I was done with work and in my apartment–a time to settle–I became unsettled. Joe had not called me since he left that morning. I reassured myself, he would in the evening–I was worried for no reason. Then pretty much lost it when there was no word from him the entire night. His stupid old SUV. Why couldn't he fly like normal people? Or was it me? Had our four days together been a dream or pot haze?

My mother called that night to ask how it went. She apparently had known Joe was coming back to me before I did; she was taking care of Holly. Her call calmed me: not crazy, not too stoned–and it wasn't a dream. So why wasn't I hearing from him? I should not have mentioned Sharon. She told me I had "no right being jealous after leaving him." I had to defend myself and prove I was not jealous. "If I really were jealous, I might suspect that he went off to North Carolina after he left me and that's why he isn't calling. I am not implying that, Mom." She told me to drop it, but it was impossible. I had worked myself into a frenzy by the time I finally spoke to Joe.

He asked me to calm down. I replied, "you have to understand; before you buzzed my door I had finally accepted we were finished and you were moving to

North Carolina to be with another woman. Then all of a sudden we are back together like we were never apart. It feels like a dream and I don't know how you can act so calm."

He said he wasn't calm. He was able to mask emotion from years of bluffing doing sales work and he even identified with me. "It felt like I was in a nightmare after you left me. We both woke up, baby, okay?"

I liked what he said, but why can't I expunge Sharon from my brain? Or wake up from the dream she inhabits?

I know why–she's no dream; she's a threatening reality.

Joe and I are back together––end of story, for both Paulee and my mother. But the story is not over because they're so wrong about Sharon. My angst has nothing to do with me being a green-eyed- monster, but Sharon is a specter. She has started to make me feel insecure: Joe doesn't love me unconditionally, Rosie hates me, and I have not secured the promised tenure. *I'm not jealous of Sharon,* but her mere existence is making negative issues resurface–I need therapy again.

Therapy helped me before in my life, but the thought of trying to find a therapist in Minneapolis is daunting. Looking for a therapist is not a simple search for a webpage. That's only the first step–the easy one. I dread having to repeat my history over and over again to each new potential therapist until

I find the right one. We have to be a good fit, like a blind date. And the worst thing about a blind date is when the realization hits mid-way–*we aren't a fit.* Blind dates are easier than meeting new therapists though. I used to have a friend call me during my date at an arranged time–a perfect escape ploy if needed. I would be reluctant to try that at an appointment with a therapist. I wish there was a way to find one similar to speed dating.

CHAPTER 21

PAULEE

I had to call forth all of the acting tips I could remember from directing my students in our mainstage school plays. I had to apply them to sound surprised and sincere when Sarah called, telling me Joe showed up in Minneapolis and they were back together. "Oh, my God, Sarah, really? He drove all the way to Minneapolis? I told you not to lose hope about you two getting back together." I sounded good if I must say so myself but I almost screwed it up when I mentioned the driving part; Sarah hadn't mentioned it. When she asked, "How did you know he drove?" I had to think fast on my feet, and the reason why I make my students practice improvisation even if they are preparing for a scripted production.

"Well, I just figured he drove. I know Joe." She bought it, thank God.

I wouldn't want her to know I told Joe she was crying her eyes out over him. She forced me to call him and lie to her about it. Is it my fault she was too chicken shit scared or stubborn to contact him herself? She'd be angry if she found out what I did; she accuses me of interfering sometimes. Which doesn't make any sense at all considering our years of friendship. The way I see it, if she doesn't want me to get involved she should keep her mouth shut. I am a part of her life. Hard to call that *interference*.

Sarah and I have been together for years and share everything with each other. Exchanging intimate details about our relationships with men has been a favorite topic since the first week we met. There's not much for me to share; she contributes more. So it goes without saying, it affords me more opportunities to offer opinions. And it has felt like I've been doing a threesome with her and Joe since their dating days right up to the present. But if she ever wanted to give Anthony a few helpful tips I would never call her out on it.

It is also not my fault she and Joe are more entertaining than Anthony and me. They were even more entertaining during the year and a half they were separated, and I was a bit player in their drama. I do get my occasional opportunities to shine though–like calling Joe for her.

It isn't fear of her anger that makes me pray she never discovers I called him. I don't want her to find out because I know how her mind works. She'll start forming negative theories: *he only came after her because I called him*; or *he felt sorry for her*; or *I persuaded him to go to her.* Not that creative, but ideas better put in a cheap romance novel opposed to serious speculation.

I only told Joe how she felt; I never told him what to do; it was his own idea to drive to Minneapolis to reunite with her. If she was thinking clearly she'd agree that nobody can force Joe to do anything he doesn't want to do, or question his willingness to return to her. But if she knew I had spoken to him, she'd overlook her own knowledge of a man she's known for two decades. Sarah can be her own worst enemy sometimes, and the more we talked I knew she was not thinking clearly.

I literally started to silently pray, "Please, Jesus, keep Sarah from *fucking it up again*." I then had to apologize to Jesus and my mother for my language. I don't like to be blasphemous, and I may be a fifty-four-year-old woman but I'm watchful of my language because of my mother and God. Sarah was making me speak profanely, but admittedly it wasn't entirely her fault. I've been with Anthony too long for it not to have an effect on my choice of words.

There's a double standard about that too in regard to my mother. Anthony can drop F-bombs left and right and my mother will say, "Oh, Anthony," and giggle like a teenager. If I slip one in she yells, "Pauline, watch your mouth. You're making baby Jesus weep." What's baby Jesus doing when Anthony is cursing, that's what I would like to know? It made me pause though thinking about my mother's warning, and I was also shaped by twelve years of parochial school. I hoped baby Jesus was otherwise occupied and glad my mother hadn't been anywhere near when I was talking to Sarah. My mother and the sisters of Sacred Heart don't have to worry about my soul though. I make a confession weekly, and by the time I finished my call with Sarah I had plenty to repent.

I dropped several F-bombs while talking to her. I couldn't help it; she was infuriating. She was making me seriously question if someone can interfere or change a tragic flaw story once it's written. I'm afraid Sarah will reset hers if she's not careful. She loves Joe, is grateful they are back together and swears she'll never leave him again. She's also sure she will never be able to forget about him having slept with Sharon while they were separated. A case of bruised hubris and proof of how strong her nemesis is. What she doesn't understand is that the nemesis can ultimately destroy her if she doesn't stop thinking about her–the same with the devil.

I was taught in my catechism classes when I was a kid that if you thought about the devil too much you called him to you. It gave me nightmares when I was six. Mostly because I could not comprehend the meaning of what they were saying; but now listening to Sarah I understand what they were trying to teach me. It was an allegory, even nonbelievers could apply to their lives. I tried to enlighten Sarah: *If you keep talking about Sharon, you risk driving Joe back into her arms, and it would be your own doing again. The only reason he was with her in the first place was because you left him.* My efforts were wasted.

"Okay, Paulee, I left Joe, but I did not sleep with anyone while we were separated." She totally dismissed her complicity and my *driving him back into her arms* point, and became self-righteous about her actions during the separation. She was self-serving.

"Well, you didn't meet anyone you wanted to sleep with, right?"

"No, that's not true and I can satisfy my own sexual urges. Apparently Joe is not able to and I'm easily replaced by the looks of it. I realized it would take years with anyone to feel the same way I did with him. He's like a comfortable old shoe." That pissed me off and I shouted out, "Now, I regret…," but caught myself. Sarah easily picked up on my anger and near slip.

"Why are you shouting at me? I'm the one who was cheated on; and what do you *regret*?"

"You say you love Joe, Sarah. Please don't tell him you love him like 'a comfortable old shoe' or I'll regret making a novena for you two to get back together." It was true; I had prayed for nine days, but it wasn't what I almost blurted out. I was grateful again for my improvisational skills.

I wished I had also been skilled enough to shut her up. Okay, Joe slept with Sharon, but Sarah continued to disregard the extenuating conditions and dwelled on the idea of not being able to accept the image of Joe being "inside" of her. I finally said, "Then stop envisioning it, and you're acting like Joe was a virgin before you met him, Sarah. He's been 'inside' many women besides you."

Did she think her vagina was some sort of *sacred vessel*? She said this was different; all the other women before the two of them had met were literally prostitutes, and if not real working girls, tramps he picked up at a bar. I reminded her about Maureen, his live-in girlfriend who he had been with only months before her. "Didn't he meet her in a hobby store selling airplane models?" She dismissed that, saying I was overlooking the most salient point–everyone was *before her.*

"I thought the prostitute idea was the salient point."

"What don't you get, Paulee? Sharon was not before or a prostitute. That's exactly why I am so upset. Rosie told me she leads a damn bible study group."

I did not know that, and would have liked to have heard more but she started on the vagina topic again, and how hers was *special* since she was Joe's wife. Which forced me to point out for the umpteenth *fucking time* (sorry, baby Jesus, another Hail Mary added), that we were having this discussion only due to her having moved to Minneapolis. Why was she harping on whose vagina was more special? I told her we should be talking about whose vagina had been more *available.* It had been Sharon's, not hers. Which made Sharon's vagina special by default–but I didn't say that in fear of Sarah's reaction.

She was incapable of changing the topic no matter what I said. Focus and perseverance are two of her admirable traits, but not commendable when it came to Joe's brief liaison with Sharon. *Brief* was the operative word that Sarah refused to accept, and she continued to stress about it. She insisted there had been no reason for him to sleep with Sharon out of need, and pointed out Joe's history with prostitutes again.

"Why hadn't he gone to one if he wanted some pussy?" She would not have been upset about that–it was this, "sweet, well-mannered" Sharon who tormented her.

I didn't know how she formed those ideas about Sharon. I never told her that, they must have come from Rosie. Sharon seemed like a bossy bitch to me. I don't care if she does lead a bible study group. If Sarah thinks that's proof to support her being sweet or well-mannered she's naive. She doesn't have my experience with so-called *pious* women. I went to parochial school for twelve years, and not all religious women are sweet or polite. Sister Veronica, my 10th grade biology teacher, had been a bitch on steroids, but she was not Sarah's problem.

I finally had to concede: if Sarah didn't check her hubris, she was going to face her nemesis once more and it would have Sharon's face, and I could not do a damn thing about it. I'm not sure why I ever thought I could play interference. For years I've taught that the tragic flaw story is a theatrical device to depict human frailty and a metaphor for destiny. Nobody can change someone's destiny.

CHAPTER 22

SARAH

Joe finally called me—one full day and night after leaving Minneapolis. It was not his usual habit when he was traveling. In the past he would call me on the road and after he settled for the night. Paulee asked me why I didn't call him. I had called but he didn't pick up and his voicemail was full. He seldom checks his voicemail on his personal phone and has a habit of turning off the ringer, forgetting to charge it or even losing it. That's why I wasn't too concerned. I left a message on the answering machine at our townhouse for him to call as soon as he arrived in New Jersey. That was at the height of my stress, before I smoked half of a joint to calm myself. And when I was more relaxed, I reminded myself that he had a cell he used for business which he was very attentive to; I didn't have the number but he could call me with that if he had had an emergency. I wasn't sure whether or not he had brought the work phone with him on the trip though. Joe could obsess over office politics, but he was not one of those people who thought about his clients once he clocked out. He wasn't like me or Paulee who had our students on our minds most of the time. I asked him once how he was able to simply forget about clients when his day was over and he said, "it's just a job." Reflecting on that made me finish the joint. I was upset; why wasn't he calling me?

I was emotional by the time he did but I didn't ask him what had taken so long, nor question his explanation of leaving the phone in the SUV. I felt awkward, like he was a man I was serious about but not sure how committed he was–and I've been with him for over twenty years. This was a problem because he wasn't *just a man*–he was my husband. I hoped this was only a temporary unease due to our separation and once we were actually living together again it would dissipate. We would return to our status quo; everything would revert back to normal. The only exception being I would stop contemplating leaving him.

Continually questioning our relationship and marriage was finished on my part, but what is the status quo since we reunited? Have our positions reversed? Would he now be the one who questions our relationship? That's my sense which accounts for some unease–I'm the vulnerable one this time. It's disturbing no matter who is contemplating, but if my emotional recall is accurate, my former position was less troubling than now. There is also proximity to consider–comparing history to an existential threat. Sharon is why I chose not to question him further about why he hadn't called sooner.

Once Joe returned to New Jersey my unease about not hearing from him sooner after he left Minneapolis became a distant memory. He called every day to keep me informed about the move. He had rented a large storage pod, and over the following two weeks he cleared out the townhouse in Jackson and filled it with all of our belongings. It was moving along as planned: townhouse emptied; closing; money pocketed; and Joe moving in with my mother while he continued to work in New Jersey. He planned to start hauling our stuff to Minnesota after Christmas. He did not anticipate a problem finding a house quickly because he was using cash for the purchase. He prefers to use cash for all of his purchases, but that's a lot of money. I cautioned him, "it makes you look like a drug dealer." His only reply was, "I'll handle the money, you handle the house," but house hunting wasn't so easy.

I contacted a realtor but I was too busy to look at houses. She probably thought we weren't serious buyers, but that wasn't true. I would have liked to look at houses if it wasn't the end of the semester with exams and grades. My mother told me to get "my priorities straight." Would she say that to Joe and expect him to stop working and fly back to Minnesota to house-hunt? I believed he should be looking at houses with me. I knew he wouldn't have cared if I chose one by myself. He would only ask, "How much?" Our budget is all he cares about, but buying a house is a big decision he should be a part of. My counter argument when my mother criticizes me, but the truth is more than that.

After I finish teaching I'm pooped; I want to relax– smoke a little pot and have a glass of brandy in front of my fireplace. I'm feeling more tired than usual. The last thing I want to do after work is to march around the frozen tundra of Minnesota looking at houses. I had to finally tell Joe the last time he called to be prepared to move things from New Jersey to Aunt Marion's barn. "There is no way I will be able to find a house on your game plan"–not happening. His response: "January is my designated moving-month, Sarah." His work ends in New Jersey a few days before Christmas and he's scheduled to start again in the Minneapolis office in February. Maybe we would be lucky to find a house in this short time frame, but the more realistic scenario is my preferred schedule–finding a house in late spring or summer. And there is no need to rush purchasing a house–we do not have to base it on Joe's time off. His refusal to hire a mover might work to my advantage, even though I continue to think he's crazy. The move is going to take time making trips back and forth from New Jersey to Minneapolis in the dead of winter. Even Paulee, who always makes excuses for him, agrees with me. It's typical Joe behavior though–he's eccentric. I don't find his eccentricity irritating in this instance– on the contrary, it's reassuring as a pleasant change. After two weeks of talking with him and hearing his plans, I knew he hadn't changed–perhaps things between us hadn't either.

It was around the same time I was feeling reassured about Joe not changing, that I discovered a change in me (or in my breasts to be more accurate). The pain the first time is what woke me up before the alarm went off in the morning. I had turned on my side and my breasts were extremely tender when crushed between my arm and the mattress. I immediately sat up in bed wide awake and felt my breasts; then I ran to the full-length mirror which hangs on the inside of my closet door to look at them. I was completely naked and it was cold in the studio but I didn't care–I was too focused on my breasts–were they swollen? I have been faithful about getting my mammograms every year since I had breast cancer and I had my most recent one four months ago. It was negative–all clear; but they are not a hundred percent accurate–no diagnostic tool is.

My doctor told me a mammography has an eighty-seven percent accuracy. It sounded good when she had said it, but standing in front of the mirror it seemed like a large margin of error. I reminded myself, it is not the only diagnostic measure. Joe found the lump on the bottom of my left breast before. He hadn't detected anything during our recent lovemaking. There was no lump this time, only tender and swollen breasts. Were those even symptoms?

My next thought was to ask my mother who was a retired nurse. Fear momentarily made me lose good judgment. She would not be helpful; fear would also cloud hers. She would start screaming: *I told you to get a mastectomy and not to choose a lumpectomy. Our family has a history of breast cancer. What were you thinking?* She'd focus on past decisions and not on what was happening right now.

I called Paulee instead. She didn't know if my symptoms were a sign that my cancer had returned, and told me to make an appointment immediately with a doctor. I told her I'd search on-line for information and she screamed: "Hang up and go make an appointment right now, Sarah." Her urgency did not reassure me but it also failed to move me in any direction. I chose to do nothing.

Why read about all the diseases it might be, in addition to breast cancer? Searching the internet could freak me out more, medically speaking, and I decided to wait until after the holidays to see someone. Christmas is less than a week away–a couple of weeks won't matter one way or the other. I might regret my decision in hindsight but I'll take my chances. My immediate plan of action is to reflect on the arbitrariness of life instead of trying to do anything about it. I'm beginning my reflection with a question.

Why did the universe choose for my breast cancer to return *now*? I finally landed a full-time teaching job, and I reunited with Joe. More importantly, I am finally sure after two decades that I want to be with him. My future is looking promising, even acknowledging the specter of Sharon. The timing absolutely stinks.

It is a stupid question to ask–why now though. When is it a good time to experience bad luck? Reflecting on that I remind myself how the timing is off for many of us: a baby dies before they get a chance to live; a newlywed couple perish in a plane crash on their honeymoon; a teenage girl is run over by her mother when she's sunbathing in the driveway. In comparison to those examples, I've been pretty lucky so far.

I won't query-*why me* either. I never asked that before and I refuse to start. I am not special or different from any other person in the world.

There is one positive thing about my dismal relationship with Rosie. It takes my mind off my physical health. Thoughts about breast cancer disappear when I talk to her but I do worry about my sanity. I had not anticipated such a strong reaction when I told her Joe and I were back together. I should have prepared myself, but I presumed she would be happy since she was angry when I left. That's not what happened. Joe was even surprised by her response but I wasn't entirely-she hates me. Joe tried to make me feel better, "she doesn't hate you, Sarah, you're her mother." Exactly my point and completely understandable.

Since day one I was forced into being the disciplinarian while Joe assumed a laissez-faire style of parenting, especially when it came to snacks, homework and bedtime. Even now in college our roles have not changed. The first semester she started living on campus Joe told her she better work or he wouldn't keep paying for school. Has he ever followed up, even once, to see if she's working? No.

Paulee defends him-*he was too upset over your leaving, Sarah*. Always blame the mother for the failure of their children. Rosie is not failing entirely but she still has two years before she graduates. On her last report card she received three C's, one D and failed computer science; a course designed especially for students who are not strong in math. Rosie is not weak in math but fails math courses repeatedly to irritate me because I teach it. I warned her that according to her program requirements she won't graduate if she does not pass a math course. I doubt Rosie's report card improved from last semester, but Joe won't say one word no matter what her grades are and will keep paying her tuition in spite of her performance.

I may not be hopeful about her grades but I am confident that her attitude towards me will be better when we are all gathered for the holidays at my mother's. Joe's presence does have an effect–he will temper her. If only he would apply his presence to her academics. Now that he is *no longer upset about me,* maybe he'll have a discussion with her about it. And who knows–she might have had an unprecedented spurt of maturity growth and passed all her classes this semester. She might not even act like she's twelve when she sees me–we will see.

I'm flying from Minneapolis and I convinced Joe that Rosie is perfectly capable of flying home from Miami by herself. He agreed to give his SUV a rest. It will be very busy in January. I am looking forward to seeing Rosie, but now I have to put up with her animosity on the phone. Joe and I should have scheduled a Zoom conference call to tell her we were back together. Calling her myself had been a mistake.

Rosie said it was "the worst news she heard all year." She didn't stop there. She said, "Sharon really loves Daddy. She cooks him great meals–all the things he likes. She isn't like you." I was naturally stunned to silence but before I could respond she described one of Sharon's typical meals. I told her it sounded like Sharon had been confusing lust with love. "If she had really loved Daddy she wouldn't have been trying to give him a heart attack."

That was one of the things I worried about when I was separated from Joe–what was he eating? I never forgot to ask him what he had eaten each night for dinner during the week when I called on Sundays. He usually refused to tell me, "If you're so concerned about what I'm eating, come home." His annoyance did not deter me. I asked my mother to make some meals for him each week. Left to his own tastes he wouldn't eat healthy. He counted ketchup as a vegetable serving.

Sharon's "great meals" were not the only reason Rosie thought she was the better partner for her father. Sharon was "a worthy person," and Joe should have never taken me back. She repeatedly kept peppering our exchange with the phrase, *you left us*. I finally said, "I didn't leave you, Rosie, I left your father. You are not a child." She only acted like one.

She told me she did not want to fly up to be with us for Christmas. She would stay in Miami. There was no way she was staying there by herself; even if, according to her, others stayed at school over the break. Her father wasn't too keen about her living arrangements in general–even when school was in session. There was no way he would agree to her idea either, and she knew it. And before she could say another word I said, "You are spending Christmas and the entire break with your family in New Jersey, Rosie."

She responded once again with–*you left us*. What kind of mother did I think I was? We were a fake family according to her. "You're no real mother. Sharon's a real mother. I'd rather spend the holidays with her, Leslie and Daddy like we've been doing since you left. Why did you have to come back?"

I shouldn't have yelled at her, but I was under stress before I called her. I screamed: "That's not your family, Rosie. And Sharon is not your mother; she's just some woman who was fucking your father."

CHAPTER 23

ROSIE

My mother called all happy to tell me she and Daddy got back together and expected me to be thrilled too. She kept asking, "Aren't you glad we're back together again?" It isn't that I'm not glad, which would surprise her. She thinks she knows me so well–she doesn't know me at all. I would have been more positive about it if I heard an apology for leaving. No words like that–just repeating the same crap for twenty minutes.

I'm also upset about Leslie. I hope she isn't going to hold it against me because my father broke up with her mother. I'm not responsible for what my parents do, and I really believe her mother is a better fit for Daddy. It doesn't mean I don't care about mine–it's simply the truth. And my mother can't stand to hear the truth or recognize it, even if it stares right at her face–one more reason why I'm still pissed at her.

It's a lie that she didn't leave me. *Not true.* She was in fucking Minneapolis and I was in New Jersey. She promised to teach me how to drive in the summer after freshman year but couldn't because she moved away. Even worse, pretends to not recall saying she'd teach me, and doesn't care that I don't have my drivers license. After I reminded her she asked me why I needed to drive at school, and if I wanted my license so bad I could ask Daddy for lessons. I remember how he taught me to play golf. He only tells you one time how to do something with as few words as possible. Afterwards if I asked him a question he would respond, "What did I tell you? Try to remember." If I had I wouldn't have asked him. Mom is a better teacher than Daddy even if she talks too much. Between the two of them, I prefer more than less when I'm trying to learn something.

Teaching me to drive was not the only thing we were planning to do that summer. We were also supposed to go to California to visit my Aunt Penny who does marketing for a modeling agency in Los Angeles. Aunt Penny promised to introduce me to some agents. I don't want to make a career out of modeling, but I wouldn't mind making some extra money. Aunt Penny put herself through college working as a model. She told me I just made the height requirement–I'm five-nine like her. My mother is beautiful but only five-five and would not have been able to be a runway model like me. Aunt Penny told me I was lucky; I got the tall gene from both sides of the family since she's my mother's sister and my father is six-three. It didn't matter; it was canceled out by having bad luck with the mother I got. We never went to Los Angeles because she was gone.

My mother never apologized about not teaching me how to drive or canceling the trip to LA. She avoids talking about it like I imagined everything. There's nothing wrong with my head; she's a narcissist–doesn't care about anyone but herself and won't admit how she abandoned me. At least with Daddy the bitch admits it; I bet she even got on her knees to apologize to him.

But more often my mother plays dumb about what she did to Daddy too, and now we're expected to play along with her and celebrate Christmas like it never happened. My parents might be able to do that, but I can't erase a year and a half from my mind–I don't want to spend Christmas with them. We don't even have our house in Jackson anymore, where Dorrie and Patty live. Daddy sold our house (thanks again to Mom) and I can't spend time on my break with my friends. When I complained she shot back, "Why not, we are staying with your grandmother in Brick? It's not that far from Jackson."

"I don't have a drivers license or a car, remember Mom?" She countered with, "don't they have cars?"

Patty has one, but she also works full time and I'm not sure I could even hang out with her on my break. And Dorrie has no car of her own; she told me she could borrow her mom's car but not every day. I will be stuck in Brick; it's not like my parents or grandmother will drive me to Jackson every day to see Dorrie. My mother and Granny Nessie would simply refuse, and Daddy will be too busy starting the move to Minneapolis. Everything is all fucked up because of my mother. That's why I refused to continue arguing with her about the car problem. I'm not going home to New Jersey for my break.

———◆————————◆————————◆———

I have decided to stay in Miami, but my mother says I'm not old enough to stay by myself if school is not in session. What sinister thing does she think happens if school is closed? And she actually said I was "not old enough." I'm no longer a child when she leaves me but I'm a child now? She can't have it both ways, and I wouldn't even be by myself. A few of my friends like Charlotte and my boyfriend Ben are staying. Of course mentioning Ben would definitely not win my mother over, and she would tell Daddy–he'd be standing at my door the next day. She doesn't trust me when it comes to boys and has convinced Daddy not to trust me too. It started when she noticed I had breasts. They popped out when I was twelve shortly after starting my period, and having breasts meant you were having sex in her mind. But sex is her obsession, not mine.

What mom gives her daughter a book on masturbation and a sex toy when she turns thirteen? I thought it was gross in spite of my curiosity. I was pretty naive, even if my mother had thought differently, and so were all my friends–Dorrie was the worst. When I showed her the sex toy she asked, "won't you lose your virginity if you use it?" I knew that was stupid even before I read the book. Dorrie was wrong, but so was my mother thinking I was having sex when I was twelve just because I had grown boobs.

I didn't lose my virginity until the summer after my freshman year in college. Mom should have taught me how to drive, and the trip to LA would have also been a distraction. I had too much free time, and I would have preferred meeting agents or even driving around a parking lot compared to my first sexual experience–the sex toy was better. I understood my mother's fascination with orgasms–those sex toys work, but what was so great about partner-sex? I needed information; I needed a mother, but mine was in fucking Minneapolis.

And she never seemed to want to hear me talk much on the phone, but I'm not being completely fair. Why would she want to when I called her a *whore* or *cunt* all the time? (Of course it's not like she doesn't deserve it). Eventually though it didn't matter if she refused to listen, I found the information I wanted on my own when I started dating a graduate student. I discovered that guys my age had no clue what they were doing. I didn't need advice from my cunt of a mother–then or now.

✦——✦——✦

I really hope my parents reuniting isn't going to mess up my friendship with Leslie. After my mother called, I was not looking forward to seeing her, but there was a good chance I wouldn't for a while. Leslie went to the library on most Saturday evenings; it was open until 9 pm and she usually stayed until closing with the other nerds. I wondered if she knew about her mother and my father. Unlike me, she spoke to her mother all the time on the phone. It's easy for her; her mother is not a cunt.

And if they had spoken, Leslie's mom might have talked about the breakup. I wasn't really sure if it was something she would quickly talk about though. It was months before Sharon told Leslie she was dating Daddy. The only thing I was sure about, I wasn't going to tell Leslie, and if I'm lucky I won't see her for the rest of the night. Charlotte invited me to a party at her sorority house. I like Charlotte but her sorority sisters are bitches so I hadn't been sure if I wanted to go. After talking to my mother, facing bitchy sisters felt preferable to seeing Leslie.

Looking back on it I'm also glad Charlotte acted as usual when I asked her if Leslie could come. She made her put-upon face like I was abusing her or something and said, 'Well, okay, if you have to bring her." She genuinely dislikes Leslie; she thinks she's a geek. She told me Leslie makes her anxious, and Leslie thinks Charlotte's a slut. She didn't call her that. She used some old word like *floozy*; she is nerdy. Charlotte doesn't want to invite Leslie to the house parties, and Leslie has no interest in going to them–she says there's too much booze and sex. In spite of already knowing in advance what each of their responses will be, I always ask Charlotte if Leslie can come, and ask Leslie if she wants to go. I like both of them, and it doesn't matter to me if they don't like one another, but I'm glad they are in agreement about these parties, especially if I wanted to avoid Leslie.

I never gave Charlotte a definite answer about her party though because Ben and I are supposed to see one another. But we have no specific plans and going to Charlotte's party is one possibility. Now my mother's call removed the inclusion of Ben from any possibility. My mother causes ripple effects wherever she goes, with everyone I know. There is no way I can see him after talking to her.

⸺◈⸺◈⸺◈⸺

Ben is a graduate student; he's twenty-six and older than a lot of other students in his class. I told my mother about him months ago but she doesn't know his age. If she did, she'd throw a shit fit, scream like crazy and tell my father immediately. It would be a kind of *wait until your father gets home* scenario–in spite of their separation or where I was living. And I wouldn't have been surprised to see Daddy showing up at my door in Miami. He's a teddy bear most of the time but he can also be lethal. He might pull me out of school, not physically, but stop paying my tuition. But remembering what he did in the playground when I was fifteen, he might throw me over his shoulder and throw me in his SUV. Luckily he knows nothing about Ben and all my mother knows is that I'm dating a student at the university. She assumes he's someone my age and only asked about his major. Second to sex, grades, and courses, majors are always on her mind.

As soon as I started junior year of high school my mother began to ask about every friend–*so what does she, he or whoever plan to major in when they go to college?* Now that I'm a university student, that's also her first question whenever I mention friends. She reminds me of people who ask *what's your sign*; a stupid and unimaginative question. I shot back at her one time, "is that the first question you asked Daddy when you met him, what he majored in?" She said no, "I asked him how much he wanted for fixing my flat tire." That was actually more interesting, it sparked my curiosity.

I was glad she did not ask Ben's age but was lost for words when she asked her usual question. I wasn't even sure if they call it *a major* in graduate school. I told her I didn't know and she was shocked, "How can you not know?" Like I said, it's a big thing to her. And I'm not saying I wasn't interested, it's just not necessarily my first question when I meet a guy. I finally asked him because she kept bugging me about it–I wanted to shut her up.

He told me his masters was psychology and his "field of concentration was cognitive behavioral studies." He tries to sound sophisticated. His way of reminding me how he's older and more experienced than me. He can be boring and irritating at times but the sex is better than with younger guys. There wouldn't be any tonight though–I have to cancel our date. I'll tell him I am not feeling well, and it won't be a lie–I know I would feel worse being with him. He's especially irritating when my mother is our topic of conversation, and I can't get her out of my head since she told me she and Daddy are back together.

Ben has annoyed me from day one when I first told him she left Daddy. I wasn't bad mouthing her, I was only telling the truth. He told me I was suffering from an *Electra Complex*. I asked him, "What the hell is that?" I couldn't believe what he said: I was in competition with my mother and wanted to have sex with my father? Gross. He said my language is the clue; not only the curse words and the names I throw at my mother. The way I call my father *Daddy* also shows how I have a *fixation* on him–*and fuck you too, Ben.*

✦━━━━━✦━━━━━✦

I didn't say that, only thought it; but the reason why I now want to attend Charlotte's house party by myself is to avoid Ben, as well as Leslie. I know I wouldn't be able to keep from talking about my mother for an entire evening, and I don't feel like being psychoanalyzed by him. I just want to have fun and say any damn thing I want without being judged.

I'm not ready to face Leslie if she's upset about her mother and Daddy either. And if she doesn't know yet, I have the same problem with her like Ben. I don't know if I can keep my mouth shut with my mother on my mind; it would only lead to the topic of my parents reuniting. A real party bummer if you ask me, and I need to party.

And it won't matter that I never said a definite yes to Charlotte. I can just show up–Leslie is right, these parties are zoos. People come who haven't even been invited and if they're asked during the night who they know a name is thrown out at random. There was always someone with that name, and as the night wears on all the sorority sisters are too wasted to care if there had been an invitation or not.

I'm not planning on getting wasted, I never do. I just want to dance and have a couple of beers. I never use drugs at these parties either. People don't even know what they're taking, it's really dumb. I feel very responsible for not using drugs but get no credit from my mother. She accuses me of taking them and using grass. She may be a pothead herself but she obviously doesn't know how to spot one. Why would I want to smoke, growing up smelling pot my entire life?

Aunt Paulee knows me better than my mother. I overheard them talking about me one day, and they were discussing whether I was vaping or smoking grass. Aunt Paulee doubted it. She always sees me in a more positive light than my mother, but her opinion was based on children growing up in cultures where wine was offered from a young age. "They aren't drawn to it when they're older, Sarah." Her example was not a true representation of my life; my mother never offered me weakened pot at any age. But Aunt Paulee was right–I wasn't "drawn to it."

I was not as wild as my mother thought–except for my clothes. And I was only trying to dress like her when I was younger. Instead of being flattered she gave me a hard time, but I never wanted to be a pothead like her. I was only tempted to steal some grass from my mother once, and it wasn't even me who wanted it. I was dating Bradley the summer before my junior year in high school and he asked me to steal a couple of joints. I was relieved when I found the cash box where she kept her grass locked. I had no desire to get high but I wanted to get Bradley–he was hot. When I told him the cash box was locked he asked me if I could break it. I refused, and I told him if he came to my house and stayed for an hour he'd probably get a contact high–we wouldn't need to smoke at all.

My father always complained about the house smelling like pot. He came home one evening and started opening all the windows, and it was cold outside. My mother complained that the house was now freezing. My father replied, "Stop smoking dope in the house and you won't be freezing." (He never says pot, he always calls it dope–he's nerdy, like Leslie). My mother got pissed at him. She stormed out of the room and marched loudly up the stairs to their bedroom. Daddy went after her, he always did, and they were up there for a long time. I guess he was warming her up. I wasn't a kid and I knew what they were doing–it was gross. Couldn't they have been more discreet and have sex when I wasn't home?

They can do whatever they want over the holiday break. They can screw their brains out for all I care because I won't be there. If I can't stay in Miami, I'll ask Leslie if I can spend the break with her and Sharon– if Leslie doesn't take it out on me for Daddy getting lured back by the bitch. If she does, I'll have to come up with another idea, but I seriously doubt she'll react as strongly as my mother did about Sharon. Leslie's not a bitch, like my mother. Sorry Ben, that's the truth and don't say I have a complex because I say it.

Ben's got a lot of nerve telling me I have a complex, just like my mother who accuses me of having a foul mouth. That's a joke; I wasn't surprised at what she said about Sharon. I've heard her scream *fucking* as long as I remember smelling pot–which is my entire life.

CHAPTER 24

PAULEE

Rosie didn't help matters mentioning *Sharon*. It set Sarah off again, but I seriously doubted that she had stopped stressing over her. Worse now though because Rosie expanded the rivalry in Sarah's mind beyond Joe. Now she's not only in competition with Sharon for him, but also for Rosie's love. Rosie saying she preferred to be with Sharon instead of her had really hurt. Rosie makes me more empathetic towards Sarah. I'm tending towards forgiving her for being annoyingly emotional. And I hate to speak ill of my godchild, but Rosie needs a good spanking.

Sarah has this cancer scare to contend with and needs to spend the holidays with her immediate family–and Rosie is acting like a little bitch. I encouraged her to tell Rosie about the scare because if she knew she would want to be with her mother. Sarah wasn't so sure about that, which is a horrible thing to think about your daughter. She also refuses to use "emotional blackmail" to make Rosie spend the holidays with her. I'm seriously considering interfering again.

Sarah's wrong not telling her family, especially Joe; she doesn't want to spoil the holidays for them. I'm the only one who knows. What about me? It is a burden on me, but she has to share it with someone. And I am comforted knowing she has an appointment to see a doctor the week after New Year's. I don't know why the hell she's waiting that long, but I can also see her point with the holidays–*why worry anyone until she knows for sure the cancer has returned*?

This idea has not carried over to herself or me unfortunately–we are both worried. I'm strong enough, but I'm not sure she is. Besides the health concerns, all the other emotional garbage she's experiencing right now is making her irrational. She said at least a dozen times in our most recent phone call, "I'm a bad mother, Paulee. No wonder she prefers Sharon to me." I had to finally shut her down or hang up, and I wouldn't hang up on my best friend.

"You have no idea what kind of a mother Sharon is and neither does Rosie. And everyone's parents seem preferable to your own when you're a teenager, Sarah." I also reminded her how teenagers often act the most vicious with people they feel the closest to (especially girls with their mothers). To make my point I told her about something that had happened to me recently. *I was shopping and was about to get in the checkout line when this guy ran up to me, "Miss Bellini, hi. I just wanted to tell you I'm sorry for acting bad in your English class. I was a real brat, you were my favorite teacher."*

Several things ran through my mind after he said it: it must have been a while ago–he called me "Miss Bellini." And if he was a *brat* with his favorite teacher, how did he act towards those he didn't like? I also felt a little chagrined if I was his favorite teacher–I hadn't taught him well; he should have said *badly*. But Sarah did not need to have all the information. I only delivered my salient point: "I couldn't for the life of me place this guy. I just stared at him until he finally said, 'I'm Scott Cooper.' I was shocked; this big brawny man was skinny little Scott Cooper with the guttermouth who had been a pain in my ass? I had been his favorite teacher, Sarah. Get my point?"

"Yes, but it doesn't apply to us. Rosie is not a teenager anymore, remember? She turned twenty this year, Paulee." Sarah knows most adolescents don't fully mature until they're twenty-five. She was not thinking clearly. She is also forever saying that Rosie is immature for her age. Probably true based on the recent actions of my godchild, but I also have a theory about Sarah insisting Rosie is immature.

Sarah wants to recapture the past. She feels guilty for not giving Rosie more attention when she was a kid so she locks her into childhood. It was not the time to have this discussion with Sarah though, and I'm not ruling out that Rosie is below average in emotional maturity, but I doubt it. She's behaving as many people her age do when they're pissed off.

I understand adolescents–empirically, from research and teaching teenagers for over twenty-five years. If Sarah wasn't so upset she would not question my judgment. I am familiar with their love-hate expressions. They really mean *I love you*, when they say, *I hate you*. But I'm not suggesting those hate messages are not triggered by something. Adolescents are overly sensitive to every action we make as adults, and rebel against any directive or criticism aimed their way. That was the discussion I needed to start with Sarah.

"What's Rosie angry about, Sarah?"

"She's angry because I left Joe." It had to be more than that.

When I returned home after my first semester at college I was pissed at my mother. I had craved the comfort of the familiar, and I was greeted with change smacking me in the face. She turned my bedroom into her sewing room. She even donated my bedroom furniture. I asked her, "Why did you take over my room? Where am I supposed to sleep, Ma?"

"You don't live here anymore, Pauline, you're grown up now. When you visit me you can sleep on the futon in the den. You'll have your own bathroom down there." She made it sound like an upgrade but I was slowly being pushed out of the house.

Joe and Sarah didn't push Rosie out of her room, but she had to deal with change. The very first semester back from college–her mother was gone–more traumatic than losing childhood furniture even if Sarah can't see it.

I am also astute enough to realize Rosie must bristle over the tight rein her parents keep on her, even from a distance. Sarah thinks she's immature, and Joe is no better; he's even worse at times. No wonder Rosie rebels. Sarah said it herself–Rosie "turned twenty this year." So why do they treat her like she's a little kid? Joe won't even let her fly to and from college so he drives her. If she does fly, she better be with someone. Doesn't he know six-year-olds fly by themselves? Sarah complains about him not allowing Rosie to fly, but she is on Rosie about her grades constantly like she's still in high school. You have to allow them to fail sometimes–it's how they grow up.

I totally understand why Rosie is angry, but it is unfair how she relentlessly directs it all at Sarah. It's the mother-daughter conflict syndrome. Sarah shouldn't take it personally, and she needs to also remember Rosie is a daddy's girl. That makes it even more predictable for her to lash out at Mommy–not because of something intrinsically flawed in Sarah.

Daddy and Mommy both drive Rosie's negative behaviors. They need to let her grow up if they want her to stop behaving like a kid. It is not terribly complicated, but if Joe saw Rosie as an adult he would have to retire from his daddy role. He might even have to give up his primary seat to some other male.

If Sarah saw Rosie as grown up she would have to accept that she's older. Getting older is a problem for her. Women who are beautiful like Sarah have a harder time contending with aging. I can't relate to that but I could share my expertise on adolescents with her: "Rosie may be angry because you are not allowing her to be independent. Why can't she stay in Miami? If you gave her permission she wouldn't be making veiled threats about Sharon. Some kids are roaming around Europe by themselves at twenty, or married with kids."

Sarah gave me a look of horror. Was it because she truly believed Rosie was too immature and feared for her safety, or was it seeing herself as a grandmother?

CHAPTER 25

SARAH

I finished with classes on December 23rd and flew from Minneapolis that day, catching an early evening flight at 6 pm. It had been a tight schedule but I made it work, and Joe was picking me up at Philadelphia International Airport at 8:30 if there were no unexpected delays. I was looking forward to spending Christmas with my family, and momentarily put my health worries aside.

I was waiting in front of the pick-up area at the terminal when I saw Joe heading my way. He ran up to me. Well, let's be real, Joe does not run. But he was not lumbering along as was his norm, and he reached me quickly, taking my face in his hands before he kissed me smack on the lips. He then said I should have waited inside, "to stay out of the cold, baby; your face is freezing." After enduring the cold temperatures in Minnesota, New Jersey's December did not feel uncomfortable. I had not minded standing outside of the terminal but I was relieved he was there to take over bag duties. I had packed light but my suitcase seemed much heavier than in the past.

Rosie wasn't with him. I didn't really expect that she would come to the airport, but I was disappointed.

I was anxious to see her, especially since our recent phone calls had been so negative. I reminded myself: it will only be an hour and a half drive until I see my wayward daughter again, and we will all be together at my mother's house to celebrate the holidays.

I didn't even mention Rosie until we had driven in the car for a while. I finally asked Joe what day he had picked up Rosie, and "I presume she had no problem with flying from Miami by herself." He answered matter-of-factly, "I didn't pick her up."

"What do you mean you did not pick her up, Joe?" I could not believe my ears, and before he could elaborate further I asked another question, "You let her stay in Miami for the break by herself?"

"No way. She's with Leslie in Chapel Hill." I was blindsided. It took me a few seconds to recover. "You mean with Sharon?"

"Well, that's Leslie's mother so, yeah, Sharon is there."

"Isn't that a little strange, Joe?" He didn't think so in spite of the disturbing history he had with Sharon. I was flabbergasted. I had not mentioned her name to him since his visit in Minneapolis. I had heeded Paulee's advice; yet the degree of separation had shortened between Joe and this woman. Was it because I never stopped thinking about her, or saying her name to Paulee? Do Paulee's crazy superstitions really have merit?

I remained silent for the rest of the drive to my mother's house in Brick. Joe did not say a word either, but he often does that. Not my usual behavior though and it finally caught his attention, but not until we pulled up in front of my mother's house. "Are you alright, Sarah?" I told him, yes–*what could possibly be wrong?*

◆

My mother was also disappointed Rosie wasn't coming home for Christmas. Joe had told her she was staying with a college friend over the holidays. She didn't make a connection until I told her the friend was her roommate in North Carolina. That's when she asked, "Isn't her mother the woman Joe was involved with?"

"Yes."

"That's odd. Why would she want Rosie at her house after Joe broke up with her?" I wanted to scream: *thank you, thank you Mom. I'm not the only one who thinks it's strange.* I told her that Joe acted like there was nothing "odd" about it. I questioned him and he replied, "Why is it a big surprise? Rosie has been going to North Carolina for her breaks since you've been gone."

I wasn't gone now, Joe. If I didn't know my husband better I would have accused him of attacking me with a passive aggressive punch to the gut; retribution for having left him, but Joe doesn't use emotional manipulation. And he never deliberately tries to hurt anyone or anything. Just like me and that damn frog when Rosie was six.

We were headed out to the car when she yelled, "Look Mommy, look at the little frog." I didn't see any frogs and continued to walk to the car until I was stopped by Rosie's cry, "You stepped on it." I felt awful: I had unintentionally killed the frog, made Rosie cry and had *squashed frog* on the bottom of my new sandals. Metaphorically speaking, Joe steps on frogs left and right every day; he is unaware of how his words squash the wind out of me sometimes. I felt like Rosie's frog when he told me Rosie was staying with Sharon.

He might not be cognizant of his words' impact, but his words and actions do confirm how naive he is; he really believes Sharon only wants his friendship. You would think with all his experience with prostitutes he'd be familiar with the idea that *women always want something from men*. His problem might be that he thinks it's exclusive to prostitutes. Sharon hopes to rope him back using Rosie and he can't see it.

I shouldn't expect him to figure out Sharon when he often misses his own daughter's manipulations. I asked Joe why Rosie didn't want to see her New Jersey friends, Dorrie and Patty, over the break. He had to find that puzzling. They've been her friends since she was six. "Is Leslie the only friend who means something to her now, Joe?" He had an answer; I was overlooking how people's preferences change. He proceeded to give me several examples of clients changing their orders before finalization. "It's clouding your reasoning, Sarah." Not true, and we were talking about our daughter; it was clear to me. She was forgoing seeing her life-long friends to stay with Sharon and Leslie for one simple reason. She knew it would hurt me, and it did.

On Christmas day my mother wanted to video call Rosie. "She has her computer with her doesn't she?" I was about to say she probably did when Joe said Sharon didn't have Wi-Fi, but my mother could video call her on her phone–her network would pick up. Who doesn't have Wi-Fi? Wouldn't Leslie need a computer for her school work? If this hadn't been directly linked to Sharon, I would have pursued the subject; it did–so I didn't.

It was early afternoon when we made the call and Rosie picked up immediately. My mother asked her what she was doing, and she replied, "watching TV." It didn't sound like much of a Christmas–watching TV. It wasn't surprising though, and she'd probably be doing the same thing with us; TV or nonstop on her phone. What was surprising–she was by herself. Sharon and Leslie were working at their church. They were helping out at a dinner the church was hosting for needy people. Rosie said she could have gone with them but she had a headache.

I began asking a bunch of questions: how long she had the headache; how many aspirins she had taken; had she tried lying down with a cold washcloth on her face? Etc., etc., until she stopped me and screamed, "I just have a headache." I was only concerned and she did not have to react so negatively. Joe piped in, "Your Mom just misses you, baby girl." To which she replied, "whatever." It would have been nice to hear her say, "I miss her too." She didn't mention missing Joe either to be fair nor did she thank us for the large gift card we sent her. She's so immature, which brings to mind all of Paulee's psychobabble about maturity and her take on Rosie. I agree with her that adolescent maturity is not binary–you are not immature one day and mature the next. But some people never mature completely (which I hope will not be the case with Rosie), and I'm not referring to adults having occasional gaps.

Paulee has accused me of acting like I am eighteen at times, but so does she. Even steady Joe is naive when it comes to Sharon; he's acting like an adolescent. We all have our moments, and the amount of open gaps not filled with wisdom and empathy is the true indicator of our maturity level, not our chronological age. Rosie has many unfilled gaps frozen in an opened position; a level equivalent to an average sixteen-year-old.

The second factor Paulee ignored when she lectured me about Rosie was–*context*. Context is not fixed, it's variable. A kid may be old enough to be potty trained but it doesn't equate to sending them into a public restroom by themselves. Rosie may be mature enough to be at a school hundreds of miles from home, but not mature enough to stay in Miami when school is closed. There's a difference between attending classes and spending all her time hanging out with friends.

It was a no-brainer to her traveling throughout Europe by herself too, even if some girls her age are married with children. I am well aware of that, and it was an artificial distraction. Paulee was describing our mothers who were married at that age. She thought it was a persuasive argument, but Rosie does not resemble them when they were married with babies in their early twenties.

Rosie assuming the responsibility of taking care of a baby is an absolute joke. She loses her house keys every other month. She'd probably forget the kid somewhere. Getting pregnant is easy and usually enjoyable; and the physical pain of birthing only gives you a glimpse of what's in store. Caring for a child is the hard labor. Rosie refused to even help out with our cats and dogs. "They belong to you and Daddy," she would say if I asked her to take the dog out or feed the cats. It was true; also true she had too many open gaps and still does.

Paulee also overlooks another major contextual factor when she is having these discussions–*motherhood*. She doesn't know what she's talking about because she doesn't have kids. There is a difference between being a mother and being a teacher. A mother lives with their kids, Paulee can leave hers when she clocks out of work. Simple math when you compare investment and time between a mother and a teacher. The most dedicated teacher will never exceed that of a kid's mother.

Another major difference between teachers and parents–the ego factor. Ego is hard to remove from the love you have for your kid most of the time. Paulee might feel awful when one of her students doesn't excel.

I feel the same way with my students. But my distress is far deeper when Rosie doesn't excel–I feel it in my genes. When she fails, I fail. She is a part of me.

I like my students, and have even loved some of them, but it's not the same kind of love I have for Rosie. A teacher's love is usually as transient as the students–children are for life.

CHAPTER 26

ROSIE

The saddest thing about my holiday break was discovering how big a bitch Leslie is. She turns out to be just as bad as one of Charlotte's sorority sisters. Maybe my mother was right when she said "all women are bitches." She shot that back at me when I called her *a bitch in heat* when I was twelve (I learned the catchy phrase from my grandfather Mac).

It wasn't the only thing my mother said that day. She followed with a lecture, and not because she was pissed off. She actually was real calm and that makes it memorable. "Rosie, do you know *bitch* is a synonym for a female mammal, and most commonly refers to a dog? So what did you call me? An ovulating female. If I substitute your words with–*ovulating female* every time you call me that, there's no bite at all."

It would eventually become insightful on many levels but she had really confused me at first; I was young at the time and hadn't even started my period. Mac had also called men bitches; he even called my father one at the previous Thanksgiving dinner. I had to look up the meaning of *ovulating*, but I wasn't dumb. It didn't take much time to realize there are different definitions and intentions for saying *a bitch in heat*. It also became clear to me that my mother got my meaning when I called her one, or she wouldn't have added the *bite* crap.

I've been thinking about my Mom's lecture, and realize now it was my first indication of how my parents are very similar, and more compatible than most people think. They're both weirdos. My father is a weirdo when he's vague and uses too few words; my mother's one when she uses too many. But she was right about bitches and Leslie, (even though an exaggeration to say *all women*). I spent a lot of hours by myself on my holiday break because Leslie is one. She wouldn't hang out with me even though I was staying at her house. It gave me time to think about my life, and it was only natural I'd review my sexual history. And I don't care if Leslie doesn't agree with me–I'm no slut.

✦——————✦——————✦

There were two contenders for popping my cherry when I decided to lose my virginity. Bradley, who was hot and experienced, and PJ, who was a geeky virgin. There were pluses and minuses for both of them.

I contacted Bradley on my socials at the end of my second semester at college; right after my mother told me she had left Daddy. We made a date to get together when we were home on summer break. I didn't mention anything else. I wasn't dumb like some people who put personal stuff in writing online. Things on the internet can follow you forever. I chose to make my proposal face-to-face.

Bradley definitely has a nice face too. I was attracted to him which was a plus. My friend Patty says that should be a prerequisite when you're choosing someone to lose your virginity with. It wasn't for me. His attractiveness would make the experience more pleasant, but it wasn't high on my checklist of requirements. Previous experience was more important for one and I knew Bradley was experienced. It was a simple deduction; he dated Janet in high school and she was one of the school's sluts. But being experienced was a minus too. I wanted someone who knew what they were doing, but I didn't want them to think I was an idiot. I was almost nineteen and still a virgin. PJ was a virgin like me.

I've known PJ since grammar school. I wasn't sexually attracted to him, but I liked him. I also knew he liked me. I decided that was a prerequisite for choosing the guy I wanted and more important than previous experience. I even liked the idea of us losing our virginities together. We had a history; we both learned to ride our bikes without training wheels at the same time.

After I chose him over Bradley he surprised me in a good way. In spite of me not being attracted and his inexperience, I was impressed when he said we needed to get protection. I had forgotten all about that. I had been too preoccupied tallying up pluses and minuses. It was a pretty amazing oversight. I've been hearing my mother say almost every day since I got my period: "It only takes one time to get pregnant," and "If you're old enough to have sex, you're old enough to use protection." I don't know why I had forgotten it but was glad PJ had the foresight. It was the only positive I'll give him though because he was too nervous to buy condoms.

It was more embarrassment than nerves even though he denied it. He insisted he looked too young; they might not sell them to him. It was true, he didn't even have a beard and he was eighteen; he looked like he was in junior high. But I didn't think there was an age restriction on buying condoms, and I told him he could always say he was buying them for his father–which embarrassed him even more. I even reminded him about crazy Ted, the manager at the store next to the cleaners. "He looks the other way when we say we're buying cigarettes for our parents." There was nothing I could say to persuade him, so I finally said I'd get them myself.

I decided to look around my parents' bedroom and bathroom first. I knew they didn't use them– "too much information, Mom." But I hoped there might be some lying around which my mother bought to give me (since she had done it once before). I didn't find any, but I found my mother's diaphragm which was surprising–she didn't take it with her to Minneapolis? The discovery made me consider for the first time that she might not be planning to cheat on my father. I dismissed the idea quickly; this was probably an old one. I remembered her saying they had to be replaced every couple of years, and I was not ready to think more favorably about my mother. But I continued to find it curious why she would keep her old diaphragm, even though it was no use to me. It wasn't like I'd ever consider using it, and I wasn't embarrassed to buy condoms.

PJ and I decided to do it at his house when his mother was at work. We could have done it at my house too because my father was also working away from home a few days a week that summer, but PJ started to stutter only at the mention of him. "What if your dad comes home early, Rosie?" He definitely was afraid of an unexpected arrival of my father. His mother walking in on us held less terror for him, and I understood completely; so we got off in his den with a TV playing without sound and Mick Jagger scream-ing *Get Off of My Cloud*. PJ liked classic rock like my dad so we were listening to the playlist I had recently made for our trip driving from school. PJ liked it until I mentioned Daddy–he freaked out again. It made him more awkward and geeky than he normally is.

It wasn't a great experience. PJ being inexperienced was one thing but I hadn't anticipated his terror. He seemed almost scared when I took my shirt and bra off. He sat there with his mouth gaping open staring at my boobs until he said, "Oh my God." He didn't say anything else and just kept staring. I finally had to encourage him to get it moving along. "You can touch them if you want PJ," and he asked, "Can I?"

He really is a geek. He asked me if he could touch my breasts and I was letting him pop my cherry? And I never thought he'd find it, bobbing around down there. When he finally did–it hurt. Why hadn't my mother mentioned that?

At least it was quick, but it was annoying that PJ had enjoyed himself some of the time and I didn't. He was the only one who really *got off* losing their virginity. At least it was shared joy the day we rode our two-wheelers together. That's why I took some pleasure in his freaking out when he saw the blood on the couch. It wasn't very much at all but he was terrified about his mother seeing it.

I only slept with PJ once–once was enough. And fortunately it didn't turn me off from trying again. When I did, I was driven by attraction and my own hard-won confidence from now being experienced. I started dating Ben after summer break when I returned to school for the fall semester. He was good looking and experienced, an additional plus–I did not have to buy the condoms. Ben was not embarrassed to go to a store when he discovered he needed to restock the first time we did it. My mother would have had a fit if she had known that I didn't routinely carry condoms with me.

When she and Daddy dropped me off for school that first semester she took me aside and pressed a small purse in my hand whispering, "Be prepared, don't depend on the boy; and don't mention this to your father." I was not about to; she was an annoying control freak but I kept my mouth shut. Daddy would have packed up the car again and not let me stay if he had seen what she had given me. She was right about what she said though, even if I did not appreciate her lecturing me at the time.

I wasn't prepared when I went to Charlotte's house party–I always left it up to Ben. I don't even know where the purse with the condoms is that my mother gave me. But even if I had been prepared, I'm not sure it would have made a difference. I also didn't follow her warning about drinking. I might have had more than two beers by the time I met Lance.

He was in my Romantic Lit class, and was one of the talkers. There were a few of them; English majors or wannabe writers. I knew Lance's name because he stood out. Sometimes it seemed like a two-way conversation was going on between him and the professor and the rest of us were spectators. It was okay with me that he liked to hear himself talk. I had no desire to say a word–I hated the class.

The Scarlet Letter was tolerable but we were now reading *Wuthering Heights* and it sucked. I asked Aunt Paulee why it was considered a classic. She said it was a perfect depiction of 19th century life and the gothic novel. It had all the elements of the genre. I asked her: "In 200 years will some class study a reality show and call it a classic too?" *It depicts 21st century life and has all the elements of its genre.* That's lame. Those shows are stupid, and this novel sucked. Aunt Paulee said I had "to stick with it; some books needed to be studied carefully to grasp their meaning and value." I had given her the impression I wasn't reading it, but I was. The real problem was I did not want to be chastised by the professor, my mother or her because I had nothing noteworthy to say about it. That's why people like Lance are useful in these classes, even though I barely understood what he was saying most of the time. But it didn't matter if you looked like him.

He was entertaining because he was very attractive; I liked his wild black hair and piercing dark eyes. He looked as I imagined Heathcliff would if he stepped out of the pages into the 21st century, but *Heathcliff* did not look like someone who would be invited to Charlotte's house party. It turned out he hadn't been; Lance was Charlotte's brother. He crashed the party looking for booze and drugs. When he saw me he asked, "Hey, you're in my Romantic Lit class aren't you?" I was impressed, I didn't think he ever noticed me. I'm definitely not his type, but we were both a little wasted. That's why it happened.

I knew I was pregnant as soon as I missed my period. Ever since my periods started when I was twelve I've been as *regular as the sunrise*. But that's a weak metaphor; or is it a simile? I need to pay more attention in English classes. But I know I'm making a weak comparison because the sunrise changes from day to day, and I never changed until the month I was late. My cycle was very predictable, unlike my mother who is very irregular. I made that deduction on my own but it took years because I did not understand what she and Aunt Paulee were talking about until I was older. And when I knew, it was embarrassing and uncomfortable hearing about *late periods, the damn diaphragm* and *pregnancy scares*, but eavesdropping on them was compelling. My mother put on a great show in distress every other month, fearing she might be pregnant. She never was, but her periods were crazy hearing her talk.

Knowing that, I would think she'd calm down but she hasn't, and it is also ridiculous how my parents screw so much–they're so old. But what was even worse was hearing her and Aunt Paulee talking the weekend I came home from school for my grand-mother's birthday party. My mother was doing her usual freak-out-pregnancy show which I have been hearing for years. It was uncomfortable, but would not even be noteworthy except for the fact that she walked out on Daddy two months later. It made her hysterics and leaving even worse. Was Daddy only another sex toy to her? Why did he take her back?

It bothers me how she used him just for sex, even if he has forgiven her. But that's not as upsetting as what she said to Aunt Paulee about me when I was fourteen during one of her bi-monthly scares. I overheard Aunt Paulee trying to comfort and reason with her, and they were oblivious to me eavesdropping on them as usual.

"Why is it so awful if you are pregnant, Sarah? I thought Joe wanted another kid. You're not that old and you have the means to support another child."

"No, thank you. I love Rosie but after her I don't want another kid." Gee, thanks Mom.

The "I love Rosie" had sounded like a disclaimer, not a heartfelt sentiment of maternal love. I slinked away from the kitchen and ran out the back door before they could discover me. I didn't want them to know I had heard them. I felt awful, but I should not have been cowering; my mother should have–for what she had said.

I'm pregnant and I could get an abortion pill if I want. Even if the student dispensary won't give it to me I would be able to get a pill somewhere on campus. Students can easily get hold of any drug. The reason why I didn't do it immediately was I am not sure how I feel about abortion. I don't want a kid but I could give it up for adoption. Growing up with loving adoptive parents is a good thing–better than hearing your real mother say she doesn't want you.

❖――――❖――――❖

I need to use my head going forward. I want to be sure I make the right decisions. Not being prepared and drunk were obvious early mistakes but it had also been a waste of money buying the pregnancy test; a minor error but a mistake all the same. I convinced myself that I might take after my mother. I bought it because I was holding on to the slim hope I was late for the first time in my life. Another was asking Leslie to help me with the test. I can pee on a stick without help, but I needed some emotional support. I didn't know Leslie would turn into such a bitch. When I first told her I suspected I might be pregnant she had been pretty neutral. All she said was, "I thought you and Ben were careful."

Her *bitch transformation* started when I told her the father wasn't Ben. That's when her eyes got real big and her mouth opened wide enough to catch flies. She also raised her chin up like she was looking down her nose at me when she said, "Oh, I didn't think you slept around." She acted like I was a slut. I've only had sex with three people, and that's if I count PJ. She also said some other crazy shit. She assumed Ben and I were getting married after I graduated. According to her, couples should only have sex if they are married or planning to be. I never told her I was engaged. She wasn't being a supportive friend.

She was also useless helping with the test. I asked her to look and tell me the results; I was only delaying the acknowledgement of the inevitable. When I handed her the stick she said, "It has two lines, I don't think you're pregnant, Rosie." She's not as smart as I thought, besides being a bitch.

After the pregnancy test she started to avoid me on campus; but it was impossible for her to do it all the time because we're roommates. When we're in our room she doesn't speak to me very often, and she moved her bed closer to the window. Does she think she can get pregnant by talking or being close to me? Pregnancy is not contagious.

The only reason I'm with her now in North Carolina is that it had already been planned for me to spend the break at her house (before she found out I was pregnant and got all weird). I asked her if she still wanted me to stay with her for the break and she had said yes; but she's not acting that way. I could have gone to New Jersey like my parents had wanted but I preferred being with Leslie. I was more pissed at them than at her when I was considering my options, and I didn't think Leslie would be a bigger bitch than my mother. I feel isolated.

I've felt that way since I found out. I don't want to talk about the pregnancy with Ben for obvious reasons so I started avoiding him. There's no way I would have sex with him now. I'm afraid he'll notice changes in my body. It would be visible evidence of me having cheated on him, even though I don't think anyone can see it, and I check my stomach every day. But I'm also afraid I might blurt out without thinking–*not necessary* when he starts to put a condom on. Pregnancy is making me paranoid.

I would like to be able to talk with someone; Charlotte would be supportive and not be judgmental. She's not prissy like Leslie, but she would ask me who the father is. She'd probably assume it was Ben but I can't lie about something this serious. The father is her brother; I don't want to tell her. If she knew she might not be any more neutral or objective than Ben and Leslie. And if my mother is right, she'll be a bitch too.

If I decide to have the baby it will take a while for me to show, and I can probably finish the spring semester without anybody knowing I'm pregnant.

But I do have to tell my parents. Daddy will be disappointed in me and the bitch will scream. Both are preferable compared to how Leslie is acting, or telling Ben I cheated and Charlotte she might soon be an aunt. And as uncomfortable as it might feel telling my parents, at least after they know I won't feel isolated anymore. Mom will be pestering me all the time. I might have to change my phone number.

CHAPTER 27

SARAH

I stayed in New Jersey through New Year's. It was now time to fly back to Minneapolis. I declined Joe's invitation to drive back with him. He was making his first trip in a medium sized rental filled with small furniture pieces, and boxes packed with dishes, clothes, and assorted stuff we had accumulated over two decades. I should have gone through the boxes before Joe sealed them and loaded the rental. I was sure there were things we no longer wanted but I hadn't been able to lighten the load. It wasn't me who packed the boxes–it was Sharon. It was a creepy thought thinking how she touched our things. Touching my husband was not enough? She had to put her hands all over my personal possessions too? It was another violation. I didn't mention it to Joe; my mother advised me not to. "You weren't here, Sarah. Joe had to empty the house and he needed help. Remember that." How can I forget?

No matter what the topic the woman insinuates herself into my life, and I am reminded once again how I left Joe. Mind-boggling–I was not gone for years and years. How had she moved so quickly? And I really don't want to talk about her. That's why I didn't mention the boxes. It had nothing to do with my mother's admonishments and my sense of culpability about leaving. But my feelings about not letting the name *Sharon* cross my lips doesn't carry over to our bed and mattress. They're in the storage pod parked in my mother's driveway. Joe told me he's moving them later when he has a larger rental and some buddy-help.

I will not remain silent, there's also Joe's culpability to consider. I told him I wanted to buy a brand-new bed and mattress; my mother could donate our old ones. There was no point in moving them to Minneapolis so he could take them out of the storage pod–*put them out on the curb for all I care.* Joe was perplexed. "Why would you want to do that? There's nothing wrong with them." The man is obtuse sometimes.

"Are you serious, Joe?"

"Yes, I am."

How could I not get upset? My mother warned me not to mention the boxes, but even she couldn't expect me to sleep on a bed where Joe had fucked Sharon. I admit, I could have worded it differently when I said as much to him. He became annoyed, and later when I told him I preferred to fly back to Minneapolis he thought I was angry. It will take a while to unravel this miscommunication but at this point I believe it will be easier than unraveling Sharon from our lives.

Joe doesn't know about my doctor's appointment. I would miss it if I drove back to Minnesota with him. I have yet to tell him anything about my cancer scare.

Paulee keeps saying I'm wrong, but I don't want to worry him. After the argument over the bed and mattress, I began to reconsider because it became a little tense between us. Imagining–*how sorry he would be for his annoyance if he knew the real reason for my declining his ride,* mitigated my anger, but not Joe's.

I chose to fabricate a reason for flying back. Which would not be necessary under usual circumstances. Ordinarily Joe would agree I should not lose money by being charged a fee to cancel my return flight ticket, but his annoyance blurred his thinking–fees were not enough. I told him I wanted to take Holly back with me on the plane. "She has to be moved eventually, Joe. It would be easier if she went with me rather than us driving across the country with her."

It was hard saying those words. I wasn't looking forward to taking her outdoors in the freezing cold once I returned to Minneapolis–*it was Joe's job to take her out.* My offer had been a ruse, but it was also intended as a peace offering. It was successful; it worked to lighten our moods. Joe and I shelved our irritations over the bed and mattress. I also felt better knowing Holly was something Sharon had refused to touch. My mother told me "she doesn't like pets."

◆━━━━◆━━━━◆

Holly is back at my studio now and it is a pain having to walk her. I'm also sorry to say that my and Joe's truce was only temporary. The contention over the bed and mattress continues, but I know I'll eventually win the battle. Our old mattress and bed may cross over the state line to Minnesota but they will never move into our bedroom. I hate to be crude, but it's as easy as refusing to open my legs.

I'm not even giving much thought to it right now. I'm not stressing one iota in fact. I discovered a panacea for eliminating stress about marital tiffs and health concerns–a behemoth stressor. I am not recommending it as a panacea, but it worked for me, and that's the only reason why I mention it. When Rosie told me she was pregnant, she was the only worry on my mind.

To say I was shocked was an understatement, even though this has been something I feared hearing from the day she began to menstruate. And I received little support from my best friend. When I told Paulee she said, "My mother was twenty when she had me, and look at your mother, Sarah; she had you and your sister by the time she was twenty-three." It was not comparable or relevant. "Yes, Paulee, but call me old-fashioned, our mothers were also both married." She had to admit, it was a significant detail she omitted and it made a difference. But she had to add, "I didn't think you were so conservative when it came to unwed mothers, Sarah." I wasn't, as long as they were self-sufficient *unwed mothers* and that wasn't Rosie.

I don't know why I always turn to Paulee. She doesn't always have the best advice and often makes me feel worse, but she's an addictive habit. I usually talk to her before anyone else. She's like a net, the first to catch my complaints, fears and problems before they filter out to other people. I wish she had been the net in front of my mouth before I said to Rosie, "Don't expect your father and I to help you if you choose to go through with this pregnancy. You're on your own." As soon as the words burst forth from my mouth I felt regret. Fear and bewilderment had propelled me to say it. Why would she even consider having a baby with a boy she hardly knew? She only had carnal knowledge of the father. She was drunk and slept with him at a party. How had she been so stupid?

Marriage is out of the question too. The days of shotgun marriages are a relic of the past. Rosie rejected the idea anyway, "I don't want to marry him, Mom. How lame." I have to agree, and it was the only intelligent thing she said. I told her she needed to terminate the pregnancy as soon as possible, to which she replied, "My baby, Mom, and your grandchild." That's when I told her she would be on her own if she made the choice to keep it.

She's not mature enough to care for a child. She was obviously not able to even take care of herself to land in this predicament. And I wouldn't trust her with a goldfish; she forgot to feed every single one she had. There was also the time she brought the stray dog home which she wanted to keep. I told her, "Only if you take full responsibility for its care." Never happened, and Joe and I ended up taking care of the dog until we found him a home. Rosie had no idea how her life would be drastically altered; no more school, parties, or freedom if she chose to go through with this pregnancy. I also feared once that hit home she'd leave a baby on our doorstep with a note–Mom and Daddy, *please take care of it?* We couldn't place a sign on a tree *looking for a good home* like we did with the dog.

But my greatest fear was for Rosie; I wanted the best for her. She was my primary concern–not what was only the possibility of a baby at four weeks of gestation. My identity was also mixed in with these feelings–what I have always tried to explain to Paulee. Being a teacher is not comparable to being a mother. If one of my unmarried students tearfully confided in me about an unplanned pregnancy–I would be patient and understanding; I'd give thoughtful advice. With Rosie–I was irrational. I became a twenty-year-old unmarried pregnant girl, and I couldn't emotionally separate from her after she told me. I was anchored as if we were attached by an umbilical cord. I had a super-charged empathy, with no apparent justification–my feelings didn't mirror hers. I was terrified while she sounded cool, but I knew it was her naivete talking. The poor girl did not have a clue, and she refused to listen. She hung up on me.

I keep calling her and she doesn't pick up or return my calls. Maybe Joe would have more success–he's arriving tomorrow if he doesn't run into bad weather. He won't be able to dodge this storm when he returns to Minnesota. I'm thankful he's in transit now–I don't want to distract him when he's driving. There's also an excuse to delay; I'm not looking forward to sharing Rosie's news. Once he arrives though, I will not hesitate one minute to tell him; hopefully he can talk some sense into his *daddy's girl.*

Rosie made me so upset I forgot about my doctor's appointment. I also forgot to take Holly outside and she peed on my rug in front of the fireplace. My panacea caveat–brain fog

---

Joe arrived at my studio exactly twelve hours after Rosie's call. When I told him he wanted to book a flight to Miami and leave again immediately. Joe was upset–he was choosing to fly instead of drive. He told me he had to have "a serious discussion" with Rosie's boyfriend. *A serious discussion?* His choice of words was nonthreatening. He was taking it relatively well since I had only recently told him that she even had a boyfriend. More wrath going Ben's way was suggested when he added he couldn't believe this guy had gotten Rosie pregnant. Joe always points fingers at others rather than his precious daughter. I had to defend Ben and set Joe straight. "Before you take a shotgun and fly off for 'a serious discussion' with Ben, he's not the father." I told him how she was drunk at a party and slept with a guy she barely knew, and she didn't want to marry him.

Joe has a full beard that he keeps trimmed very close to his face; I can't really see his skin well beneath it, but I don't think it was my imagination. His face blanched after I told him. After he recovered, he asked me why she wanted to have a baby if she didn't love the guy. My husband is such a babe himself; did he really think we all arrived on this earth because every pregnant woman loved the man who impregnated them? I wasn't so naive, but I wondered too why she wanted to have the baby knowing full well–to paraphrase Tina, *love had nothing to do with it.*

Joe wasn't happy about his daughter's behavior but he didn't like what I had said to her–*move over Ben.* Joe took his rancor out on me now. "Why did you ever say something like that to her, Sarah? We will help her."

"I was upset, Joe. I reacted without thinking, just like you were flying off to Miami without having all the details." We both took a deep breath; and I told him I had been calling her non-stop since I said those things to her but she wouldn't answer her phone.

"Maybe you can talk some sense into her."

"Well, I'm not going to tell her to have an abortion."

"Does that mean you think her having a baby is a good idea?"

"No."

At least he agrees with me on that point and he did call her. He went into the bathroom for privacy. I remained outside of his good graces apparently, that annoyed me as much as my studio apartment. We really need to move into a bigger place with more than one bathroom. He was in there for close to an hour and I had to pee. It was a long conversation for Joe. When he finally came out I asked him how it went. He said he asked her: *how she thought this would impact her life; where would she want to live; did she want to continue with school; etc.,etc.?* I asked him, "Why all the questions, Joe?"

"I always find with my prospective customers you get better results when you let them talk. Find out what they want." I couldn't believe it. His call was supposed to be making Rosie aware of all the problems and difficulties she would face if she chose to go through with the pregnancy. No wonder the call had been so long, Rosie did most of the talking.

"Joe, you weren't selling an air conditioning unit to a customer or practicing the Socratic method of argument. You were supposed to be guiding her to make the right decision."

"What's the right decision? It has to be hers to make, not ours, right?"

My husband never formally studied the Socratic method but he was a natural. He liked to pose questions and let his respondent find the answers with minimal interference on his part. Was he also naturally drawn to a theory of binary maturity? That a person could be immature one day and mature the next? I don't think such a theory has ever been posed or validated but even if it was confirmed–we're talking about Rosie. The girl Joe had refused to give permission to stay in Miami by herself over holiday break. I reminded him of that, and how she brought a stray dog home when she was fifteen. He asked, "What's a dog have to do with Rosie being pregnant?" I can practice the Socratic method as well as he can. I posed a question of my own: "What happened when she brought the dog home, Joe?" He couldn't recall.

An observation about the Socratic method I made long ago teaching. Sometimes lecturing is preferable to questioning.

CHAPTER 28

SHARON

Rosie stayed with us for the holiday break in spite of her parents reuniting. I don't relish seeing her but it does keep me connected to Joe, even though he doesn't call anymore since he and Sarah got back together. I wait for a sign from God on how to save him, and I draw comfort from the bible: "Be still before the Lord and wait patiently for him; do not fret when people carry out their wicked schemes." Sarah has Joe in her clutches now, but it won't be forever. I also know somehow Rosie is part of the Lord's plan in reuniting me with Joe, as much as I dislike her. That's why I did not object to her staying with us over the break. Rosie seemed more restrained than usual too–thanks be to God. She and Leslie weren't talking very much with each other, but I didn't give it much thought. It wasn't until later when I discovered their friendship had cooled that I understood their behavior during the holidays.

I became aware of their estrangement when I went to Edith's in Miami and did my usual stop over to see Leslie. We went to our favorite fish restaurant which was our regular habit, but everything was not as usual–Rosie was not around. Leslie didn't ask if she could come with us or even mention her until I asked, "Where is Rosie?" She only shrugged and said she didn't know. She finally told me she wasn't friends with her anymore. "We weren't even friends when she was at our house for the break, Mom." This was something I had prayed for but it was puzzling. How could this forward God's plan? I should know better than to question the ways of our Lord though, and I believe Proverbs 14:29 "that whoever is patient will be granted great understanding."

The bible also stresses individual effort. It was up to me to find out what had happened no matter how difficult it might be, and after much cajoling, Leslie finally told me. She realized Rosie was a "tramp," but it had taken her more than a year to discover it. I could have saved her time. I knew Rosie was a tramp on day one, but I'm glad Leslie finally saw the light–even if her new-found wisdom bewildered me more. If my daughter disliked Rosie, how would that help me fight Lilith and save Joe? I tried to be patient to be afforded *greater understanding* but I had to find the missing pieces to this puzzle. I needed more details. "Why this new insight, Leslie?"

She finally told me Rosie was pregnant and her mother told her she was on her own if she had the baby. Sarah wanted her to have an abortion. I gasped. "I know Mom, she's a tramp, and she's being pun-ished." I am pro-life; Leslie probably thought my gasp was due to what Sarah had said. That was not the reason my words had been sucked out of my mouth. I realized this was the sign I had been waiting for from God.

The behaviors of both the mother and the daughter aren't surprising–Rosie is a tramp and Sarah is Lilith. Those are not revelations–God providing me an opportunity to save Joe is. Rosie needed help and I will offer it to her. The obvious contrast between Sarah and me is God's way of showing Joe Sarah's wickedness. I'm not clear why it's not obvious to him right now, but remind myself that Joe is a man after all, and I'm also not going to question the ways of God.

And there is an obstacle in my path beyond Lilith and the frailty of men–*my own daughter*. Rosie will not turn to me for help if she and Leslie are no longer friends. I am encouraging Leslie to befriend Rosie again, but she's strongly against it. I told her it was unchristian to turn away from Rosie in her hour of need, even if she was not an honorable woman. She softened a bit after I reminded her of Mary Magdalene, but she remains stubborn. I also cautioned her: "Be not like a horse or a mule, without understanding," but in the end I might have to buy her some new clothes or agree to some concessions. She needs a carrot, and I can't fault her too much–Rosie is horrid. I hope Leslie will not want a tutu skirt or ask to keep her cell phone when she's home. If it weren't for Joe, I would be celebrating that she no longer wants to be friends with Rosie. There is also a fear–how low will I need to go to justify the end?

I never thought in my wildest dreams I would be praying every morning and night for Leslie to reach out to Rosie, or how hard it would be, but I am humble enough to acknowledge I cannot understand the mystery of the Lord's actions. It gives me the strength to pray: "Let us not grow weary of doing good, for in due season we will reap, if we do not give up." Amen.

CHAPTER 29

SARAH

Joe is only staying for two days and then he's return-ing to New Jersey in an empty truck. A ridiculous waste of time and gas. Thinking that made me recall the furniture and boxes I saw at Aunt Marion's which belonged to my mother. Aunt Marion told me when my mother left Minnesota she was so upset about my father having asked her for a divorce, that she only took some clothes and fortunately my sister and I. After hearing more of our family history, I would have thought my mother could understand the emotional significance of my old bed and mattress and be empathetic.

She's either a hypocrite or time can soften emo-tional triggers. When I asked her if she wanted Joe to bring her furniture and other stuff to New Jersey since the truck would be empty, she was thrilled. She had forgotten the pain those items had once evoked, and had entirely forgotten she left anything in Min-nesota–confirming the latter. She was eager to rum-mage through her belongings and offered to pay for Joe's gas and tolls. She also had a great idea: "You can have my four-poster bed since you made such a fuss about your old one." She delivered this generous offer very sweetly but the subtext was clearly criticism, not generosity. I could play this game too.

"Or maybe you can hold on to my old bed and mattress instead of selling them, Mom, and when I'm seventy-six I'll be emotionally desensitized to them." She replied, "I don't know what on earth you are talking about." She was being disingenuous. I told her to "think about it." She then told me I always had to create dramas, and she couldn't understand it. I hadn't been like that until I hit thirty. Was that true? If so, it would be around the time I met Joe.

Before I met him all the men I dated were *bad boys*. They supplied plenty of excitement in my life. If my mother is right, maybe I needed more after I met Joe–he is the antithesis of a bad boy. It's a shortsighted theory though; there was never a need for me to add to the spectacle of our lives once I found out I was pregnant, six weeks after we were married. Rosie was the perpetrator in utero, and continues to stir things up. If my mother thought I created drama–wait until she hears Rosie got herself knocked up.

I hope she'll never find out, but Rosie has only five weeks left until the abortion pills may not work as effectively. I keep telling her if she waits any longer she may have to undergo a more invasive procedure; I get no response from her. She doesn't seem to understand that delay can increase more chances for complications, and worry for all of us, including my mother's. I leave at least fifteen messages every day on Rosie's voicemail and she never returns my calls.

Joe says, "Stop trying to persuade her to get an abortion, Sarah, maybe that's why she isn't answering or calling back." He tells me to let her be, or only ask how she's doing. He makes me sound so cold, almost evil. I only want to make her aware of the ramifications of what's happening. Unlike Joe, I am aware of Rosie's maturity level. She complains about having a chipped fingernail. Wait until she sees what pregnancy does to her body–bad enough when you are fully committed and want a baby. She isn't even sure she wants one, and she's not married. The latter used to be enough to deter a girl but not anymore–maybe I am old fashioned like Paulee says. No one fully appreciates the magnitude of what's happening. It's understandable: Rosie is immature, Paulee was never a mother and Joe is *Joe*.

He says he is trying not to interfere. I get it and it's a positive take, but there is another way to look at his behavior. Joe is someone who buries emotions. He has a personal history of suppressing his own trauma from experiences he had as a kid. It wouldn't surprise me if he's trying to block out Rosie's pregnancy–he calls her less now. When I query him about it, he always says he's "giving her time to figure things out for herself." We are running out of time, Joe.

I'm not clear what he's really feeling concerning the pregnancy. I hope he doesn't actually want her to have the baby. What a wild idea for him to think she's mature enough to make any life-changing decision by herself, and even more absurd that she would be able to make the right choice concerning motherhood. He has indulged her since she was a child though. It usually fell on unresponsive ears much of the time when I'd say, "she can't have everything she wants, Joe." Is he extending it to a *baby* now? If that's *yes*, he's as crazy as his daughter, but I'll agree to stop pushing my agenda–only as a strategy to encourage her to answer my calls.

I'm only leaving "how r u doing" on text messages now. For the time being I'm redirecting my persuasive energies. I'm focusing on Joe–who also needs some prodding. Does he really expect me to choose a house without him? I want him to check out houses with me before he heads back to New Jersey.

When we met with the realtor I could see she seemed relieved–*I really had a husband and we were serious buyers; I hadn't wasted her time*. Her upbeat mood didn't last long. I had told her we were in the market for a three-bedroom house walking distance from my work, and she had a few listings to show us. To her surprise and mine, Joe said he preferred a townhouse. "I don't want to be cutting a lawn." It was the first time he expressed this to me. I asked her to show us the houses anyway, and smiling, mentioned how "summers in Minnesota are shorter than New Jersey summers; less mowing time." Joe frowned so I added we could look at townhouses too (and my mother says I'm the one who always creates dramas).

The realtor said there were several townhouse complexes near my work, but she would need some time to see what was for sale and to pull up listings. They were more popular than free standing homes in that area of the city, suggesting a number of people share Joe's point of view. She added, "Perhaps you two should first decide which way you want to go. There's no point showing you properties you're not interested in." It was a professional way of saying–*don't waste my time*. It was clear to me we would not be moving out of my studio apartment in the near future, and I was right; when Joe left two days later we had not even made a decision "which way" to go.

Looking at properties was put on hold leaving more time to worry about Rosie. But I continued with my laid-back strategy, and it worked–Rosie finally answered her phone. I avoided any talk about pregnancy. It was all about school, but there was a huge elephant in the room for the entire conversation–*a pregnant one*. On the next call no matter how difficult it might be, I had to ease back into the subject of pregnancy. I had no idea how complex a subject it would morph into, but my calls were not accomplishing my true objective. The only benefit? They reminded me of my own gynecologist.

———◆———◆———

It has been a couple of weeks since I missed my appointment, and I keep forgetting to reschedule in spite of their voicemails. I finally called them this morning right after my call with Rosie. I was very apologetic, and told them there had been a family crisis. The receptionist said, "Oh, I'm sorry, I hope it wasn't anything serious." I responded, "No, only the rabbit died." Rosie was still on my mind, and I momentarily made the doctor's receptionist speech-less. She probably thought I was mental so she waived the missed appointment fee, and I was able to get an appointment for today due to a cancellation.

"You don't have breast cancer," were the happi-est words I had heard in weeks. It was the first time seeing this doctor, but I had no reason to doubt her competency or seek a second opinion until she added, "You're pregnant." She had to be looking at another patient's chart.

"But I'm fifty-one." She then asked me if I had gone through my menopause yet.

"No."

"You're still ovulating, so you can still get pregnant."

"Are you sure? I would think it is highly unlikely." She smiled, but I could see she was growing weary, and annoyed for questioning her expertise.

"The chances of getting pregnant at your age are slim but obviously possible."

"I wouldn't think my eggs were any good." When she said, "good enough, Sarah," I knew she had lost her patience, but I was also annoyed. Why did she address me by my first name? She didn't know me, I was a new patient. I looked up at her diplomas hanging on the wall behind her. I wondered how she would like it if I called her *Christine* instead of by her title.

I held myself back, and I actually apologized for questioning her competency–*even though that's exactly what I was doing.* I told her I just found what she said shocking. She asked, "Did you have unprotected sex, Sarah?" Again with the first name, distracting me. My only excuse for replying, "Yes, but it was with my husband." I knew as soon as the words left my mouth how stupid my statement was.

It was ultimately *Christine's* fault for making me sound like an idiot. She had put me in a time warp when she asked the question. She made me feel ashamed and defensive, like a teenager being asked the question. Her use of my first name created this *out-of-age* experience making me feel like a teenager again. I had asked Rosie the same question when she was fifteen (that meant I was grown up if I had asked my daughter). I felt spacey.

Christine brought me back to my senses and the present when she said, "I am glad to hear it was with your husband, and I'm sure he'll be very happy when he hears the news." Would Joe be happy? Probably, if he survived the shock, and even though this doctor had been telling me I was pregnant for the last five minutes I had to ask one last time.

"Are you sure?"

She looked down at her desk and did not say a word. She picked up her prescription pad and wrote

something on it. I figured she was giving me a prescription for vitamins or a tranquilizer safe to take
while pregnant. After she finished writing, she folded
it in half and handed it to me. I opened it and read:

Yes, I'm sure. You're pregnant.

CHAPTER 30

PAULEE

Sarah and I have remained friends for years because we usually agree on the best vacation spots, restaurants, books and movies. More importantly, we share a similar worldview. We usually think and react in similar ways, with a few deviations. She silently endures offensive drivers, and with the exception of Rosie most people she disagrees with; I don't take shit from anyone. I choose to respond differently to bumps and turns I encounter in life. If the little *Christine* doctor had addressed me by my first name and I didn't like it or her attitude, I would have told her where to go. A doctor has some damn nerve getting annoyed at a patient asking questions. Sarah can also be frustrating at times with her rationalizations: "In her defense, I guess I was making her impatient, Paulee. I asked her the same question at least four times." *Forget that bullshit.* No doctor has a right to be impatient the way they can make us wait for hours.

I told Sarah to find another doctor, especially since she told me due to her age her pregnancy is considered high risk. There is a chance of her developing high blood pressure or diabetes, and a greater probability of delivering a baby with chromosome problems. She doesn't need a doctor who gets impatient answering questions on top of all that. I have never been pregnant, nor am I an obstetrician, but I am interested in hearing Sarah's concerns about her pregnancy. And I expect a doctor to listen–they're paid to do it.

I never had a strong urge to experience pregnancy. I have been sufficiently fulfilled to have experienced it vicariously through Sarah, but she was not a big breeder like other females in my family so it wasn't a current theme in our relationship. The recurring interest between us fostering our camaraderie is obvious to most people, and has nothing to do with babies. We are both teachers.

We spend many hours discussing our work. I'm not suggesting that constitutes serious academic discussions on epistemology, although we have done that on occasion. Our *shop talk* is more centered on gossiping about students, colleagues and administrators. Sarah has also spent much of our time complaining about her poor pay over the years, until she landed her full-time position at the college in Minnesota. Salaries were the only topic I could never relate to. I always made more than her and still do, but I didn't mind her talking about it. She made me thankful I chose to teach at the secondary level. She can have her doctorate and professor title; I'll take twenty-five thousand more in my paycheck.

The other draw between us is a matter of personal taste and may be obscure to many people. Sarah and I find each other entertaining. She always says watching Anthony and I interact is like watching a reality show. She exaggerates, we are not feuding. I keep telling her just because we speak loudly doesn't mean we are going to have a food fight. She's also way too modest. Anthony and I pale in comparison to *The Janack Family Show.* I have been watching it for twenty years and I'm still not bored.

One of the reasons it's not boring is the sex. It has been a central theme of the storyline for years and is an attention-grabber. There are always surprises too which moves the arc of any good story. For years I expected Sarah to walk out on Joe due to their "dysfunctional sex life." That was according to her even though it always sounded pretty hot to me (that lent a bit of tragedy to the story). The surprise element kicked in when she didn't leave him when I expected. She waited until everything was seemingly good in their lives.

There have been engaging subplots too. Sarah having breast cancer, and Rosie with her slutty clothes and filthy mouth. That was foreshadowing with Rosie. Her pregnancy was not that surprising, and I thought the story was becoming too predictable and boring, then–*wham.* I'm hit with a shocker–Sarah's pregnant. I was the first one she told–like the TV critic who views the show before the public.

Of course The Janack Family is not a real reality show where I want to see someone punched, or laugh when a glass of wine is thrown in a person's face. I don't want anything bad to happen to Sarah, and I want her to deliver a healthy baby. And whatever Rosie chooses to do, I hope Sarah will accept it. I also hope Joe will be happy when he hears another Janack woman in his family is pregnant. Joe is like the straight man in a comedy of errors and the Janak women generate pandemonium around him—otherwise it wouldn't be an engaging plot. But I'll forfeit my entertainment for this show. I want a happy ending for everyone, even if it is boring.

⸻ ❖ ⸻ ❖ ⸻

After Sarah told me she was pregnant along with Rosie, I told her she should ask *Christine* if there is a family plan for prenatal services. She didn't think it was funny and ordinarily she would have laughed. I've read that being pregnant can make a woman moody, even though I don't remember Sarah being that way before. I'm ignoring her grouchiness without saying a word. Afterall, I am her best friend and her biggest fan.

CHAPTER 31

SARAH

When I told Paulee she first said, "A joke right, you're kidding?"

"No, and I don't know how it happened."

"Well, you did tell me you and Joe were fucking like rabbits on that reunion visit. So I guess you know how it happened, Sarah."

"Not what I mean, Paulee. I'm too old to conceive a child so easily, don't you think?" She then lost touch with reality and told me it was almost like an *immaculate conception*, and I'm not even Catholic. I had to get her on track. "Isn't 'fucking like rabbits' antithetical to an immaculate conception, Paulee?" That did not dissuade her one bit and she countered with, "Joe is Catholic," and gasped. "Oh, my god, his name is *Joseph*," and blessed herself. I wish we hadn't been on a Zoom call; seeing her bless herself made it worse, like I was watching some whacky ministry service online. From that day on she referred to my pregnancy as a *miracle*.

Since Joe has not been inside a Catholic church since he was ten, and I don't believe in an omnipotent deity, I prefer a more secular term over miracle–*rarity*.

Rarity or miracle, it continues to be hard to believe, and I keep asking–*why me?* I'm happy about the baby, even though it means giving up my glass of brandy and pot for almost two years, but I feel a little guilty about it too. Women many years younger than me go through the expense, time and emotional strain of fertility treatments, and here Joe and I come along without any help at all. Besides being a rarity, our coupling is unlikely to produce twins or triplets like hormone-induced pregnancies often do–*vive au naturel*. When I considered that I was grateful. I knew I could never handle more than one (having momentarily forgotten about Rosie's).

Paulee was the first one to know when I was pregnant with Rosie and it was the same this time. This is my norm; my habit is to tell her first about any happening in my life. Joe was the second person I told twenty years ago and he would have been the second again if he hadn't been in transit. I can't wait to see his expression, but every time there's important news lately he's driving on the interstate. I didn't want to tell him on a phone call; I wanted to tell him face-to-face.

My mother was the second person I told. That's how I learned Joe was on his way to Minneapolis in the big rental truck with Rocky. Finding out Rocky was with him was distressing. There has been a sexual tension between us for years; he's always hitting on me. Sometimes right in front of Joe who acts like he doesn't care. When I complained about Rocky to my mother she reprimanded me, "Joe is a big guy but I hope you didn't expect him to move all the furniture and boxes himself. I don't think you, your Aunt Marion or your ninety-three-year-old grandmother would be much help."

She was right; that's why I had wanted Joe to hire a moving company. But he refused, and Rocky was his only close male friend who could help. I'm still upset, and it isn't only about Rocky being a lecherous creep. It means I will have to wait until Joe and I are alone before I can tell him about the baby, no matter who is helping him. I don't want Rocky or anyone else with us when I tell him the news.

My bet is Joe will be happy but I'm not absolutely sure. We've been together for years but sometimes it feels like I don't know him at all. I had no clue he wanted to buy another townhouse. I'm feeling good about the pregnancy, but what if he doesn't feel the same? Rosie had not been an accident; she was planned and wanted by both of us. We were also twenty years younger. The shock might kill him.

When I told my mother she screamed at me. "Sarah Elsbeth Janak, are you still annoyed because I said you always create drama? This is ridiculous, I'm an old lady. Are you trying to give me a heart attack?" I assured her I was not, "I wouldn't kid about something like this, Mom–I'm pregnant." She then started to cry, and told me if I was kidding she would never speak to me again.

After I convinced her I was serious and she recovered from her shock, she asked what I was doing to assure my and the baby's health. Since it had been less than forty-eight hours since I found out I was pregnant I had done nothing besides having a prescription for vitamins filled. My doctor had given me the prescription along with her snarky note. They were the size of horse pills and I planned to take one with dinner. I already missed my glass of brandy thinking about it; I usually take my evening supplements with Hennessy in a large crystal sifter. My mother says I cancel out the benefits of the supplements when I do that. I disagree with her but I am concerned about the liquor. Unfortunately, I've been imbibing it for a month and I had no idea I was pregnant. I didn't mention that to my mother; it would be just one more thing for her to worry about. Who knows though, she might have some advice for how to counter adverse effects from one large glass of brandy each day for the past thirty days.

She's a retired nurse and a big advocate of alternative medicine. She told me vitamins were not enough, especially at my age. She advised me to immediately find an acupuncturist and to begin using herbs. She told me to buy lemon balm supplements and to start drinking teas: stinging nettle, red raspberry leaf, and chamomile. She also encouraged me to start using ginger when I cooked. I asked her, "How about pot for morning sickness?"

She completely forgot that recommendation she made years ago when I was pregnant with Rosie. She doesn't deny its medicinal properties, but she insisted these herbs were better, "but don't try to smoke them, Sarah." I wasn't planning to, but I also didn't think a little grass would hurt. I asked her to make a list and email me. I wasn't sure about the acupuncturist, but I would use her herbs and buy lemon balm. I'd stop using everything when I started breastfeeding, including pot.

Our call ended on a positive vibe. I told her I was really grateful for her help and I meant it. I wasn't like my sister Penny. I didn't think our mother was a "whacko" because she touted herbs and exotic supplements, but thoughts of Penny compelled me to say: "Mom, please don't tell anyone about the pregnancy. I need to tell Joe before anyone else knows, okay? Not even Penny."

◆———◆———◆

Joe was one hour and a half from Minneapolis when he called me from the road. He told me they were going to drive straight to my Aunt Marion's to unload the truck then head to my apartment. He asked me what I wanted to do for dinner. I told him we could go to Jimmy's, but dinner was not what I was concerned about. "Where is Rocky staying? I hope you don't expect him to stay here in a studio apartment with us." Joe told me the plan was to find a motel room for him someplace nearby. He also asked, "what's wrong?" I told him nothing was wrong but when he said, "after dinner we can find a bar and we'll all have some beers,"

I lost it. I screamed, "I don't drink beer remember, and aren't you two tired from all the driving?" He told me no, and that's when I learned they hadn't driven straight through. They had spent the night before in a motel. I also learned that Rocky was planning to stay a few days. He had never been in Minneapolis and wanted to see the sights. They were planning on finding activities for each day of his stay. It was beginning to sound like a buddy road trip.

My question was what were they planning on doing–ice fishing? Not that Minneapolis doesn't have other attractions, and I love going to the Anthony Falls Historic district to view the falls and there are parks in the area where I like to walk. My favorites are Loring and Mill Ruins Park, but it was January and freezing. And I never had the impression Rocky was big for museums. I told Joe they could bar hop without me, I was tired even if they weren't. They could also exclude me from all their activities they planned for the coming days. Joe said I sounded "out of sorts." His way of saying he thinks I'm acting like a moody bitch.

I'd prefer to be called a *moody bitch*–it was clearer. *Out of sorts* could cover a range of negatives. And after hearing Joe say it a number of times, especially when we were first married, I was even curious about the origin of the phrase. I asked Paulee; she told me the saying had to do with typesetting. *Sorts* were the individual metal type printers used. "He's saying you have no patience, you little bitch." Very funny, Paulee. But Joe was right, then and now; I had no patience left. I wanted to tell him why I was tired and unable to drink liquor (no beer, thank you), but when would I have the chance?

As soon as I hung up I made a motel reservation for Rocky. I didn't trust Joe to remember to do it. I then took a shower and decided to take a short nap for an energy boost. It wasn't because I changed my mind; there was no way I was bar hopping with them. I should have set an alarm; I was more tired than I thought. It was dark when I woke up and I still had to dress.

I wanted to wear something warm and nothing that was in the least way provocative. I put my jeans on and could barely zip them up. I was way too early in my pregnancy for that; they must have shrunk in the wash. I found another pair that fit fine but was on my third sweater. There were no laundering issues mitigating this predicament. My boobs were bigger and all my sweaters were too tight, and I only own a single bulky one. I never wear it outside–it's too big and not very warm. A shame really, it was so loose I could wear it seven months pregnant. It wouldn't work then, or now–it was on the bottom of my dirty clothes bag.

I looked at myself in the full-length mirror which hung on the back of my closet door. It was hopeless. My third sweater looked no better than any of the others I had tried. My boobs were too large. I looked like a sausage encased in angora. Now that I know I don't have cancer I'm not upset about my swollen breasts, but I need to buy some new clothes. I was about to take it off to look for something else to wear when my doorbell buzzed–it was Joe and Rocky. I hadn't made an extra key for Joe yet.

I let them in and Joe took my face between his hands and gave me a long lingering kiss. He then quickly ran off to use the bathroom. He has been doing that quite often lately. It made me ask myself two questions: were we too old for this baby? And when did Joe last have his prostate checked? I was unable to ruminate about the answers due to distraction. I was left alone with Rocky who gave me a crushing hug copping a feel–no accident, it was his intent. After that he had the audacity to kiss me right on the lips. It wasn't a sensual kiss like Joe's but still uncomfortable. He continued to be close and I could feel his breath on my face when he said, "Glad to see you're back in the family again." I was back with Joe; I wasn't part of his family. I responded, "How is your family, Rocky? How is Liz these days? I haven't heard from her for a while." Did I really have to remind him he was the husband of one of my good friends? He ignored my question and chose to stare at my boobs instead. Joe was back with us when Rocky said without lifting his gaze, "You're looking healthy, Sarah." What a pig.

When Joe helped me with my coat I quietly complained to him about Rocky hitting on me. He said it was my imagination.

"It's not my imagination, Joe. Don't you see how he looks at me?"

"Men look at beautiful women. It doesn't mean they're hitting on them." That may be true for Joe, but not for most men I have met, especially Rocky. I couldn't wait until Joe and his buddy were off on their own for the evening. I would only have to endure Rocky at dinner. Nobody could ever accuse my husband of being a jealous man, but his lack of concern is sometimes irritating. I have never given him a reason to be jealous though–I never seriously considered cheating, in spite of men's attention and my periods of discontent. There was no *Sharon* in my history.

❖   ❖   ❖

As soon as we arrived at the restaurant Joe made a beeline to the restroom again. *Thank God for enlarged prostates?* I ran after him, I had to speak with him away from Rocky. I told him to please drop Rocky off at his motel after bar hopping, and not to bring him back to the apartment for any reason. "As soon as I return home I'm putting my pj's on and relaxing, Joe. I'm in no mood for a slumber party." I was acting like a moody bitch, but Joe laughed. He thought I was trying to be funny. He agreed, and told me he wouldn't be out too late. Rocky was the one who really wanted to party, and he "had to be a good host." He was grateful to Rocky for helping with the move, and we could have "our own private party" when he returned. I was so tempted to tell him I had a big surprise but I kept mum. I had waited this long, what was a couple of hours more?

I was snug in my bed reading a book when Joe returned. Holly was also cozy and content sleeping against my side. I hated to disturb her, but Joe wanted to take her out. Holly didn't like the frigid cold any more than I did; I had started to use wee-wee pads which we both preferred. It wasn't Joe's preference. He put on her little sweater and booties and took her for a short walk around the block. It allowed me a little more time to consider how I was breaking my life-changing news but they were not gone long. Minnesota winters are very different from those in New Jersey. Joe might change his preference yet for wee-wee pads but that was another discussion for later. Now it was time for my announcement, but I waited until we were all settled on the sleeper bed for the night–*two humans, an incubating third, and one canine.* I had to ease into it. This was not something I could just blurt out.

"Joe, I need to tell you something. There's a reason why I feel so tired."

"Are you sick?"

"No. A good reason. Or I think you'll agree it's a good reason."

"What, are you training for a marathon?" He was serious. Joe will say things like this and it makes me think he's one of the strangest people I've ever met. Who has he been living with for twenty years? I am the person who purchased seven gym memberships since he's known me. My practice with all the gyms was to take their tour and use a few machines and then never to step through their doors again. I also purchased an exercise bike which I've only used as a clothes tree (I hope he didn't move it here to Minneapolis; I have enough closet space). And I never choose to walk a distance over five tenths of a mile if I can drive. There's no way I would be training for a marathon.

The only exercise I enjoy doing is swimming. I finally found a gym with a pool which I actually used three times a week when I lived in New Jersey. I didn't do strenuous laps but I did swim, and then floated around the rest of the time. And I was the one who taught Rosie. Joe believes swimming is "instinctive." According to him all a parent needs to do is throw a kid into the deep end; his father *taught* him that way. As an adult Joe occasionally swims but doesn't really enjoy it; he prefers to play golf. I asked him once, "Do you think maybe how you were taught contributes to your dislike of swimming?" He said, no; he has no memory of his father throwing him into the pool because he was two-years-old. "And I don't remember ever being unable to swim, Sarah. I hate to say it, but my father had the right idea." A frightening thought. I refuse to relinquish my title as family swim instructor.

After I moved to Minnesota I started swimming in the pool at the college where I teach. I don't swim in the winter though due to the cold. Paulee asked, "Why not? The pool is inside isn't it?" It was a stupid question. To be sure it was inside, but it still feels cool. I freeze when I venture into it. I've been advised to take a plunge and some strokes to warm up but I prefer to be a seasonal swimmer, swimming only in the warmer months. But if I wish to retain my title as a family instructor I'll need to start swimming now. If I wait until the weather changes I might be so big I'll sink, but I was getting ahead of myself.

First, I need to tell Joe I'm pregnant.

After I assured him that I was definitely not training for a marathon I asked him: "Do you remember another time in our lives when I was extremely tired?" He was quick to respond; no longer acting downright delusional but now thinking I was. "Don't tell me you think you're pregnant." I let his words linger in the air until he asked, "You're pregnant?"

That's how it went down and we celebrated with a *private party*. I was tired but at least we didn't have to worry about using birth control. Joe is happy about the baby but troubled by the possible health risks due to my age. He said it's totally up to me. He understands if I don't want to go through with the pregnancy. I never considered not having the baby but I do wonder if we are too old. I needed his reassurance. "I want to have the baby, but do you think we are too old, Joe?" After him repeating a number of cliches like *age is just a number* and *you are only as old as you feel* he went to pee again. I voiced my concerns; he said he "just had too many beers." I'm not so sure, and have visions of us racing each other to the bathroom in a few months when the baby is pressing on my bladder. What are we doing?

I told four people about the baby, and three were happy over the news. Three out of four isn't bad, and no surprise who the person is who spoiled the good run. I hadn't even intended to tell Rosie about my pregnancy because telling her she would soon have a sibling had not been a priority. It was too early yet, and her situation is paramount and urgent.

"You are running out of time, Rosie. Are you wanting a complication or a surgical procedure?"

"Mom…" I didn't let her finish what she wanted to say before I continued.

"I know how it feels when you're pregnant. It's hard to think straight sometimes even under the best of circumstances due to hormones."

"Don't tell me how it feels, Mom. How can you remember? You had me twenty years ago. You always think you know everything." She was irritating as usual, and I reacted without thinking as I so often do.

"Well, it just so happens I do know what I'm talking about, and I don't have to rely on an old memory–I'm pregnant." A full minute hung in the air before she replied; I thought she hung up. I called her name out a couple of times before she responded. Although *responded* is too soft a word–she exploded.

"What? You're making a sick joke, right? You're too old to be pregnant."

"Apparently not because I am." After she recovered from her shock she turned indignant.

"You always have to grab the attention, Mom. You always need to compete with me."

"I'm not trying to compete with you, Rosie. My pregnancy wasn't planned. It was an accident like yours." It was probably wrong of me to introduce a similarity between us. She became more upset over the idea that I was planning to have my baby.

"Why is it okay for you to have a baby when you're old but you want me to have an abortion?"

"Ever since you turned thirteen you think you are equal to me, Rosie. I hate to break it to you but you force me to do it–*you're not my peer.* Having said that, it remains ultimately your choice to decide what you want to do; even though the circumstances around our pregnancies are totally different." I then began to list them for her: "I'm married; I have an established career; your father and I have the means to support a child; and since you are the one who brought age into this–I know you don't want to hear it–but frankly, I don't think you're mature enough to have a baby."

There was another long pause with no sound for at least a minute. It went on and on until I realized she had really hung up on me this time.

CHAPTER 32

ROSIE

A few weeks after the holiday break Leslie went out with her mother to a restaurant. I wasn't invited; Leslie barely talks to me these days. I'm a fallen woman in her eyes. I have an invisible *scarlet letter* emblazoned on my chest she only sees. One thing I am grateful for–she keeps it to herself. She really doesn't have that many friends other than me to gossip with, but I'm pretty sure she's not bad mouthing me. The few friends she does have act nice when I see them on campus.

Sharon came last Friday evening to pick up Leslie, but I didn't see her. She waited for Leslie downstairs, and when Leslie left she told me she was spending the weekend with her mother at her grandmother's. She added the only reason why she was telling me was she didn't want me to report her as missing or something. "It's not like we're friends anymore, Rosie." I wouldn't have done that; she was with her mother, why would I think something bad happened to her? She only said it to me because she wanted to throw that *no friends* crap at me–she's a snotty little bitch, and when she walked out of our room I called out to her: "Take care of yourself. I wouldn't want you to get kidnapped because I'm not going to report you missing."

I didn't see her until Monday evening, and things were weird. It was as though Leslie had really been abducted and a new Leslie returned as my roommate. She was wearing stylish clothes I had never seen before, and she had also cut her hair. She didn't look like a geek, and it wasn't only the packaging that had changed. She apologized for having been so mean, and hoped I would forgive her. She also said I could count on her if I needed anything.

Her words were nice but they sounded a little rehearsed like she had practiced saying them in front of a mirror. She didn't sound natural, more like a bad actor. I doubted her sincerity, but I finally decided that her awkwardness was due to her embarrassment and not an alien abduction. She could buy new clothes and change her hair style, but it's impossible to remove all of the geek out of a geek. I also suspected Sharon had something to do with Leslie's change of heart.

If I wasn't feeling so alone I wouldn't have accepted her apology. I have other friends, I'm not a social outcast, but Leslie is the only one who knows I'm pregnant. I need someone to share with; I'm going through a lot. I'm not ashamed to tell other friends, but I don't want to be a topic for public discussion; I have a social presence to consider.

Leslie's sudden acceptance of my pregnancy was so weird that I truly had no idea what her reaction would be when I told her I was considering an abortion. She was pro-life with no exceptions, even if the mother might die or the baby might have something wrong with it. Remembering the former Leslie, I expected her to stop talking to me again but the new Leslie surprised me once again–she wouldn't shut up. She tried to change my mind with talk and creepy pictures of aborted fetuses from pro-life web pages. She was as annoying as my mother who was pro-choice. It was like they were having a debate–screaming at each other inside my head. I wished they would both mind their own business. I would make my own decision without advice from them.

I decided to get the abortion pill from a clinic. It was actually two pills and they each cost three hundred dollars. Thankfully, they accepted a credit card; I was given the pills and instructions and sent on my way. It was so easy; I didn't even have to stay at the clinic to take the pills, but they told me I should be with someone when I took them. Would the new Leslie go for this? It was also safer to be near a hospital in case of an emergency. Complications were rare but they could happen because the pills induced a miscarriage, like ones that occur naturally and there was a chance of hemorrhaging. I would have to tell Leslie about my intentions, and I wasn't sure how she'd react. That's why I still hadn't taken the pills four days after I got them. It was also why I was still pregnant when my mother called. I was happy she did–I didn't need Leslie. I'd tell my mother my decision and ask if she could be with me when I took the pills. Maybe she could fly here, or I could go to Minneapolis–but she didn't let me get one word out.

I don't believe my mother's pregnancy was not planned. I've never even heard of anyone at her age getting pregnant without some medical help. She always has to grab attention. It would be just like her to get pregnant because I did. Didn't she get enough attention when she bewitched Daddy to reunite with her? It must have annoyed her when he was calling me all the time when he found out I was pregnant. He was very supportive, too, unlike her, throwing her weight around as usual and screaming at me every time we spoke: "How could you be so stupid, Rosie? First you get yourself pregnant and now you refuse to think logically to help yourself."

How about them? They are pretty stupid to have a baby in their fifties. What really pisses me off though, she wants me to have an abortion and at the same time she plans to have her baby. I don't want a baby but there is no way I'm having an abortion after she tells me she's pregnant. If she had let me speak I was going to tell her my decision, but she was too busy talking about herself–I'm glad. If I had taken those pills and then found out later she was pregnant, I would have been more pissed than I am now.

She'll be surprised when she sees the credit card statement–they're sent to her. She's the one who gave me a card. My father didn't want me to get my own, and he doesn't even have one. He pays with checks and walks around with a big roll of cash–Daddy is pretty geeky. He wanted me to wait until I'm finished with school and have a job with an income before getting a card, "if I had to have one." Against his "better judgment" he compromised by letting my mother authorize me to use one of hers. I'm actually surprised he agreed to that knowing his philosophy about credit cards. I became aware of it when I was just a kid, long before I wanted one or even knew what a credit card was.

My parents and I were at the mall shopping and my mother wanted to buy an expensive item. I don't remember what it was but I do remember my mother wanted to use her card. My father said not to bother, he'd pay with cash. He pulled out his big roll of bills and she asked, "Aren't you afraid you'll get mugged carrying around that cash all the time, Joe?" He said no and since her first statement didn't leave much of an impression on him, she then told him he looked like a drug dealer. He was probably annoyed but it's hard to tell with my father. He replied, "I guess that means your friend Anthony carries around a big roll of cash." Paulee's husband Anthony owns a restaurant and is not a drug dealer, but he is the person my mother bought her grass from when she lived in New Jersey. She was clearly pissed after my father said that. She abruptly moved to a different checkout leaving my father standing there with his load of cash–he bought me two candy bars and some gum; they continue to disagree about credit cards.

I love them, and charged those pills with her card. She'll see six-hundred-dollars paid to a clinic when she gets the statement, but she would have known about my intentions and purchase much earlier if she hadn't been so preoccupied with her own pregnancy. It's also because of her that I flushed the pills down the toilet after hanging up. What a waste; it was like flushing six-hundred-dollars down the toilet. But the clinic wouldn't take them back; there was no point in keeping them. I could have tried to sell them by posting a notice on the student bulletin board: *Pregnant, need help? Text: xxx-xxx-xxxx*, but it probably was illegal to sell those pills, so I chose not to do it. I'm not stupid like my mother always screams at me, but I'm thinking that a post might still be useful with some editing–*I need help.* I refuse to ask my mother for anything though; I rather take care of myself. I'm also a little pissed at Daddy. Why is he so pussy whipped by my mother and okay with her being pregnant? He's got a kid already–me.

CHAPTER 33

SARAH

Rosie is not very happy about relinquishing her role as an only child. She doesn't think I should have the baby. Joe thinks her behavior is only because "she's in shock, like we all are." He also thinks my pregnancy is not her concern. "It isn't her business about us having a baby; just like we have no right to pressure her to get an abortion–that's her concern."

I don't agree with Joe at all. It is Rosie's right to voice her feelings about us because she is a member of the family, and we have rights because she's our daughter. One who doesn't have a job or income; she can't support herself and a baby. Who is going to do that, if not us? *Who* and *us* are the operative words here, and if she chooses to have the baby it will be a drastic mistake. She would have to drop out of school, and her life would become very challenging for our entire family. Yet Joe believes that Rosie's pregnancy is only her concern? Maybe that is what allows him to get a good night's sleep.

I decided to pretend the same thing for a while. I needed a little rest too, and if I stopped worrying about Rosie I could catch up with all the things I've been neglecting. I had homework to check, grades to upload and household chores: laundry, cleaning, and paying bills. Since Joe moved in with me the dirty laundry bag filled more quickly and dishes seemed to magically multiply in the sink overnight. There were also some outstanding bills I had to pay before the Wi-Fi was turned off or my credit cards were declined. I had been so distracted lately I had even forgotten to check the balance on my card that Rosie uses, but I'm sure she was distracted herself. It's doubtful that she is doing her norm, spending too much on shoes and dresses, which necessitates me to monitor her activity. That's why when I saw the balance my first reaction was–*you've got to be kidding*–until I discovered the six-hundred-dollar purchase was made at a clinic not a dress shop. My daughter wasn't as foolish as I thought. She had made the right choice this time.

I didn't discuss the pregnancy or abortion with her in any more voicemails or texts. I honestly never would have mentioned any of it again, but that is conjecture. After I told Rosie I was pregnant, she returned to the habit of not answering or returning my calls, assuring no chance of it happening. There was communication though; she answers Joe's calls. It doesn't bother me that she does not want to speak to me if she's okay–and not pregnant.

After Rosie had the abortion Joe didn't call her as frequently as he had in the past because he was very busy with his job. It wasn't a new company, but he was acclimating himself to a new office and boss. When he finally talked to her a month after I paid the credit card bill–she told him she was still pregnant–she had not gotten an abortion. I assured him he was wrong–she was lying. I showed him the statement. He could see for himself she had paid for abortion pills if he didn't trust what I said. "Our daughter is a liar but she did finally come to her senses, Joe." He told me to call the credit card company. "Maybe you got billed by mistake. I hate those cards. I've been telling you for years, Sarah–use checks or cash."

In the middle of April Joe asked me again if I was positive that Rosie had an abortion. He didn't think she did: "Why would she keep lying to us about something so important?" He is so clueless when it comes to Rosie.

"To get attention, Joe, like she has done all of her life."

CHAPTER 34

SHARON

We didn't talk long–but he called. Thanks be to God. He thanked me for offering my home to Rosie and said if there was anything he could do to help I should not hesitate to contact him. God continues to shower me with his blessings. "I will bless the person who puts his trust in me," Jeremiah 17:7-8. I did trust the Lord and could see the divine plan he had for Joe and me unfolding before my very eyes. I had always trusted God but it still felt like a miracle. It started when Leslie told me Rosie was pregnant, and predictably, her mother did not support her. Lilith only thinks about herself. Then Leslie told me Rosie was upset about her mother insisting on an abortion; that was not too surprising. It was the next step in God's plan calling me to act.

I told Rosie when the semester ended she could move in with me. God was using her as a way to help me banish Lilith–as he had banished Lilith from Eden. Rosie and I were God's instruments.

Pete wanted to know why I didn't want him to drive me to the university to pick up Leslie at the end of the school year. Leslie accumulated a number of things at the end of the two semesters, in addition to what she had brought at the beginning of the school year. I appreciate my brother carrying the boxes and other belongings, and Leslie has more wardrobe this year; all the clothes I bought to encourage her to reunite with Rosie. But I told Pete that there would be less things than last time and I did not want to "put him out." He's basically lazy so it did not take much convincing, and I was not telling a lie. I told Leslie to donate her old clothes and other belongings she no longer wanted. She and I could carry all the things ourselves without his help or Rosie doing any lifting or carrying. Leslie still asked me why Uncle Pete wasn't coming and I told her the whole truth; I didn't want him to see Rosie. He would eventually find out she was pregnant but I didn't want to hear his crass and lewd statements on the long drive from Miami to North Carolina.

Leslie told me Rosie's pregnancy was not obvious yet in spite of her being five months along. I didn't care, I wasn't going to chance it. If my luck was bad she would suddenly blossom and choose to wear a tight shirt with her baby bump showing on the day of the move. I thought pregnant women who flaunted their pregnancies like that were exhibitionists. Rosie should also be ashamed of herself since she is not married, but I haven't picked up a hint of shame.

After I informed Leslie about Uncle Pete not coming, she asked me: "What about all of Rosie's things? How will we carry it? And there isn't enough room for Rosie's junk in your car."

Leslie was friendly with Rosie but truthfully, she was annoyed at me for inviting her to nest at our home. She would simply have to get over it. I told her it was the Christian thing to do, and part of a divine plan. She asked, "What divine plan?"

"The plan where we are all expected to help one another." It was all she needed to know.

I had honestly forgotten about Rosie's belongings and how it came about that I saw Joe on moving-out day, which reinforced my belief in God and his ways. It truly is his divine plan for Joe and I to reunite.

❖——————❖——————❖

I arrived at the school at four pm; it was a long drive, in spite of stopping for a sleepover mid-way. I made the trip regularly though to see Leslie so it was not out of the ordinary, and I planned to spend the night at Edith's with the girls after Leslie and I packed the car. When I got to the school Joe was loading Rosie's belongings into his SUV. She was standing there wearing a big loose-fitting shirt over a skirt. Leslie was right, she didn't look pregnant. She was not flaunting it, but she still managed to show off with her long legs. She had not learned a blessed thing in spite of having been caught once already.

Joe was very gracious; he thanked me several times for taking Rosie into my home. He also wanted to take us all out for an early dinner–just like old times. Fortunately, Rosie had gone back inside when he added, "Hopefully, she won't be staying with you for long; she'll get over her anger with her mother in a couple of weeks, and then we'll make plans for her to fly to Minnesota." I felt like shouting back–*no, you don't understand–this is how it's supposed to be.* I then realized I would have to fight even more to banish the devil from his life–by any means. "Put on the full armor of God, so that you can take your stand against the devil's schemes," Ephesians 6:10-11.

❖———❖———❖

As soon as the girls got in the car the next morning for the drive back to North Carolina I asked them to hand over their cell phones. Leslie was used to the routine; she only used one at school because it was impossible for me to reach her otherwise. Unless it was a dire family emergency the school refused to give her my messages. Rosie rebelled and whined when I asked her to give me hers. "You've never asked me for my phone before when I stayed with you." I told her this was different, she was not visiting, she was becoming a member of the house. If she wanted to live at my house that is how it had to be–no cell phones allowed. I also added that she shouldn't be using one while she's pregnant. "Don't you know mobile radiation can alter the genes in your unborn child?" She was surprised; the little know-it-all didn't know everything. But she didn't stop giving me grief until I told her she could use my landline, and her father had that number to reach her.

After Rosie moved in I reinforced my armor to fight Lilith. Rosie was not only angry with her mother, she felt unloved by both parents after a short time. It sounds cruel but she needed to continue to feel that way, and I would use any means to fight Lilith, even lies and deception. Every time Joe called to speak to Rosie I made an excuse of why she couldn't talk to him. I always added she was fine; and still angry with Sarah. He never questioned me further. Then Sarah started calling; she wouldn't rest with my explanations. She insisted I tell Rosie to call her back. I never did, and I never told Rosie her parents called.

When Rosie started to ask to use my phone to call her parents, I'd say, "Don't you think it's better if you let them come to you to measure their love and devotion?" Rosie was easy as Joe, but the last time I talked to Sarah she screamed at me, "Let me talk to my daughter you bitch." I hung up on her and started screening my calls.

It was not only to further the divine plan that I needed Joe and Sarah to stay away from Rosie. I needed to protect Rosie's unborn child. Rosie told me she didn't want to keep her baby; she wanted to give it up for adoption. I almost shouted–*praise be the Lord* when she said it. I didn't want this innocent baby to be raised by Rosie. Before I stopped taking Sarah's calls she told me to tell Rosie she was okay with the baby now; Joe and she would help her as much as they could. I didn't want Lilith to be anywhere near this baby any more than Rosie.

I told Rosie there were resources through my church; they could place her baby in a good Christian home with loving parents. "There aren't enough white babies, Rosie." She asked me what I meant by that. I explained to her how there were too many colored babies–which is simply a fact, and they should be raised by their own kind. Now she's not sure she wants to give the baby up. She changes her mind from day to day. I need to help her; I also need her to stay away from Sarah, and God forgive me–Joe.

CHAPTER 35

LESLIE

When I first met Rosie I envied her; she was so pretty and worldly. Rosie says people don't say *worldly* anymore–it was lame. "Say *an influencer*, Leslie." She was so sophisticated; I felt like a child in comparison. I wanted her to teach me about important things, and my mom never said anything unkind about her. She only encouraged me to branch out to meet other people. Spending so much time with one person wasn't healthy according to my mother, but it was no longer a concern after she started dating Rosie's father.

After they broke up I expected her to start telling me, "to cast a net out for more friends." It was one of her favorite expressions and started saying it to me when I was in grade school. She surprised me. She didn't say it and started to talk about a "divine plan" when I overheard her praying. I never eavesdrop on private conversations between her and the Lord though, and would leave the room immediately if I heard her.

I didn't give it much thought until later when she spoke of "the divine plan" directly to me and I don't get what Rosie has to do with it. I also don't understand why my mother has been pushing Rosie on me since she heard about her being pregnant. I no longer admire Rosie or think she is sophisticated–I definitely don't want to emulate her.

And I don't want to share my room with her for an entire summer. My mother kept imploring, "We need to show her kindness and make her feel welcomed." I pointed out how Rosie would probably be more comfortable in her own bed and room, being pregnant and all–it worked. My mother agreed and Rosie is staying in the guest room.

I'll be going back to school in the middle of August. My mother wants me to fly back for the birth in September, but I don't know why. We wouldn't be celebrating a happy occasion. The organization arranging the adoption doesn't even let the birth mother see or hold the baby. As soon as she gives birth they take the baby from her. My mother says, "That's exactly why Rosie should have her friend here to comfort her." I'm not her friend anymore and doubt she would even want me with her. I replied, "What about her parents, can't they come?" My mother didn't even answer me, and I know she talks to Rosie's father every week.

I pray when Rosie has her baby I have a huge term paper due, or an exam I can't miss. I don't think my mother will insist I fly back for the birth if it jeopardizes my grades, but she's acting strange–a little unbalanced actually. I am not absolutely sure about anything or what my mother's thinking at this point.

CHAPTER 36

SARAH

It wasn't until the middle of May when I discovered how wrong I was and had to reset my opinion about Rosie–she wasn't as wise as I had thought. She was pregnant and told Joe she was moving in with Sharon at the end of the semester. Sharon was helping her–she didn't want any help from us. I asked Joe, "Are you okay with this?" His response, "Rosie is going to be okay. Sharon is a good, decent woman. She's one of those religious types who wants to help people." I had to also reset my opinion about him. It prompted me to say, "Oh, like that good, decent religious person you met when you were ten?"

As soon as I said it I regretted it and apologized. It was a cruel thing to say. Joe looked at me for at least thirty seconds not saying a word until he replied, "Sometimes I wonder if I should say anything to you." That would also be cruel. I felt miserable, along with a headache, a queasy stomach and ankles so swollen they looked like tree stumps. Joe came over to me and put another pillow under my feet and asked if I needed something before he went to work. I said no, only his *forgiveness*. He took my face in his hands and said, "You already have that. Stop worrying about Rosie. She's going to be fine, but you should probably tell your mother about her."

He was right. Rosie was going through with this pregnancy; I had to finally tell my mother. When I did, she said, "Oh, my; what's going on in your family, Sarah? Two babies?"

❖————————❖————————❖

At the twentieth week of my pregnancy my blood pressure soared; I was given Labetalol and told to restrict my activities and reduce stress. Rosie was killing me with worry, and she continued to ignore all of my calls and texts. Joe did not understand why I was worrying about her; he wasn't worried. When Rosie's school semester ended he went down to Miami to get her things from school before she went off to stay with Sharon. I wanted to go with him but was in no physical condition for the drive. Joe saw Rosie, and according to him she was fine. He continued to be the family liaison between my daughter and me.

But from my perspective as soon as Rosie moved in with Sharon there was a complete communication blackout. Her phone didn't ring anymore and went straight to voicemail. I kept leaving messages until it was filled and wouldn't accept any more. Joe said the same thing happened when he called her cell. It wasn't a problem in his mind. He called Rosie on Sharon's landline, but his role as liaison was unproductive from my take–he never spoke directly to her. Sharon always answered his calls but the only thing she relayed after an hour of conversation was that Rosie was out with Leslie, or napping. She also said she didn't know what was going on with her cell phone. She said she would check it out but never did.

There was only one deviation from Sharon's behavior and standard replies to Joe's queries about Rosie that made me feel better about what was going on. She told us she was helping Rosie place the baby up for adoption. It was good to hear, but I wish we were more actively involved with it. We are Rosie's family, not her.

It was causing me stress but Joe was okay with Sharon's answers and never questioned why Rosie did not call him back. "She's pissed at me Joe, not you. It's really out of character for her to cut you off." Why wouldn't she want to tell us about the adoption, and was she really so busy going out and napping? The napping part was the strangest. I finally questioned Joe, "You don't wonder why Rosie is always napping?"

"She's pregnant. You nap often too."

"Yes, but she's twenty-one. I'm more than twice her age." He told me I had to stop worrying–it was bad for me and the baby.

"She's in good hands, Sarah. Look how Sharon is helping her with the adoption."

On the surface it appeared a good thing but it made me worry about my marriage. Sharon was re-establishing her ties with Joe. They had a solid long-distance relationship. Rosie might not be available but Sharon always was, and they had long conversations. It was out of character for Joe even if Sharon did most of the talking. The length of these talks was also puzzling because we received so little information about Rosie. Joe said Sharon asked him questions most of the time. He never cut her off; it would be rude since she was caring for Rosie. What was going on? It wasn't surprising my insecurities rose to the surface.

They prompted me to question him about his meetup with Sharon when he went down to get Rosie's things from school. "I just took Sharon and the girls out to eat. It was the least I could do for her taking Rosie in." I wasn't upset about Joe treating Sharon to a meal at a restaurant or him making our daughter sound like a damn orphan. But then my mind went to places where it shouldn't have. "When we were separated and you were dating Sharon, did you remove your wedding ring?" I always wanted to ask the question and never did. That's when I discovered he could answer Sharon's questions for an hour but couldn't answer one of mine with a simple *yes* or *no*.

"Are you going to start up with that again?" I didn't dare say another word, even though I don't trust Sharon. I knew I'd be wasting my time trying to convince Joe she wanted to steal our family. Even Paulee said to me, "Remember Sarah, you were pushing Rosie to get an abortion. She didn't want one, she sought refuge with Sharon."

I would not have continued to encourage Rosie to abort after it was too late. She knew where I drew a line on abortion, but she chose to turn a blind eye to it. She chose instead to draw a line on me, and turn to Sharon as her refuge when it was not necessary.

CHAPTER 37

ROSIE

After the cars were packed my father took us all out to dinner. When we finished our meal my father was driving back to Minneapolis. I almost wanted to say–*I've changed my mind. Can I come with you?* I didn't. I reminded myself: my stay with Sharon and Leslie will only be a month at most, and even though it was already May, I figured the weather in North Carolina would still be better than what I'd find in Minnesota.

I'm pissed off at my parents but there's no way I want to stay with Leslie and Sharon for long. Leslie and I aren't even real friends now. She talks to me but she sounds mechanical most of the time, like she's a damn computer or something, and she no longer asks for advice about guys, clothes or socials. Disregarding socials is understandable once we get to her house though since her mother confiscates her phone as soon as she gets out of school each break, and there's no Wi-Fi. We have to go to the public library if we want to use our laptops, making it a little hard to maintain a social presence. I don't really care though. Due to my present condition I want to keep a low profile, but

I didn't expect Sharon to take my phone. That is even more intrusive than my mother, and I don't believe in that mobile radiation crap she's spewing.

After she confiscated it, I started having second thoughts about teaching my mother a lesson about *letting me live my own life*, but it was too late to change my mind. I was in a car headed for North Carolina and Daddy was off in a different direction. After four weeks, I now know my lesson was a waste of time but I learned something. I never thought both parents would abandon me. I don't understand it.

My father hadn't acted annoyed with me on moving day. He hugged me and asked me how I was feeling. He also said my mother sends her love and misses me. She would have come, but she was not feeling well; she was told to restrict her activities. It had sounded like a lead-in to talk about her pregnancy which I had not wanted to happen. I haven't told Leslie or Sharon about my mother being pregnant; I'm too embarrassed. I abruptly told my father I had to get something from my room; I was pretty sure he wouldn't keep talking about my mother to Sharon. Sharon is nosey but I knew my father would not share my mother's personal stuff, even if she asked; he's very private that way. I thought I got personal messages from him that day–he loved me and my mom was thinking about me.

Once I settled into Sharon's house my parents never contacted me. I couldn't believe it. My mother is always interfering and in my face. She never stopped before, why now? Even when she left Daddy and I did not want to talk to her, she wouldn't stop pestering me. Daddy is also acting out of character. Why did he suddenly stop calling me? I asked Sharon, "Are you sure he has your number?" She assured me that he and my mother both had her landline number, and I should give them some time. It didn't matter how much time I gave them. Sharon doesn't have all the information. I know what's happening, I'm no longer on their minds–they're already replacing me with their new kid.

◆――――◆――――◆

Being pregnant sucks. Even when I didn't look pregnant and could pretend I wasn't, I was nauseous all the time. When I moved in with Sharon she asked me if I had been seeing an OB/GYN for prenatal care. Why would I do that since I was planning to get an abortion for most of my pregnancy? I thought better about mentioning that so I simply told her no, and she made an appointment. The doctor told me my nausea would ease up soon. When it still hadn't a month later, he said unfortunately I might be someone who would experience this mild discomfort all through my pregnancy. Other *mild discomforts* started to surface, like heartburn and headaches.

I could live with nausea, heartburn and headaches but I hate getting fat. At first I was fascinated by the change in my body, but now I feel like a bloated cow with big swollen udders–which in my case are boobs. I wonder if cow boobs hurt like mine?

I can't wait for this to be over, but I'm not sure I want to give the baby to the agency Sharon is suggesting. I'd rather have an adoption which is open, where I can be a part of the kid's life. Sharon says those kinds of adoptions are confusing for a child, and many would-be adoptive parents dislike open adoptions. She keeps asking, "Don't you want your child to have a good home?" I do, but not necessarily with Sharon's agency, and I wish my parents would call me.

I need to talk to Daddy and my mother even if they don't want to talk to me. I told Sharon I want to call but she insists that it's better if I let them reach out to me. I finally asked, "Why?" I also asked for my phone back; she said she didn't remember where she had put it and started leaving pamphlets on my bed about mobile radiation. That's when I asked to use her landline and she said it was out of order–I don't believe her.

It sounds overly dramatic; it's not like I'm being held captive, locked in my room. I'm not trapped–I can walk right out the door to buy a burner phone or go to the library. The only problem about that plan is Sharon's house isn't walking distance to any store or the library. Maybe before I was pregnant I could have done it, but I feel so tired much of the time now that I know trying to walk there is a joke. I have asked Sharon for rides but every time she gives me an excuse. Leslie doesn't help either, she never wants to leave the house with me for anything. Maybe I'm a pregnant embarrassment to her. How does she explain me if we run into people she knows?

Just trying to figure out how to get in touch with my mother is exhausting. I wish she would call me. I have so many questions to ask her about pregnancy, like why am I so fucking tired for one? Is this normal? I don't believe much of what comes out of Sharon's mouth anymore, and I want answers from my mom. But I don't think I'm getting any soon because she has abandoned me–just like before.

If my parents don't call me, I am going to call them. I have come to a decision about the adoption that I want to share with them. I don't want to give my baby to Sharon and her agency. I asked Sharon if I could use her phone again so I could call my parents; I told her I was tired of waiting for them to reach out to me. Her big surprise? She told me her landline wasn't working again. I know she's lying and she's going to keep doing it. That's why I decided to sneak into her bedroom to use her phone when she was hosting her bible study group. She keeps it on the nightstand next to her bed, and when I first picked up the receiver I panicked. I wasn't even sure how these old things worked, but I figured it out and it started to ring. I felt like screaming–*hurry, hurry, pick up,* and when I heard my mother's voice I blurted out "Mom" --but it was only her voicemail. I also heard a noise. Was

Leslie or Sharon coming upstairs? I needed to be quick and my mother's message kept droning on. She really needs to record a shorter greeting. I thought it would never end and when it finally did, I distinctly heard someone in the hall near Sharon's bedroom. I only had time to say, "Mom, help me."

I had to hide and there was no way I would have fit under Sharon's bed. I ran to her walk-in closet that smelled like moth balls. I knew I wouldn't be able to stay long before I retched on the floor. A few minutes felt like an hour until I heard the upstairs toilet flush but I still waited in spite of feeling dizzy. I was afraid to come out from behind Sharon's sweaters and dresses, but I couldn't stay hidden there all night. I slowly opened the door and peeked out. Sharon's room was empty; I crept as lightly as a big fat cow could back to the guest room.

CHAPTER 38

SARAH

When I first called her *Christine* she gave me a strange look. I thought she was going to say something but she didn't. It might have only been a look of surprise rather than indignation. She gave me the same look when she told me she was scheduling me for an emergency C-section and I refused. I wasn't refusing the C-section; I simply did not want to be admitted to the hospital immediately like she wanted. The procedure wasn't scheduled until the next morning. How much of an emergency could it be? I explained to her that my husband was out of town and I preferred to have him take me to the hospital after he returned.

Joe was in Chicago and I expected him to return by the evening. If he was held up for any reason, Aunt Marion was already prepared to step in for him. Christine reluctantly agreed and told me I had to be at the hospital by 6:30 am. All the more reason not to spend the night at a hospital. Every time I've been a patient in a hospital I've never gotten any rest, and I'm sure it would be the same this time with their frequent interruptions throughout the night.

During my appointment I heard my phone vibrating. Christine prefers for her patients to put their mobile phones on airplane mode. She probably thinks I'm a very defiant patient since I refuse to follow her instructions, in addition to calling her by her first name. I had honestly forgotten about my phone, but I'm grateful it was on, in spite of what Christine might think about me. I knew someone had called and as soon as I was in my car I checked my voicemail. When I heard Rosie's plea a chill went right down my spine. A jolt of fear like an electrical current hit my bladder making me feel like I was going to pee in my pants; fortunately it was only a feeling and did not come to fruition. Rosie's voice triggered a primal response–*protect your young.*

I was suddenly filled with energy. I hadn't felt this good physically for weeks. I called Rosie immediately, in spite of being aware that her phone has gone to voicemail since May and her mailbox is always full. It had to be different today–she called me, but there was no change. I then called Sharon, and not surprisingly there was no change there. Her answering machine picked up and I left a message. I didn't curse at her, but I was very firm, "I'm warning you, as soon as you get this message tell Rosie to call me." I wasn't sure what my warning was, but it felt good saying it.

I called Joe next and he picked up immediately. "What's wrong?" After I told him about Rosie's call, he asked, "Is that all she said?" She asked for help, wasn't it enough? For a man who normally uses so few words, couldn't he appreciate that? He then asked if I had called Rosie and Sharon. I felt like screaming–*stop wasting time,* but told him Rosie's mailbox was filled as usual and Sharon never picked up or returned my calls.

"Really? I know that's the case with Rosie's phone but it hasn't been my experience with Sharon. She always answers my calls." I wanted to reply–*I'm not the one she wants to fuck.* He got annoyed all the same when I admitted, "It's probably because I called her a bitch the last time I talked to her." He stopped speaking, but at least he didn't chastise me for being uncivil to *Saint Sharon.* I was still the one who had to get us back on track: "Please do something, Joe. If you heard Rosie's voice, I know you'd feel the same as I do." He said he was sure if something was really wrong Sharon would have called us. He was unbelievable.

I sat in the car for ten minutes waiting until Joe called me back. He told me Rosie had a scare because she thought she was going into labor, but it had only been a false start–she was fine. I asked him if Rosie had said it to him directly. He said, no.

"Joe, do you realize you haven't talked directly to Rosie since May? You need to go to her. Even if we accept she is fine, she still is our only daughter who is about to give birth. She needs to have someone from her family with her. Sharon is not family–and I'm not saying it because I'm jealous of her. I'm saying it because that's true, and I love Rosie."

Did it suddenly register with him that it had been weeks and weeks since he actually talked to Rosie? Or was he picking up on my fear? I don't know what it was but he agreed to go to North Carolina, even though he was concerned about leaving me. I told him I'd be fine; I wasn't the one calling for help, and I had Aunt Marion. I didn't tell him about my C-section scheduled for the following day. I was afraid he would change his mind because I wasn't getting a sense of urgency from him about Rosie. Especially when he said he'd probably drive to North Carolina instead of flying from Chicago. I ended the call with my own plea, "Please fly, Joe." I wasn't convinced he would–and Rosie needed help. I needed more helpers.

My mother was not someone I had to convince about Rosie. She thought Sharon was a little-off ever since she invited Rosie for Christmas after Joe broke up with her. I can still recall her words verbatim: "Who does something like that? I would think she wouldn't want to entertain her ex-boyfriend's daughter, even if she's friends with hers." After Rosie got pregnant and Sharon offered her home, my mother said Sharon was "mental." I don't know if Sharon is mental or not, I only know I want to get Rosie out from under her roof. I asked my mother if Rosie could stay with her for the rest of her pregnancy. She told me she was going to suggest it before I asked: "Certainly she can stay with me. She's my granddaughter and she's having my great-grandchild, and you're in no shape to take her in." It was true, and I didn't know if Joe could handle being a nurse if my studio apartment turned into a maternity ward.

◆——————◆——————◆

As soon as I got home I set up my web-cam to call Paulee. She had to hear Rosie's voicemail since she considered Sharon a *refuge*. After she heard it, she agreed that Rosie sounded distraught. When I reminded her we hadn't talked directly to her since May she was ready to sign up–she would go to North Carolina. She had already scheduled days off to help me, but I convinced her that Rosie needed her help more than I did.

"Should I bring the police with me, Sarah? But then again, you did just get a message from her–she's still alive."

"Paulee, you are not making me feel better. You don't have to bring a SWAT team; just book flights and get her." I also warned her that Joe might be there. "He might try to persuade you to change our plans. Don't let him."

"Are you serious, Sarah? I coach the debating team. He is not going to be able to change my mind or plans. I'm booking flights, getting a rental car at the airport and when we're back in Jersey, I'm taking Rosie to your mother's. Trust me, Joe will be helping me." I told her to concentrate now on making all of the arrangements for getting Rosie safely out of Sharon's house, and not on her powers of persuasion with Joe, but I trusted her completely. Rosie would be okay.

I was exhausted after talking to Paulee, but calmer. I was relaxed enough to become aware of how lousy I felt. I stretched out on the Victorian settee and propped my legs up on a pillow. I looked at my swollen ankles and wondered, was it here where it happened? Is this where my child was conceived? It happened somewhere over that four-day period when Joe visited me. If the baby was a girl I could name her Victoria in remembrance of my settee. But we also did it on the couch, bed, floor and up against the closet door–no appropriate names from any of those locations.

The settee felt uncomfortable but I had no energy to move. I also knew the problem wasn't the settee, it was my body. I was burning up. They say pregnant women glow–I'm combustible, and if I ever hear another man say "we're pregnant" again I will need to be restrained. Nobody should utter that platitude if they're not experiencing swollen ankles, hemorrhoids and pain–spare me. I was grateful Joe never said it because it was an asinine statement.

What I wouldn't give for a glass of brandy, but I can't drink. I can only adopt it for a name. Brandy is a nice name and also meaningful. I blame alcohol for making me horny, but I can't forget the pot. It made me forget we weren't using birth control until it was too late, but I would never name my baby girl after pot–even though Mary Jane is a girl's name. I like the name Brandy better. The first time I heard it was when my friend Liz told me one of her babysitters was named Brandy. I said at the time, "What a nice name." I never thought in my wildest dreams I would be pregnant in my fifties considering *Brandy* for my own baby girl.

I need to come up with names for a boy too. There's no guarantee my baby will be a girl. Paulee insists I'm carrying as though it were a boy. When I bared my belly on the web-cam to show her my baby bump, she said it looked different from when I was pregnant with Rosie. She fails to notice or mention that my entire body looks different than it did twenty-one years ago, but I hope she is right.

I want a boy. I want Joe to have a son since he already has a daughter. I doubt we'll have another rarity pregnancy and my body wouldn't be able to survive it if I did. I also hope I have a boy for Rosie's sake–l want her to be able to retain her title as *daddy's girl* in the family.

Tomorrow I will know if we have a Brandy or a Joe, Jr. Yes, we will definitely name our boy Joe, Jr. There is no chance in the world that Joe would want to name him Mac after his father. I can hardly wait to find out the sex, and there had been no need to wait so long to find out. Christine could have told me after eighteen weeks, but I wanted to be surprised. On the day she asked me if I wanted to know I said–no. She asked "Are you sure?" I told her I was and she looked at me with a strange expression. She frequently throws that look my way. I have the distinct impression that she will be as happy as me when my pregnancy is finished. Thankfully it will soon be over for both of us, and so will Sharon's abduction of Rosie. Both thoughts make it easier to ignore my fatigue and swollen ankles but I'd feel even better if I could smoke a joint.

CHAPTER 39

PAULEE

The voicemail was melodramatic but what was left unsaid was more disturbing. I had to agree with Sarah, even considering her obsession with Sharon–something was off. Why hadn't she and Joe heard directly from Rosie since she moved in with her? I know it's driving Sarah crazy that she can barely move, and would like to be on the next plane to North Carolina to rescue Rosie herself.

I'm still not sure we should view this as a *rescue*– I was only kidding about the police. I should have known better to joke with Sarah in her delicate condition, but I'm willing to fly to Sharon's and take Rosie to her grandmother's in New Jersey.

As soon as I finished my call with Sarah I went to work: booking flights, a rental car and one night's stay at a motel near the airport. I found two flights to North Carolina, one going from Philly in the early evening, and another which left from Trenton the following morning. I wasn't bothering Sarah about which to take, I knew what she would say already, but I had my concerns over the evening flight if there were delays. I might not get to the courtesy desk in time to pick up the rental car–the desk closes at 8 pm. If I didn't arrive in time I wouldn't be able to get the car until the next morning. I worried about it until I finally said to myself: I'll find another way to Sharon's house if the desk is closed–screw the rental car.

The next thing was calling out sick, and when I told Anthony he said, "Aren't you afraid they're gonna fire your ass? You already put in a request for extended leave to help Sarah." "They can't fire me, I have tenure." That fueled his spiel about how teachers have it so easy and all we do is complain all the time.

"I'd sure like a job where I could sit around on my ass all day reading books."

"Nobody forced you to go into the food and beverage business, Anthony." I also added he should worry about his own ass. It was going to get sore from all the hot air he was spewing out of it.

My job was not sitting around reading books all day, and he knew it. He often said he could never handle all the papers I had to correct, or take the lip from students every day like I did. But his real gripe wasn't with the teaching profession, he was just sore because he wasn't able to take off from work to go with me. He loved to fight. I didn't anticipate one, but if I did have to claw my way out of there–I could handle little mousy Sharon by myself; I did not need Anthony as a backup.

I arrived at the airport and only had minutes to spare to get my rental car which meant foregoing picking up my suitcase. I wondered how long the airport lets luggage go around the carousel before they throw it into an unclaimed freight pile. It was a recurring question since it took longer than I had anticipated getting the car. After I did the paperwork, I followed the clerk to a restricted lot to check out the car for defects. I didn't see any but watched him circle it twice kicking the tires. I finally said, "Everything looks fine–let me sign-off on it." I wasn't buying the damn car, only renting; and based on my maps, I would be driving a total of thirty-six miles round trip to and from Sharon's house.

I finally retrieved my suitcase after getting the car, but I wouldn't have cared if I had lost it. What's a suitcase in the big picture? Just like what Sarah said about Rosie's luggage: she didn't know how many suitcases she had "but what is important is getting her out of Sharon's house as fast as possible. We can replace things–I can't replace Rosie." Talk about melodrama–Sarah was in rescue mode when she said it. She and Anthony had to calm down. I continue not to anticipate a high drama escape or fight.

I was in the car and about to pull out of the airport lot when my cell phone rang; it was Sarah's Aunt

Marion. She told me she had to take Sarah to the hospital. I was surprised, Sarah had told me her doctor had called it an *emergency* only to be able to admit her earlier than the previously set date for her C-section. Sarah had been mistaken or her condition had changed since I last talked to her. Aunt Marion then began a convoluted story about Sarah repeatedly calling Joe on his cell and he never answered. She had also called Sharon's landline multiple times but nobody picked up. "Sarah finally asked me if I would call. She said this woman Rosie is staying with never takes her calls." Aunt Marion went on to say that when she called it also went to voicemail, but Sharon turned off her answering machine and picked up. "Isn't that quaint? She still has an answering machine."

I never met Sarah's Aunt Marion and I hope I didn't sound rude but I shouted out, "I hate to interrupt Marion, but what's the bottom line? I'm on the way to Sharon's house to get Rosie."

"Oh, I'm sorry, dear. I told this woman to have Joe call me, it was urgent. But Sarah told me I should also tell you."

What was all this phone intrigue with Sharon? Was she playing games or was there really a sinister intent? I call this episode of The Janack Family Show: "Sharon's Phone Caper." Or better yet? "Dial M for Mousy Bitch."

✦   ✦   ✦

There was a very bright porch light on Sharon's house. I not only saw her little brick house, her entire front yard was illuminated. Ceramic and resin ornaments in the form of frogs and mushrooms were placed along the border of her driveway. Religious statues are acceptable–paying honor to the Virgin Mother, Jesus or Buddha–but this was lawn trash.

I parked on the street because there wasn't any space in her little driveway. There were two cars already parked there; one of which looked like a rental. Sarah was afraid Joe would choose to drive to North Carolina, since according to her he didn't act like he thought this was urgent or a caper being perpetuated–was she wrong? Maybe he had flown, and rented a car from the airport like me?

As soon as I stepped on the porch, my question was answered. The inner door was wide open and I could see Joe through the glass of the storm door. He and Sharon were standing in the living room facing one another. They were positioned in such a way it looked like they had just kissed or were about to kiss. How dare he? –and with Sarah in the hospital having a C-section with his baby. I was momentarily startled (I had always thought better of Joe). I was pissed and anger took over; when I charged into Sharon's house I had the energy and fierceness of a bull. Lucky for her the storm door was unlocked; if not, I would have knocked it down. When I burst through Sharon let out a little gasp, and Joe turned towards me.

"Hi, Paulee. What are you doing here?" He didn't act like a man who was caught cheating on his pregnant wife–was I wrong? It didn't matter, my adrenaline remained high and helped me to finish the job I had signed up to do. The first thing was addressing these phone calls.

"Joe, where's your phone? Sarah has been calling you." He told me he couldn't find it; he thought he might have lost it at the airport. The last time he saw it was when he texted Sarah.

"Sarah called Sharon's landline too. So did Sarah's Aunt Marion, didn't Sharon tell you?" I stared at Sharon when I added, "Don't say you didn't get the call, Sharon; I know you did." Joe wasn't interested in a discussion about Sharon's Machiavellian skills as a receptionist. He asked me if Sarah was okay, but before I could answer, we heard Rosie cry from upstairs. "Daddy?"

I ran up the stairs and Joe and Sharon were behind me. Rosie was standing in the doorway of a bedroom; she was really big. Was she having twins? When Joe saw her, he said, "Oh my God, you look just like your mother." It was a silly thing to say, but I guess it was a shocker. Sarah told me in May Joe had said she wasn't even showing yet. Perhaps seeing Rosie in her last weeks of pregnancy made him realize at last she was really pregnant. Sarah believed he had been deliberately ignoring it for nine months. It was impossible now and I couldn't help myself when I said, "Yes, Rosie and Sarah both look like they're ready to pop, Joe. And Sarah's in the hospital as we speak having your baby. That's what the phone calls were about."

I had barely finished my statement when I heard a blood-curdling scream:

"Lilith is pregnant?" I didn't think such a loud cry could come out of such a little mousy woman and it was the first time since this all started that I was inclined to think like Sarah and Anthony. Maybe this was high drama and a possible fight, but who the hell was Lilith?

The next thing I knew Sharon ran off somewhere, and Joe was just standing there with a dazed expression on his face. I had to take control of the situation. I asked Rosie if she wanted to leave or stay with Sharon. She started whining, "Get me out of here Aunt Paulee." Boy, do I hate whiners. I told her to pack her bags, "but make it quick before Sharon starts boiling pet rabbits and comes after us with a knife." That set her off again. "What are you talking about Aunt Paulee?" I took her by the shoulders–gently. She was a pregnant woman, she only acted like a kid having a tantrum. I repeated again, "pack your bags so your father can put them in my rental car." That's when Joe asked, "Can someone tell me what the hell is going on around here?" Not really.

I replied, "Better to leave now and figure it out later. The important thing is for you to return to Minneapolis and be with Sarah now. You might already be a new daddy, and I have to escort your firstborn to New Jersey."

Sharon never resurfaced, and as soon as my car was packed Rosie and I left for our motel, leaving all the frogs and mushrooms in the dust. We were on the same route as Joe, ahead of us on his way to the airport. He didn't have to be told to get his ass back to Minneapolis as fast as he could–he was no longer dazed.

Rosie seemed very nervous. This was too much excitement for her–words poured out of her mouth nonstop. Then the tears started. She told me how Sarah and Joe hadn't called her even once since she moved in with Sharon. It was untrue and I told her so, but even if it had been true I would have lied. I feared that her emotions would induce an early labor. We had to get through that night, the plane ride the next day, and the drive to Nessie's house.

I was Sarah's labor coach when she was having Rosie, along with Joe, who was pretty useless and dazed that day. I was an extraordinary coach compared to him, but I would probably be as inept as him if I was left on my own with Rosie. I needed the security of a delivery room with doctors and nurses–surrounding me like a comforting womb.

I told Rosie her parents had never stopped calling her; it was Sharon–she was not giving her their messages. Her parents loved her.

"Well, maybe my father does, but not my mother so much."

"You know she does. Why would you call her asking for help if you really believe that?" She didn't say anything, and I thought we could now move on to more neutral topics–but we weren't finished.

"Then why did she always say she'd never have another kid after me all the time?" Sarah did say that frequently, but I didn't think I needed to clarify. Rosie must know her story, but maybe the baby hormones were making her brain mushy.

"Your parents didn't wait at all to start a family and your mother was so happy when she found out she was pregnant with you. There were some issues in their marriage at the time too, but she was determined to have you," (Paulee, why did you open your fat mouth and mention issues?). And sure enough, Rosie asked, "What issues?" I told her she could talk to her mother about that, but I made it clear–she had not been a stupid mistake; she had been planned; (only to kick myself again–would she think I was making a reference to her stupid mistake?). I continued to plod along in spite of my blunders.

"After your mother had you she realized the enormity of being a parent and she didn't think she could do it again. It was nothing about you, and I agree with her. That's why I never had kids, but it doesn't mean I don't like them. Your mother loves you."

"The enormity of it didn't stop her from getting pregnant now."

"This pregnancy was not planned, Rosie, but she views the baby as a gift to your father. She feels guilty about leaving him; he always wanted another kid and she refused."

This discussion was too emotionally charged for my liking. I did not want to deliver a baby in the rental car. Not only would I not have a clue what to do, I would most likely be charged extra for a cleaning fee. I had to move to a less impassioned conversation. I asked her if she was hungry; we were almost at our motel and according to their web page they had a restaurant open for bar food items until 1:00 am. She said she was, and I was feeling good until I thought: is it wise to eat late and then sleep on a full stomach when you're pregnant? Tacos were certainly less exciting for Rosie, but not so much for me.

I was not going to rest easy until I dropped her off at her grandmother's. My emotions were too heightened for my taste. Motherhood makes a woman hysterical. It's probably the reason why Sarah acts like she does. I was not enjoying this job; I was Rosie's godmother, an honorary title at best–I couldn't wait until the real mothers took over.

CHAPTER 40

SARAH

I called Aunt Marion about a ride to the hospital for the following morning, and she asked if I had packed a bag. I hadn't even thought about that and Christine said I'd be in the hospital for three to four days. Aunt Marion said she'd come over to give me a hand. By the time she arrived I wasn't feeling well. I was very dizzy and had a terrific headache. I got worse after telling her about Rosie, Joe, Sharon and my battle plans to rescue Rosie. She did not want to hear another word–she was taking me to the hospital immediately; and if I didn't call my doctor, she would.

* * *

Aunt Marion's pushiness continued after we arrived at the hospital; she insisted I call Joe. "I don't want to scare you or be morbid, but what if something happens to you, Sarah? Joe doesn't even know you're in the hospital and you're having complications." Is it ethical to use fear tactics to persuade someone? No, according to Paulee who coaches debate, but it worked–Aunt Marion convinced me; even though I had already planned to call him. Only once I was in the hospital–which was supposed to be tomorrow. I had wanted to wait until he was with Rosie. She was more important than me; I had support.

Joe had texted before I called Aunt Marion to say he was about to board his plane for Raleigh, which I took as a good omen–he wasn't driving. Later he texted when he landed in North Carolina. That's the real reason I acquiesced to Aunt Marion's direction. It wasn't her scare tactics that moved me to contact him. He was probably with Rosie already or very close. The problem now was he wasn't answering my calls. I called Sharon's landline too, even though I knew that would be a big waste of time.

I finally asked Aunt Marion to try. She had no better luck reaching Joe on his cell than I did, but there was progress forward–Sharon picked up on her landline after two rings. Aunt Marion introduced herself as Rosie's great-aunt. She told her that Joe was on his way for a visit, which put me into a panic. I was having second thoughts about tipping Sharon off. We were so close to getting Rosie out of there to screw up now. Aunt Marion read my distress as coming from my condition and patted my hand. She continued her conversation. She asked Sharon to give Joe a message from Sarah–to call as soon as he arrived.

"I still don't know why you didn't want me to tell her you were in the hospital and it was urgent, Sarah."

"If you said that she'd tell him I died and it wasn't necessary for him to return to Minnesota. He could just move in with her and Rosie." That's when she was convinced my pregnancy complications were affecting my mind, and maybe she was right. It was a ludicrous thing to say but I had enough wits to tell her to call my friend Paulee. I didn't trust Sharon to deliver any message from me to Joe, urgent or not. I told her she could give Paulee all the details as I was being wheeled away. I was confident that Sharon would be outmatched. She might be able to manipulate Joe but she didn't stand a chance with Paulee.

The day I scheduled my non-emergency C-section, Christine asked me if I preferred an epidural or general anesthesia. I remember thinking at the time–*you're the doctor, shouldn't you know which is best for me?* In retrospect I have to admit that I never cut her a break. Whether she gave me agency or not–I complained. I blame it on hormones and the on-going friction we have with one another. In spite of this, I had replied politely that day, "What do you think?" She preferred general anesthesia due to my high blood pressure. She didn't verbalize it, but it was clear to me she thought if I were awake there was a good chance of it going higher. It was also to her advantage–she wouldn't need to hear my questions, comments, screams and curses. Do women even scream or curse during a C-section? I didn't know anyone personally who had one, and I had nothing to compare the experience to since I had a vaginal birth with Rosie. Vaginal delivery had met my expectations, and I screamed and cursed during a significant part of the birthing. It was one of the most painful experiences in my life–worse than breaking my arm in the third grade when I fell off the jungle gym.

For the emergency-C I wasn't given an option, but it was a no brainer. Christine didn't have to convince me. The idea of having general anesthesia was appealing. I wouldn't mind skipping the pain of labor. Yes–knock me out and when I wake a sweet babe at my breast? Sounds good to me.

❖

It wasn't clear at first where I was when I opened my eyes, until I felt pain in my lower body; it also felt like I couldn't move my legs. It registered–I was in a hospital. I must have been in a car accident, or a truck had crushed me from the navel down. When I looked for the button to summon a nurse, I noticed my breasts were leaking. They were also tender, which was only a mild irritation compared to the pain in the lower part of my body, and why it took me so long to realize: I hadn't been in an accident where all the organs below my navel were crushed; I had awakened from my C-section operation–where was my baby?

My question acted like the cue for the nurse's entrance, but I wasn't sure if she was indeed a nurse. She looked like she was twelve (she might have been one of those high school volunteers, but she was dressed like a nurse). It didn't matter, nurse or a volunteer, I wanted to see my baby so I asked her: "Where is he?"

"He, who? Your husband?"

"No, my baby." She then laughed at me. Is this something they were encouraging in nursing school now–laughing at your patients?

"You had a baby girl. You've been waking up and going back to sleep for twelve hours now, but we did tell you. You must have forgotten." I didn't completely trust her, and then I got annoyed. She wanted me to sit up and move around– "Doctor's orders." It hurt moving around; and didn't she realize I wanted to see my baby before I started an exercise program? She must have flunked new-mother/new-born etiquette in nursing school. When I asked if I could see my baby first she replied, "Oh, of course." She acted like it had been her original idea and not mine; she added, "Your husband is around somewhere too. I'll tell him you're awake."

She cranked up my bed and left, and when she returned with only the baby, no Joe, she placed her in my arms. She asked me if I had breastfed before. I told her I had, I didn't need her help, but I asked her to find Joe. I needed his help. This was definitely not our baby.

She was a pretty little thing but she didn't resemble Joe or me at all. It was her hair more than anything else which convinced me there had been some kind of mix-up. She had a full head of dark straight hair which capped her head. A look reminiscent of British rock singers on the covers of my mother's vinyl records from the 60's and early 70's. I had blonde hair and Joe had been blond when young.

She wasn't mine, but she still rooted around on my chest. She was hungry and I had leaking breasts. I figured I'd let her nurse and hoped someone was doing the same for my baby. I looked the picture of maternal bliss when Joe and the little nurse walked into the room. It made it all the more shocking when I said, "Joe, they gave us the wrong baby." He didn't ask me to expand but turned immediately to the nurse and asked, "Is she okay?' I couldn't complain about him not addressing me directly, I hadn't said hello to him or asked about Rosie either. But when the nurse said, "She may still be a little disoriented from the anesthesia," I had to clear this up for both of them–I was not disoriented.

"Joe, this is not our baby. She doesn't resemble us; look at the hair. We don't have dark hair." I saw the nurse shoot a glance at Joe when I said that, which made me add, "You were blond when you were a kid, it got dark when you got older." He knew that of course. I only said it for the nurse's benefit. Joe replied directly to me, ignoring the nurse.

"I don't think newborns resemble anybody but other newborns in spite of what people say. And don't forget genes in the family–my mother had dark hair." When he mentioned his mother and genes, I remembered that my maternal grandmother had also been a brunette. How had I forgotten it? Perhaps I was a little foggy and this was our baby.

After she finished nursing, Joe held her while my nurse (who I learned was named Angie), helped me get out of the bed and walk to the bathroom. It hurt terribly to walk, squat and pee–so much for skipping the pain of labor. I hadn't anticipated this much post-operative pain. Why hadn't Christine prepared me for this? The birth is over, shouldn't the big pains be over too? I wanted to shriek, curse and shake my fist in the air, but I didn't. And I wasn't trying to be a well-behaved patient. No; the reason for my subdued behavior? It hurt too much to express myself.

There won't be a next time for me, but if a pregnant woman asked for advice I'd tell them– "If there isn't a medical emergency and you have a choice–choose a vaginal delivery. It will be painful but you're able to scream and curse and you're forgiven–they expect you to do that." You'll also be awake throughout, less chance of a baby mix-up.

CHAPTER 41

ROSIE

I was surprised by my mother, but more so by my father who didn't call me. My fears had been confirmed–they were replacing me with their new kid–they were starting a whole new family. That's when I decided I could do the same. I didn't need them. I would not give this baby up for adoption. I would start a whole new family of my own. I started to think of the baby as mine–instead of *it* or *Heathcliff's mistake*. If it was a boy I might even name him Heathcliff.

My decision to keep my baby didn't change after I found out my parents hadn't replaced me, it only strengthened. Even after Aunt Paulee told me how Sharon had lied and deceived me. What a weirdo, I never thought she'd try to keep me from my parents. I only suspected something at the end, and I thought she was trying to steal the baby for her agency when I told her I changed my mind about giving it to them. But the thing now is Sharon has made me doubt everyone–I no longer trust the very idea of adoption. I don't want to give my baby to anybody.

It bothers me too to think Leslie might have been aware of her mother's deception, even if we weren't really friends anymore. If she knew what her mother had been doing all along and didn't tell me, it sucks. Nerds aren't all the same; there is no universal morality. My father would have told me about Sharon if he had known.

It was pretty exciting when my father and Aunt Paulee showed up at Sharon's house after I called my mother–like a covert rescue team. Aunt Paulee scared me though suggesting Sharon might attack us with a knife. She told me later she was only making a joke. She said Sharon was so hung up on my father she was acting like the woman character in *Fatal Attraction*. I didn't know what she was talking about except she scared me with the knife shit. And the way I see it, the only thing that suffered anything *fatal* was my phone. I never got it back from Sharon. Aunt Paulee said "fuck the phone you can get a new one," when I complained. She apologized for scaring me but was more annoyed because I said her joke was lame.

She's always making jokes and references to movies she saw when she was a teenager. The 1980's must have been good film years for her and I asked her if *Fatal Attraction* was satirical like *Villains*. She never saw that one, but said her movie was not funny. That's why I still don't get why she said she was *making a joke*. She needs to see new movies so she can update her references and get better jokes. And there was nothing funny about Sharon taking my phone. I also blame her for my mother's high blood pressure because she lied to her and raised her stress level. Probably the reason Aunt Paulee said *fuck the phone;* a person's health is more important than any phone.

Sharon is another bitch, she lied to everyone including my father–so much for being madly in love with him. It didn't stop her from deceiving him. I'm glad they got me away from her, but my father should have kicked her butt. At least three times, for him, Mom and me. Aunt Paulee said talking like that is not good for the baby, and the important thing had been a safe exit from her house with no one harmed. No matter how much she protests I think she really thought Sharon might have hurt us. Some joke.

✦━━━━✦━━━━✦

Later in the evening when Aunt Paulee and I were settled in our motel room my great-aunt Marion called to let us know my mother had a baby girl. She said my mother and the baby were fine, but it was "a little touch and go" for a while. Why can't old people be straight and simply say what they mean? I asked Aunt Paulee what she actually meant and she said, "Your mother had a narrow escape–she almost had a stroke." That's when I found out how serious it was but I would have preferred that Aunt Marion had said that. *Touch and go* has a more playful tone than a *stroke.* I wanted it straight-out even if it makes me feel bad for all the mean things I've thought and said about my mother. And I'm glad she's okay even if I was right–she was too old to have a baby. Sharon might have made my mom's health worse, but the real stressor was her pregnancy.

I'm happy I finally got a sister though. A real one–I don't need Leslie, and I hope I never see her again. She's a nerdy bitch. My baby sister has a genetic chance of becoming one too, thanks to our parents. But the odds of her becoming a weirdo are even higher than becoming a bitch or a nerd. I'm having a kid the same age as her–she'll be my kid's aunt. It is not supposed to be this way–it has to affect normal development.

The next morning Aunt Paulee dropped off the rental car and we flew to New Jersey. We were heading to my Granny Nessie's house when Aunt Marion called Aunt Paulee again. I answered her phone this time because I was playing games on it. Aunt Marion told me she was still the official messenger. "I called to let you know what your baby sister's name is. They're keeping your mother so drugged for the pain she can't keep her eyes open."

They named her Brandy but Aunt Marion didn't think my father liked it very much. It was a pretty name but it sounded like one my mother would choose, not my father. He probably agreed because he didn't want to upset her. Aunt Marion ended the call saying my mother would try to reach out to me in the evening; it was how the discussion of names for my baby came up.

Aunt Paulee was surprised, she thought I was giving the baby up for adoption. I told her I had changed my mind. I asked her not to mention it to my mom; I wanted to tell her and Daddy myself. Aunt Paulee is one of those people who often starts a conversation with my mother: "I'm not supposed to tell anyone this–swear you won't tell a soul," and then blabs a secret she had been entrusted with. She swore she would not say a word about me keeping the baby to anyone, but I got the impression she thought my change-of-mind was a bad idea.

Still, I don't think she'll blab this time because she said Mom needed rest. She might get upset about me keeping my baby, but I could talk about it with *Aunt Paulee* as much as I liked. I told her if the baby was a boy I might name him Heathcliff. She asked me how I came up with the name. I told her to take a wild guess, and added it shouldn't be too hard for her because it was related to her job. She immediately said, "Heathcliff, from *Wuthering Heights*? I'm impressed, Rosie, so erudite of you." I am going to have to look up *erudite*; I'm not completely sure of the meaning, but it was clear she was really impressed I had chosen a name from literature. It's also my nickname for the guy who knocked me up, but she doesn't need to know that. Besides, there's still a connection to *Wuthering Heights*.

And Aunt Paulee never asked me about the father of my baby. My mother had told her I got pregnant with some guy I barely knew when I was drunk at a party. A positive thing about Aunt Paulee, and my mom–they didn't moralize about it like Leslie. They never shamed me about sleeping with a guy I hardly knew. My guess, they both had done it themselves. Of course Mom said I was stupid because I was drunk and didn't use birth control, and had actually screamed, "For the future, if you want to drink at parties–get on the pill." It was about lack of judgment, not morality.

She and Aunt Paulee are pretty liberal in their thinking when it comes to sex, but clearly out of touch on other current ideas, which is surprising since they both teach young adults. That happens when a teacher listens to their own talk too much and not enough to their students. When I told Aunt Paulee I was going to name my baby Billie if she was a girl, after my favorite female singer, she actually asked if it was Billie Holiday. She makes references to moldy-oldy movies and doesn't know one of the most popular singers of the day. Yet, she and my mother will blame people my age for the miscommunication between generations.

Aunt Paulee said she didn't like the name–too masculine sounding. After she said that I was firm about naming my baby *Billie* if I had a girl. I even decided Billie would be the name if I had a boy. It didn't matter; it was to honor my favorite singer and gender is fluid these days. A concept people like Aunt Paulee and my mom don't understand–they're too old.

The discussion with Aunt Paulee over baby names motivated me. I made the decision right then to take an active role with my baby sister's education. The age of parents and relatives was definitely a factor–increasing the odds of Brandy getting weird. I had to try to save her.

CHAPTER 42

SARAH

I was in the hospital for four days, and when Joe brought Brandy and me home he had set up the crib, which had been in a box for two months. Neither one of us had been moved to put it together–we did not have a room for a nursery to encourage us. Joe moved the Victorian settee by the windows to make space for the crib. For me, it was an intentional arc: lust, conception, and Brandy in her crib where the Victorian Settee had been. Joe also put Mother Goose wallpaper on the wall next to the crib, and attached a mobile of cows and moons, which dangled over the crib like astronauts bouncing around in space. He was trying his best to make a little alcove of sorts for our baby in the studio apartment, but it was clear we needed to find a bigger place to live.

Brandy had not only been a *rarity baby,* she was instrumental in making Joe soften to the idea of buying a free-standing house which would afford more space than a townhouse. I am amenable to anything at this point but wish we could buy one online the way people buy cars. I am in no shape to walk around looking at real estate. I find it challenging enough to walk to the bathroom, kitchen, and my desk where I keep my computer, and it's a shame too since the weather is pleasant to look at properties; it will turn cold in eight weeks or less.

We are going to be a very close-knit family for a while, but it won't be a problem because we do not need marital privacy. For the first time in my life sex is the last thing on my mind and sometimes I worry a new arc will never be reset. I don't need sex, I need sleep, and fortunately Brandy is a very good baby and settles quickly. Rosie had been the same until Joe spoiled her. He hadn't been able to stand even the slightest whimper before running to pick her up when I put her down for a nap or the night. It may be too early to determine for sure, but it seems as though he has evolved. He agrees with me that it is possible to spoil a baby? Or maybe he's just not as energetic as he was twenty-one years ago.

A week and a half after I had Brandy I had to start my online classes making it a necessity to walk; my computer sat on a small desk a room's length away from where I usually lounge. At least I had the foresight to ask for online sections for the fall semester. I hadn't expected to feel so lousy, but I knew I didn't want to teach in-person if possible. My department head had approved my request but I had to take a teachers' course for online teaching during the summer before the semester started.

When I put in my request, I envisioned the type of online classes I had taken as a student. I only took two, but I remembered how I would often work into the middle of the night–stoned out of my mind; it didn't matter. There was flexibility as long as my assignments were in on time. I was able to choose when, where and how I did my work. I planned to breast-feed rather than smoke pot now but it was with the same mindset. The flexibility to arrange my instruction and class around my schedule with no structured class times, only structured due dates. I was surprised when I discovered the online classes I would be teaching were hybrid. At first I panicked, did it mean I would have to teach weekly in-person classes? It wasn't that challenging, but I was teaching five sections and each class required a real-time web-cam session each week.

I had no autonomy to change it, and I had to function with a baby, a dog and a husband sharing my teaching space. It also meant I couldn't wear my baggy tops–convenient for pulling out a boob on short notice, and I had to wear makeup and fix my hair. In other words, I had to look presentable. I was a professor, not a lactating woman with a sore twat who needed ten minutes to walk across the room.

I decided to take my neighbor Mimi up on her offer to watch Brandy while I was teaching. Mimi had approached me when she saw I was pregnant, and had asked if I would be needing a babysitter. *Approached* is not really the correct image. I was about to go into my apartment and Mimi called out to me. She stood inside her door shouting and gesturing until I walked over to her. She told me she had hurt her back in a car accident and was on permanent disability, but she needed to earn more money. Even though she said she was on disability for her back, I also suspected it was more. I had never seen her outside of our apartment building since I moved in two years ago. My gut feeling was she was harmless though and it was convenient–she was directly across the hall from my apartment. If there were an emergency I could tell my students to work independently while I checked it out. (After I had Brandy I only pleaded with fate if something did warrant me to leave a class that it happened later in the semester–allowing space for my walking-time to improve).

I continued to debate with myself about hiring Mimi until she said she'd watch Holly too, it was hard to pass up. I only had one reservation–Sid. Sid was Mimi's large African Gray parrot who was bigger than Brandy and my dog. Mimi said I shouldn't worry, "Sid is a lamb." She told me he slept right next to her in bed every night wrapped in a towel, but I also saw him break a shelled nut with his beak like it was a soft cookie. She assured me she would keep him in his cage when she was babysitting. We agreed to that and there was only one slight problem–when he was caged he shouted obscenities. Mimi had inherited Sid from her father who taught him his spicy lexicon. I already had one daughter with a guttermouth and now my infant daughter would be hearing a parrot cursing. What would her first word be after listening to a cursing parrot for fifteen and a half weeks? It was kind of funny but I knew Joe wouldn't see the humor–so I didn't tell him, and I never asked him to get Brandy from Mimi's if I was late ending a class. I was afraid Sid would tell him he was "a cock-sucking bastard" when he walked in the door.

On the days I taught my real-time classes I pumped my breasts and prepared bottles for Mimi before bringing Brandy and Holly to her apartment. If Joe was home he'd offer to take Brandy to Mimi's and I always told him no– "I need the exercise." It was true, my doctor told me I should move; but I didn't start my exercise program due to what my doctor had said–it was because of Sid and his foul mouth.

Crying or barking weren't the only distractions I was concerned about when I taught–Joe was also one. He did not have a nine to five job and often worked from home. I felt awful that he was making business calls from the bathroom. Occasionally when he had to make a video call, he hung up a sheet as a make-shift backdrop to block out his surroundings. I was grateful he wasn't asking me to teach in the bathroom, but the thought of him in there bothered me. It didn't bother our dog at all; she was happy when Joe worked from home–she stayed in the bathroom with him. Mimi told me Holly was terrified of Sid and she hid under her couch the entire time when she stayed with her. She tried to coax her out with dog biscuits but she wouldn't budge.

Mimi assured me Brandy didn't mind Sid. "She laughs at him and recently started cooing and making sounds like a little pigeon when he talks." Was this supposed to make me feel reassured? Talks? "Fuck Irene" was not a laughing matter no matter who the woman was. I did not anticipate hearing my baby's first words like most mothers because of her exposure to Sid. Imagining *bitch* coming out of her sweet little mouth kept me up some nights. How would I ever explain it to Joe?

Rosie had her baby three weeks after I had Brandy. For two and a half weeks prior to the birth we talked more than we had in years. She was nervous about labor, and I told her it was a natural phenomenon. In some parts of the world women delivered while working and then went immediately back to work. She countered by bringing up my recent experience. I stressed how my second delivery was not normal, and how she was young and healthy. She also worried about the pain–she had a low pain threshold. She took after me in that respect but I assured her: "the pain is intense but it comes in waves with breaks in-between." And the proximity of the intense pain to them placing the baby in my arms had been near enough for me to forget about it. But I decided it was better not to mention this last stage when the pain is an overpowering crushing force. Instead I said, "If I could take it, you can too."

She took my last statement as a criticism rather than a compliment about her strength as it was intended. It was the exception to an otherwise positive experience talking to Rosie over those two and a half weeks. I had nearly forgotten about the friction which usually exists between us because our conversations were so pleasant, until it fully resurfaced.

It happened shortly after Rosie told me about Sharon and the adoption she was instrumental in arranging for her baby. I always say if I know someone long enough I will eventually find some common ground with them, no matter how different they may be. Joe was not the only thing Sharon and I agreed on. *Rosie was not able to care for a baby–adoption was a good idea.*

Sharon had not handled it well though by pushing one particular agency. She had focused on the agency over the welfare of the mother and baby so it was clear Sharon and I were not about to become buddies. I offered many different types of adoptions Rosie could explore–private and those arranged through different agencies; religious and secular. Rosie should have the autonomy to choose what was best for herself and her baby, and if she wanted an open adoption she could choose that. She let me rattle on about adoption options until four days before she gave birth, and I finally asked, "Don't you think you should start making some plans for the adoption?" She told me she planned to keep her baby and I replied– "You can't care for a baby." It was a reflex, without forethought or temperance–no measured volume or critical tone removed.

Joe was working at his laptop during my call with Rosie and after it was finished asked, "What was that all about?" Joe has this way about him which suggests he is not aware of what's going on, but he always seems to know what's happening most of the time in spite of it. He doesn't usually eavesdrop but he was being a little disingenuous. He must have heard enough even hearing only one side of the conversation to figure out what was going on. I indulged him anyway and gave him all the details–only to be rewarded with a reprimand. "Why are you always trying to control her, Sarah? Let her make her own decisions about her baby."

Curious how one single word can change the entire meaning and intention of a communication. Joe chose the word *control*, I would choose *protect*. I needed to protect Rosie from making another mistake, but I was not going to get any help from him.

When I called Rosie back my mother answered the phone. "She doesn't want to talk to you, and I don't blame her. I just can't believe you are urging her to give up her baby. It's unnatural, Sarah. How on earth did you come up with this idea about adoption?" I defended myself–it wasn't my original idea–it was Rosie herself who had wanted to give up her baby.

"Well she doesn't want that anymore. Enough said. You upset her," and my mother told me she didn't want to discuss it further. Another person I wouldn't be getting any help from.

I asked Paulee if Rosie had mentioned keeping the baby when she was with her. She told me she knew about it since North Carolina, but Rosie asked her not to say anything because she wanted to tell me herself. I started to moan and lament about Rosie's decision until I was abruptly cut short by Paulee.

"It's her baby. If she wants to keep it, why shouldn't she? I think you're more upset about being identified as a grandmother." Paulee could be surgically cutting at times.

It was such an unfair thing for her to say. Rosie was about to ruin her life if she kept the baby–that was what I was upset about, even if there was a miniscule thread of truth in what Paulee said. She knew I held a different perspective on the notion of grandparents from other women my age. We had friends who as soon as their daughters hit a viable age urged them to marry and have children as soon as possible. They couldn't wait to be grandmothers.

"I've told you before, Paulee, becoming a grandmother only reminds me I'm one step closer to death."

"Exactly, Sarah, and that's why people are so happy to have grandchildren–they know they will live on through them. Your sister has no children; aren't you happy that Rosie is able to give you a grandchild, and the Laarsen side of the family will continue?" What was wrong with Paulee? I do want Rosie to have children in the future, even if grandparenting is not a big priority in my life, but the operative word is *future*–not now. Rosie has no husband, job or degree, and she's in no position to care for a child.

Paulee switched to other topics as though Rosie and her baby were mere blips in my life, but she ended our conversation with, "I gotta go, talk to you later, Grandma." I told her if she ever called me that again I would hang up on her. She said she was only joking around, but it was clear I wasn't getting help from her. I struck out three times.

Is it because Joe, my mother and Paulee all think I am a controlling, unnatural woman who doesn't want grandchildren?

CHAPTER 43

PAULEE

Nessie called me at 8:30 am to tell me Rosie was going into labor. She also pleaded with me to get there as soon as possible–she couldn't handle Rosie's "histrionics." I asked her if something was wrong and she said she didn't think so. She explained how Rosie had been okay until she called her mother. "Rosie wanted Sarah to fly to New Jersey to be with her, and Sarah told her she was in no shape to do that, and she had her three-week-old baby sister to consider. Joe is coming, but it doesn't calm her. Now she's saying she can't stand the pain, which is ridiculous at this stage."

It was too much to take in and I never had a kid, I have no idea how labor pain feels. Nessie had experienced it twice. She was in her late seventies though, did she forget what it was like? The only response I could come up with was that I was sure they would give Rosie something for the pain once she got to the hospital. Nessie shouted at me then, "They won't this early. I know, I was a nurse for forty years. Please get here as fast as you can, Paulee. I'm too old for this."

I wasn't working; I was on my previously scheduled leave to help Sarah. Rosie's delivery was falling in the time frame of Sarah's originally scheduled C-section when I had planned to be in Minneapolis to help her. I joked with Sarah how it was very convenient, a coincidence that she and Rosie got "knocked up at the same time." Sarah did not think it was funny; she's lost her sense of humor.

I left my house as soon as I could, but I was going to hit the tail-end of the morning commute. I wasn't that concerned because I thought Nessie had to be exaggerating. I've only experienced one woman in labor and Sarah was only loud in the final stages–when Joe was no use at all. He made me understand why the tradition started to keep husbands out of the delivery room. If Joe was coming, I prayed that he would arrive after the birth of his grandchild because I don't want to take care of him and Rosie.

◆―――◆―――◆

Nessie left the room as soon as I arrived; she needed a break. She wasn't exaggerating, but Rosie seemed to be in real pain. I flagged down a nurse and demanded she give Rosie an epidural. My sister and sister-in-law had been given them so why wasn't Rosie given one? The nurse said the doctor wouldn't prescribe one until Rosie was dilated two to three centimeters. I asked why and she simply said it was too early. I didn't think she was brushing me off, in spite of her curt manner, but I continued to argue with her. I was telling it to her as I saw it; I didn't care if she was a nurse. We both had eyes and ears–she wasn't using hers: "Can't you see she's in great pain? I don't care if she's in an early stage of labor. There must be something wrong." She gave me a funny look but didn't sound argumentative when she replied, "Trust me, if something is wrong, it has nothing to do with the labor or the baby." Was she trying to politely say Rosie was a drama queen? I wasn't sure, but her statement made me take notice for the first time that I did not hear any other women screaming, crying or cursing on the entire floor. It was going to be a long day and it got worse. Rosie was even scolded by one of the nurses. I thought she was rather rude, but she only said what I wanted to say–I couldn't fault her.

Rosie calmed down a little after she got the epidural but not enough for my liking. I asked a nurse why Rosie continued to complain about the pain, and she told me while epidurals reduced about eighty percent of the intense pain they didn't eliminate all of it. Couldn't they knock her out and give her a C-section like her mother? Since that was not an option I had to put up with her, and like Nessie, I needed a break.

Nessie hadn't left the hospital, but like the nurses only made occasional drop-ins to see how Rosie was doing. Yes, she was a retired nurse, but was she confused–mixing up her role description now? She was Rosie's grandmother and a soon to be great-grandmother of Rosie's baby–not some fucking nurse. I was only *Aunt Paulee*; I wasn't even Rosie's real aunt, but it didn't matter–I was left alone with Rosie by myself for most of the time.

I tried to distract Rosie with gossip about my students; it didn't work. I guess she had to know them personally for it to be of interest so I massaged her feet and neck to ease her distress until I had to stop. I couldn't trust myself not to strangle her. This was not good; I came to help her, not kill her. I was finally joined by nurses and the doctor when Rosie went into the final stage of labor. My role now was to keep wiping her brow and to yell–*push*, and after eight hours of labor I also needed my brow wiped. When they put her baby boy in her arms she said: "Please take him away. I'm so tired." She wasn't the only one, but when she refused to hold him the nurse handed him to me.

I have held my nieces and nephews but I was so tired I was afraid I'd drop him. Fortunately his mother hadn't drained all of the strength from my body, and I held him steady in my arms for a few minutes. There was definitely a family resemblance, he could be Brandy's twin. He had a full head of black hair just like his aunt. I looked at his little scrunched-up face and whispered, "Good luck, kid. You're going to need it."

◆————◆————◆

After my long day of labor was over I headed to Nessie's house. I was staying with her for three days to help out with Rosie and the baby. Rosie would be coming home from the hospital the following day (if they didn't throw her out earlier). Her screaming had stopped after the birth to be replaced with whining and complaining. She was only quiet when she slept (a blessed relief for the staff). I felt sorry for Nessie; how will she be able to handle Rosie once I leave? I will never complain about Anthony being high-maintenance again.

I was exhausted but it was too early to go to sleep. Nessie and I took to her deck looking at the river–drinking some very good South African port. It was pleasantly warm; the weather was stalled in summer and there wasn't even a hint of imminent fall. Around 10 pm I went into the kitchen to get some more chips and I heard a knock on the door–Joe had arrived.

He told us he had gone to the hospital but it was past visiting hours. They wouldn't let him see Rosie or the baby. There were no exceptions made unless you were the father. I told him he should have said he was the father since he and Rosie had the same surname.

"There's men your age who divorce their wives, marry younger women and start second families, Joe."

"Not funny, Paulee." He didn't sound angry exactly but he was looking at me like I had just suggested he was having an incestuous relationship with his daughter. It annoyed me. I have to admit Sarah is right when she says he's odd at times. Give me a break, I did hard labor with his daughter all day–but I was too tired to defend myself. I changed the subject instead.

"So, how does it feel being a grandpa, Joe?"

"I don't know yet, but I can't wait to see him." At least Nessie and Joe seemed happy about his arrival, and I mentioned how Rosie didn't want to hold him after the birth.

"Well, she just went through an emotional experience. She has to gain her footing." She wasn't the only one (another thought best left unsaid). He then continued to advocate for his daughter.

"It takes time for some women to bond with their babies, I guess." It wasn't my experience with Sarah and other women I knew, but what did I know about any of this? I never had a baby; I've only had kittens. They're easy to bond with immediately because they are so damn cute and easily potty trained. I agreed with Joe that women are not all the same though, which prompted me to say, "Humans should be like ducks; ducks bond with their babies as soon as they hatch." Joe then made one of his razor-sharp observations: "Well, Rosie's not a duck, Paulee." He irritates Sarah when he says stuff like that, ignoring the main point of a discussion (which this evening was Rosie's lack of maternal instinct). He seemed to be also irritating Nessie by the sounds of it when she entered into our conversation. She had her eye on the main point.

"She didn't even want to nurse him. I told her there were important nutrients in mother's milk that the baby needed immediately. I encouraged her to at least nurse him for a few days and then she could switch to formula. They are only going to pump her breasts and toss it out." Nessie continued describing how she finally got Rosie to nurse, but only for a short time. I had missed that; it must have been when I went to get a sandwich and coffee from the vending machine. Joe appeared to be too uncomfortable with this topic to continue defending his daughter, and I wanted to change the direction of the conversation–I had enough of Rosie for one day. Sarah would be a welcomed neutral topic for us.

"So, Joe, why do you think Sarah is so averse to being called grandma?"

"She has a hard time facing the fact she's getting older, like all of us."

I believe she also has a fear of her beauty fading. There's an advantage to not being a beautiful woman. I don't have to worry about not looking good when I'm older because I never looked that great when I was young. I read a biography about the 1930's film star Hedy Lamarr who had been a great beauty in her day, and when she aged had a number of cosmetic surgeries. This was when they were uncommon and more dangerous–and not very effective. At least Sarah was only kidding when she said she'd like to have a complete body make-over when she was out during her C-section, but it was on her mind–the plight of beautiful women.

Another truth is, I do not worry about my visual appearance as I'm getting older because I'm actually improving with age. My boobs are bigger. The rest of my body is fatter too, but I continue to view myself as a fine red wine–better with age. Sarah must think of herself as a sparkling white wine. She still sparkles and she's a good vintage, but it's true–they don't age well.

CHAPTER 44

SARAH

Rosie gave birth to Brandy's nephew in the same month Brandy was born. It was also a few days before great-great Aunt Elsbeth's birthday, who would turn one hundred and six if she were still alive. My mother bakes a cake (buys one more often these days) to celebrate every year; Aunt Elsbeth had been her favorite aunt. "We have three September birthdays in the family now," my mother gleefully pointed out–she was thrilled.

Rosie named her baby Billie Joseph Janak. Was the middle name a diplomatic ploy to win over Joe? If so, it had not been necessary. He was truly happy about Rosie's baby–he even got a son of sorts in addition to a new daughter. I was the one who was not thrilled or happy and I wished I could be. I wanted to keep the lines of communication open between Rosie and me. There were plans to be made–she couldn't do this alone and Joe wanted Rosie to be part of all the decisions that were made–with one exception. We had to work out between us what we were able to offer her before bringing her into the discussions. Spoken like the professional salesman he was for the majority of his working life. Joe was insightful and helpful mapping out our negotiations with Rosie. But there was one position not changing–Rosie was hell-bent on keeping this baby. I had to accept it–Rosie and I needed a mediator.

My friend Evelyn came to mind. I met her at a departmental meet-and-greet the first semester I started teaching at the college. I was growing weary of only men approaching me the entire evening, and at the first chance I had to break away I saw Evelyn sitting by herself on a window box seat with a glass of wine. If no women wanted to take the initiative to meet me–I'd do it myself. The only reservation I had was I hoped she wasn't trying to avoid people. The meet-and-greet was taking place in a lovely old Victorian house with lots of nooks and crannies where one could hide. She had chosen a place set off from the main room where the festivities were taking place, but it's not like it was a closet space under a staircase. She could be seen and I found her, but if she didn't want to engage, I'd get it–unlike many of the men who had approached me.

As soon as I went over to her we made our intro-ductions, and I asked her what she taught. She said psychology; I didn't say a word in response but she caught my puzzled expression. "I know, I'm not in this department at this school. I get confused sometimes because I also teach at the university and there my psychology class is in the Mathematics and Sciences department. I saw the notice for this event and after I arrived it hit me: psychology is housed in the liberal arts department here. I figured they wouldn't mind if

I had a glass of wine before I left. Don't tattle on me." I assured her, "your secret is safe with me," and she didn't leave. We spent the rest of the evening together, and I didn't meet anyone from my department for the rest of the meet-and-greet.

It was really preferable. The truth was I identified with her more than the full-time professors in my department. She was an adjunct–teaching at two schools–a rank I had held for over ten years. It went beyond simple identification though; I was more comfortable with her than I was with my colleagues. She seemed to share those same sentiments when she told me I was the first full-time professor she met who acted like they wanted to be friends, and we have remained friends ever since.

◆———◆———◆

Evelyn wanted to visit me and to see Brandy. We made a date for her to stop by on a Friday–the only day we both weren't teaching. It would be just the two of us and the baby. Joe was in New Jersey visiting Rosie and our *grandson*, whom I preferred to call *Rosie's baby* or Billie. Joe told me to get over it. "It doesn't matter what you call him, Sarah, he's still your grandson." That is true but at least I know his name. Joe calls him *William* most of the time.

"His name is Billie, not William, Joe."

"But isn't Billie a nickname for William?"

"Yes, but his name is Billie." In spite of me correcting him, he continues to call him William, Will or Bill.

I was glad Joe would be gone, I wanted to seek some advice from Evelyn to improve my relationship with Rosie. I wasn't afraid of him interfering, but I wanted to have a private *consultation* with her. She held a PhD in cognitive psychology and taught a course called "Using Psychology to Solve Conflict" at the university. She was also a certified mediator in addition to teaching. She only worked with couples going through divorces, but also taught Adolescent Psychology, and I was sure she could combine principles from her class with her mediating skills to help me with my conflict. She wouldn't be truly mediating anyway–it was only me she'd hear–no Rosie, but any advice would be welcomed. I needed help.

Joe told me I had to listen to Rosie more. I always retorted– "I do listen to her." That was the problem–I heard her and didn't like what she said. I needed a mediator, and Evelyn agreed to help. Surprisingly she voiced similar *do's and don'ts* that Joe did, but for some reason when she said them they sounded reasonable instead of annoying. It might have been simply because she was more structured than him. He was too abstract, and his *do's and don'ts* sounded like criticisms. Evelyn was clear, specific and non-judgmental.

When she discussed listening, she didn't open by telling me it was something I *should do*–instead, she asked me if I did it. I responded with "of course–I'm not hard of hearing." She countered with: "There is a difference between hearing and listening. Hearing takes very little effort, but you need more energy to listen. You need to use your mind as well as your ears." She then asked me how I knew I was listening. I didn't know how to answer her question so I said for a second time that there was nothing wrong with my hearing, and she said, "I'm not talking about your ear health, Sarah. You may be able to hear but not be able to listen effectively at the same time, because hearing is not listening."

I was an obtuse *student*. She had to approach her question from a different direction– "Sometimes understanding a concept is easier when we explore what it's not, instead of what it is." She asked me if I interrupted Rosie or multi-tasked when I talked to her. I admitted to both. "You're not listening when you do either of those things."

I assured her (just like I had Joe), that when I interrupted I was listening. I heard every word and it's why I needed to interject my opinions. Evelyn asked me to explain the intention of my conversation– "Why are you talking to Rosie?" Rosie needed help and I wanted to help her. "Okay, but you can't help her if you don't listen to what she needs. Presuming she really wants your help, of course. When we want to help someone we need to use empathic listening–which requires the most energy of any listening objective. You don't judge the other person when you listen empathically and it takes energy to be nonjudgmental." In other words, with academic framing, she was telling me to stop interrupting Rosie.

She explained how every time I interrupted I was judging her. "We all need to feel autonomous, Sarah, especially people of Rosie's age." Evelyn told me if I wanted to help Rosie I couldn't threaten her need to be independent–she'd turn away from me and I wouldn't be able to help. Evelyn suggested I pose a set of questions– "let Rosie answer them, and don't interrupt or evaluate her answers." In addition, she told me not to give advice unless Rosie asked for it, and to frame my responses with: *If I were you*–I would whatever, and never say–*you should* whatever. I now could see why Evelyn said it took energy to listen–I was drained already.

Evelyn also told me I had to stop multitasking. "I don't care who is doing it. There is no way each task can be addressed equally. You need to give Rosie your undivided attention, especially with your history of estrangements where she has felt abandoned by you. And I'm just curious, Sarah. What kind of multitasking are you doing?" I told her it wasn't like I was balancing my checkbook or correcting papers, I was nursing Brandy.

"Oh, my God, Sarah; you have a sister, you should know better. What about sibling rivalry?" Sibling rivalry? Rosie was twenty-one and Brandy was a four-week-old baby. Besides, Rosie was thrilled about Brandy. She had only seen her on our webcam calls but couldn't wait to meet her in the flesh.

"It doesn't matter. For Rosie to feel you are really listening to her you need to give her your full attention. And I am not disputing that she doesn't love her little sister, but where siblings exist there's always sibling rivalry–it's innate. And age has no bearing. My mother is seventy-eight and continues to argue with her seventy-five-year-old sister about their mother favoring one over the other–and their mother has been dead for eighteen years."

Evelyn's last question: "How do you indicate you're listening when you talk to Rosie?" I finally understood if I interrupted or nursed Brandy I sent unintentional messages that I wasn't listening, but now Evelyn was asking me how I showed I was. I did not have an answer.

"You can repeat her words back to her from time to time. Paraphrase what she has said so she knows you were listening to her. Simply say: *If I understand you correctly*–and paraphrase away. When you are on a webcam call you can also lean forward more in your chair and shake your head periodically to indicate you understand her." It truly was exhausting, but at least now I was aware of some concrete behaviors to avoid and practice–opposed to Joe's abstract criticisms which only made me fume. Evelyn had helped me enormously, and I was eager for my next conversation with Rosie to apply what I had learned.

After working with Evelyn I wasn't that surprised to discover Joe was a poor communication coach, but it was an eye opener to discover how weak I was as a communicator. This made me even more inclined to give Joe more credit where he was effective–as a skilled contract designer. When we discussed what we were able to offer Rosie he was clear and specific. Help was not an abstract idea but a detailed plan. We would ask Rosie what she wanted and in return tell her what we were able to give. Our main offer was to support her and her baby for one year. If she wanted to continue with school, she would need to move to Minneapolis where she could attend my college–free on my teacher's perk. We couldn't do both–support her and pay for school. I feared she would say she wanted to return to Florida. Joe told me to stop speculating and focus on what we were willing to give–he was firm. I realized Rosie was soon to meet Joe– *the skilled salesman*. Her overindulgent daddy would not be present.

CHAPTER 45

ROSIE

When I was pregnant old ladies would smile at me all the time, and younger women would sometimes ask if it was okay to touch my stomach. It was weird but I let them. It had to be they were women who wished to be pregnant themselves but due to health problems or no partners weren't. It's why I always said okay. They weren't truly weirdos–only sad or wishful. When I told Aunt Paulee about it she said I shouldn't allow strangers to touch me; she told me I had been lucky- "there are crazy kooks out there, Rosie." To make her point, she told me a gruesome story about a lady who tried to cut the baby right out of the stomach of a pregnant woman. I hoped it was a fictional account of something she had read or seen in a movie and not true–but it didn't matter. After she told me that I stopped letting women touch my stomach, and after I moved back to New Jersey nobody ever asked. It was probably a Southern practice; I always found people friendlier in the South compared to the North.

There's a natural niceness shown to pregnant women no matter where they are though. After I moved to New Jersey I still found total strangers who offered their seats or let me cut in front of them in lines. When my grandmother and I went to the grocery store, guys often volunteered to carry my bags to her car.

I also got attention and consideration from people I knew. Sharon had always asked if I was comfortable–did I want more air or less? Did I want an extra pillow for my feet or back? She also made me special dishes to eat, and Granny Nessie continued to do that. There were perks being pregnant, people were concerned about my comfort and well-being. After I had the baby–it shifted. It didn't matter how tired or sore I was–all the concern and attention was directed towards the baby.

I am not saying a newborn should not be considered but I had gone through an ordeal and nobody cared–strangers or people I knew. The pregnancy was awful–heartburn, headaches, and hemorrhoids, which I can't believe I still have. They won't go away, just like the memories of the labor. They told me it wouldn't hurt if I got the pain killer–they lied. They also didn't tell me they were going to cut me between my ass and cunt. The nurse explained, "the doctor needed to widen your vagina a bit so your baby's head could come through more easily." I'm glad he finally got out, but now it hurt even more when I tried to poop. First hemorrhoids, now this? Granny picked up where the nurse stopped and said, "It's called an episiotomy and it should heal in about three weeks, Rosie."

I don't care what the fuck you call it–another pain in my ass. I thought once the kid was out the pain and discomfort would be over. I'm still fat too. I asked Granny Nessie why I continued to look pregnant after the birth. She told me I had been all stretched out–it would take time to get my shape back. Aunt Paulee interjected how her sister never got her figure back. She wasn't helping, which is exactly my point. After I was no longer pregnant, nobody cared about how I felt–mentally or physically

My mother said I would forget all of the pain and the discomforts when they placed my baby in my arms (hard to believe how a thing that small hurts so much to push out). I didn't want to hold him. He was too small, and I had never held a newborn before. It took me an hour after his birth to finally get the nerve. Granny showed me how to support his head and it wasn't so scary. I cradled him in my arms just like Granny demonstrated–and I waited. My mother told me when I held him I would bond with him immediately. I felt nothing–another lie.

I tried and tried to bond–how do you do it if it doesn't happen naturally? No matter how I tried to have a positive outlook, I was an objective observer when I peered down at his little red, blotchy face and his black hair–which looked as though it had been glued to his head. I wondered: why do people say newborns are cute? There was nothing cute about him, unless they were referring to his size. His smallness was cute, but it didn't change my feelings of nothing-ness towards him. What was wrong with me? Was I a sociopath or a psycho mother? I'm not telling anyone what I'm thinking because I'm afraid I really am.

It's one of the reasons I finally gave in to Granny and nursed him. Maybe the bonding was delayed because I hadn't done it. My mother told me breastfeeding was one of her favorite experiences when I was a baby. She breastfed me for ten months and would have done it longer but she really wanted to smoke a joint and drink wine again. It was an indirect expression of how great breastfeeding is if a pothead like her was willing to stop smoking for ten months.

Breastfeeding is not a new topic for my mother. It has nothing to do with us both having newborns. I've been hearing her talk of its virtues my entire life. I always found it so embarrassing when she did it in front of my friends. She actually said once, "my boobs are not only decorative, they're functional," in front of Dorrie and a guy she was dating. Apparently her equipment continues to be functional–age hasn't dried them up. She nurses Brandy during every webcam call I have with her.

I told her my whole life that when I had a baby I didn't want to breastfeed–I was going to use formula and baby bottles. I feel that even more strongly now since I have a baby. I felt like a cow when I was pregnant, I don't want to continue feeling like a cow breastfeeding. My mother doesn't push it directly, she only suggests I at least try. I know by nursing in front of me she's trying to use a subtle form of persuasion. She repeatedly says how much joy she gets doing it. She always adds, "nursing is not for everyone, of course." She only says that so she can convince herself she isn't trying to convince me.

My mother can't say I'm not at least trying, but I have to ask her– "Why didn't you tell me it hurt?" Granny had been a pediatric nurse and she knew about nursing. She also knew it could hurt. She told me Billie isn't latching onto my nipple deep enough and that's why it's painful. It figures I'd give birth to a baby who doesn't know how to nurse–but it doesn't matter if Billie is slow, I don't want to breastfeed. We are a perfect match if you think about it that way. Granny says it sometimes takes a while for "mother and baby to get the knack," but there isn't any point to continue when the pain isn't helping me to bond any quicker.

On my last call with my mother I complained about my weight. She told me I could lose 1 to 2 pounds a month breastfeeding. It was the most positive thing I've heard about breastfeeding but I don't believe her. I've been told too many lies from everyone about everything.

◆――◆――◆

I only had to stay in the hospital for one day which was a good thing, but at the hospital there had been a bunch of nurses to take care of the baby. I was more comfortable holding him now but thinking about caring for him by myself was frightening. I worried for no reason. Once I got to Granny's house, Daddy, Paulee and Granny took over for the nurses where Billie was concerned.

I watched my father holding him. He was cradling him in his arms, singing and speaking softly to him. I was fascinated, I had never seen him with a baby before.

He had always taken care of me when I was young, but I didn't remember how he did it when I was an infant. He looked so comfortable and natural. Maybe there really was something wrong with me. He told me he was beautiful too. I still don't think that's true, even if he does look better now than he did after he was born (being born must be as traumatic as giving birth).

The only time I hold him is when I'm nursing, but I don't want to breastfeed anymore. I keep asking Granny when I can stop and how I do it exactly. She always changes the subject. I'm realizing for the first time how controlling my grandmother can be; I always thought it was only my mother who behaved that way–I was wrong. They are more alike than I ever imagined, but at least my mother is helping me, in spite of being a big proponent of breastfeeding.

When I told her I wanted to stop nursing she explained how to do it. She told me I needed to pump my breasts for a while and gradually switch Billie over to formula. I might also have to use ice packs if my breasts swelled, but according to her it was easy to stop. On a webcam call she showed me her electric breast pump. She paid over two hundred dollars for hers–it reminded me of an automated milking machine farmers use for their cows. She told me I could buy a cheap manual one for twelve bucks at a pharmacy since I wouldn't be using it for long and I could pick one up when I bought the baby formula. I didn't think Granny would drive me to a pharmacy. She told me to ask my father if Granny refused–which she did; I then asked Aunt Paulee.

Aunt Paulee was the first one to leave Granny's house, and when Daddy was leaving two days later, I cried. I asked him if Billie and I could go with him to Minneapolis. He said, "sure, baby girl," but I would have to stay with Aunt Marion–there was no room in the studio apartment for Billie and me. I changed my mind; I had never even met Aunt Marion before and I also figured it would be better to stay with Granny because she had been a pediatric nurse. It was painful to say to Daddy that I'd rather stay with Granny but not as painful as when she said, "Remember Rosie living with me is only a temporary arrangement. You can stay with me for six months, and then you're going to have to make a decision about where you want to live permanently when your time is up."

I was shocked; I had thought I could stay with her indefinitely–she had a big house with plenty of room. I had to look at it with a positive light though, at least she was giving me six months. Sharon would have probably thrown me out immediately after I gave birth. I also think Granny is just pissed at me because I don't want to continue breastfeeding. She has to be pissed, why did she sound so mean using the phrase– "when your time is up." It sounds like I'm being executed.

Another perspective is that it's just one more example to support my original idea: once I had Billie–I was overlooked. My feelings and comfort were no longer given the same consideration I had enjoyed while pregnant.

CHAPTER 46

SARAH

Rosie did not stay with my mother for six months. Three weeks before Christmas she told me she wanted to move to Minneapolis to be near Joe and me. She felt isolated and had no friends. The only people she saw were friends of my mother's, and they were "a bunch of old ladies." She also didn't drive and had to depend on my mother to take her everywhere. I agreed; she needed to get a driver's license if she chose to stay in New Jersey, or move somewhere with decent mass transportation where she didn't need a car. I questioned her about her friends though–where were Dorrie and Patty? They had cars and didn't live far from my mother's. She told me both of them live out-of-state now. After graduation Dorrie took a job in Wisconsin. She lived closer to me than to Rosie, and Patty was working on her masters degree in California.

Rosie was depressed; she saw her friends moving forward with their lives while she was stuck and left behind. She asked me if it was still okay about her taking classes at my college. I assured her, her father and I were true to our word. We'd pay for an apartment and she could take classes on my teacher's perk. It was also an opportunity to meet people her age.

I approved of her plans and ideas–I listened emphatically (without interruption or judgment). It was only when she said she planned to move back to Florida in the fall to finish her degree that I realized *approving* was also judging. I hadn't been listening emphatically at all, and it took all the energy I had in my body to suppress being judgmental; I wanted to scream: *How can you move to Florida? How are you going to support yourself and Billie? You'll need a job and a place to stay.* Joe and I did not have the means to pay for school, an apartment, childcare and her upkeep in Florida. And did she think her school was going to let her move into student housing with a baby? Even if such a wild idea were a reality–she needed a job. Where was Billie going while she worked?

Her university extends grace time to complete degrees, and I had envisioned her getting a job and saving money before she moved back to Florida. When Billie was old enough to start school even. In other words, not until she could stand up on her own two feet more–without total support from Joe and me.

It was fortunate we weren't on a video call when she told me about moving back to Florida. She didn't see me clamping my hand over my mouth. I had to at least try to keep all of the critical comments inside. It was exhausting, but I managed to mask my true feelings and maintain a neutral tone when I said, "Well, you have a number of plans. The first thing on my agenda will be to find you an apartment in Minneapolis, walking distance from school, and if you take evening classes your father and I can watch Billie." I was careful not to tell her she *should* take evening classes if she wanted us to watch Billie. If she chose day classes it would cost more money because it would require paying someone to care for Billie. Rosie has an obvious lack of consideration about that since she's planning to move back to Florida without giving it a single thought.

I had to respect Rosie's need for autonomy and monitor my every word before I spoke–I needed to end the call as soon as possible. I knew I couldn't keep my charade up much longer.

◆

Finding an apartment for Rosie was not difficult. There were always students wanting to sublet in the spring. Not students at my school (the majority of them were commuters), but students from the University of Minnesota. They were a mixed bag. Some were studying abroad but had a lease they were responsible for until May, and others had dropped out or finished their degree work in December but were stuck with apartments until spring semester ended. Those apartments were usually empty–all furniture and personal belongings removed when the students removed themselves. I chose to sublet an apartment from the former demographic. He was a student studying for one semester in London, and his apartment was completely furnished. There was a big advantage to subletting Samuel's apartment, we didn't need to buy any furniture other than a crib. Joe was getting quite proficient in setting up cribs–this would be the third one he assembled in the past five months.

There were disadvantages renting Samuel's apartment though. We were responsible for all of his things and we would need to find another place for Rosie after he returned. Joe didn't think those concerns were a worry. Rosie was no longer a messy teenager in his view, and when it was time for her to move out– "she can find her own place." I wondered how that would work where money was concerned since she didn't have any. "Aren't we even going to have a say about the cost, Joe?"

"Yes, we let her know how much we're willing to pay and she finds her own apartment. Stop worrying, Sarah." Was I worrying about nothing? Joe told me I was all the time and he encouraged me to let Rosie do as many things herself as possible. I made the arrangements to sublet Samuel's apartment but Joe discouraged me from doing anything else–even when it concerned school and classes. The apartment would be ready for Rosie in January. I wanted to advise her to move in early enough to check out the campus and register for classes before they filled up–Joe stopped me. "Forward all the information about school to her. Let her see the deadlines for herself. Stop telling her what she should do, Sarah."

Rosie did sign up for two classes in time, and moved into the apartment one week before they started. Joe was right, she was able to do things by herself. It was hard for me not to do more, and aside from subletting the apartment and filling out the necessary paperwork for tuition reimbursement, I did nothing else. Joe wouldn't even let me fill up her refrigerator the day before she planned to arrive in Minneapolis. "I'll drive her to the supermarket, Sarah. She can choose her own food." It seemed a little silly; we were paying for the groceries, and taking care of Billie on the two evenings when she had classes. Why was he drawing arbitrary lines? Paulee called it– "independence with training wheels."

I finally relented and deferred to Joe. I even refrained from visiting her after she moved in, unless she invited me, but complained because she never did. Joe said, "give her space," and it was true when he said, "it's not like you don't see her." After her classes we spent time together before Joe drove her and Billie back to her place, and Rosie and I shopped every week– with my money. The point Joe missed, both did not alter the fact that I never went into her apartment but it only seemed to bother me, not him.

After moving-in-day it was over two months before I set eyes on Samuel's apartment again, and Joe hadn't been inside since he assembled the crib. When he picked Billie up at the apartment, Rosie always met him in the lobby, and when he drove them both back, he left them at her door.

"Don't you go inside, Joe?"

"No, she doesn't invite me." I guess I should not take it personally then but it bothers me. What is she hiding?

"Why don't you go into her apartment, Joe? You're her father, not Dracula, you don't need an invitation."

"Yes, I do, Sarah." He was infuriating sometimes, and I'm afraid Rosie is not taking care of Samuel's apartment–her room was a total mess when she was a teenager. I reminded Joe that we were responsible for Samuel's apartment and his personal belongings. "In essence, we are quasi-landlords, right?" Joe wasn't worried: "Like I said before, Sarah, Rosie is no longer a teenager." He told me I was having trouble letting go of her–just like it troubled me to be called *Grandma*. Two discrete topics not having anything to do with my concern but the way we ended our discussion, accomplishing nothing.

CHAPTER 47

ROSIE

My apartment is a twenty-minute walk from the Liberal Arts building where my classes are located, and five minutes from my parents' apartment. If my mother had told me that in the past, I would have thought–oh, no, she is going to be here all the time. But not anymore–I crave more interaction with her. I felt so isolated living with my grandmother and an infant (even though he was my own baby). Babies are boring–even more boring than grandmothers. I finally realized what my grandmother meant when she said, "Billie is such a good baby," –he slept even more than her most of the time.

At four months he still sleeps a lot but he also plays with his toes, looks like he's body surfing in his crib when he's on his stomach, tries to stand up with my help and babbles for hours. He must have gotten the talk gene from both sides of the family. His father–who never stopped talking in Romantic Lit, and my mother. I love my father, but I'm glad Billie doesn't take after him–I want Billie to talk to me. The only problem is I can't understand *babble language* and I need to interact with a person my age–or even closer to my age. My mother is preferable to Granny and her friends. Living with Granny Nessie I had heard all of their stories more than once because they kept repeating them. It was so boring I wanted to crawl into the crib with Billie to take a nap with him.

———◆———

After I told my mother I wanted to move to Minnesota, she sent me a heavy sheepskin coat, thick gloves and a ski mask. I thought she was crazy, but she didn't tell me it was so cold that my snot would freeze in my nose when I walked outside. It feels like an expedition to the North Pole just walking short distances. I used to complain about winters in New Jersey but a very cold day there would probably be considered *balmy* in Minneapolis. People who have lived here all their lives say the summers are beautiful. They also say–they're not too hot–which tells me weather is relative and *not too hot* will be too cold for me.

I was late registering for classes. I didn't think it would be a problem because I could take anything–I only had to satisfy electives but I wondered how many course offerings there would be. The college where my mother works sucks. She defended her dinky little school telling me it was a satellite campus. The main campus was located in a town in the middle of Minnesota. At least I was in Minneapolis but I would have preferred to be attending the University of Minnesota and not her school. I can't believe she left New Jersey and Daddy to work here. She said, "Considering your circumstances at the moment Rosie I would think you'd understand. I needed a full-time position." Daddy supported her–it was bullshit and she knew it, but I didn't want to piss her off, and I had no choice about schools. But I could choose my electives and I refused to take heavy courses–no sciences, math, English or languages. When I said that to my mother she replied, "I don't think they have basket weaving 101, honey." She just can't stop being bitchy, it's her natural inclination. She was right about basket weaving but there were art classes offered. The problem was they were all filled. There weren't many open classes left in anything by the time I registered. I also needed evening classes, since it was the only time my parents could babysit. Music Appreciation and Creative Writing were the only things left.

Creative Writing is technically an English class but I will not have to read boring novels and write papers about them–I can write my own shit. I figure it's an easy course load and I'll be able to transfer the credits to Florida with no trouble. The problem with both classes is there are absolutely no students my age. My mother said there is usually an older demographic in the evening, and they also aren't required courses which reduces the number of students overall in a class. It would have been nice if she had given me this information earlier. Why didn't she give me some advice? I didn't know anything about this school, she works here. The only old people I saw at my university were the professors. When I complained, she said, "at least they're free," which has nothing to do with why I am upset.

In Music Appreciation there are a number of students who aren't even *real* students–they aren't taking it for a grade. One woman, my mother's age, told me it was her third time auditing, and she knew several other people in class from previous semesters. They are all her age or older. It feels more like a goddamn club for retirees than a class.

The first meeting of the Creative Writing class was just as dismal but more annoying than Music Appreciation. It was not just that I was the only young person in class–I had to write and read aloud my poem the first day and listen to a bunch of people reading their poems. Even when somebody's poem wasn't half-bad they sounded stupid when they told the class how they hoped, "to make a living someday as a poet." Even poets who are good don't make a living writing poems. Not to mention that these people were my mother's age or older. Did they seriously think they were going to make a career change now?

My classes only meet once a week, and after the first week I realized not much was going to change in my life from living with my grandmother. The only change is now I am totally responsible for Billie's care, except for the two days when my parents babysit. I'm okay with it–Billie is "a good baby." I'm no longer scared to take full responsibility for him, but I continue to be lonely and isolated.

Things changed at the second meeting of the Creative Writing class. Back at the University of Florida I probably wouldn't have given Christopher a second look. He was a little short and too thin for my taste (he reminded me a little of PJ), but when he showed up in Creative Writing it took a concerted effort not to stare at him. He was definitely my age and had a nice face. We were continuing to write poems–haiku poems that evening, and Christopher's poem was pretty good. After he read it, he introduced himself because he had missed the first class. He said he wanted to be a professional writer; he didn't want to be a poet, thankfully. He hoped to make a career writing screenplays–more realistic than making a living writing poetry. The most we would be doing in this class were short stories but he said he "got ideas from hearing the work of other writers." I thought he was being very gracious, based on the poems I and the other students had written, to call us "writers." When he approached me on the break I doubted it was based on the strength of my haiku.

He asked me if I wanted to get coffee after class. There was a kiosk on the main floor of the Liberal Arts building. I called my parents and told them I'd be a little late–I had to have a conference with another student about a group project. It wasn't a complete lie–we were required to do some sort of collaboration during the semester. The professor hadn't given us the full details yet, but I could mention it to Christopher when we were having coffee since he missed the first class.

It turned out he was younger than me, but I didn't care. He was nice and I liked him; I was also in need of a friend. He asked me if I wanted to go to one of the pubs on campus to grab a couple of beers after coffee, but I refused. I wanted to go but couldn't push my lie to my parents any further. I told him "maybe another time." He suggested we plan on it for the following week, or if I was free– "on the weekend?" We exchanged phone numbers and two days later he asked me out for beers again at a campus pub. That's when I asked how he could buy beers since he was underage. He told me he had a fake id card. I didn't tell him I had a baby.

I agreed to the date because I figured my parents would agree to babysit–they were already tied down with Brandy. They didn't seem to care how their own activities had been cut short since her birth–probably because they're old and tired. The thing I dreaded and feared was telling Christopher about me having a baby, not asking my parents to babysit.

His reaction was unexpected. His first response was, "You have a baby? No way, are you married?" There was absolutely no disdain or disapproval in his voice when I told him I had never been married. I was surprised but I had probably spent too much time with Leslie and Sharon. They had made me expect everyone to act like them. He told me I was "really brave" to choose not to have an abortion and to keep my baby. He wouldn't get off the subject; he acted like I had told him I had walked on the moon or something instead of having a baby by myself. I started to think he was kind of a jerk, or really inexperienced. Was I the first girl he had met who was unmarried with a baby? He was a college student in Minneapolis.

Christopher couldn't wait to meet Billie. He suggested coming to my place instead of going to the pub; he offered to bring wine, pot and take-out. His suggestion might have been enough alone in the past to decide he wasn't for me because he wasn't taking me out. But there wasn't anybody else wanting to date me, and at least he was paying for the food and wine. He also seemed genuine–he really didn't seem to mind that I had a kid. I said okay, but told him not to bring the pot–I wasn't my mother.

❖———❖———❖

I wasn't very attracted to Christopher. I even asked myself–why are you agreeing to see him? I finally realized it had little to do with him. It was more about the idea of having a boyfriend, or any friend, which made it appealing. And I had no intention of having sex, but in spite of that I still prepared since I had agreed to the wine. If I was drinking wine, there was a chance I might do something I wouldn't do if I were completely sober–it's how I got Billie. I wasn't planning on getting drunk, but in the past I've thought some guys were more of a catch than they really were after only one or two glasses. I made an appointment at a women's health clinic.

There were two types of birth control pills: one took effect after two days, and the other after seven. I was about to get the two-day pill until the nurse told me one of the possible side effects was weight gain, and it was the same with the seven-day pill. There was no way I was taking them. I hated how my body looked right now–I didn't want to get fatter. I was about to leave when I heard Billie babbling in his stroller. I do understand some babble language after all, I got fitted with a diaphragm.

<hr>

We moved quickly after that, and I saw Christopher three or four times a week outside of class. The diaphragm was put into action. The sex was okay, he wasn't a jerk like PJ, but his appeal wasn't based on my attraction or the strength of the sex. Christopher allowed me to fantasize *a family*. He liked Billie and had no problem taking him with us wherever we went. I would bundle Billie all up and the three of us would go to a restaurant or store. If it was an unusually warm day and not raining we sometimes took Billie to a park. Even though there was snow on the ground, some of the parks had clear walk-ways where you could easily push a stroller. But more than not Christopher carried Billie, and people seeing us often mistook us for a young married couple with our first child–neither one of us ever corrected them. When a server at a restaurant we went to frequently asked us how old our baby was–Christopher answered, "five months." He was fantasizing too, and after every outing we'd go back to my place, put Billie down for his nap or for the night, depending on the hour, and have sex–like a real married couple.

The only time we are without Billie is when we go to Christopher's dorm room after class. My parents continue to think I'm meeting with my project partner. It isn't a lie because Christopher told me he would work with me. So far that's not what we've been working on though, and I'm not telling my parents I'm seeing someone. I'm afraid my mother will say–*you're a mother now Rosie. You should be thinking about Billie, your school work and getting back on your own two feet–not dating.* My own guilty conscience is driving these thoughts. The only thing my mother ever mentions is a job, but she isn't pushing me to get one. She told me if I wanted to find part-time work in the evenings, when I don't have classes, she and my father could watch Billie on those nights too. She recently asked me if I had given the work idea any thought. I told her I was too busy with Billie and my school work. She would not be happy if she knew what was really keeping me busy.

◆——————◆——————◆

The last time Christopher and I had sex in his dorm room his roommate walked in on us. I was embarrassed; I was on top–he saw my ass, and my tits when I turned around (my fat stomach too which upset me more than my ass and tits). He was very apologetic, and as embarrassed as I was. Only my mother would think someone walking in on her while she was having sex would be funny and not get embarrassed. She told a story about Granny walking in on her and Daddy having sex in Granny's living room before they were married. This had been when she lived with my grandmother. It wasn't funny. It was one of those occasions when Daddy was annoyed by one of my mom's sex tales and said, "Sarah, could you please come into the kitchen for a minute." There wasn't any reason for my mother to tell the story since Granny, Aunt Paulee, and Daddy knew it already. I was the only one who hadn't heard it before. She told it for my benefit and I always wondered why. Was it a warning or foreshadowing?

Christopher and I didn't talk about what happened that night or at any time after because I never saw him again. When I went to class on the following Tuesday he was a no-show. I called him but his phone always went to voicemail. People in class asked, "Where's Chris?" I wished they would leave me alone–they made it worse. When he was absent again a week later, Professor Buckley asked to see me during break. He told me he had gotten word that Christopher had dropped the class; he would have to put me into another existing group for the final project. He said he was sorry, but "there is always a chance this kind of thing will happen when working with only one person. If they drop out, the other member is left in the lurch. It's better to be in a group." It's good advice for life in general. I had focused entirely too much on Christopher these past eight weeks. If I had found a part-time job, like my mother suggested, I would have possibly met other people my age—made other friends.

I felt like dropping the class myself, it was depressing being there without Christopher. I wasn't in love with him; he didn't leave me with a broken heart, but he did leave me isolated and lonely again. I also realized for the first time that a one-night stand mentality can exist for multiple fucks. I had thought he was a nice guy, but I was wrong. He tossed me like a soiled tissue without warning or a single word of explanation. He definitely was a jerk.

Billie chose to stop being "such a good baby" at the same time Christopher chose to leave me. He was crying all the time and wouldn't stop. I was going crazy and sometimes when he wouldn't stop, I locked myself in the bathroom with the shower running full blast to drown out his screams. What the hell was wrong? Did he miss Christopher, or was it only coincidental, and his nonstop crying was just untimely bad luck? Whatever its cause, it spiraled me down further into a big black fucking hole—until I could barely crawl out.

CHAPTER 48

SARAH

The first week Rosie texted us, she said she wasn't going to her classes because they were canceled. They were told they should work on their group projects outside of class. I texted back– "You have group projects in both classes?" There was no immediate response, but she finally answered: "I don't have a group project for Music Appreciation but the professor canceled too–I don't know why." It was strange that both of Rosie's professors canceled their classes in the same week having nothing to do with the school itself. I experienced a blend of annoyance and envy.

Some professors canceled their classes frequently for non-emergencies, and also dismissed their students twenty minutes early from seventy-five minute classes on a regular basis. I didn't know how they had the nerve, and during my period working as an adjunct I believed the department heads at orientations when they had said they wouldn't tolerate such behaviors. I now know these kinds of rules are ignored by many full-time tenured professors, and I have also known adjuncts who ignored them. I was never so daring then or now, adjuncts and untenured professors can be easily replaced. I wondered–were Rosie's professors tenured and secure and felt entitled, or adjuncts who were just bold and didn't give a damn?

Of course there could have been real emergencies for Rosie's instructors. If that was the case, I empathize–especially if they are adjuncts. They are usually only entitled to two personal days each semester. It doesn't matter if they need more time, there is a pile of applicants waiting in the wings for their positions. It was standard policy to simply hire someone new rather than extend time off; or that was what I was led to believe when I worked as an adjunct for over ten years at several schools.

My initial preoccupation with those first texts from Rosie focused on teaching, privilege, and the life of untenured instructors, and it wasn't until she didn't want to go shopping with me that I became concerned.

"I think I should go over to the apartment to see if she and Billie are okay, Joe."

"Why, what did she say?"

"She said she was too busy with her assignments." Joe told me to take her at her word, be happy she was working so hard at her schoolwork. He reminded me of Sid, without the bad language when he kept repeating: *give her some space; give her some space.* He said it so many damn times I felt like shoving a cracker in his mouth, but I deferred to him instead. He made me question myself–was I overreacting? It's what Joe thought, so I *gave her some space*–but something continued to feel off.

I received a call from Rosie at work a week after her texts; unfortunately it almost felt expected. She was crying and I could hear Billie screaming in the background. Not sounding good, but at least they were both alive. She wanted me to come over to her place, but I had two more classes to teach. Fortunately, I was able to contact my department's administrative assistant to tell her I had a family emergency and I needed to leave for the day; there was not a problem—even untenured, I was higher up than a poor adjunct.

◆——————◆——————◆

I buzzed and knocked on Rosie's door with no response but I could hear Billie screaming inside–perhaps she couldn't hear her buzzer or me knocking? I used my keys to go inside and there's no polite way to say it, the place was a mess and smelled like shit.

Baby shit to be specific. Billie was in his crib with a soiled diaper and there was a pail filled with dirty diapers which hadn't been tossed for a while. Rosie was nowhere in sight so I was presented with a con-flict–deal with Billie, or look for Rosie.

There weren't many places for her to go, this was a studio apartment like mine, Rosie must be in the bath-room. I could do both; I picked up Billie and headed for the bathroom. I could hear the shower running and I yelled, "Rosie, are you in there? Are you okay?" There was no answer and the door was unlocked so I walked in to find Rosie sitting on the floor. She was on the blue bath rug I had bought: long legs up to her chest with her head on her knees and hands tightly clamped over her ears.

"Rosie, are you okay?"

"He just won't stop crying, Mom." I didn't mention he needed to be changed because it was obvious. I grabbed a towel and went back to the studio to find the diapers. Rosie hadn't wanted a dressing table, she said she'd change him on the couch. First, I had to find the diapers, and thankfully I spotted them and the baby wipes on top of Samuel's computer table. The couch wasn't an option for changing Billie though. It was covered with clothes, three pizza boxes filled with crusts, soda cans, plastic cups and paper plates–at least a week's worth by the looks of it. More shit.

I put Billie back into his crib and put the towel on the floor and got the diapers and wipes leaving him to continue to scream his head off. I had to agree with Rosie–he had powerful lungs but he needed them. *It was called self-preservation.*

All cleaned and changed Billie continued to cry; he must be hungry but I couldn't find the formula. I went to the bathroom only to discover from my daughter that she had run out of it.

"What is wrong with you, Rosie, when was he fed last?" She told me in the morning but that was hours ago. Billie continued to cry and my breasts responded like Pavlov's dogs. Would he accept breast milk? I knew how to switch from breastmilk to formula but never read how to do it in reverse. I cleared off a section of the couch, piling things on one side like a tower of refuse, and sat with the screaming Billie and offered him my breast. I didn't need to worry; it was his natural instinct as a baby and a male, he sucked on my nipple immediately, and for the first time there was a welcomed quiet.

Billie nursed like a pro, but he did occasionally bite my nipples, causing a little pang of pain. Billie made me remember a guy I dated named Justin who used to bite. Justin told me it turned women on. It might work for some women but I didn't care for it very much and our dating was short-lived. Billie didn't hurt as much as Justin, but he opened up that long ago memory and made it stick. That's how I started to call him *Justin* as a nickname. Joe overheard me one day and after I told him the story, he said he didn't need to know about the lovers I had before I met him. Better than hearing about lovers I had after I was married–which was zero, unlike him and Sharon. I have yet to totally eradicate her from my mind, but on that first day nursing Billie, I was very much at peace. My calm was abruptly shattered when Rosie came out of the bathroom and screamed, "What are you doing, Mom? Gross." She had moxie, I'll give her that. Billie had been hungry and soiled and she was upset because I was nursing him?

"I guess you have never heard of a wetnurse Rosie, and I'm a walking milk bottle with a convenient double spout. If you don't like it, go buy your son some formula."

"I will." But stood there staring at me.

"Just go, Rosie, and we have to talk when you get back." Billie was peacefully sleeping in his crib when she returned. She walked over to him and gently placed her hand on his little tummy, and let it rest there for a moment. "Is he okay, Mom?'

"Yes, he'll survive. Babies are tougher than people think but what were you thinking, Rosie?"

"I'm sorry, he wouldn't stop crying even after he ate this morning." I told her he might be teething. Babies will often bite nipples when they're nursing if their gums hurt. It had to be more than teething which made Rosie lose it though. Billie was also soiled and the apartment clearly hadn't gotten this dirty in one day. Whatever was bothering Rosie to make her overlook Billie had been going on longer than that morning.

"What's up, Rosie? This looks really bad. What if someone had reported you because they heard Billie screaming? Children services might have shown up and they would have taken him away seeing him and this place." I would have continued but Rosie stopped me.

"I know, Mom. I fucked up. How were you able to stand all the crying?" I wanted to say the crying was easy compared to her mouth when she turned twelve. It was better left unsaid, there were more important things to say. I couldn't excuse her actions, but at the same time I didn't want to only scold her. As disturbing as the incident was, I needed to say nobody is perfect–we all make mistakes and she replied, "I thought if you could do it I would be able to."

She needed to finally stop this competition she's been having with me since she started junior high. Paulee believes it's her way of showing how she admires me and wants to be like me. But I never had a baby out of wedlock, and the circumstances surrounding our pregnancies were too different to compete fairly even if she chose to. I tried to warn her about that when she was contemplating having a baby but she didn't listen–she had to live it to get an understanding.

She was feeling badly about herself now and self-evaluation was called for, but I also wanted her to consider the differences between our situations. Maybe she would finally listen to me: "It's a lot easier when there is another person who is invested in the child, like your father was in you, and you were never hungry because I was a walking milk bottle. Breastfeeding also encourages mothers to keep their babies clean, it's the proximity." The last part was truly a gift for Rosie, excusing her for the filth.

It was hard to see if my words had been meaningful because her response was that I had lied to her. I lied when I said she'd forget the pain of labor once she saw her baby and would bond with him as soon as she held him. They weren't lies, they were my truths, and I thought it would be the same for her. The only lie I ever told her was when I said if her father hadn't helped clean the house when she was a baby it might have looked as bad as her place. That was a big, fat lie. Joe did help, but if he hadn't, there was no way in hell my house would have looked like this. It might have taken me hours to clean, because I suffered from inertia the first year of Rosie's life, but it would have been cleaned eventually. And there was no way soda cans, pizza boxes and other trash ever cluttered my house when Rosie was an infant, and that's when I remembered Samuel. What poor quasi-landlords Joe and I have been.

But the apartment was a secondary problem. We could clean and hire an exterminator if there was a need—Billie was a more pressing concern. This was also obvious to Rosie by her next statement. "I want to give him up, Mom, I should have never kept him. But I want someone in the family to adopt him."

Did she give this a lot of thought? Whom was she wanting to adopt her baby? She didn't have any siblings old enough to adopt and she didn't like her cousins from Joe's side of the family very much. My sister was always moaning about never having had a child, but I doubted that she and her wife were interested in having a baby now when they were in their mid-fifties. And I'm sure Rosie thought her Aunt Penny was too old like us—in spite of Brandy. That's why I was surprised when she said she wanted Joe and me to adopt Billie.

It wasn't only our age, Rosie has been telling me what a horrible mother I am since she was twelve. Why did she want me to take on a mother role with her son? How did she come up with the idea? Paulee said later, "Are you serious, Sarah? Don't you think it was obvious when she saw her son suckling at your breast?" Paulee often has a very blunt way about her–always bursting my balloon. It was my hope Rosie didn't think I was such a horrible mother after all, and that's why she chose me to be Billie's mother.

Plans were somewhat settled but all the details would be ironed out later with Joe. He was going to have to agree to this arrangement but I didn't anticipate any resistance from him and it was getting late. I told Rosie I had to leave to pick up Brandy from Mimi's. She literally shouted in response, "Aren't you taking Billie with you, Mom?" He was sleeping and I hadn't wanted to disturb him, but Rosie shouting made him whimper. He didn't actually wake up–it was more like he was having a bad dream–most likely about hunger and soiled diapers. I told Rosie I would be back later with her father, she could start cleaning while I was gone. I saw the fear on her face; she acted like she was afraid to be left alone with him. It made me change my plans and I told her to get Billie ready. She then asked if I could do it instead. Apparently the surrendering of the child had taken place already in Rosie's mind. I had to wake the poor little guy up for the short trip to my place, but I wanted Rosie to come with us too. It would be better that she talked to Joe herself. Otherwise he might think this was my idea if I was the one who told him.

◆————◆————◆

As expected, there was no resistance from Joe about taking Billie but maybe he was just in shock.

He had a blank expression on his face for hours. Joe often has a blank expression though so it was really hard to judge what he was feeling, but we did discuss the details of Billie's care. Joe wanted to formally adopt Billie instead of Rosie giving us power of attorney to raise him. It would be easier that way for her to take over custody again when she was ready. I don't know how he figured that since it seemed it would be the opposite from my perspective, but I didn't argue with him, I was probably in a state of shock.

After the discussion the relay between our place and Samuel's apartment began. Joe went first, he was going to take the crib apart and bring it back to our place to reassemble it. He was toning his skills; it would now be the fourth time he assembled a crib in seven months.

While Joe was gone Rosie talked freely about this guy she had been seeing and how he had abruptly dumped her. As painful as that is, I was surprised how she would become so unhinged by it. She told me she felt really bad after he left and she couldn't handle caring for Billie who was crying all the time. It piled up too much until it finally tipped her over and she broke. Joe and I caring for Billie would definitely help her to get herself together. She'd have more freedom to look for a job, and to get involved with activities at school where she'd meet more people her age. I agreed she needed to socialize; but she also needed therapy. That's when she yelled, "I'm not crazy, Mom."

It took a while, but she finally accepted the idea. She might not be crazy, but her behavior in reaction to her despair had jeopardized her baby and herself. She asked me if I thought Billie would hate her when he was older because she gave him to us to raise. I told her if she thought she was unable to care for him right now–it was the right thing to do. I also pointed out that her question indicated another need for therapy. She had to come to terms with her decision and also accept the reality–no matter what a mother does or doesn't do, they will ultimately be blamed for everything that goes wrong in their child's life. It's like when I told Paulee what happened with Rosie, she said, "Why weren't you checking up on her? The way you describe the condition of her apartment it must have been going on for more than six days, Sarah–she needed you." I told Paulee I was doing what Joe wanted–*giving her space.*

When Joe returned to our apartment with the crib it was my and Rosie's turn to start cleaning Samuel's apartment. It would definitely take more than one evening but we had to begin sometime. I grabbed garbage bags, disinfectant and sponges and Joe shot me a look at one point and shook his head. What was he trying to communicate? He had seen the mess Rosie had made. Was it–*I can't believe how her apartment looked,* or like Paulee, *why weren't you checking up on her, Sarah?* I wouldn't be surprised if it was the latter because it's like I said to Rosie–*mothers ultimately get blamed for everything.*

CHAPTER 49

PAULEE

The Janak Family Show continues and as usual I am surprised. I never thought Sarah would turn into an earth mother with a babe at each breast. She calls them her family's "glorious mistakes." She is starting to remind me of these women at work we used to complain about who wouldn't stop talking about their kids. I pray she'll snap out of it, and based on my previous experience with her when Rosie was a baby, I'm confident my prayers will be answered. Sarah likes babies but she is more drawn to older children, and I relate. We both chose to teach on the secondary level and that's not arbitrary. Just thinking about teaching k-8 is enough to fill me with dread.

The problem from the way I see it with Sarah is that there are two babies at the same time, too much distraction from the rest of the world–she doesn't even talk about her job anymore. I'm grateful she at least doesn't look fat and dowdy. On the contrary she seems to be younger since she had her baby and more energetic breastfeeding two. Is it breastfeeding? Is it releasing some kind of youth hormone into her body, or is she pricking their little fingers and putting little drops of their blood on her tongue? It was a joke, and I was only trying to say how great she looked but she didn't appreciate my creative expression. She's gotten her figure back but not her sense of humor apparently.

Sarah is youthful these days but Joe looks a little haggard. He has more gray hair on his head than he had two years ago. I worry about him and I hope Sarah is not denying him sex like she did when she was nursing Rosie. Sarah won't use pot or even drink wine when she is nursing and gets a little grouchy because of it. I said to her, "My mother smoked cigarettes and drank a martini every evening when she was pregnant and we all turned out okay, Sarah." She refuses and she's so much into her earth mother role she won't even have a cup of regular coffee. It's why I was afraid she was denying Joe sex, and also because she doesn't even mention sex since the babies–which is so out of character for her. I finally asked her if they lost their mojo.

She told me Joe is tired much of the time. She shouldn't feel so bad; I replied, "Welcome to married life–finally. Anthony and I are lucky if we have sex two or three times in six months." She then says, "Yeah, we are down to three times a week." She's got to be kidding, but she wasn't. Joe may look haggard but he is obviously not that tired. He must be on energy reserve most of the time since he barely talks, enabling him to have a good sex life.

◆———◆———◆

There's only so much I can accurately assess on phone calls and webcams. I was better able to determine how everyone was seeing them in-person, but I was confused. Not about their general welfare–about labels and language, which is the basis of our reality and my profession. I flew to Minneapolis to help them when they moved into their house, and sometimes I seriously had a hard time figuring out to whom they were referring or addressing. Joe calls Billie– "William," and Sarah keeps switching from Billie to Justin, and Joe often uses a catch-all label of *baby* which can refer to anyone in the family–Sarah, Brandy, Billie or the dog. When he told me, "hand the steak knives to *baby*," it was clear he hadn't meant the babies or the dog but it was not always so obvious. Shakespeare said, "A rose by any other name would smell as sweet," but he was never in the Janak family house. Children form their conceptions of the world through language. Will they have the ability to conceptually understand it, as well as their own identities? They could develop identity crises in their own house with all the name switching. Their language development could also be delayed by Joe and Sarah using different labels for them as well as for themselves. Joe is Grandpa for Billie and Daddy for Brandy; Sarah is Mommy for Brandy, and are you ready? Sarah for Billie.

I offered Sarah a suggestion to mitigate damages and strengthen reality: "Use–*Mama*–it could cover

Mommy or Grandmother. Sarah thought it sounded too much like *Mommy*. "I don't want to confuse him, he has a mommy." As though calling herself *Sarah* and him Justin or William isn't already confusing. And how does he understand her name switch while he is suckling at her breast alongside Brandy. Is there one *mommy tit* and one *Sarah tit*?

My suggestion that Joe could be *Poppy* which would cover daddy and grandpa was completely ignored by Sarah. Fathers apparently have a lower status in this household–the earth mother rules. And as for Billie's biological father–he is never mentioned, as though Rosie was impregnated with fairy dust. I finally asked Sarah if she had ever contacted Billie's father. She unbelievably replied, "who?" I know he was some guy Rosie hardly knew but she acts like he doesn't exist. I often wonder if it's a true story and if Rosie even knows who the father is. Maybe she was sleeping all around and even telling the drunken one-night stand story sounded better. But known or unknown, it should be acknowledged that there is a father out there somewhere. Sarah, as well as Joe, are going to have to address the father question one day when Billie asks the question. If sooner, it could be an exciting episode on the Janak Family Show– "The Phantom Father Returns to Claim his Son," wrestling him away from Sarah's breast. For the time being Billie doesn't hear about him or see him, and except for video calls, he doesn't see very much of his biological mommy.

Rosie moved back to Florida. Sarah insists that, "it's only to get her degree, and she'll be back in Billie's life full time eventually." I question whether *independence with training wheels* is the right thing for Rosie. My mother had the better idea when she turned my bedroom into her sewing room when I took off to college. I thought she was cruel after I graduated and she made me pay rent to sleep in the den. She definitely was no earth mother, but she made me grow up fast and seek full independence. Sarah says my situation was completely different because I had my degree and the means to support myself. I also did not have a baby out-of-wedlock. The last time I checked the stats, only about thirty percent of the people in this country go to college and not all of them finish to obtain their degrees. Is Sarah suggesting that seventy percent of the population in this country can't support themselves and none of them have children out-of-wedlock? Sarah and Joe refuse to look at it the way my mother did, and Sarah ignores my stats. She prefers to point to the trend of grandparents assuming a parental role for their grandchildren. "There are a number of people 'practicing independence with training wheels' with their adult children as you like to phrase it, Paulee. It's not so unusual what we are doing with Rosie." She might be right, but their arrangement is still unusual. Most grandmothers don't breastfeed their grandchildren or encourage them to use their first name. Billie can call her *Sarah* for the rest of her life though and it won't change a thing–she's still his grandmother.

Anthony says she is the sexiest grandmother he ever saw. I love Sarah, but after so many years, I'm sick of hearing Anthony tell me how great she looks. He's worried about her tits though and won't stop talking about them. Every time I mention that I talked to her he starts moaning, "She's gonna ruin those beautiful tits of hers with all of that breastfeeding." I finally said, "I hate to break it to you Anthony, but that's why God gave women tits–to feed their babies." I failed to mention grandbabies specifically and fortunately Anthony overlooked it, which worked to my advantage. I would have had to agree with him about unnatural use, and it wasn't my salient point. "It doesn't matter if they're ruined or not because it's not your problem, Anthony. Joe is not going to let you get near her tits–so why is it your concern?" I also told him he was a "fucking pig."

Father Gallagher gave me ten Hail Mary's and one Apostle Creed for cursing. It was too severe and I complained. He then added an additional Hail Mary and said, "Pauline, every week you come in to make your confession and every week you tell me you cursed at your husband. Are you truly feeling remorse and trying to change your behavior?" Father is right, I have to try harder. Even though Anthony might sometimes deserve to be cursed I don't want to make the baby Jesus weep, but then again, I am sick of all babies no matter who they are.

I blame babies for the transformation of my best friend. Ever since she had Brandy she cares nothing about my life, and it's gotten worse since she became her grandson's guardian–or wet-nurse, whatever you want to call her. All she wants to talk about is them and I have very little to contribute. What do I know or care about the pros and cons of pacifiers or the best time to introduce solid foods to your breastfed babies? She also bombards me daily with pictures. Okay, they're cute, but so are my cats. I don't send pictures of them to her three times a day.

I don't understand it. She was never this way with Rosie. She talked about her but she wasn't possessed. She never spoke about her first words, teeth or boring baby growth accomplishments constantly, but apparently she had been aware of all the markers. It took her over twenty years to share them with me and the infant Rosie's milestones are now thrown into the mix with Brandy and Billie's. I complain to Anthony and usually he has nothing worthwhile to say, but occasionally he deserves applause instead of a curse.

"You know they aren't gonna be babies forever, Paulee. And Sarah and you are not in–*a friends today enemies tomorrow* situation, like me, with the lying scumbags I've known in my life. You two are best friends forever, right?" Right.

CHAPTER 50

JOE

I was never good with women–I don't understand them. It was just dumb luck how I got Sarah. Or it might have been due to her not maintaining her tires so well, she was going to have a flat sooner than later from the looks of them. However it happened it did, and I thought after twenty years I had at least figured her out. I know she's passionate, stubborn and often impulsive, but I never thought she'd leave me. It's not that there weren't rocky times in our marriage, there were a number. It was the timing of it that threw me. She left me when I thought things were going really well. I never saw it coming and I never saw it coming with Rosie and my grandson.

Sarah and Rosie remind me of the time working on the fishing boats when a crane broke loose and hit me. One minute I was standing and the next I was flung clear across the deck. I was lucky I didn't get seriously hurt or thrown overboard. From that day on I checked the wire ropes every day even though it wasn't my job. I wasn't going to allow a chance for it to happen again. But women are not as easy to handle as wire ropes. There were people who told me I should stop working on commercial fishing boats after I got hit with the crane and those who told me I should not have taken Sarah back after she left me. I didn't listen before and I refused to listen twenty some years later. I never regretted continuing my work on the boats or reuniting with my wife. I loved working on the boats too much and I feel the same way about Sarah. I love her too much not to have her in my life even if I may get knocked over.

Sarah always makes life interesting. My father once said I lived mine through her–meaning I was too dull and unimaginative to shape one for myself. My father was never one for compliments–but he's wrong, even if I do agree with him in part. My life would not be better without Sarah, and Rosie. They are the best things about my life and now I can add Brandy as another female in it. I was hoping for a son, but I can't blame Sarah at all for her sex. It was my X chromosome again–I'm destined to be surrounded by women. And my wish for a son hadn't been a need to carry my name or anything like that; I don't have good father-son memories I want to replicate. I just didn't know if I could handle another female even though I love them.

I'm glad Rosie had a boy. William and I are still outnumbered but at least I'm not the only male. When he gets older maybe he can offer me some insights about the women in our family. He's only a baby, but my hopes are not high. I already see how Brandy domi-nates him. Sarah reminds me that Brandy is three weeks older than William, and it makes "a big difference with babies–that's why they measure a baby's age in weeks and months." Sarah might be right and I hope so because William already doesn't seem to know what's coming next from his little aunt. A toy can be pulled out of his hand in a flash. His mother left him in a flash too–a surprise for him and me.

Rosie is emotional and stubborn like Sarah, but I always thought she was more predictable than her mother–I was wrong. I never anticipated her giving up William. My mistake was thinking she would be the same as Sarah where babies are concerned, but it didn't turn out that way. It just highlights my limitations in understanding women. People who know Sarah and Rosie well might say that I don't understand them because they're too complicated. It's just them, not all women. I might have agreed–before I met Sharon.

Sharon's personality is the total opposite of Sarah and Rosie. She's very quiet and reserved and I never heard a bad word come out of her mouth. She was predictable. I always knew there would be a good meal waiting for me when I arrived at her home, and the sex, while not exciting, would always be satisfying. And a curious thing about the sex, after a few months it felt like Sharon and I were a long-married couple. It still feels fresh and new with Sarah after twenty-two years and two kids–another plus for chancing a dodge with a crane. And predictable sex has nothing to do with predictability; I was wrong about Sharon. She turned out to be a dormant volcano who chose to erupt when

I least expected–confirming my general weakness. It's not only Sarah and Rosie I don't understand, I don't understand any woman.

I sat on the couch and watched Brandy and William playing and once again saw how Brandy was grabbing his toys. I finally asked Sarah, "Why isn't Brandy satisfied with her own toys? Why does she take William's?" Sarah replied, "For heaven's sake Joe, she's only eighteen months old. It's what babies do. Don't you remember?" I don't, it's been a long time since Rosie was Brandy's age and I don't even recall a time when Rosie played with another baby when she was that young. I probably have forgotten, but I can't stop from thinking that it's less about memory and more about my weakness–exposing another layer–like a frayed wire rope. The message is clear: you don't understand females no matter what their age. *Caution Ahead-Crane Area*.

CHAPTER 51

CHARLOTTE

heard rumors about Rosie when she didn't come back to school but I didn't believe it–it was too backward. I defended her until Mavis told me it was true and I believed her–not that weirdo Leslie. Then I ran into Cammie; she was on the decorating committee with me junior year. She told me Rosie had her baby and the father was some, "bohemian deadbeat, usually stoned, but indisputably hot," and supposedly I knew him.

"You have to remember him, Charlotte, he crashed our house parties all the time." Was she talking about my very own brother? She had to be, so naturally I lied and said–no. I was not about to admit any connection with Lance to Cammie, but I was going to have a word or two with my brother.

I asked him if he remembered my friend Rosie. At first he had no recollection of her but I persisted. "You must remember her. She has curly blonde hair and big brown eyes like a doe."

"Oh, yeah, she was in my Romantic Lit class. She also has a body like Aphrodite."

"That's the one. Did you sleep with her, Eros?" He told me I was crazy; Eros was Aphrodite's son. He never slept with his mother and it was Romantic Literature not a Roman orgy. I was not to be distracted by his joking around. I asked him if he had ever met her at one of my sorority parties that he crashed. That's when a light went on in my brother's brain.

"Oh, yeah, I did see her at one of your parties."

"Did you sleep with her?"

"I don't remember." How could someone not remember something like that? He told me he was pretty high whenever he was at those house parties.

"Well, the rumor is you got her pregnant and she had your baby."

"No way. Where's the kid?"

I told him I didn't have a clue and I did not care to find out. I was satisfied with my contribution to this mess. I was not going to pursue it any farther and made him promise not to mention he was my brother to anyone if he chose to make inquiries. He acted hurt when I said that, but let's get real, my brother Lance is an embarrassment. I don't care that he thinks he's evolved working as a graduate assistant now. He needs to get a real job, and I only told him because I thought he had a right to know what people were saying about him.

Maybe he'll forget about what I told him since he seems to have a memory problem. I hope that for Rosie and the baby's sake he is not successful in tracking them down, especially since he had the nerve to say, "I never realized what a bitch you were, Charlotte." That's the thanks I get for trying to be helpful.

ACKNOWLEDGMENTS

I owe a special thanks to my editor Kera Voigtlander for her help and advice that go beyond that of a typical editor.

I would also like to thank Ricky Villane, Joann Lay and Amanda Evans for their insights.

ABOUT THE AUTHOR

Marjorie Duryea has worked as an actress, director, choreographer and educator, teaching dance, acting and Communication on the college level. She is a member of SAG/AFTRA and AEA and holds a masters from Monmouth University. She lives at the Jersey Shore.

Thanks for reading our book. If you enjoyed it, please consider leaving an honest review on your favorite store or social platform

—SACADA LIBROS PUBLISHING